the WIZARD of
CRESCENT
MOON
MOUNTAIN

the WIZARD of CRESCENT MOON MOUNTAIN

Oldman Brook

Matador
9 Priory Business Park,
Wistow Road
Kibworth Beauchamp
Leicester LE8 0RX, UK
Tel: (+44) 116 279 2299
Fax: (+44) 116 279 2277
Email: books@troubador.co.uk
Web: www.troubador.co.uk/matador

ISBN 978 1848767 621 (hardback)
978 1848767 614 (paperback)

British Library Cataloguing in Publication Data.
A catalogue record for this book is available from the British Library.

Typeset in 10.5pt Palatino by Troubador Publishing Ltd, Leicester, UK

Matador is an imprint of Troubador Publishing Ltd

Printed and bound in the UK by TJ International, Padstow, Cornwall

For Ella

You are the key who unlocked the door

CHAPTER 1

THE WIZARD'S GUESTS ARRIVE

It is a dark and frosty night. A small man smartly dressed in a fine brown suit and fine brown leather boots, well kept but windswept, is being chased by something, or someone, through snow-covered woods. The man being chased is called Connor Perrywinkle.

Plumes of smoke, created by warm breath catching cold air, swirl behind him as he attempts to run faster and faster away. Looking back, over his shoulder, it becomes apparent that it is not something that is chasing him but some *'things'*, and they are gaining ground quickly. Shadows holding swords, axes and daggers high up above their heads bay for his blood and will not stop until they get it. Perrywinkle has been running for a long while now and cannot keep up his pace.

And then, Perrywinkle's attempt to escape is brought to an abrupt end by the simplest of things. Sliding on the slippery, snow-covered ground, his foot catches on a stray branch, tripping him up. Flying forward, unable to control or balance his body, he falls heavily onto the cold, hard ground. It is not long before he is surrounded by his attackers. With his face down in the snow, Perrywinkle whimpers and closes his eyes, hoping for someone or something to take him away from his tormentors.

"Oooh, we're gonna do nasty things to yer – just like he asked!" he can hear one of the bloodthirsty creatures threaten.

Suddenly, everything goes black. The woods, the trees, the snow and his attackers have all gone. He is in another place now, full of nothingness and silence. The face of an old man with a long grey beard, surrounded by a bright white light, appears out of the darkness.

"Connor Perrywinkle! Connor Perrywinkle! You owe me a favour, and it is time for me to come and collect it," the old man bellows in the most intimidating of manners. "Do you remember your promise to me?"

"Yes, sir. No, sir. Yes, sir, I do," replies Perrywinkle with a whimper and a cry, half-hoping for the 'things' to come back and take him.

"Good, because I'm coming for you, and you'd better be ready for me. I have something special in mind for you, Connor." And with that, the old man is gone.

Connor wakes up with a scream, his bedclothes and red-blanketed bed are wet with sweat.

"It can't be. I've just had a nightmare, that's it! A nightmare. Have I just had a nightmare? It felt so real and he *is* a wizard. But no, it cannot be. Invading dreams? Impossible!" he says, trying to reassure himself.

The morning sun tries to peer through worn, grey curtains. Cream-coloured paint on old walls stained yellow, flaking and peeling, glistens in the sunlight. An easel sits in the middle of the room by the bed. A painting of a middle-aged woman wearing a green headscarf sits on the easel, paints and paintbrushes littering the floor immediately around it. Paintings propped up against walls fill all sides of the room, as do stray pieces of paper, books and journals.

To the right of where Perrywinkle lies is a wardrobe full of expensive-looking suits. A chest of drawers with socks and underpants hanging out of them sits to his left. On top of the chest of drawers is a bowl with water in it. Next to the bowl is a bar of soap and a toothbrush that has been used too many times.

Connor pushes the red blankets away from him and jumps out of bed. Barefooted, he walks along his dusty, dark brown, wooden floor, opens his dour grey curtains and looks out towards a mountain in the shape of a crescent moon. Hidden on the side of that snow-covered, crescent moon-shaped mountain is a house in a cave. Little does Perrywinkle know that in that house, looking right back at him, is the wizard: the Wizard of Crescent Moon Mountain.

"No good looking back at me through your window, Connor. Why do you imagine an escape? You'll never get away from me," comments the wizard.

The wizard, sitting at the window in the house of the cave, is very tall and wiry, so much so that ordinary men pale in comparison to his stature, although it must be said now that wizards come in all shapes and sizes.

"That Perrywinkle fellow... lazy, very lazy, but bright – special even. I'll make sure he pays me back well enough," mumbles the old man under his breath.

The old man's long grey hair and long grey beard curls and winds, covering the most part of his face, right down to his chest. His eyes are dark brown and he has long, bushy eyebrows. The wizard's nose is reasonably long but not overly pointed. His forehead is wrinkled, and so is the skin around his eyes when he smiles or frowns. This old wizard can be caught smiling and frowning regularly, if you wait long enough, although today he is frowning a lot.

Dressing in garments typically associated with wizards, he wears a long olive-green coat with an olive-green hood over a long olive-green smock that stops at his ankles, so as not to drag on dirty floors. He refuses to wear a pointed wizard's hat, as that would make him look silly and this old wizard is not silly at all – at least he would have you believe that. Whilst the old man prefers to wear sandals, because they allow his feet to breathe, he also likes his feet to be warm. So, when he ventures outside into the cold, harsh snow, he likes to wear a warm and comfortable pair of sheepskin boots.

"And where are those guests of mine? They're always late. You'd think that I wasn't important. Surely they could have made their way here by now. Time is precious. I'm sure I've mentioned that once or twice before," grumbles an increasingly grumpy wizard.

The fact is that this old man is a dominant figure in the world of Everlast (called Everlast as most creatures here assume this particular world will be around forever). He has lived for an age, and his adventures are recounted in many tales told by many creatures. But, at present, he is taking time out from adventuring.

For the past ten years, this wizard has chosen to live in a cave deep in the Falcon Gorge mountain range, which sits at the very centre of Everlast. The mountain range is the only one of its kind here. It splits the north and the south and the east and the west of this land. Hundreds of mountains make up this range, many touch the sky, and for the most part, the tips of these mountains are unseen due to a constant cover of cloud. Very few creatures have traversed the range, though some creatures, much like the wizard, call it home.

Although the wizard lives in a cave, it is not how you would imagine a cave to be because, from the outside, this cave looks cosy, homely and light. The front of the cave-house is made of red brick, and the roof of this house is the natural curvature of the cave itself. Protruding out from the centre of the red-brick frontage is a porch with glass-paned windows and a small, pointed, red-tiled roof.

Upon entering the porch, you are greeted by a large, red, wooden front door, with an ornate knocker in the shape of a falcon's head. If you knock on the door using the falcon-headed knocker then, invariably, the wizard will come to meet you… as long as you are friendly that is.

On either side of the porch are two large, oak-coloured, wooden sash windows. Etched into the stone and brick on the upper half of the house are a number of smaller, oak-coloured, wooden windows. There are many of them, generally circular in shape, like the eyes of a spider. On the far right of the house, set a little way in front of the cave, a brown, wooden shed contains lots of wood the old man has chopped for the fires that keep this house warm.

"Hmm! Where are they?" the old man grumbles. "I'd better turn down the heat on the stove. We can't have the rabbit stew sticking to the pan, can we? Oh and where did I put that cake? Ah yes, it's in the pantry. I'd better not forget that – I'm sure they'll be very impressed by it. Book, I'm very sorry to have to move you but I need you to go back from where you came."

A book, that was indeed content to sit on the wizard's warm lap, closes shut, levitates off his knee and hovers to the back of the room, where there is a bookcase spanning the whole wall. The book tucks itself back in to its designated place on one of the shelves amongst the old man's favourite books and parchments.

"Where was I? Oh yes, I need to check on that rabbit stew," he remembers.

Forgetting in an instant about the stew, the old man looks out of the lounge window again. Light snow has started to fall outside. Admiring the vast landscape from his window, he can see the village of Kardarnath in the distance and on its outskirts, the Whispering Woods. There is a track from this village that leads all the way to the wizard's front door, it is so well established that even in heavy snow you can find your way.

A quarter of the way down the track from the mountain, next to a river that weaves its way to Kardarnath and beyond, is a solitary tree. On this tree there are a thousand branches, and on those branches thousands more twigs shoot out in all directions. For the most part, it is a dark and leafless tree appearing dead to those who happen to see it. There is a time, however, when it does come alive, and at this time many leaves and small pink-coloured flowers adorn it. Sometimes, generally every twenty to thirty years, it bears a perfectly round, rich red-coloured fruit the size of a cherry. The fruit is called a dangleberry because it dangles precariously on a long thin stalk off the twigs of the branches.

Prized by the villagers of Kardarnath due to its healing powers, it is said that dangleberries have brought creatures of all races back from the brink of death. Growing very, very rarely and only in small harvests means that, when it is collected, the fruit is dried to preserve it for as long as possible.

All of a sudden there is a knocking of the falcon-headed knocker at the door.

Knock, knock, knock!

The old man, who had been waiting with a feverish expectation, runs out through the door next to the window and into the hallway. With the front door to his left, directly ahead is the kitchen and dining room.

Against the wall, by the front door, there is a long staff made from the branch of the strongest tree. Carved out of the wood at the top of the staff, about the size of a fist, is the ornately-decorated head of a bear, mouth wide open and baring its teeth. Sitting in the mouth of the bear is an opaque pearl-like ball. The ball is called an oric; it has a magic about it and is a good friend to the wizard, although more about it will become apparent as this tale unfolds.

Opening the front door, the old man bellows, "Hello. Welcome, friends."

On the doorstep are three dwarfs wearing dark brown cloaks, dark brown boots, light brown tunics, chain mail around their chests and bellies, large black belts around their waists,

5

The Wizard's bear-headed staff

helmets on their heads and backpacks on their backs. The dwarfs look identical, most probably because they are brothers. All have dark bushy hair, long black beards hiding large full lips, large flat noses and deep-set dark brown eyes.

The only way to tell these three dwarfs apart is by observing the weapon they choose to carry. Igralf, as he is called, has an iron hammer which could, if wielded correctly, cause the earth to move violently. Gendralf carries a large axe which can chop through the largest of trees with one swing, and Wattlespalf wields a sword which can cut through stone itself. The weapons of the three dwarfs were all forged in the north-eastern mines of this land; all were made of the same metal and all have a touch of magic added to them.

"Greybeard," the dwarfs holler. Greybeard is one of many names this wizard is known by and the most common one used. One by one they hug the wizard, and in turn Greybeard hugs each and every one of them back.

"Please come in, Igralf. Good afternoon, Gendralf. Wattlespalf, you look very fine today."

The dwarfs head straight into the kitchen in search of food and ale. Dwarfs are partial to the finer things in life, and will always seek those finer things out before committing themselves to idle chatter.

In the kitchen there is a large iron stove burning brightly. A pan sits on top of it, and inside the pan is the rabbit stew that Greybeard talked of earlier. It is filled with potatoes, carrots, peas, lentils, sage, rosemary and thyme – oh, and rabbit, of course. Rabbit stew wouldn't be rabbit stew without rabbit in it. The smell of the stew infuses the air in the kitchen and it is glorious.

"Ah, smell that hearty stew. Greybeard, it smells better than my own grandmother's cooking," enthuses Igralf.

"Anything is better than grandmother's cooking," laughs Wattlespalf. "Although, saying that, the stew does smell absolutely delicious."

"It is obvious to me that you have been practising becoming perfect in pastimes other than magic since your retirement, old man," compliments Igralf.

"I am not retired, Igralf, and as for age, I still have many, many years ahead of me… so less of the old," grumbles Greybeard.

Towards the back of the kitchen is a long, wooden table with eight wooden chairs. There are two bottles of blackberry wine on the table, surrounded by a number of clay mugs. Three freshly-cooked loaves, a block of churned butter, bowls and spoons also grace it. Nearby, on two stools, sit two kegs of ale.

"I see that you have got us some ale," says Gendralf eyeing up the brew. "There is nothing better than a strong ale after a long journey's end."

"May we?" asks Wattlespalf, gesturing his head and eyes towards the ale.

"Of course you may," replies Greybeard.

At Greybeard's response, all three rush towards the table. Each grab hold of a mug, run over to the kegs and pour the ale into them, before supping it quickly down their throats.

"Be warned, you three. It is a strong brew, and as we have much to talk about, I don't want you falling over yourselves – or worse, asleep! Besides, I am expecting other guests soon and I can't have you making fools of yourself," the wizard says grumpily.

"I will heed your advice. Don't worry," comments Igralf.

"Yep, every word," adds Gendralf.

"I will try my best not to fool anyone," promises Wattlespalf. Greybeard rolls his eyes.

"Now you have your refreshment, would you mind telling me if you had a good journey or not? You think of your bellies over pleasantries too much, where others think of pleasantries over bellies," continues the old man.

"Oh, sorry. Where were our manners? Pleasantries… erm, yes. Well, we had an eventful journey," informs Gendralf, not declaring whether it was a good or a bad one.

"Yes, especially at night. A lot of creatures are stirring, mainly the bad sort," reveals Wattlespalf.

"They are becoming more confident – a plethora of unpleasant things, the ogres, and goblins and other foul beasts. It is a long time since we have had to keep our wits about us even at night," interjects Igralf. Greybeard is unsurprised and remains silent.

"Needless to say, we had a lot of enjoyable battles, though all were small and easy to overcome," hollers Gendralf.

"I take it we can help ourselves to the stew?" asks Wattlespalf.

"It is there to be eaten," replies Greybeard.

No sooner has Greybeard made his reply when there is another knock at the door.

Knock, knock!

The old man makes his apologies to the dwarfs, leaves them mid-conversation, runs to the front door and opens it.

Standing out in the cold are two young-looking men, well armed, tall, slim, weather-beaten and with deep blue eyes. Both are dressed in long, brown leather coats, which drape against their ankles, and underneath they wear white collarless shirts, dark hemp canvas trousers and brown leather boots. Again, these two are obviously brothers, though distinguishing them is quite easy. Stryker has long, dark hair, is unshaven and has a broadsword strapped to his back. Forester, in contrast to his brother, has short hair, a clean-shaven appearance, a bow over his left shoulder, a quiver of arrows over his right, as well as a sheathed sword hanging from a belt holding up his trousers.

"It is a long time since we have seen you, old friend," Forester says quietly and gently, his voice deep but clear, "but it is a blessing to see you all the same."

Stryker continues in the same tone of voice. "It will be interesting to hear why you have called us. I dare say that it can only be exciting news on the back of the journey we have had."

"Hmm, by the tone of your words it sounds as eventful as the journey had by my other guests. You might well be pleased to see them," Greybeard reveals. "Stryker, Forester, come in and make yourselves at home. I have ale, blackberry wine and a stew to greet you. Let us make a little merry and tell each other stories of what we have experienced since we last met." Greybeard smiles and pats both Stryker and Forester on the shoulder as they enter the house.

Walking into the kitchen, Stryker and Forester are greeted by the dwarfs, who have all grabbed a bowl and are ravenously tucking into the rabbit stew.

"Hello... what has the cat dragged in? I can see two vagabonds coming to steal this gorgeous-tasting food and fine ale," teases Wattlespalf, talking with bits of stew running down his beard and a large grin on his face.

"Ha, it is a long time since we've had the pleasure of *your* company. How are you all? Merry yet?" asks Forester with a laugh and a grin.

"Ha! Merry? Remember the last time we met? We shared an ale or two, and if I remember rightly, you two were passed out at the end of the night," Igralf says jokingly.

"That's right! We had to carry you two to your beds. Isn't that right, Wattlespalf?" Gendralf goads the two new arrivals.

"Yes, I think you're absolutely right," confirms Wattlespalf. "It is safe to say that these two cannot take their ale at all."

Stryker and Forester can be seen visibly wincing. The dwarfs snigger and Greybeard pulls a wide grin, enjoying the banter and horseplay.

"So, Greybeard, can we partake in this stew before these pigs clean out the pan?" asks Forester.

"Less of the pigs," shouts Gendralf, pulling his nose out of his bowl.

"Of course you can. Grab a bowl and help yourselves," gestures Greybeard. "I've also made a cake with the finest jam and cream for afters. If the stew is not enough to fill you, that is."

The room goes quiet. A few sniggers and then all-out laughter fills the room.

"What?" asks Greybeard. "It is a lovely cake." His cheeks fill with a red hue, as he becomes more and more embarrassed at his friends' playful derision. The laughter gets louder.

"The last few years must have been very interesting, making stews and baking cakes," patronises Igralf.

Greybeard's embarrassment at Igralf's jest is quite clear, but the wizard has a wizardly retort. The old man is not going to let himself be outdone by a dwarf. Turning his head away from the others, so no one can see or hear him, he mumbles, "Bubbilous mouthir."

Igralf's laughter suddenly turns to a cough and then, as if by magic, clear bubbles begin to come out of his mouth (of course it was magic). One by one they leave Igralf's mouth until dozens of bubbles float around the kitchen, popping randomly.

Pop, pop, pop.

Igralf looks at Greybeard, mouthing curses at him, but as he does even more bubbles are created. The others, including Greybeard, laugh hysterically at the absurdity of what is happening.

"Sorry, Igralf. It was a little unfair of me to use my magic on you as I did," the wizard apologises, ending Igralf's blushes with the wave of a hand.

As suddenly as it started the last bubble leaves Igralf's mouth.

"Yes, that was unfair, you old goat. Obviously you have lost your sense of humour during your self-imposed exile."

"I've said I'm sorry, but you've got to admit it was funny. My 'self-imposed exile', as you call it, has not drained me of my humour, so much as changed it a little," protests the old man.

"Yes, well, I suppose I would have found it funnier if your trick had been aimed at someone other than myself. Just make sure you don't do it again."

"Of course I won't, I promise," assures the wizard. "Hmm, bubbles. Yes, of course. Have you all finished your stew?"

Everyone nods.

"Then I'll set about the washing up," comments Greybeard, staying firmly seated.

"No, please let us do that. You have been too kind to us already," offers Stryker.

"You are my guests. Please, it will only take me two seconds. Watch!" Everyone looks at the wizard, wondering what he might do. "Washus Uppus," the old man mumbles. And with that, the plates, knives, forks and spoons begin to fly up off the table. By the kitchen window is a sink, and in it the plates, spoons and knives are washed clean before a tea towel, held by no hands, rubs them dry. Next to the stove is an old dresser housing all matter of kitchen things. Once dry, well-behaved plates, spoons and knives fly back into the dresser, which opens its drawers and cupboards to let them in.

"Shall we take our conversations into the lounge now the washing up is done?" Greybeard says, pleased with himself. "Better there sitting on comfortable chairs next to a roaring fire as opposed to here on chairs that are stiff and straight," suggests the wizard.

"Oh yes, that would be very nice. Travelling is all very well but the comforts of a home are always welcome, and a nice comfortable chair would be more than that," Igralf enthuses, stretching his limbs.

"Come on then. Let us all retire and chat some more," Greybeard orders, rising up from his chair.

Dwarfs and men, upon the wizard's suggestion, arise from their seated positions at the dining table and proceed to make their way out of the kitchen, through the hallway, towards the lounge.

Walking into the lounge, cream-coloured walls are the first thing our friends see. Scattered all along the walls are pictures, some drawings and some paintings. Portraits of people and places, past and present, invariably their subject matter.

At the right-hand side of the room there is a large, arched, iron fireplace, a wooden mantle sits atop it and a mirror hangs above the mantle. Logs burn slowly on this fire and the room is warm (in contrast to the wintry chill you can feel outside).

In the centre of the room are two large, wooden settees at angles to each other, adorned with feather-filled cushions and covered with multicoloured blankets in bright reds, greens and blues. The dwarfs, Stryker and Forester jump onto the settees with glee and begin to remove their shoes and socks. Some of the smells which emanate from some of the creatures' feet are very unpleasant and noses turn as horrid whiffs invade them, but they are happy for this comfort.

A handmade green rug sits between the settees and the fireplace. The floors, which were originally a cold stone, are now a soft, warm wood.

After everyone else has made themselves comfortable, the wizard sits in his rocking chair. Positioned right next to the fire, he puts his feet in front of it and lets them toast in its warmth.

So it is, everyone talks and chatters. Time flies by with tales of the past and present. The copious amounts of ale, wine, rabbit stew, cake and nettle tea consumed makes those telling the tales exaggerate and exploit facts, albeit no one tells a lie. Stories told of glorious battles involving the slaying of ogres, goblins, alluan, trolls, barghest and erlking are delivered eloquently. Tales of sword-play satisfies the warrior element in these men. Indeed, these are warriors talking, well-travelled miscreants protecting the boundaries of their kingdoms and others. Some warriors fight for honour, adventure and the knowledge that they are fighting for what they believe to be right, whilst others do it for the money and riches. Let it be known now that these men believe in the former. Greybeard, after his initial bout of merriment, remains silent; he is bothered by something.

"Friends," Greybeard says solemnly. Everyone stops talking. "It is time to tell you why I have called you all here. I have been passed information that a small goblin army has gathered in the south, and it is growing at a pace. They appear to be led by an armoured soldier calling himself Warrior. He is not of the goblin race, and no one knows who he is or where he has come from. He is a giant in stature… "

"Is he taller than you?" interrupts Wattlespalf.

"Yes, yes, he is much taller. Where was I? Ah yes, he wears a seemingly impenetrable armour, is well-skilled in warfare and can also control magic. Worryingly, he wears the skulls of the more esteemed kings and men he has killed, and it appears he is adding to his collection quickly…"

"Do we know how many skulls are around his neck?" asks Wattlespalf, trying to be studious.

"No, I do not know how many skulls are around his neck but assume that there are a good few," retorts Greybeard grumpily. "He appears to be able to travel for short distances between two points in the blink of an eye. Warrior carries a talisman which is embedded in his sword: a red oric. If it is what I think it is, then the world is in grave danger – anyone who masters the power of this particular oric will potentially have the power to make all races bow before them. This Warrior fellow does not appear to have mastered the oric fully, or at least he has not utilised its full power, but it can only be a matter of time."

Wattlespalf raises his hand.

"Yes, Wattlespalf?" Greybeard mutters, a little peeved that he is being constantly interrupted.

"Erm, how much time do you think it will be before he masters it?"

"Wattlespalf, I have no idea. Now can I please get back to explaining what I know?"

Wattlespalf nods and winces.

"What is more, he is protected by things not of this earth. The description given to me was vague, however, those who have seen them say that they are dark creatures, vicious, scary and full of hate. Swords have been unsuccessful in penetrating, never mind killing them."

"I bet my axe could cut through these creatures," Gendralf shouts.

"Gendralf, you don't even know what they are or what they look like. Maybe it will be my hammer that tames them," scorns Igralf.

"Where do we come into it?" Stryker interrupts, trying to cut short the argument developing between the dwarfs.

"We have to stop this Warrior and his army, Stryker." Greybeard's tone becomes grave. "They are already formidable. The bloodshed has already started – a small number of villages have already been burned to the ground and many more will fall, I have no doubt.

"So what is the plan?" asks Stryker.

"That, my friend, I don't fully know. We must find out more about this Warrior before we make any move to face him. Therefore, the plan at the moment is to travel to the south of this land, gathering information and an army along the way," Greybeard informs, looking into the eyes of everyone in the room. "I have called you here for your help. My question to you now is will you join me in exploring this adventure further?"

Everyone around the table looks at everyone else several times over. No words are spoken, as if everyone is talking to each other by more mystical means. In turn everyone nods their head.

Stryker breaks the silence. "This is what we live for."

Greybeard smiles graciously and thanks everyone. He wanders towards the window; it is starting to get dark outside. The sun is showing a deep red glow as it descends closer and closer to the horizon. The night lights in Kardarnath begin to flicker as they are lit one by one. The snow is still falling lightly. Footprints of the two men and the three dwarfs can still be seen where they made the long-winding walk up to the house in the cave.

Greybeard lights all of the candles in the lounge with the uttering of one word. "Flamien."

The wizard walks from the lounge into the hallway. To his right, the hallway opens out. In the middle of the hall there is a wooden staircase winding up to the floor above. On either side of the staircase is a locked door; keys sit in the cast iron keyholes of both doors. Greybeard is just about to utter his magic word to the candles against the walls in the hall, when he is alerted to his staff.

The ball in the bear's mouth has begun to glow; the oric is calling Greybeard to it. The staff starts to shake violently. The old man moves quickly towards his staff and takes hold of it. His friend immediately stops shaking, as if calmed by the steadying touch of its master. Greybeard looks into the ball. The oric produces a swirling light, flickering rhythmically as if to a beat, while it focuses itself into the wizard's eyes. His pupils contract to the size of pin holes, and he appears as if in a trance, his eyes firmly fixed to the oric.

Coming out of the lounge, the others gather round Greybeard. All are alarmed but no one disturbs him; they have seen this before. The glare gets much brighter and it begins to fill the room. The swirling light inside the ball begins to produce a whirring sound; it gets louder and louder until the sound becomes deafening. Everyone but Greybeard puts their hands over their ears. In the midst of this deafening sound and blinding light, Greybeard is bombarded by a series of images, rapid and precise.

The wizard can see that it is dusk and two figures are wandering in the snow. Both appear to be boys – one is taller than the other and must be a few years older. Dressed in dark green from head to toe, they cover their heads with the hoods of their cloaks. The attire they wear is not for this weather; they are freezing, finding it hard to walk, and they stumble at every step. The snow is too deep for them, and it is falling heavily.

"Tell me where they are," whispers Greybeard. At the very moment he asks, an image of the tree at the bottom of the mountain appears before him.

"Hope," he mumbles. The next image is more distressing. Laid out in the snow, the larger boy holds the other, trying to keep him warm. Snowflakes land on top of them with ferocity. A blanket is forming over their bodies. Soon they will be lost.

"Stop!" exclaims Greybeard. No sooner said than the light and the noise have gone, as if the event had never happened. "Stryker, Forester, I need you to shift your shape and find two boys. They are close, near to the tree at the entrance to the mountain, and they are being covered rapidly by the snow. You need to hurry or they will be lost."

Stryker and Forester look at each other. Stryker asks, "May we have some privacy while we change?"

"Ah-hmm. Yes, of course," replies Igralf, stumbling on his words.

"No problem," adds Gendralf.

"We'll go into the other room," says Greybeard. "Come, dwarfs. There is not a second to spare."

"Yes, back into the kitchen," mumbles Wattlespalf.

The dwarfs and the old man wander back into the kitchen whilst Stryker and Forester begin to strip out of their clothes.

"Greybeard, we will be back shortly," shouts a resolute Stryker from the hallway.

The door opens and the men scuttle out. One can be heard saying, "Bit brisk out here."

"Bitterly cold," the other says. The door is shut quickly behind them. Seconds later there is a growl, then a trotting of heavy feet. The dwarfs run to the kitchen window and they are sure that they can see two large white bears rushing off into the darkness.

The dwarfs in turn rush into the hallway, finding Stryker and Forester's clothes and weapons lying in neat piles against the wall. Igralf opens the front door. He can see the first few footprints of both men in the snow, switching suddenly to become the prints of bears.

CHAPTER 2

ELVES RESURRECTED

Faster and faster down the mountain Stryker and Forester rush in their polar bear forms. It is hard to see as it is now dark and the snow is getting heavier. The faster they go the more snow lands on their faces, and more importantly, their shining blue eyes, blinding their paths temporarily every few steps they take. The wind accompanying the snow whistles louder as the bears pick up their pace. To the left of them is a sheer drop to the earth below; both move into a single file formation as the ledge becomes narrower and narrower. The weight of their bodies makes the ground rumble with every footfall. Small amounts of loose snow from higher up on the mountain drop behind them. Both are aware of the threat an avalanche poses but carry on regardless.

"Come on, slow bones. Halfway there," shouts Forester.

"Just pacing myself, Forester," replies Stryker, at which point he accelerates and jumps over Forester into the lead. "Come on, slow bones, ha ha!"

Both Stryker and Forester belong to the Otso clan. This race of men has been given a gift that has, more often than not, cursed them through the ages. Otso have the ability to shape-shift into whomever or whatever they want. Anyone belonging to the clan keeps very much to the shadows as all races are suspicious and generally do not trust them. Woe betide a member of the Otso clan revealing themselves to ordinary men.

Tales throughout the ages have blamed the Otso for numerous murders and killings, when the crimes were actually committed by shape-shifters unable to control their animal halves (such as the 'were' clans).

In reality, the Otso clan can control both their shape and behaviour throughout their transformation. It is the character of the man or woman that influences the behaviour of the animal he or she becomes, and as we all know, there is good and bad in all races. Needless to say, the Otso have been demonised, hunted and killed in their thousands. Recently the killing was more prevalent with the burning of practically all the Otso villages. The clan is now fragmented, without a real land to call home, members of it destined to live a nomadic existence.

After a long while, the bears get close to the bottom of the mountain which gradually opens up onto the plains. They can hear the river flowing at the side of them and can see a small patch of open sky hanging onto the last remnants of daylight, exposing the tree ahead. The pace slows as the snow gets deeper. Large, strong, padded feet of the polar bears shovel snow into the air as they struggle forward. Close to an hour later, they are at the tree – now the search begins. There is no sign of the young men; they are hidden. Both bears lift their noses into the air hoping to pick up a scent, but they smell nothing.

"Forester, we need to take different sides of the tree. I'll take the left side – you take the right!"

The bears split up and search the area immediately round the tree. Where there are mounds the bears dig, hoping to uncover the boys. Surely they have not survived. The search is frantic, as round and round the bears hunt for them. Both bears start to move their search outwards, further and further they traverse away from the centre of the tree. As they move outwards, there is more ground to cover and the search is starting to take longer and longer. Stryker and Forester begin to question whether they will ever find them at all.

"Please, please let us find them," prays Stryker. "Please, please."

Then, to the surprise of Stryker, a fist forces its way out of the snow. The fist unravels itself to become an open hand before falling back onto the snow. Stryker growls loudly, forcing the attention of Forester.

"Forester, they are here!" shouts a relieved Stryker.

Stryker runs towards the hand and gently starts brushing away the snow to slowly reveal the bodies of the young men. Forester arrives and helps Stryker complete the job at hand. The boys are covered by their cloaks. Forester, expecting the worst, pulls back one of the cloaks with his paw, exposing one of the boys. Stryker uncovers the other boy. The skin on their hands and faces is swollen, their colour a mixture of pinks and blues, both are frostbitten and barely alive. Both Stryker and Forester realise that these are not ordinary children. The boys are fair; they can see golden hair and pointed ears beneath the hoods covering their heads.

"Forester, take the smaller boy. I'll take the other."

Stryker takes hold of the larger boy by the scruff of the neck with his teeth, and flings him as gently as he can over his shoulders onto his back. Forester does the same. Both boys are motionless and limp on the soft white fur of the bears. Stryker and Forester begin what will be a slow journey back to the house, heading across the plains and back up the mountain.

At the house, Greybeard prepares for his two new guests, hoping that both have been found alive. He rushes over to the locked door to the left of the staircase in the hall, and holding a lit candle, turns the key. He opens the door and inside there is a small room full of shelves filled with jars of many shapes and sizes. The majority of the jars contain powders and liquids of all colours and shades: reds, greens, blues, yellows, oranges, browns, and of course, black and white. But here and there are jars with very strange things in them, such as pickled frogs, spiders and beetles, dried herbs, flowers and fruits. It is a fruit Greybeard thumbs his way towards.

"Dangleberry, yes. Yes, this will do... but only a pinch," he says to himself.

Greybeard opens the glass jar containing the large dried red fruit and snaps a little bit off it. Putting the jar back onto the shelf, the wizard shuffles out of the room, locks the door and walks down the hallway into the kitchen. He puts the candle on top of the dresser next to the stove. Rooting inside one of the cupboards, Greybeard pulls out a small pan. Also in the cupboard is a blue bottle containing water. Taking hold of it, he pours a little into the pan, adds the dangleberry and puts the pan on the stove. The old man then fumbles in a drawer and pulls out a wooden spoon before walking over to Wattlespalf, who is sitting silently with Igralf and Gendralf at the table.

"Wattlespalf, here is a spoon. I want you to go over to the stove, put the spoon in the pan and stir it. Make sure that the pan does not boil over and remove it from the heat once the water has turned a deep red," he commands. Wattlespalf gets up with a jolt and does as he is told. Igralf and Gendralf, in contrast, sit and watch Wattlespalf work with smirks on their faces.

Greybeard leaves the kitchen, makes his way to the staircase and begins running between ground and top floors, upstairs, downstairs, upstairs; for a man of his age he is quite nimble. On the top floor there are six rooms. At the top of the staircase, the first room on the right is being prepared for the young guests.

The room has two single beds, and on both beds there is a large duvet sitting on top of what appears to be a comfortable feather mattress. Two pillows adorn each bed and there is also a folded patchwork quilt on top of each duvet. A smouldering fireplace, which incidentally shares the same flue as the large fireplace in the lounge downstairs, is situated against the wall, facing the door. The room is warm. There are several rainbow-coloured rugs on the floor. Two chairs and a set of drawers sit against the front wall. Inset into the front wall are two circular windows and one oval-shaped window which lets in a significant amount of light, especially in the morning as the sun rises in the east. Greybeard makes one more inspection of the room, making sure everything is ready for his young guests.

Outside, Stryker and Forester are nearly back at the house. To signal their arrival they let out deafening growls. Inside, Greybeard and the dwarfs hear the call. The wizard runs towards the drawers in the bedroom and pulls out two blankets. He rushes out of the room and down the stairs towards the front door. Opening the front door he leaves the blankets in the porch. They are not for the boys; these blankets are for Stryker and Forester. The old man then moves into the kitchen and stands over Wattlespalf.

"The dangleberry brew is ready, Wattlespalf. Can you please remove it from the heat? In the drawers there are some cups. Get two of them out and put a little of the liquid into each cup," Greybeard orders. "Then take the cups upstairs into the bedroom."

"Yes, of course," replies Wattlespalf.

"Igralf and Gendralf, come outside with me. I need you to help carry our guests upstairs," continues the wizard.

Igralf and Gendralf quickly stumble and wander outside. The bears can be seen coming up the path with the boys, who appear still and lifeless on their backs. Greybeard joins the two dwarfs as the bears pull up at the front of the house. By now, both Stryker and Forester are breathing heavily, exhausted from carrying the weight of the boys uphill on their backs. Igralf and Gendralf quickly grab the still unconscious older boy off the back of Stryker and begin to carry him towards the porch.

"Remove the cloak and shoes off this boy, and put him into one of the beds I've prepared for them," says Greybeard.

Igralf and Gendralf disappear through the front door into the house. Almost immediately, Wattlespalf comes out to help, having taken the dangleberry potion upstairs.

"Grab the legs of this smaller boy, Wattlespalf," Greybeard tells him, taking hold of the boy by his arms. "This is very grave," he continues. "The boy is dying."

Wattlespalf and Greybeard begin to carry him into the house. As the light hits the boy's face it becomes very apparent to Greybeard that this boy is special. What he sees troubles him, though; this boy is an elfling but elves do not inhabit this world anymore, or at least so he thought.

Carrying the boy slowly up the stairs and into the room, Greybeard and Wattlespalf lay him gently onto the bed. His wet cloak is removed as well as his shoes. The quilt and the blanket are pulled over him.

Wattlespalf picks up the cups of the bright red dangleberry concoction off the drawers in the bedroom, and puts one of them into Greybeard's hand. The wizard sits at the side of the smaller boy's bed, pours the liquid into his mouth and rubs the boy's cold throat to make him swallow it. He checks the boy's eyes by parting his eyelids. The boy's eyeball flickers; his eyes are a deep green. The wizard takes the boy's hand; it is freezing cold and limp.

"The boy is obviously in poor condition, but he is stronger than I thought. I cannot believe I'm in the presence of an elfling." Greybeard claps his hands lightly together, unable to hide his excitement over his concern.

The elves were gone, dead, and never expected to grace this world ever again. Greybeard's thrill is justified; elves disappeared thousands upon thousands of years ago. Old texts allude to the genocide of elves instigated by dark forces, but those who wrote about it could not prove this to be true.

The dwarfs look at each other surprised. All have heard of elves, but none have seen an image of one.

Greybeard sits at the side of the larger boy's bed. Wattlespalf hands the wizard the second cup of dangleberry brew. Everyone takes the time to study the young elflings' faces. This group of men and dwarfs are standing in the face of history, and if these elves survive, it is likely that they will be responsible for their protection.

"How can it be?" asks Wattlespalf.

The old man makes the same checks on the larger boy.

"It is an impossibility that these boys are here, but here they are. All we can do is hope that they survive and are able to shed some light on how they came to be here. This boy is very strong. He has a very good chance. Gendralf, could you add some wood to the fire? We need to keep these boys warm," Greybeard asks. Gendralf does so without question. Lying fully covered in comfortable beds, the young elflings do not move. It appears the shock of being in the snow for a prolonged period of time has induced them into a deep sleep – one that they may never arise from.

Greybeard and the dwarfs leave the room. The door is closed behind them. They go downstairs and are greeted by both Stryker and Forester, who have taken human form again and gotten dressed.

"Thank you, friends," says Greybeard.

"How are they?" asks Stryker, wondering if he and his brother reached the boys in time.

"The situation is not good, Stryker. The boys are close to death. One might survive but both… I am not sure. I hope the warmth of the house and the healing powers of the dangleberry can revive them," Greybeard informs. "There are beds upstairs for everyone. I suggest after this night's events that we all get some sleep. You have all had a long journey and a long day to boot." It is late. Everyone looks at each other wearily, and with that, all head upstairs to bed.

Connor Perrywinkle twists and turns in his bed. Greybeard has invaded his dreams once more.

"I hope you were watching and listening to everything that has gone on before," bellows the wizard.

"Yes. Yes sir, I did. Dwarfs, Otso, Elves, magic plates, rabbit stew and the like. I remember all of it," Perrywinkle answers the wizard in his nightmare.

"Good, very good. Remember it well because tomorrow we might meet again, Connor. I know what you're thinking, so don't even think it. Escaping me is not an option. If you even so much as consider it, I will deliver you to those who sought to do you harm. You know I can and will, if prompted to do so. Do you remember that night?" threatens the old man.

"Yes, sir. Thank you, sir. Of course I won't escape. Why would I want to escape from you?" gulps Perrywinkle.

"Hmmm, we'll see, won't we?" replies the wizard before disappearing from the little man's nightmare.

Perrywinkle wakes with a start.

"Please. No," he laments.

CHAPTER 3

WHERE DID THEY COME FROM?

It is the morning after the night before. Everybody is in bed on the upper floor of the wizard's cave-house, apart from Wattlespalf, who is downstairs preparing some toast on the stove to feed his very real hunger.

Wattlespalf sings and moves his body to the rhythm of a tune playing in his head. Pulling slices of toast out of the stove, the dwarf quickly puts them on a plate so as to avoid burning his fingers. Wattlespalf takes a knife out of a drawer and turns round to walk to the table. Suddenly, he notices what he thinks is a moving shadow out of the corner of his eye in the hallway. Standing still for a short while, Wattlespalf looks in the direction of the door before shaking his head and walking over to the table.

The dwarf sits down on a chair facing the door into the hallway (just so he is not taken by surprise by anything dangerous), places the plate of toast in front of him and proceeds to scoop butter onto his knife, spreading it all over the toast. There is also a big pot of marmalade on the table; Wattlespalf adds lashings and lashings of it onto his toasted bread.

The dwarf begins to eat the toast covered with butter and marmalade, getting some of the sticky, gooey mess on his beard. And then, again, out of the corner of his eye, Wattlespalf notices movement by the door. This dwarf does not like ghosts and the hairs begin to lift on the back of his neck, but he does not move to investigate. The dwarf continues to eat, preferring to stay where he is. All in all, he has three slices of toast, which is a fair amount for even a dwarf to consume. Leaving the table, he walks over to the door leading into the hallway. Wattlespalf takes his time getting to it as he is a little frightened.

"Any ghosts out there, leave me alone," the dwarf says, peering around the side of the door. Seconds later he gathers the courage to jump out into the hallway.

"Boo!" he says to himself and any ghost that might be close by, hoping to frighten it.

Wattlespalf goes to the front door and opens it. He walks into the porch and then outside towards the chopping block by the shed. Spending some time looking out at the view of the village in the distance, Wattlespalf eventually turns round, and as he does so, thinks he sees a figure looking out at him from the lounge window. Turning his head slowly to face the window he looks again, but the figure has gone.

"I'm being haunted," he mumbles to himself.

Wattlespalf muddles back through to the porch, opens the front door, walks through it, turns to close the front door, turns again to go into the lounge, and gets the biggest surprise of his life. The surprise is so great that Wattlespalf nearly jumps out of his skin. He starts screaming and yelling because there, standing directly in front of him, is the larger elf.

"I'm hungry," the elf says, dazed and slightly confused after his long slumber.

Wattlespalf screams even harder. "He's going to eat me. He's going to eat me!"

There is movement upstairs. Footsteps beat quickly above Wattlespalf's head, doors start opening and closing and finally, to his great relief, he can hear his friends running down the stairs. The first to arrive is Stryker.

"What's up, Wattlespalf?" Stryker asks as he gets to the final step of the staircase. "Hello." He smiles. "One of our young guests is up and awake." Stryker strides onto the hallway floor, followed by Greybeard, Igralf and Forester. Gendralf is still fast asleep in bed.

"I thought he was going to eat me," Wattlespalf says in the process of calming down after his fright, at which point everyone laughs.

"Young man, were you going to eat our friend?" asks Greybeard.

"No, sir. But I am hungry. Where am I?" the elfling asks, slightly overawed by the amount of people in front of him.

"Do not be alarmed. Please follow me into the kitchen. It appears we both have a lot of questions to ask and answer. Let us prepare you some food and talk."

Everyone is sitting at the table except Greybeard, who is slowly pacing up and down the kitchen. The attention is firmly focused on the elfling. He is young, entering the first years of manhood, only fourteen or fifteen years old at best. His features are striking: his face is etched with pointed nose and chin, lips are thin, eyes a deep green and his golden hair drops down to his shoulders, covering his pointed ears. The elf is reasonably tall, standing taller than the dwarfs with room to grow, which is quite understandable considering his age. He is slim, not really muscular at all, but he does appear to be very agile. The elfling's dress is smart: he is wearing a green waist-jacket over the top of a green tunic, green pants that appear to be made of hemp and light brown leather boots. The elfling eats plenty of food including meat, cheese and four slices of toast, all in silence. He is obviously famished, which is not surprising under the circumstances. Questions begin to be asked.

"So what is your name, elfling?" asks Stryker.

"Finn," comes the reply.

"I am Stryker. Sitting next to me is my younger brother, Forester. You've obviously met Wattlespalf. Sitting next to him is his brother, Igralf, and there pacing the room is our esteemed host, Greybeard. The laziest of our dwarf friends, Gendralf, is still in bed, sleeping off the ale he drank last night."

"Finn, I've got to say your recovery is remarkable. You were gravely ill, close to death, but this morning you appear as if the events of last night had not happened at all. Even a dangleberry potion cannot provoke a recovery as speedy as yours. I am truly amazed," gawps an enthusiastic Greybeard.

"Sir, we elves heal quickly. We are very..." Finn pauses, trying to find the right word, "robust."

"Did you get a good sight of your friend in the bed next to you? How is he?" asks Wattlespalf.

"Sir, my younger brother, Beezle, appears well. He was stirring when I left him. I suspect he will wake soon."

"That is good news, young elfling. I would like to ask how you came to be here, Finn," probes Greybeard. "Do you understand how you came to be in the snow?"

"Yes, sir, my brother and I were exploring the forest where we live."

"Which forest do you call home?" Greybeard interrupts; everyone around the table is listening intently.

"Windrush," is the reply.

"Windrush Forest?" replies Greybeard. "In the southeast, by the coast?"

"Yes, sir."

"Please continue," says Greybeard.

"Yes, we were exploring the forest near to our village. We came to a small pond and decided to rest a while. Whilst looking into the water, we heard a bang and there was a flash of blinding light. Behind us, only a short walk away, was a hole in the forest surrounded by a swirling red cloud. Round and round it went, the hole getting bigger with every second that passed. Beezle challenged me to get closer to it."

"Sounds like a time portal. I have read about these before," interjects Greybeard.

"My brother is undisciplined – he's always getting in trouble. Anyway, he ran towards the hole, and I ran after him asking him to stop. He did stop, for a brief moment, at the entrance to it. Looking at me he grinned as if the hole played some part of a game. Beezle ran through it, and the hole and the red cloud surrounding it started to get smaller. I didn't want to enter. I didn't know where it would lead or what dangers might be lurking within it, but I had to because he is my brother and I couldn't just let him go through it on his own. So, I dived into the hole."

"And what was inside?" asks Greybeard, interested to know.

"There was a path surrounded by space on all sides, full of moons, planets, stars, suns and blackness. I could almost touch them. It was beautiful. And then, as I walked further and further through space, I began to feel colder and colder. I could see an exit, much like the one I dived through, and through it I could see snow. It was falling onto the ground lightly. I had never seen snow before but I had heard of it, seen it in books and recognised it instantly."

"So, what happened next?" interrupts the wizard.

"Before long I was on this side of the hole, standing in the snow. I could see my brother walking ahead. I turned back round to face the hole and the reddened cloud, but to my surprise the hole and the cloud had gone. It was then that I realised we were trapped. I chased after my brother and caught him up. I was annoyed with him, I told him we were lost, but he was unconcerned. This didn't surprise me. He told me that it was better we were away from the forest, that this would be a great adventure. All that I knew was that we needed to find shelter but there was none to be seen. Snow was falling and it was freezing. We continued moving and for at least an hour we walked; our legs became weary. Suddenly, I saw a tree – it could offer us shelter but we were too tired. We moved very slowly because we were both freezing cold and we couldn't feel our feet. My brother fell onto the snow. I covered him and tried to keep him warm," Finn pauses, thinking back to his experience.

"And?" prompts the old man.

"I don't remember much after that. I do remember hearing a thud, thud, thud and what I thought were voices, and I think I punched through the snow cover with my hand. And now, here I am," Finn says, ending his tale.

The story has captivated everyone; there is silence.

"From what year have you come?" Greybeard asks Finn.

"The year is 8976." Everyone looks at each other, showing surprise and alarm; they look at Finn. Terrible news must be dispatched in his direction. "Sir, where am I?" Finn asks, looking at Greybeard, confused and unsure.

"You are in the same world, though some distance from the hole you entered. The problem lies in that it has brought you a great many years forward in time," Greybeard reveals, looking at him solemnly. "You, my young friend, are in a place where elves no longer exist except in tales of old. You and your brother are, as far as we know, the only elves seen in this world for over three thousand years." Finn looks visibly horrified.

"Three thousand years in the future, that's brilliant. I knew this would be a great adventure," a young voice cries out enthusiastically. "What's even more brilliant is the ball on top of this staff. It keeps talking to me, but I don't understand what it is telling me. Can any of you tell me?"

By the kitchen door, holding Greybeard's staff, the group are introduced to Beezle. Being the smaller of the two elves, Beezle stands around the same height as the dwarfs; he is, of course, younger than Finn, maybe eleven or twelve years old at the most. His blond hair is cropped short at the back and sides, revealing his elven ears, which are a sure sign of his race. Unlike his brother, he has a round face with a round button nose, full lips, small round chin and slightly chubby cheeks. His eyes are a deep green, like his brother's, but Beezle's eyes show a petulance and mischief, whereas Finn's show strength and innocence. Like his brother, he is thin, agile, but less muscular; we must remember that this elf is still a child. Beezle looks smart enough, dressed much like his brother, but his clothes are a bit dirty, as if he has enjoyed rolling around on a dust-filled floor just a little too often. And now, Beezle has his hands around Greybeard's staff, and like a child might, pretends to make it do magical things.

"Please put that down! It does not belong to you, young elf," Greybeard shouts.

"Stop it, will you. You could cause someone some harm," Finn adds.

Beezle waves the staff around in an uncontrolled manner, aiming it at the men sitting at the table. Beezle thrusts the staff forward, at which point a blast of lightning, as seen in the skies on thundery days, exits from it. The blast narrowly misses Stryker, who flinches at its ferocity before it hits and shatters some of the plaster on the wall behind him. Beezle looks shocked and in awe of what he has achieved, and a wry smile cuts across his face. Greybeard puts out his arm and stretches out his hand. Under his breath he calls for the staff to come to him. Obeying the wizard's words, the staff flies out of Beezle's hand and returns to its master.

"You're a wizard," Beezle says enthusiastically. "Wow, I've never met a wizard before. You must be very powerful."

"Yes, I am a wizard. You are correct in your assumption – I am indeed very powerful. And you, Beezle, yes I know your name, well, this staff can turn you into a frog, and worse still, make you disappear for good. If you ever attempt anything like what you have just done again, I will make sure that you are adequately punished for it," warns the old man. "And adequately means something suitably nasty and horrible."

"Oh my, I've read about your kind in the books at the library," Finn whispers under his breath.

"This boy should be beaten," booms Stryker, reeling at Beezle's misguided attack.

"I second that. It was a very disagreeable and dangerous act if ever I saw one," agrees Igralf.

Grudgingly, Beezle listens to the old man's advice and rumblings from the others but stops short of apologising. The little elf wanders over to the table, and looks at everyone around it before grabbing some meat and some bread. Sulking, he gorges on the food, not saying a word as he does so.

"Much like wizards, I haven't met dwarfs and men before. It really is quite exciting to see a good few races being social with one another. Do you all live here together?" asks Finn, breaking an uncomfortable silence.

"Well no. I am the only one living in this place. These men and dwarfs have travelled here much like you and your brother did. I called them here for a purpose. We have a quest to be getting on with," informs the wizard.

"A quest?" pipes up Beezle, coming out of his sulk. "You mean like an adventure?"

"Yes, I suppose it is an adventure of sorts, but one which will be filled with danger and dread. The world is in trouble and intervention is needed to halt what it faces," replies Greybeard.

"Would I be right in saying that you are all fabled warriors, then? I mean, fabled warriors save the world over and over again, and you are going to save it, are you not? You are good, aren't you?" asks Finn.

"Hmm, I suppose you could say we work for good, although much like anyone else we are flawed. And fabled, possibly, but none of us would admit it. Anyway, we are but a handful of warriors. We need a good few more to even stand a chance of beating this particular foe, which is why we must journey to find others before we face our enemy," remarks the old man.

"So, if you are heading off on a journey, what of us? Are we to be abandoned? Are we a hindrance? I'm sure you must be very busy," gulps Finn.

"Wouldn't surprise me if we were. We can look after ourselves anyway," mumbles Beezle.

"Right, brother. What a great job we've done looking after ourselves so far. We would have died if it weren't for these people and don't you forget it," tuts Finn.

"Please, neither of you will be abandoned if you do not want it. As for being a hindrance, I believe you two are quite the opposite, and very special. It would be a pleasure if you would travel with us. My friends and I would like it very much. And, whilst I cannot promise you this, I know how strange this world will be to you and I will try to get you back to your own time, in time. Anything is possible if we find the way," assures the wizard.

Finn looks at Beezle excitedly; Beezle looks less impressed, but faced with an adventure, nods his head in agreement. "Please, anything to get us back. Besides, where else are we going to go, and who better to travel with than good-hearted wizards and warriors?" replies Finn.

"Then so be it. As you two are obviously well enough to travel, we will set out this morning," Greybeard announces with glee.

At this point, Gendralf walks into the room after enjoying what was a good, long sleep. Surprised to see the two boys alive and seemingly well, he asks, "What, they're alive and walking around? Have I missed something?"

After breakfast, Greybeard goes upstairs to prepare three backpacks for the journey ahead: one for himself, one for Finn and one for Beezle. His own backpack is very light, carrying only a spare smock, a pair of his favourite sandals (for when he gets to warmer climes), a small tin with a few magical powders (each carefully wrapped in paper), a few dangleberries (for obvious reasons), a small flask of nettle tea (his favourite tipple), a bar of soap wrapped in cloth, a toothbrush, a loaf of bread, some meat and a good slab of cheese, all of them wrapped in paper. For the boys, he provides them each with a bar of soap (again wrapped in cloth), a toothbrush, a towel, a flask of water, bread, meat and cheese.

Searching the dark recesses of his wardrobe, the wizard selects clothes that will protect the elflings from the cold. He finds the boys a wool jumper each, and both these jumpers have shrunk in the wash. Greybeard is not the best at washing clothes, in fact, he is terrible at it. Two woollen hats are picked out that will not only cover the boys' heads, keeping them warm, but will also hide their pointed ears, which are unique to their race.

Any educated creature would instantly recognise an elf, and any acknowledgement that there are elves alive in this world could provoke some unwanted attention. Finally, he gets them each a pair of woollen socks to keep their feet warm for the long walk in the snow; there is nothing worse than cold feet, Greybeard muses, thinking a little of his own.

The others wait for the wizard as he packs things for the journey ahead. Doing what they can to keep occupied, Stryker and Forester sharpen their swords and the dwarfs raid the pantry for apples, cheese and meat. Beezle runs round the house, pretending to be a bird, bumping into, knocking off and breaking things.

"Beezle, will you please be careful," implores the wizard, shouting down from the top of the stairs.

Finn is busy flicking through books from Greybeard's extensive library, and to his surprise, the pictures in some of the wizard's books move. The elf, taking in as many tales as he can, marvels at the events of one particular story entitled 'The Battle for the Horn'. In this story, the elf can see battalions of men fighting trolls and ogres for a magical horn, stolen from them by the King of the Trolls. As the story unfolds, the battalions of men are beaten back by trolls and ogres, who are too large, too strong and too many to defeat. The King of the Trolls, sensing victory, holds the horn aloft to rousing cheers from his army. But the story doesn't end there; Finn is suddenly enthralled as a big blue dragon swoops down from out of the clouds and steals the horn from the King, before flying off into the distance, never to be seen again.

"Right, I'm ready," Greybeard hollers as he makes his way back downstairs. "Finn, Beezle, I have some warm clothes for you to wear out in the snow. Come on, this adventure is about to begin!"

CHAPTER 4

SETTING OUT TO KARDARNATH

It is time to set out. Everyone in the hallway is ready and eager to get underway. The two young elves, covered in their wool garments, are very warm – almost too warm. The wizard has wrapped them up all too well. Backpacks are on backs and weapons in their rightful places. All, bar Greybeard, head into the porch and then outside, in single file.

The old man finishes fastening his sword to his side, and covers his head with a white woollen bobble hat. He then takes hold of his staff, closes the red front door of the house and locks it shut. Even here, in the ice and snow, there are vagabonds looking for easy riches.

The wizard pats the red door and mumbles, "Constantus protectum." It is a spell protecting the house from all that is bad or with poor intention. The falcon-headed door knocker, saddened by the old man's departure, sheds one hard metallic tear, the tear falling to the floor with a small clink. Turning his back on the house, Greybeard walks onward with the others and does not look back.

Descending down the side of the mountain, the company moves slowly so as not to slip on the icy patches on the path. Everyone is mindful of the cliff edge and the steep fall they'd experience should they drop off the side of it. Looking upwards to the sky, walls of grey rock are exposed along the cliff face. The enormity of Crescent Moon Mountain and the mountain range behind it cannot be underestimated, but then neither can its beauty.

A while later they step onto the plains. The dangleberry tree can be seen in the distance ahead. The snow is deep on the plains. Indeed, the snow has been so heavy that the tracks created by the bears only last night have been covered. It comes up to the knees of Beezle and the dwarfs, who find it hard to maintain the pace that the others are setting (not that you would hear any complaints from the dwarfs).

Everyone breathes heavily. The companions are still very high up in the world of Everlast even though they are at the bottom of the mountain and the air is very thin, so much so that there is little air to spare for talking; even the dwarfs are quiet.

Eventually, this group of men, dwarfs and elves arrive at the dangleberry tree and rest. Finn and Beezle look back at the view of the mountains. They stretch across the whole land, or at least as far as Finn and Beezle's eyes can see. Many mountain peaks are so tall that they are hidden behind the clouds, smaller white-tipped peaks dance below the larger ones. It is a wondrous sight to see for two boys who have never been out of the forest before.

The dwarfs each take some bread and water out of their backpacks, ripping into the bread and chewing on it greedily. Stryker and Forester each drink some water out of a flask. Greybeard rests his staff against the tree. He looks up at the branches, and to his surprise, one twig has one solitary leaf growing from it. He is a little put out by this leaf being there as he might miss the event of a dangleberry harvest because of this adventure. "Hmmph! Just my luck," he grumbles to himself.

Greybeard notices that, in the distance, the cloud is becoming a very dark grey, and a mist created by heavy snow is rapidly coming towards them. "We need to get a move on. The snows are coming and I suspect that they will be heavy," he commands, pointing towards the storm in the distance.

"Oh, no, here we go again. I'm not sure I want to be a part of this adventure after all," says Beezle, remembering his last encounter with a snowstorm. The backpacks are hastily packed, the party set off and everyone begins to walk on just that little bit quicker than they did before.

Onward they plough, through the snow, following the river towards the village. A row of stone-bricked houses of varying colours, all with smoking chimneys, can be seen in the near distance. From behind this row of houses others peer out from behind, as if trying to get a better view of the mountains. The houses are all different shapes and sizes. Some houses are tall whilst others are short, some are wide whilst others are narrow, and some are square whilst others are rectangular, but all are well-maintained. Kardarnath appears tantalisingly close in the race to get there before the storm gets them. But the snowstorm is faster than those travelling on foot, and at its edges, snow begins to fall lightly on the group, whilst a wind starts to blow.

"There is no escaping this, so brace yourselves for what is going to come at you," hollers Greybeard over the whistle of the growing wind.

The storm has caught up with them; the snow is relentless and the company are thrust into partial darkness. The group can barely see each other now, let alone what is ahead.

"Stick with me," Stryker shouts over the winds, taking Beezle's hand. The dwarfs take hold of each other's hands, find Finn and take hold of his. Stryker and Beezle are next to join hands with the dwarfs. Forester takes hold of Greybeard's arm, and seeing the party just ahead, joins them. The company walk in a line holding hands, protecting each other, making sure none are lost to the storm. They know that they are heading in the right direction as they can just about see the river to the left-hand side of them. At the very back of the line is Greybeard, and for a moment, he thinks he hears something through the wind behind him.

"Was that a growl?" he mutters to himself, looking over his shoulder. He hears another growl, and through the blanket of falling snow, he is sure he can see a large, shadowy figure. No, two large, shadowy figures.

"We are being stalked," Greybeard tells himself. Calmly, he taps Forester on the shoulder. "Ice Wolves," he shouts above the winds. Forester looks back; he too can see dark, shadowy figures stalking them.

Forester in turn taps Gendralf on the shoulder. "Ice Wolves," he shouts to the dwarf.

"Keep moving, we will follow shortly – we have business to attend to," Gendralf informs Wattlespalf. Gendralf lets go of Wattlespalf's hand.

Greybeard, Forester and Gendralf stop walking and get ready to defend themselves. The dark shadows promptly come to a halt as well, as if still believing that they have not yet been seen. After a brief pause, one of the wolves begins to run, propelling itself towards Greybeard. Greybeard swings his staff just as the jaws of the wolf become visible through the blanket of snow. The staff hits the ice wolf squarely on the nose. The wolf yelps and it is stunned momentarily. Shaking its head, the wolf gets up and growls at Greybeard, annoyed that he has been outplayed by the wizard.

The wolf is larger than you would imagine a wolf to be. Its long coat is pure white, blending in perfectly with the landscape around it. Its legs are long and its paws are wide, enabling it to travel on top of the deepest of snows. The wolf has a long snout with a wet, white nose on the end of it; its teeth are long, its eyes are pools of pure blue and its ears are long and pointed.

The second wolf (which looks much like the first) circles around the side of Greybeard, both Forester and Gendralf are tracking its movement. The second wolf stops and turns its head towards the first wolf, and the first wolf does the same, as if indicating to each other that they are ready to launch their respective attacks. Growling at their prey, both start running towards them; the first targets Greybeard and the second targets Gendralf. Gendralf raises his axe in readiness for the impending assault. Forester removes his dark wooded bow from his shoulder and pulls out an arrow from his quiver. He pulls the string of the bow back, the arrow is ready and it is aimed perfectly at the wolf.

The first wolf runs at Greybeard – he leaps and grabs at Greybeard's staff with his teeth. The old man holds the top and bottom of the staff and wrestles with the wolf. Soon, it lets go of the staff, only to make another lunge at the old man with its sharp clawed paws, hoping to catch him off guard. A quick-witted Greybeard turns to the side just in time to avoid being struck.

The second wolf makes his jump towards Gendralf. As the wolf jumps, his chest becomes exposed. Forester lets go of the string of the bow, propelling the arrow forward. The arrow penetrates the chest of the wolf, and it hits the snow-covered ground writhing wildly, snapping indiscriminately in pain. Gendralf raises his axe and strikes it; the wolf stops moving almost immediately, except for a few twitches, and then it is dead.

The first wolf wrestles the old man to the ground. Its jaws snap close to Greybeard's face, so close that the old man can smell its breath. He pulls back his staff, and with the end of it, he hits the wolf twice on the nose. Head shaking, nuzzling the cold ground, the wolf tries to numb its pain. Greybeard picks himself up and quickly unsheathes his sword. The white wolf looks up at the old man once more and growls. His eyes showing frustration and determination, he makes one more lunge. The wizard's sword is quickly extended, the blade of the sword pointing in the direction of the wolf. The wolf, unable to stop its lunge, pierces itself onto the wizard's naked metal blade. Caught on the sword, the wolf's weight pushes it further down on the blade. Standing on its hind legs, the blade appears from out of its back. Face to face with Greybeard, the wolf looks into the old man's eyes until the life ebbs out of them. The essence of the wolf is gone.

A startled old man pulls the sword out of the wolf, its carcass slumping slowly onto the blood-covered snow. Greybeard falls back and scrambles across the snowy floor, putting a safe distance between himself and the lifeless wolf. Joined by Forester and Gendralf, the three of them look at each other, relieved.

"That was not a battle I wanted to fight," comments the old man, breathing heavily. He is exhausted. "I have never seen a wolf that big. Not even an ice wolf."

"Indeed, look at the size of them!" Gendralf exclaims, pointing at one of the wolves.

"Hopefully there are no more. These conditions do not favour us… we need to make a move now – other wolves might be close by," calls Forester.

The snowstorm starts to recede. The three men are able to see the others who, by now, are a good distance ahead and close to the village. Cleaning the blood off their weapons and hands in the snow, the three men resume their hike towards Kardarnath.

Stryker, Igralf, Wattlespalf, Finn and Beezle arrive at the outskirts of the village. The village is quite large; there are many houses lining scores of streets. Kardarnath is the last village before the mountains begin, and as such, many explorers and mountain climbers enjoy the final few nights and days here whilst acclimatising to the altitude. And so it is that many guides line the streets looking for work. They are not shy, and ask anybody and everybody who are not residents of the village whether they want someone to lead them into the mountains. In addition, there are many shops in Kardarnath selling mountain gear such as ropes, boots, jumpers and sheepskin jackets, as well as numerous tourist shops selling moon cult deities, artefacts, souvenirs and novelty potions pretending to be magic.

Kardarnath appears reasonably prosperous. The village has many inns, stalls selling food, horse traders and there is even a jeweller selling the finest gems mined from the mountains themselves. Many come to spend their currency here. But there is another side to Kardarnath, one where villagers shy away from the distractions provided for tourists. People from this village are hard working. The village has many builders, farmers, woodcutters, blacksmiths and weavers who work and live their lives quietly. Greybeard, coincidentally, knows most of these people. Gendralf, Greybeard and Forester walk up to the wall where the others are sitting.

"Busy?" asks Igralf.

"A little… nothing overly taxing," replies Gendralf.

"A couple of ice wolves distracted us," says Forester with less bravado.

"Ice wolves? What are they?" asks Beezle.

"Monsters with big teeth," Forester replies.

"And what are monsters?" asks Beezle.

Everyone goes quiet; they forget that these two boys have not seen or heard of the things that others take for granted.

"Monsters come in many forms and their overriding purpose is to scare or even harm you," replies Greybeard.

"I see," says Beezle. "So if I want to scare or harm someone, am I a monster?"

"You might well be," replies Stryker, with the hint of a smile.

"Let us move on into the village," orders Greybeard, changing the subject. "Finn, Beezle, pull down your hats over your ears."

"But the hat itches," says Beezle.

"Just do it. It is very important that you do so. Many people might do you harm should you expose yourself here, or anywhere for that matter."

"Like monsters?" asks Beezle.

"Yes, like monsters," replies Greybeard.

The company walk northwards into the village along wide, cobbled paths. The paths are wide enough for a horse and cart to travel through with room to spare as they pass the houses and shops that line the main street. The streets are busy. It is market day. On this day, people from the outskirts of the town come in to trade their wares or stock up on essentials such as clothing and food. Men, suited and booted, wear scarves and gloves and all manner of hats, from the woollen kind to ones which can be tipped. The men, more often than not, walk alongside ladies with long thick skirts, cardigans, headscarves and other ladylike things to keep them warm. Traders usher the people into their shops. Rag tag children play in the snow that lines the paths and roads, throwing snowballs and making snowmen. The paths are slippy in this wintry wonderland; people walk slowly so as not to fall and hurt their heads and bones on the snow-covered stone. The villagers of Kardarnath tip their hats, wave and shake Greybeard's hand as he walks through.

"You have lots of friends here," says Wattlespalf.

"Yes, it is better having lots of friends rather than lots of enemies. Wouldn't you agree?" smiles Greybeard.

Finn and Beezle look in wonder with eyes wide open and beaming smiles on their faces as they peruse the goods in shop windows; they have never seen so many wondrous things. Stops are made to look at toys in the toyshop and cats and dogs in a pet shop. Outside a chocolate shop, Beezle points through the glazed front window at plates which are filled full of chocolates.

"What are they?" he asks.

"Those are chocolates. They're made of sugar and cocoa and other nice things," replies Wattlespalf.

"Nice things, eh? Well, I would like to try some," Beezle declares, before marching into the shop. Without any prompting the little elf begins to grab handfuls of chocolates off the plates and begins to stuff them into his mouth.

"Beezle, put those chocolates down. They're not yours to have," Greybeard growls, trying to persuade the elf of his errors.

"No, I won't. They're so lovely and yummy, and they're mine," retorts Beezle impertinently.

"Beezle!" Finn says, grabbing hold of the little elf's hand. "Put them down now, before you get us all into trouble."

"These chocolates are not yours until you have paid for them. You do not usually get things for free, you know," adds Forester, taking money out of his pocket to pay the shopkeeper for Beezle's intrusion. "Come on – out now!"

Like a spoilt child, the little elf stamps his feet as he comes out of the shop and proceeds to have a tantrum. Shouting out loud, he screams, "I want, I want, I want." Beezle's protestations cause people to look at him; some even comment at how poor this boy's behaviour is. Greybeard and the others stand awkwardly, unsure what to do with this unruly child, and blush with embarrassment as people pass by.

"How can I discipline him?" Greybeard cringes as he looks to Stryker for guidance. "I am not his parent, and at present he comes willingly on our journey. I don't want to persuade him to do anything otherwise by shouting at him, but he is somewhat wild and wilful and needs a firm hand. What do we do?"

"Let us see how events progress, old man. The longer he is with us, the better we might know how to calm him," replies Stryker, equally unsure.

It is quite plain to see that Beezle is not like an elf. Finn is considerate, logical and reasonable; he needs facts to make his judgements. If you were to read the old writings, Finn fitted the stereotype given to the elves, but Beezle… well, he behaves more like a man. He is more emotional in his responses. Men are surrounded by other men who harbour the same emotions and are brought up to understand them. Beezle has been surrounded by elves who did not share the emotions he feels. This elf is unable to control his feelings, and worse still, understand why he is this way, so unlike his father and brother. Beezle has been made wanting, he yearns to be accepted, but wants it on his own terms.

After a short while, this group of creatures come to the centre of the village, where there is a small square. In this square is a market, with fruit and vegetable stalls, butchers, breadmakers and a horse trader with at least thirty horses lined up in a row against the eastern wall.

Greybeard goes up to the horse trader, a man called Pantus. Pantus is an old man, slim and wiry. He has no hair on top of his head, although wisps of hair at the side of his head fall onto his shoulders. His face and hands are dirty. His dull, green eyes are surrounded by heavy and leathery wrinkles. He has an abundance of hair coming out of his long pointed nose but few teeth in his mouth; those that he has retained are yellow and painful. He wears an old, battered grey suit, with a dirty handkerchief in the top pocket of his suit jacket and an off-white shirt underneath it. His black leather boots are well-worn and he has an old walking stick. Despite Pantus' appearance, his horses are immaculate and well looked after. It is obvious that he values his horses over himself.

"Hello, Pantus. How is business?" Greybeard asks.

"Ah, the old man on the mountain. I am doing well – very well – and business is good," Pantus enthuses, shaking the old man's hand vigorously. "Your horse is still waiting for you at my stables, and he is in fine spirits."

"That is good. I would like to put some more business your way. We need three horses and five ponies. They must be strong and able to last a journey to the far southern reaches of this land."

"Ooh, it's a long way to ride – a very long way indeed. Hmm… no problem. Look at these horses. All of them are bred from kings… please, please, look," Pantus gestures for Greybeard to look down the line.

Men, dwarfs and elves walk along the line looking at all the horses and ponies, checking stature, muscle build and character, whilst testing for defects such as lameness.

"I'll take this one," Stryker says, putting his hand on the head of a large, sturdy, dark brown horse with a short brown mane.

"This one will do for me," says Igralf, rubbing the nose of a bright white pony with a long white mane. Wattlespalf and Gendralf also pick white ponies with long white manes.

"You don't make it easy for us, do you?" laughs Forester, alluding to the fact that it was hard enough to tell the dwarfs apart without having the added confusion of three ponies that also looked the same.

"We like the same things," informs Wattlespalf.

"Apart from weaponry," Gendralf laughs, waving his axe about.

Forester looks up and down the line several times, and stands by a large light brown horse with patches of white all over it. "I'll take this one."

"Finn, I want you to choose a horse. And Beezle, I want you to choose a pony, not that you deserve one," says Greybeard, casting a disapproving eye over the little elf.

"Really, my own pony?" asks Beezle, missing or ignoring Greybeard's point. He smiles excitedly and takes his time. After a while he chooses a black pony with a black mane and the darkest black eyes. "I want this one then."

Finn is drawn to a tall, slim horse, almost red in colour, with deep blue eyes, a long black mane and a patch of white on his forehead. "I'd like to take this one, if I might?" asks Finn, stroking its back. Greybeard nods in approval of the elf's choice.

"Old man, you asked for eight horses in total, but if your horse is in Pantus' stables then we have one spare. Are you sure that your numbers are right?" asks Forester.

"We have one more man to collect, Forester," replies Greybeard. "I am confident he will come and we will need a horse to accommodate him. So, the need for eight is correct."

Greybeard pulls out a purse from his backpack. He empties some of the contents of the purse onto his hand. In the wizard's palm are numerous gems, all very precious. The wizard picks out a red gem, a green gem and a clear gem, putting them forward in Pantus' direction. Pantus cannot believe the wealth he is about to receive, or his luck. For a man who has spent his life working hard for relatively no gain and much struggle, this payment will secure his retirement.

"Will this do?" asks the old man, knowing that he needn't have asked the question in the first place.

Pantus nods his head. "This is too much and besides, I don't have any change to give you."

"Pantus, you do not owe me anything," insists Greybeard. "You deserve it. Do as you will, but at my request, treat yourself well whilst you do it."

"Thank you, Greybeard. Your generosity will ensure my last few years of life are more than bearable," Pantus answers, with a tear in his eye.

"Pantus, please equip the horses with everything we need. Bring them to the Old Mill Inn before dark, along with my horse," Greybeard orders, avoiding any possibility of getting into a deeper conversation with him.

"Yes, yes, without question."

"By the way, Pantus, do you know where Connor Perrywinkle might be hiding? I need to speak with the ruffian."

"If you are here then he may well be at your house removing its contents," frowns Pantus. "I'm sure the man stole one of my horses a while ago, and I gave him a good hiding with my stick when I saw him last to make up for it. If he is not at your house or somebody else's, then I dare say he is with his vagabond friends getting merry in the Old Mill Inn, where you are headed." Pantus is getting angry just talking about him.

"Thank you, Pantus. I'll start my search for him there then."

CHAPTER 5

DANGER AT THE OLD MILL INN

The companions walk through the square, towards the far end of the town where the Old Mill Inn is situated. The streets are less busy here; there are no shops to entice people onto them. A number of establishments offer a bed for the night, and a few inns offering food, ale and beds litter the street in between houses of varying sizes. After some minutes' walk, the Old Mill can be seen at the end of the street; it is instantly recognisable because one part of it used to be a windmill.

The windmill has been lovingly restored by the villagers of Kardarnath after becoming dilapidated over many years. Holes in the roof have been repaired, old broken bricks have been taken out and replaced, and rotten wooden windows have been fitted with new timbers. A new brick building has been extended outwards from the side of the windmill. As the Old Mill is the last building on this particular street, and the village for that matter, the new building has been made to be as big as it could be.

Set on three floors, the new building has large, wooden windows and plenty of rooms to house the many tourists and mountaineers who come to rest in Kardarnath. From the top floor of the building, the best views of the mountains in the whole village can be observed. The food is renowned to be the best there could be. The ales and wines have been sourced from all around the land with the specific intention of making any creature who happens upon this place feel a bit closer to home.

Greybeard, Stryker, Forester, the dwarfs, Finn and Beezle walk through an open gate which leads into the courtyard of the Old Mill. In front of them are the front doors to the inn; they can hear music from a fiddle, laughter and many people talking inside. Walking into the inn through two large, oak front doors, the group notice that the place is clean and bright inside. Wooden floorboards that span all floors are stained a dark brown. The walls and the ceilings are white. A number of large windows all let in a good amount of light, and large mirrors in different spots reflect that light around the main bar.

Behind the bar they are greeted by the Innkeeper, Willy. The Old Mill is owned by Innkeeper Willy and it was he who realised its conception. It was his vision that had made the Old Mill what it is today.

Innkeeper Willy is a big man with a big, bushy moustache and shaven head, who keeps an ordered bar. He was a decorated soldier, who fought with the King's Guard in the Western province of Mericusa, before he went into business. His reputation precedes him, and as such, there is rarely any fighting seen at the Old Mill, although unsavoury types such as buckriders, bandits and bounty hunters are regularly to be found here. If there is any trouble brewing, all it usually takes is for Innkeeper Willy to pull out the club he keeps under the bar and tap, tap, tap it on top of the bar until he gets the creature in question's attention. Willy himself is a very pleasant man, very well-mannered and very happy, or at least so far as anybody else can see. Willy is also aware of Greybeard's place in this world and they have a mutual respect for each other's exploits.

"Hello, Greybeard, been a few weeks since you visited these parts. Have you been well?" Willy asks.

"Yes, Willy, very well. I've been taking in the fresh mountain air, using the time to do a spot of reading, walking and the like. How are you faring?"

"Oh, very well – very busy. Seems everyone wants the same mountain air you're having. I would have some myself but I can't seem to get the time off to breathe it."

"I hope it is not too busy that there are no rooms available for tonight," comments Greybeard, a little concerned.

"Oh, let me have a look. We've had a lot of bookings recently, but we might still have a few rooms available for special guests such as your good selves." Willy looks in his book for an empty set of rooms. "Ah yes, here we go. We have two rooms, both with four beds, unfortunately they're not on the same floor, though."

"That will do, as long as we're able to get some rest," sighs a relieved Greybeard.

"Oh yes, the rooms are generally quiet. There you go, old man. One key for room 214 on the second floor, and another for room 308 on the third."

"Thank you, Willy – much appreciated. You two," the wizard calls, pointing at Finn and Beezle, "can spend the night in the same room as Stryker and Forester. I'll take my chances with the dwarfs." The dwarfs look perplexed and a little annoyed at that final comment, but then realise that they do grunt, burp and fart quite a lot when sleeping, and often when not.

After sorting out the formalities of who will go where, the group split up and go to their allocated rooms. Greybeard stays downstairs in the bar area and begins to look around the inn for Connor Perrywinkle. The inn has many nooks and crannies, with rooms spilling off other rooms and so on. There are lots of creatures making merry in the bar, including men, dwarfs, brownies, sprites, trolls and the odd goblin (obviously from the Hob clan, as they denounced the other goblin races in order to maintain the peace they enjoyed with other creatures). A few of the more unsavoury customers look Greybeard up and down as he walks through, staff in hand, searching for Perrywinkle. Most ignore him, more content to sup ale, however, he cannot help but feel he is being watched by something more sinister. From a corridor he hears Perrywinkle's voice.

"I had her jewellery in my hands when all of a sudden her husband came back. Like any good thief, I slipped out of the house undetected with it…"

"Connor Perrywinkle! Vagabond! Remember that favour you owe me? Well, here I am, as promised, to collect it," Greybeard bellows as he walks into a room off the corridor he has just come from. Perrywinkle almost jumps out of his skin on hearing him and tries to hide under the table he is sitting at.

There are several men in the room; all turn round and scowl at the impertinence of the old man standing in the same room as them.

"You want us to show this old man a lesson, Perry?" growls one of them, upon noticing Perrywinkle's fright.

"No, I wouldn't do that, Peter," warns Perrywinkle, trembling, his eyes peering up from under the table.

"Oi, old man, you wanna rumble?" Peter grimaces, standing up to face Greybeard before staring the old man square in the eyes.

The old man remains silent. He stares at Peter and the other men in the room and then begins to laugh at them. Perrywinkle looks horrified at what is happening; he obviously does not want to be in the old man's bad books. The other men stand up, puffing out their chests and rolling up their sleeves, angry at this old man's insolence. Their bravado is misplaced, not knowing who this old wizard is and of what he is capable.

Greybeard says to all of them bar Perrywinkle, "You will all leave this room, go home and spend a wonderful night in with your families. If you don't have a family then you will read a book, and if you do not own a book then you will go to bed, fall asleep and enjoy a beautiful dream about rabbits and kittens." The men look at each other bewildered for a few seconds, only to become even more annoyed at this old man's tone.

"Are you mental?" Peter laughs menacingly, raising his arm as if he is going to punch Greybeard.

Greybeard mumbles an incantation under his breath, "Legus hypnotinium." And, without a moment's hesitation, Peter and the other men start to walk out of the room, legs obeying the old man's original instruction.

"I'm gonna get you," Peter curses as he walks into the corridor towards the front door.

"Yes, goodnight, Peter," patronises Greybeard. Peter can be heard cursing all the way down the corridor along with everyone else. "So, Perrywinkle, how are you?" asks Greybeard, as if luring Connor into a trap.

"Fine, Mr. Beard. Fine, anything you want. I'll do it for you," Perrywinkle answers, trying to stop his body from shaking with fear and apprehension.

"Good, because I want you to come with me and some others on a journey to save this land, and I want you to play an important part in it."

"Yes, sir... journey? Save the land? Oh no, sir. I can't do that – I can't, sir. I wouldn't be up to it. You see, I've had this terrible illness plaguing me. Oh, it is very nasty... horrid in fact. Oh and contagious, very contagious," responds Perrywinkle, almost begging to be let off the hook, feigning coughs and splutters.

"Poppycock, you useless, self-satisfying weasel. You will and you are, that is the end of it," booms the wizard, scaring Connor into submission.

"Yes, sir, I will. I would never upset you, Mr. Beard. After all, you saved my life, I can never forget that, can I?"

"Hmm, I'm glad you remember. I have a particular role in mind for you… scribe."

"Scribe, sir?"

"Yes, Perrywinkle, you are going to write about this tale that is about to unfold."

"So it wasn't a dream I had then?"

"No, you are quite right in assuming that it was me talking to you in your dreams, Connor."

"How did you?" asks Perrywinkle.

"Just know that I can," replies Greybeard menacingly. "Oh, and if you decide to slip away out of my sight, or choose not to join me on this very, very important quest, I promise you that your dreams will turn to nightmares from here on in. Goblins and fires or much, much worse will plague you from this day on, that is, until you see fit to rid yourself from this world. By that I mean die."

"Oh no. Oh no, sir, not nightmares. I would never want to have nightmares for the rest of my life," Perrywinkle whimpers. "So the elves returning, the men who turn into bears, goblins and a warrior with skulls and spikes in my most recent nightmares, given to me by your good self, it's all true?"

"Yes, Connor, it is all true," admits Greybeard, calming his tone. "Back to the job I have for you. You have developed quite a skill with pen and paper."

"How do you know?" asks Perrywinkle, wondering why the wizard would take an interest in his ditties.

"Just know that I do and that I want you to share that skill with us. This journey will give you some good practice, and may even make a good man of you. Go home, get your belongings and come back here. If I do not see you back here soon, remember that I will make sure that your dreams turn to nightmares for the rest of your life. Be quick!" he orders. Perrywinkle shakes, unable to move. "Go!" the wizard commands. Perrywinkle does so, realising that something worse may happen to him if he does not.

Meanwhile, in the bedroom, Finn and Beezle have removed their woollen hats; both scratch the itches out of their warm, red ears, which have finally been exposed to the air again. They are safe here but to let them out in the bar area could potentially turn out to be a disaster. Stryker and Forester know this. The decision is made to get everyone something to eat and drink. Forester will go downstairs, see Greybeard and the dwarfs and then go to the bar. Stryker will look after the boys, furthermore he will ensure that they do not wander out of the room. Beezle cannot be trusted; his boisterous, often disturbing behaviour has not gone unnoticed.

Connor soon returns back to the Old Mill with a backpack and wearing a heavy coat. He walks up to a waiting Greybeard, who has, by this time, sat down with a small cup of wine.

"Ah, good man. I knew you would return – your dreams are safe... for now. Shall we make our way upstairs to meet your travelling companions?"

"Yes, sir, why not," replies Connor, who has butterflies in his stomach.

Greybeard and Perrywinkle walk upstairs and along the corridor to the room. Reaching the room the wizard raps on the door with the bear-headed staff. Igralf opens it and lets the wizard and Connor in. The dwarfs have already taken the initiative of ordering several flagons of ale and are quietly sitting on separate beds supping them.

"Igralf, Gendralf, Wattlespalf, this is Connor Perrywinkle, a vagabond who wants the chance to redeem himself. Isn't that right?"

"Yes, sir," answers Connor with a trembling in his voice. The dwarfs all wave, acknowledging their new companion.

Perrywinkle is a young man, only in his early twenties. He is very small and slim, smaller than the dwarfs. His face is boyish, eyes are wide and blue, hair is short and well kept, he has a small button nose and terse, thin lips. Connor is smartly dressed in a clean, grey, buttoned suit, white shirt, red tie and sparkling black leather boots. Don't be fooled though – his dress belies his real station, much like the room he rents, because Perrywinkle is known to be a thief, not a gentleman.

This small man comes from a poor family with poor morals, but he is gifted and did well at school. Unfortunately, as Connor got older, he could not overcome his urge to follow in his family's footsteps. Perrywinkle ran in the wrong circles, and the people with whom he hung around taught him to steal: first it was pick-pocketing and then it was burglary. But the people who taught him could only teach him so much and he surpassed their skills. Soon, Perrywinkle was hired by important people to steal from other important people in the large towns and cities. He had a talent for figuring out traps and riddles, finding and stealing many priceless treasures. His downfall was that he could not keep quiet about his talent and the things he had done.

After saying the wrong things to the wrong people at the wrong time, he found himself in big trouble. It was rare that he got caught, but eventually he was. The creatures who caught him in the woods that night were vicious, and they sought to spit roast him over a fire much like you would a pig. He was close to death when out of the blue, Greybeard saved him. Eternally grateful to Greybeard he took some learning from him.

From that day onward, he did not steal anymore. But he found that when you have a reputation, you are linked to all manner of crimes committed, even if you were miles away from them. Connor has since earned his money writing poems and tales, although in reality he doesn't need to earn a living, as he had saved much of his earnings from his previous life. Now, after accepting Greybeard's command, he is in the employment of the great wizard, for which he will not be paid. The chance now is to change his fortunes and maybe, just maybe, his reputation as well.

No sooner than Connor and the old man enter the room, there is another knock at the door. *Knock, knock.* Igralf opens the door to Forester.

"Hello," responds Igralf with a smile.

"Evening," says Forester, in a joking sort of manner. "Ah, I see our new friend has joined us. I hope everyone has made you feel welcome."

"We've made him feel very welcome," interrupts Greybeard, just as Perrywinkle opens his mouth to answer. "I take it the boys are upstairs with Stryker?"

"Yes, safe and sound," replies Forester. "I was just wondering what you want to do. We were thinking that we could order some food to come up to the room, and then sit and wait for morning to come."

"That sounds sensible," replies Greybeard. "Actually, I am feeling a bit peckish myself. Would you order me some steak and vegetables?"

"I suppose so," answers Forester, rolling his eyes.

"I'll come up shortly to check on all of you and eat my meal there," adds the wizard.

"Do you lot want to order anything whilst I'm down there?" asks Forester.

"Don't worry about us, Forester. The ale will keep us going for a while. We'll order something later," answers Igralf.

Forester nods his head and leaves the room. He walks down the corridor and stairs to the bar. The innkeeper greets him, tells him Pantus has delivered the horses and that they are tied up with the other horses at the back of building. Forester is about to order some meats, vegetables and bread when he senses that he is attracting some attention. He turns his head slightly so that he can just see over his shoulder. There are a couple of large figures looking his way, all are hooded and all hide in the shadows. One thing is certain, if they are hiding their faces, they do not want to be seen.

"Are they bounty hunters? Are they trackers? Do they know I am Otso? Have they seen the boys?" Forester asks himself.

"You're being watched, you know," Innkeeper Willy whispers over the bar to Forester.

"Yes, apparently so. Who are they?" whispers Forester.

"I don't know. I've never seen their like here before – bounty hunters I suspect. We get a lot passing through here. If it weren't for me knowing Greybeard, I'd say you and your friends were trouble," observes the Innkeeper.

"Hmm, normally I would say you were quite right in your assumption but on this occasion trouble, it appears, has found us," replies Forester with a hint of a smile. "I must warn the others. Could you do me a favour and make sure I'm not followed by any of them?"

"Don't worry. I don't let anyone who isn't a resident here past the door to the rooms. None have paid me to stay here or drink my ale, and for that they are not welcome," reassures the innkeeper. "You're safe here, I promise you that."

"Thank you, Innkeeper – you're a good man."

Forester goes back upstairs and along the second floor corridor to the room where Greybeard, the dwarfs and Perrywinkle are situated. He knocks on the door. Wattlespalf answers it and Forester walks in.

"I think we're being watched," announces Forester.

"I got that feeling, too," responds Greybeard. "Someone or something must have gained information of our expedition. I cannot see any other reason unless you lot have been getting up to unnecessary mischief," he says, looking at the dwarfs, Forester and Perrywinkle. "Well, have you?"

Shoulders are shrugged and all show elements of guilt in their faces.

"Hmm, I thought that might be the case." Turning round to face his oric, he asks, "Do you know?"

The oric talks to him in a language only the wizard understands. Greybeard nods and grumbles at the knowledge being imparted to him.

"Hmm, thank you, oric. I think we have been spied upon. Warrior appears to know we are coming and has obviously known for some time," reveals Greybeard. "His red oric is powerful, and he appears to know his oric much better than I thought he might. Unfortunately, he could have infiltrated mine."

Greybeard resolves to make his oric inaccessible to other wizards. This old wizard had allowed his oric to be responsive to other wizard's calls; therefore told his oric not to remove itself from the loop that connects all orics and all creatures who behold them. Generally, no oric is more powerful than any other. Spying upon another, whilst forbidden, is unlikely ever to happen without the knowledge of the oric that is being infiltrated. The red oric Warrior possesses is different though, it is seemingly more powerful and Greybeard's white oric might have unknowingly been used to give away the location of the group. The old man looks into his oric and utters, "Exilium influences. There, that should do it. Warrior will have little chance of getting any more information out of my oric. If he tries to break my spell, he will have to answer to me," Greybeard informs them. "Forester, get Stryker and the boys, and bring them back down here."

Forester acknowledges Greybeard's command. He rushes out of the room and up the stairs to the third floor of the building. Knocking on the door to his room, Stryker promptly opens it.

"Where have you been?" Stryker asks.

"All of you, pack your things. We're going to stay with the others," urges Forester. "It appears that we have been noticed."

Everyone quickly shoves their belongings back into their backpacks. Stryker grabs his sword. Forester takes a hold of his bow and quiver of arrows. Stryker opens the door, looks left and right, making sure that there is nothing there to surprise them. He walks out onto the corridor. The boys follow. Forester is the last to leave the room, closing the door behind him. A run down the corridor into the stairwell and down the stairs means, only seconds later, two men and two elves are outside the door where the others wait. They are quickly let into the now cramped room where the rest of the group greet them.

"Now the boys are safe here, I think it is time a few of us went downstairs to deal with these miscreants and mercenaries, if indeed they are who we think they are," storms Wattlespalf. "Who's coming with me?"

Perrywinkle holds both hands up, indicating that he wants to play no part in this. Perrywinkle may be a thief but he is not a fighter, although he will help when the situation needs him to act and when he is surrounded by friends.

Stryker is the first to volunteer. "Why not, I could do with a stretch of the legs and an ale to carry me through."

Igralf pipes up, "Yes, I'll come with you, too."

"I'm out. I've already had enough excitement today, so I'll leave this in your capable hands," yawns a tired and weary wizard.

Forester volunteers. "I'll come down with you."

Gendralf declines. "I'll stay here with the old man and the boys – make sure those who get past you lot get no further."

"We can handle weapons," says Finn. "I can use a bow and a sword. We are trained to use these items. We can help you."

"Yes, I'm sure we can help," adds an enthusiastic Beezle. "I have killed many things, animals mainly, large and small," he says smiling, as if proud of his exploits.

The room stays quiet and a few glances are exchanged.

"Alright, you take my bow and arrows," Forester says, pointing at Finn.

"You," continues Stryker, Beezle's face lifting in expectancy, "keep out of trouble."

"We'll be back soon," Forester adds, and with that the men and dwarfs leave the room.

Beezle looks around at his new surroundings. In the room are four beds, and on the outside wall there are three square windows that all open out to views of the town. He walks towards them and opens one of the windows situated above one of the beds. It is dark outside. The room is stuffy and warm. Greybeard is rocking in a rocking chair close to the door. He is chewing on his pipe and appears to be in a trance. Gendralf is lying on one of the beds, his eyes heavy – this dwarf is close to falling asleep. Finn examines one of the arrows he has pulled out of Forester's quiver, twisting and turning it with his fingers so as to take in different views and angles of it.

Beezle gets onto the bed underneath the open window and pokes his head out. Looking into the town he can see fires burning inside fireplaces through the windows of numerous houses. He finds the idea of fires burning inside houses quite strange. In the forest, fire has to be well-controlled – it certainly isn't permitted in houses, but here everyone appears to have one. The streets are emptying although people continue to trade. Children still throw snowballs at each other, whilst some villagers walk home after a hard day's work. Beezle sighs as he wants to go out onto the streets and play with the other children. He looks up at the dark skies above.

The elf is able to see only stars as the moon shines out from the other side of the building. Suddenly he notices movement out of the corner of his eye. On the outside wall above him there is a figure, and a large one at that. The elf looks directly at the spot where he thinks he saw whatever he saw, but there is nothing. Beezle looks down the wall to the floor below; this time his assumptions are confirmed – there is something climbing the wall! Quickly looking to the side, he sees there is another, and above there is another. Beezle is horrified and exhilarated at the same time. He pulls his head back into the room.

This elf says nothing when he should be saying a lot – he knows they are coming to this room. But Beezle wants to be involved in a battle to prove that he is able to fight alongside the others.

"Beezle, are you alright?" Finn asks.

"Yes, of course I am," Beezle replies with the slightest shudder in his voice.

Gendralf has left his dagger unsheathed next to him on the bed. Beezle walks towards the bed and takes a hold of it without anyone noticing. He keeps his eyes on the window. It is quiet outside. Out of the darkness, a head partially covered by a hood slowly appears and rises up from the window's ledge. The head belongs to that of a man but the parts of the face that can be seen appear to be decomposing. This monster does not have a nose or lips or skin, just teeth and flesh. The hood covers the rest of the face – all the better as the sight of it would not be pretty. A sickening stench flows into the room on a light breeze. Hands quickly cover mouths and noses in reaction to it.

The monster's green rotting hands grab the sides of the open window. This alerts Finn who screams, "Greybeard, Gendralf!"

With a sharp pull, the monster slides into the room. It is tall, fully covered by a dark brown robe, a rope is tied round its waist and a sword sits comfortably at his side – the monster begins to unsheathe it. Beezle walks up to it with the dagger, unfazed, he thrusts it towards the monster who grabs his hand, picks him up and throws him against the back wall. Perrywinkle quickly dives under the bed.

Finn, who by now has been able to pull back the bow string and aim a shot at the monster, lets the string of the bow go; the arrow goes through the hood worn by the monster and sits in its skull. Finn takes another arrow and shoots it through the monster's heart. Arrows fly another seven times, each one coolly piercing the monster, until there are no more arrows left in the quiver. The monster falls, and Gendralf is quick to make sure it is dead by beheading the monster with one chop of his axe. A black smoke rises up from its corpse, and with it everyone is sure they hear a hiss of the words, "Thank you". The monster's body dissolves until seconds later there is nothing left of it except an empty robe and an abandoned sword.

A second monster comes to the window. Greybeard rushes

towards it and closes the window before it can make any further moves to grace the room as the other one had.

The thing at the window is a draugar. They are the dead and were once men. Men with feelings, experiences, ideals, dreams, friends, family and children – who loved, hated, worked, played, wanted, needed, gave and they were flawed. Once they become a draugar they do not remember their past. They do not live in anticipation of the present or dream of the future; they are lifeless and their only desire is to eat. Possessing superhuman strength, they can also increase their size at will and often travel as wisps of black smoke. The draugar kill their victims by crushing them, cutting them with their weapons, devouring their flesh or drinking their blood. Those who spend only a small amount of time close to the draugar have the potential to be driven mad. A desire soon comes upon those affected to end their lives, submitting their souls to an endless wake as a draugar.

One way to kill these creatures is to drag them back to where their graves lie, the problem being that finding those graves is not an easy task. The other, and quite frankly, easier option is to behead them. Generally hunting at night, they are rarely seen in the day but have the ability to travel when their form is covered in a heavy cloth able to block out the sun.

Greybeard looks at Beezle.

"Did you know they were there?" asks Greybeard. Beezle is quiet and sheepish and does not say a word. "Beezle, did you see them coming?" he asks again. Beezle looks up at him and nods with a guilty stare.

"What do you think you were doing, boy?" shouts Greybeard. "What possessed you to put our lives in danger?"

"Please, Greybeard, he is young and foolish. Beezle, promise me you will do as you are told in future, and not do things that are deemed unusual, dangerous or mad," asks Finn.

"I wanted to prove my worth," Beezle replies. "Brother, I want nothing more than to please but my head sometimes wants other things. Please help me learn to be wise." Beezle begins to cry. It is not clear whether his tears are sincere or not, but every now and again, the little elf looks round to see if he is gaining sympathy from his actions.

"Beezle, listen to those who have experience of this world. We

A Draugar at the window

are new here – become wise by wanting to learn from these men," Finn says gently, putting his hand on his brother's shoulder.

"I'll try, I really will," says Beezle, sobbing through the gaps of his hands, which are firmly pressed against his face.

The draugar taps on the glass of the window. *Tap, tap, tap.* Lipless teeth smile, chatter and chomp as it contemplates eating the creatures in the room.

"I think it is time to leave this place," says Greybeard. Gendralf agrees, bending down to get a view of where Perrywinkle is hiding under the bed. Connor's hands cover his head and he is trembling uncontrollably.

"Come on, it has ended," Gendralf reassures, hoping to usher Perrywinkle out from under the bed. He takes hold of Perrywinkle's hand.

"Is it really alright to leave?" Perrywinkle asks, not wanting to move an inch… if that inch moved endangered his life.

"Yes, come on. Keep your eyes closed – although the things you would not want to see in the room have gone, outside of it is a different matter."

Perrywinkle comes from under the bed, and he keeps his eyes shut. Gendralf guides him around the empty robe once worn by the draugar. He holds his nose; the stench is unbearable to him. Finn picks up the arrows caught in the draugar's clothing and puts them back in the quiver. The draugar, still looking into the room through the window, follows the movements of everyone in it.

"Come on, everyone," insists Greybeard. Finn opens the door to the room. Everybody fills their hands with the backpacks and weapons belonging to themselves and those in the bar downstairs. Emptying the room, the door is closed behind them.

Whilst the events experienced by those in the bedroom unfold, the others have made their way down into the bar area of the inn. All of them hastily grab a mug of ale at the bar. The place is busy; it is hard to move through the throng of people who are laughing and talking loudly. No one appears to be interested in the men. Making their way through the main room, slowly they look from left to right and in the nooks and crannies for something or someone peculiar, but there is no one. Forester and Greybeard must have been mistaken.

Wandering outside, the men check the horses – again nothing.

All this time they are unaware of the attack taking place in the room upstairs. Satisfied that there is no threat, they saunter back inside, into the main bar area and sit down at a recently vacated table. Supping their ales, the men take in the atmosphere which is smoky, merry and bustling. Today's long walk has tired them out. Exhausted, they would rather retreat into their own minds than socialise amongst themselves – not that their minds are thinking of anything other than supping their ales. Everyone sits in silence for a number of minutes and it is bliss.

The bliss the men feel is soon disturbed by a booming, bellowing voice calling out, "You lot sitting there, whilst you have been enjoying yourselves, drinking yourselves to sleep, we've been doing the job you were meant to be doing." Greybeard is obviously not happy. The room has gone quiet, seemingly because of the old man's outburst, but this is not the case. In the rush and panic to get down the stairs, it has been forgotten by all that two pointy-eared elves are in their care, and the elves are not wearing their woollen hats or hoods to cover their mark. Everyone's mouths are wide open, including men, trolls, hobgoblins and Innkeeper Willy's – the shock is overwhelming. The group all say a hasty goodbye and make their way to the back of the Old Mill through numerous rooms, corridors and crannies. It is cold; everyone breathes out clouds of icy smoke upon their first steps outside.

They are greeted by four draugar; hands immediately cover mouths and noses. The stench of four is overpowering.

"Phew, do these dead men wash? They stink," says Wattlespalf, not mincing his words.

"We will take on these beasts. You get the horses." Stryker indicates to Greybeard, affording him, Gendralf, Finn, Beezle and Perrywinkle a break from fighting.

"Why, thank you. It's about time you lot did something useful!" chastises Greybeard.

The stables are up a small path to the right hand side of the back door, situated directly behind the Old Mill. They run up the path, able to distinguish their horses amongst a group tied to a long horizontal pole.

Finn and Beezle have never ridden a horse before but

understand, from watching people in the village riding them, that they need to sit on the saddle of the horse and hold the reins to control it. Finn and Beezle untie their horses, and using the reins, get the horses to clip-clop out of the stable. Finn promptly jumps high up into the air before landing on top of the horse, and indeed the saddle, perfectly. Beezle does the same to the mild amazement of Greybeard.

"Connor, that is your pony. Please get on it," orders Greybeard, pointing to a little yellowy-brown pony. Perrywinkle rushes over to his pony, unties it and moves it out of the stable. Not to be outdone by the elves, he too jumps high up into the air before landing perfectly on the saddle. Looking over at the elves, Connor pulls a huge grin.

Greybeard is slightly perplexed. "What is this, a jumping competition?" The wizard turns his attention to his horse now. "Hello, Thundercloud. Time for another adventure," whispers Greybeard, stroking the horse's face.

Thundercloud is tall, muscular, has a fine belly and long, agile legs. Thundercloud's body, mane, tail and eyes are a deep blue-grey in tone, much like clouds filled with thunder. Greybeard unties him from the post and Thundercloud walks himself to the outside of the stable. The old man ties his staff, backpack and sword onto the saddle sitting atop this noble horse. The wizard climbs onto the saddle using a stirrup as a step and positions himself so that he is comfortable. At that moment, the shadows of men can be seen approaching. Stryker, Forester, Igralf and Wattlespalf walk up the path; they all have smiles on their faces.

"This is already turning out to be an excellent adventure," Wattlespalf cries with excitement and happiness in his words.

The four men quickly get on their horses. Other draugar are beginning to appear from behind trees, on buildings and paths.

"I think it is time to make our move before the draugar become too many. We must go into the Whispering Woods and make the journey southwards," announces Greybeard. Heeding Greybeard's warning, the creatures pull on their horses' (or ponies') reins, and set off onto Kardarnath's streets with the intention of getting to the woods safely.

CHAPTER 6

INTO THE WHISPERING WOODS

Horses gallop through the village, their riders constantly looking over their shoulders. Black mists follow them, twisting and turning, huffing and puffing. It is the draugar, transformed to be as quick as they can be. Scaling the snow-covered rooftops, cobbled stones on the road and the walls of houses, black clouds try to gain an advantage on their prey. The black mists are everywhere and must be many in number.

Through the empty square and along streets where only a few people now walk, horses and the dangerous dead weave. People minding their own business, strolling these bitterly cold streets, appear to be in the wrong place at the wrong time. Draugar indiscriminately bear down on an unlucky few as the horses pass. The wails and cries of their riders warning people to run and hide go unheeded, or at least come too late. The black mists drop away from the main pack, stopping to wrap themselves around screaming unfortunates before turning back into rotting, smell-ridden figures. Holding men, women and children, they will bite and suck them until these people have nothing more to give.

It is not long before the horses gallop past the final house in the village. The woods are not far away. Once out of the village, the cobbled roads end, turning quickly to a track; this is better for the horses and they are able to gain speed. On either side of the track, snowy verges rise above the village, climbing upwards towards the entrance of the Whispering Woods in the distance. The entrance to the woods is protected by a barrier of snow-topped trees, and much like the mountains, the woods dominate this side of the immediate landscape.

The riders make haste, hoping that they can lose the black mists following them amongst the trees. There is still a long while before the dawn can help them, turning favour from the draugar back onto the riders. Draugar do not like travelling in the day; the sun burns through their flesh and their pupil-less eyes, and what is left of their minds is blinded by the brightness of it.

Greybeard utters a magic word: "Windswell." Suddenly, the black mists begin to fall behind. The horses are fast but the pace of the draugar is now hindered by a westward wind, created by Greybeard, blowing their misty forms in the opposite direction to the woods.

The riders break through the entrance to the Whispering Woods. Light from the moon is drowned out by the sheer amount of leaf cover the trees provide, so the path is hard to make out. Greybeard leans to the side of his horse as it runs, and carefully unties the cord holding his staff. He takes hold of his staff and asks that the oric light; it does so immediately, lighting the riders' way through the thick woodland ahead; the draugar seep into the woods a good few seconds later.

Whispers can be heard by all in the distance. The riders' immediate thoughts are that the draugar must be communicating with one another, but the sounds are not coming from the dark wisps.

The whispers are almost silent at first, as if one or two creatures are speaking to others who are listening intently to every word. Those who have listened add their voices, passing on the message to even more. So it is, the whispers become a deafening wave of sound, showing displeasure towards the draugar, who have soiled their homeland with their presence. The black mists stop moving and instead hover silently above the woodland track, hesitant to move forward.

The men pull on the horses' reins, slowly bringing them to a halt; they do so to watch this strange set of events unfold. The whispers remain deafening, and there is a movement on the forest floor amongst the bracken.

"A fern leaf over there moved," says Igralf. Heads turn to look.

"There, another," Forester points into the undergrowth.

"And another," adds Wattlespalf, looking in the opposite direction.

Suddenly, there is movement everywhere, as if an army is moving forward towards the draugar, but those attacking cannot be seen under the mass of fern leaves they hide behind. The mists retreat back to the entrance of the forest – they obviously know this foe and do not want to fight it. With screams of disappointment and anger, the draugar disappear into the night.

"Well, that was interesting! The draugar didn't much like what the forest had to say about them. Saying that, I doubt they will cause us any more distraction tonight…" says Greybeard.

"I'm just wondering whether we will be the next to be attacked by those creatures, or whatever they might be," warns Gendralf.

"They won't attack us – they're pollymins," announces Finn.

"What was that you said?" asks Wattlespalf.

"They are not creatures. Pollymins are woodland spirits who look after everything in these woods, from the trees to the animals, insects to the rivers and ponds. They sensed we were here, my brother and I, and seeing we were in danger they came out to protect us in the best way they could," explains Finn.

"Hmm, why do you think the pollymins were protecting you?" asks an intrigued Greybeard.

"Because we are of the forest," Finn replies, as if what he was saying was obvious.

The pollymins withdraw back into the woods and the whispers subside. The riders, now safe, breathe a sigh of relief. The vigour they felt in their rush to get away from the draugar is replaced with a tiredness that swiftly overtakes them, and their eyes become heavy.

"I think we need to find a place to rest," yawns Stryker. "This has been a very interesting but very long day and I, for one, will be glad to see the back of it."

"I know somewhere we can stay which is only a few minutes away. There is a cave and I'm sure it has room enough for us all inside," Perrywinkle reveals, to the delight of everyone else.

"Good man," praises Greybeard. "I knew you would be of some use to us. Please lead the way." Greybeard passes Connor his staff; the oric's light is still strong.

Perrywinkle sets off down the track, around trees and a few boulders, and the others follow. As promised, they end up outside a cave. It has a reasonably large mouth opening up into a relatively deep passage. The men lead their horses inside the cave, away from the elements. Snow has begun to fall again. Greybeard retrieves his staff from Perrywinkle and balances it against the wall of the cave, the oric providing everyone with light. Taking the horses to the back of the cave, this company of men, dwarfs and elves unload the items they are carrying off their steeds and onto the floor of the cave. The horses drop to the ground and rest. Stryker, Forester, the dwarfs and Finn go outside to collect as many dry broken twigs, bracken and thicker pieces of wood as they can from nearby.

Inside, Greybeard, Perrywinkle and Beezle prepare a fire at the front of the cave. They make a circle with large stones, and the others come back in with the twigs, bracken and wood. The bracken is laid down in the stone circle first, the twigs are laid on top and the thicker pieces of wood will be kept to one side until the fire is lit.

Greybeard mumbles two words, "Finger flamian." At the very tip of his finger, a flame appears. Cupping the flame with his other hand, he lights a small amount of the bracken in the fireplace. The bracken begins to curl as the dry leaves smoulder. Forester cups his hands around the burning bracken, protecting it from stray winds. Greybeard stands up and extinguishes the flame on his finger with one outward breath. Forester blows gently onto the bracken until it smoulders some more, catching the broken twigs laid out in the fireplace. He blows a few times onto it and then, eureka! A small set of flames appear, creating others which start to fold and flicker their way around the fireplace, catching leaves and twigs until they encompass everything in it. Gendralf gets a few of the larger pieces of wood and puts them on the fire. All sit round in silence, taking in the fire's ever-increasing warmth. Greybeard asks his staff to extinguish its light and it does so. Everyone watches the flames of the fire dance until one by one, and with big yawns, they all fall asleep.

The morning light peers through the mouth of the cave. The last embers of the fire are slowly burning out and it is becoming cold. Stryker is the first to awaken. He gets up and stretches his arms and legs. Moving around the cave, he checks on the horses; they appear to be content. Half of them are asleep, dreaming of fields full of sugar lumps and apples. The other half are standing, ready to continue on. The dwarfs are all snoring, mouths wide open, saliva running down their beards onto the cave floor.

Perrywinkle and Beezle are close to waking, both have one eye open, and half asleep, their eyes follow Stryker's movements. Forester is also half-awake. His hands are behind his head as he looks up at the roof of the cave. Greybeard sits against a wall, head down and asleep, his hand holds onto his staff which is propped up beside him.

"Finn! Where is Finn?" Stryker asks himself before running to the outside of the cave. "Finn!" he calls out loudly again.

Forester, Beezle and Perrywinkle get up, slightly alarmed at Finn's disappearance. Stryker looks around the front of the cave for signs of movement which will indicate which way he might have gone. He looks on the ground and can see the treading of feet from the previous night; he can tell this by the way the footprints have turned from compacted snow to ice. Stryker looks to the right of the cave and ahead of it – there are no fresh tracks. Looking to the left there is a trail, the footsteps are fresh, the snow, although compacted, is still soft. Footsteps lead up by the side of the cave and beyond. Stryker runs back into the cave, quietly indicating to those who are already awake to come with him. Going over to his sword, he picks it up and straps it to his back, while Forester picks up his bow and quiver of arrows. Stryker and Forester proceed out of the cave and begin to follow the tracks, while Perrywinkle and Beezle tag along.

"This way," Stryker says, pointing in front of him, noticing that the footsteps move in the same general direction.

The others follow Stryker. Footprints in the snow lead around trees, in between them, under branches, through bracken and nettles.

"He's gone to see the tree spirits," reveals Beezle. "He is close. I can hear them talking. I'm unsure as to what they are saying, though."

After a few minutes of following Finn's tracks, Stryker, Forester and Perrywinkle are also able to hear the whispers. They walk more slowly, creeping up onto ever louder words as they get closer and closer to Finn's whereabouts. Finn is talking. He is explaining how he and Beezle came to be in this world at this time. In front of the others is a large, wide rock. They climb the rock silently, in anticipation of seeing Finn and the tree spirits.

Stryker, Forester, Perrywinkle and Beezle peek over at Finn from behind the rock.

Finn is standing on a clear piece of ground. The clearing is circular in shape. Numerous rocks surround the clearing and on those rocks are dozens of strange-looking creatures – pollymins. The pollymins appear short in stature, only a foot tall at best. The skin on their round, hairless, naked bodies, is as white as snow. At the ends of their short arms and legs are hands without fingers and feet without toes. Large, deep blue eyes and a small mouth without lips adorn their oval-shaped heads. When they whisper you can just make out that they have a small red-coloured tongue but they do not have teeth. They do not appear to have ears, a nose, or a neck, either. Despite their strange appearance these creatures appear friendly and are invariably captivating.

Standing next to him, and no doubt the one Finn is talking to, is something very large and very much taller than Finn himself. The creature has the head and the neck of a stag with large antlers and a long tuft of hair pointing downwards from its chin. Its body is like that of a man, its figure and torso slim and defined. Standing on two long legs, its feet look like a man's but are larger in size. Thin, bony arms come down to its knees, and long fingers at the end of its equally long hands almost scrape the floor. The creature is covered in thick red and brown hair.

"What happened to our race? How did we die?" Finn asks the creature. There are prolonged whispers coming from the mouth of the creature but there is no movement of its lips. No one on the rock, not even Beezle, can translate.

"How did he come to be?" Finn replies.

More whispers.

"Time? Worlds?" Finn asks, understanding everything he is being told but requiring more information. "If he is that powerful, how can he be defeated?"

The whispering continues.

"The old man and the others? Yes, I can sense that," Finn says. He continues with his questioning. "Dragons and the Jotunn?"

The stag-headed creature calls to the pollymins, and moments later three of them walk forward in Finn's direction holding an item. Finn bends over and holds out both hands. The pollymins hand the elf what appears to be a rod made of silver; it is three palms long and three fingers wide. The rod is emblazoned with ancient writings and numerous precious stones of many different colours. The whispering becomes more solemn and the tone changes.

"And I must join the rod with the other piece? I understand. But why me? I'm surely too young for such a quest... what about Stryker or Forester?"

The whispers explain why.

"Fated?" Finn interrupts, only for the whispers to carry on once his statement has been made. "Beezle? What about Beezle?"

Perrywinkle slips, and a stone click, click, clicks down the rock. The stag-headed creature turns and stares at those looking down from behind the rock, and the Pollymins do the same. Within seconds they have fled and are nowhere to be seen.

"Sorry, I didn't mean to..." Perrywinkle cowers, looking at everybody.

"How did you get the reputation of being a master thief?" Forester asks, tutting at Perrywinkle for his clumsiness.

Finn stands alone in the circle. He looks up at the others and smiles with an air of disappointment that he did not finish the conversation, but he knows enough.

"I need to speak to you all. We need to get back to the cave," Finn mutters apprehensively.

With one huge jump Finn stands on top of the rock the others hid behind. He then jumps off the rock and begins to walk back to the cave, following the footsteps in the snow. The others try to keep up behind him.

"So... what did we just see then?" questions Perrywinkle.

"The small creatures were the pollymins who saved us last night. The large one I have no idea – I have never seen anything like him before," replies Beezle. "Brother, who was that creature?" he asks Finn.

"That creature is the lord of the woods. He has no other name but Lord. I'll tell you more when we get back to the cave," Finn answers.

After a short while, they return to the cave. Greybeard and the dwarfs have woken up, and having raided their backpacks, eaten the last of their bread, meat and cheese for breakfast.

"This is not good enough," bellows Wattlespalf. "We need more food or we will starve."

"Quite right. Where is the next inn?" asks an impatient Gendralf. "Those pesky draugar have spoiled our night, caused us to neglect our already empty stomachs and made us hungrier by making us do more than we ought."

Greybeard notices Finn is desperate to talk.

"Be quiet, you three, and stop thinking about your bellies. We will have a hearty amount of food soon enough. Now listen, because this elf wants to talk and no doubt has more important things to tell us than you do." Greybeard gestures for Finn to begin.

"Sir, I have spoken with the lord of this forest. It was he who sent the pollymins to save us last night. He lived in our time and saw some of what happened to the elves who lived in these woods. It began with a poisoning of the water. He does not know who administered the poison into the pools the elves drank from, only that the poison killed many in the villages. Deaths were painful and long, and by the time the villagers knew what was happening most were dead. Those who survived the poisoning were left weak. An army of goblins led by a huge warrior filtered into the woods. The spirits tried to ward off the army and the trees moved this day – branches became arms, twigs became fingers and roots became feet. Some trees were able to catch the goblins and crush them, but most were too slow and the goblins too fast to be caught. The elves were too weak to move too far; those who did manage to hide were easily found."

It is unusual for an elf to cry, but one single tear comes to Finn's eye as he retells the information imparted to him. Beezle is unfazed and his attentions have wandered; he is looking intently at Greybeard's staff, or more precisely, the oric encased in the bear's mouth.

"The warrior in the south..." Everyone looks surprised as Finn has not yet been told the finer detail of this quest. "He is the same one who appeared three thousand years ago. He is not of this world or at least not of this time, and he has travelled through it to get here. The red oric on his sword has been loaned

The Rod

to him – it is not his. Someone or something is using him to achieve an aim. His power comes from the oric, which is bound to the sword by a powerful ancient magic much like the oric on your staff, Greybeard. The only way to dispel the power in him is to get this rod to touch the oric in his sword. I'm assured the rod will do the rest." Finn reveals and passes the rod over to the wizard. Greybeard marvels at the rod and the writings on it, and examines it for a long while.

"Hmm, this writing… it comes from the very beginnings of this world. It is too ancient for even me to understand with any great confidence," he says, studying it further. Greybeard starts mumbling to himself as he tries to decipher the words on the rod. "We are playing into the hands of much danger. If the rod and the oric in the warrior's sword are meant to be together, then they were produced to be as one. A third element, be it man or beast, will make it wield its most destructive of forces. Beware, he who tries to become this weapon's master – as you will fulfil its purpose, you will not likely fulfil yours. Warrior must not get his hands on this," warns Greybeard. "Put it in your backpack and forget about it until we need it," he says, handing it back to the elf. Finn does as he is told.

"Were you told anything else?" Greybeard asks probingly.

"Yes, Lord mentioned Pengwellen the dragon. He said he may be able to help. He also spoke of the jotunn, the giant men of the south," recounts Finn.

"Humph, dragons and giants – both formidable enemies in times past, and Pengwellen… dear, oh dear." Greybeard is visibly shaken, as are Stryker and Forester. He ponders for a few seconds then calls on the others, "I suggest we make a move away from this place."

Whilst everybody is loading their belongings on the horses, Beezle taps Finn on the shoulder. "Finn, when we were looking down on you from the rock Lord mentioned me. What did he say to you?"

"I didn't get to hear that part, Beezle. He was gone before he could say anything more. I suspect he was going to say that you will play a major part in this quest." Finn smiles, putting his arm around Beezle. "Come on, let us get a move on, brother."

The men lead the horses and ponies out of the cave. It is still very early in the morning. The sun is beating down through the leaves at the top of the trees. It feels warmer than it has done recently, and will become warmer still as the men descend and get closer to the eastern plains.

"We should get a good run if the weather holds out," advises Igralf.

"Are there any inns off the beaten track? We didn't see any on this road coming up it," asks Wattlespalf, still hankering for some food in his belly.

"There is a guesthouse, Wattlespalf, many miles from here. We could make it by nightfall if we travel well and are not distracted by your moaning and complaining," replies Greybeard.

"Good, as we have already run out of provisions," sighs a relieved Wattlespalf.

"That's because you eat too much," jokes Stryker, reaching over to pat Wattlespalf's belly.

They all climb onto their horses and the journey begins once more in haste.

CHAPTER 7

TELLING TALES AND A SPOT OF FISHING

Perrywinkle leads the line as he guides the company back onto the main track through the woods. The Whispering Woods are particularly stunning in the daytime; the trees tend to be of one type – they are tall and the trunks are not very wide. Branches do not appear on the tree until halfway up its length, and the leaves are small but many. The branches are long and meet the branches of other trees; the effect is a ceiling of leaves, varying in shades of green. The roots of the trees are often exposed and spread the width of the track, causing the horses to take minor diversions or jump over them. Birds large and small, coloured and dull, dart in and out of the trees, singing wonderful tunes to the riders as they pass by.

The general condition of the path on this day allows the horses and ponies to trot at a decent pace, although they are careful of sharp descents. The track itself is made up of hardened earth and small stones; if it rained hard it is easy to imagine that it would become a flowing river of mud. At times the track becomes treacherous, with narrow passages and steep drops falling away into rocky or watery abysses below. Every now and again, smaller, narrower paths split off from the main track, leading to small villages, farms, fishing holes and shrines. To both sides of the track are the faces of tall, wide rocks interspersed amongst verges with long brown grasses, felled trees and the occasional boulder. The road runs alongside rivers and waterfalls which can always be heard, even in the distance and when they are out of sight. Sometimes the woods disappear for a time, opening out onto pools of water and rocks, with hiding places where picnics could be had. Occasionally, you can see the mountains peering over the trees, although views of the peaks disappear as the track descends or the tree cover thickens out.

There is much wildlife here. Squirrels hunt for nuts. Rabbits shoot in and out of holes. Foxes sniff on the floor, looking for a scent that will lead them to food. Deer stand atop rocks and look out over their territory. Boar chew on grasses, leaves and nuts found on the woodland floor. It is an amazing sight to see and the pace set has been good; the men are relaxed.

"Finn, I've got to say that your aim, speed and precision with Forester's bow when tackling the draugar last night was exceptional," praises Gendralf. "Where did you gain the skill?"

"I gained it at school. My father..." Finn stumbles on his words, this will be the first time he has spoken of his family. "My father used to teach us elflings how to hunt and defend ourselves – it was a compulsory part of our learning."

"What of your mother and father? What were they like? If you don't mind me asking," probes Gendralf.

Finn's eyes glaze over and he goes into a trance momentarily. "They were good people. My mother died when I was a very young elfling. Apparently she went to meet the Creators after giving birth to my brother. I have no recollection or picture of her but I am told I have her eyes. She was very intelligent and understood the history of this world well. Unlike the others in our village, she had travelled to many parts of Everlast to see and experience the places where history had been made. My father accompanied my mother on her journeys but he did it out of love for her as opposed to having the need to travel. He had many tales to tell of their adventures. We may even retrace some of their steps on this one."

"Do you know that dwarfs do not like to travel, preferring to stay around the place they call home?" reveals Gendralf. Finn shakes his head. "Well, for that reason, my brothers and I could be considered trailblazers. Many in my clan disapprove of our behaviour but history tells me that dwarfs, much like elves, shared this world once. It seems we have much in common. I believe our races both hid themselves away from the rest of this land, and to be frank, I don't understand why. I mean men aren't that bad – look at those four in front. They're not scary, not one bit," he jokes, pointing at Greybeard, Stryker, Forester and Perrywinkle, although they are hardly typical of their race.

"Yes, I see what you mean." Finn smiles. "I have read that our races once shared villages, towns and cities in the beginning."

"Anyway, we digress. We were talking about your parents,

weren't we? Tell me more about your father, lad." Gendralf probes further.

"Hmm, my father was…" Finn stops and corrects himself. "Is a very good man – he has looked after us well. He is one of the most agile of all the elves. Sometimes I think he can jump over mountains. He works hard hunting for food, whether it be fish or meat. He also spends a lot of time teaching the children about weaponry and how to hunt. He is a very good teacher. He knows every part of the forest, and sometimes he takes us with him to explore. I enjoy going with him to the beach on the far eastern side of the forest to look at the sea. Whilst we are exploring, he teaches me a few survival tricks. Unfortunately, I haven't learnt anything about surviving in the snow, though." Finn smiles at his joke.

"Ah, you told a joke! Elves can tell jokes – I am learning much today," laughs Gendralf. "Keep going."

"He encourages Beezle and me to be the best we can be. He has taught us to read and takes me to the library regularly. Father always says that I have my mother's intelligence and that I should use it well. I miss him already," Finn admits.

"My father was a good old soul but always merry. He liked his ale far too much – so much so that it eventually killed him," reveals Gendralf, with fond memories of him in his mind.

"I'm sorry," offers Finn.

"No, he died a very honourable death. Our mine was being attacked by a large fiery dragon. My father, in his drunken wisdom, jumped into the dragon's mouth with a flask of his finest spirit ale – it is highly flammable stuff, you know. Once inside, he worked his way into the belly of the beast. It is suspected that he poured the spirit ale in the beast's stomach, pulled out a match and set light to it. To cut a long story short, the dragon exploded from the inside out. Some dwarfs say he was in that dragon a good while, so I like to think he had a few swigs of the ale himself and a sing-song before he died. Oh, how he liked to sing. Hey, Forester," Gendralf shouts.

Forester turns round to face the dwarf. "Yes, Gendralf?" he responds.

"Do you know this boy could quite well be more skilled with a bow than your good self?" Gendralf playfully goads Forester.

"Oh, really. You think so? Young Finn, do you think you can beat me in a contest?"

Finn starts shaking his head, indicating that he could not, whilst Gendralf nods his head mouthing silently, "Yes, he can."

Forester pulls back his horse, settling in between both Finn and Gendralf. "I would like to see this skill you possess, be it this afternoon or tomorrow morning. I'll lend you my bow and quiver."

"Can you use a sword as well as you aim a bow, young fellow?" asks Gendralf.

"I don't know. Why don't you tell me what you think when a chance arises?" replies Finn.

"And what of your brother?" comes another question from Gendralf.

"Again, you will have to make your own assessment," replies Finn.

"You're also a diplomat," laughs Forester. "A man of many talents."

Whilst this conversation reaches its end another begins between Beezle and Greybeard.

"Greybeard, why are you considered to be a great wizard?" asks a curious Beezle.

"I have lived a long time and I have learnt a good many things."

"What have you learnt and what can you *really* do?" asks Beezle, hoping to appeal to Greybeard's ego.

Greybeard looks at Beezle, knowing he has nothing to prove to anyone, but he nonetheless unties his staff from the side of his horse, taking hold of it with both hands.

"That is a very good question, Beezle. Can I do anything at all or is everything just an illusion? For example, when you were being irresponsible with my staff and I took it from you; was it me using my magic to take it from you... or did I suggest to you so strongly to throw it back to me, that you did? Or, indeed, is it my staff that possesses the magic, and as such, did it choose to come back to me of its own accord?" Beezle looks a little bewildered.

Greybeard raises his staff into the air and whispers an incantation to himself. Out of the blue, a red butterfly flutters by.

The butterfly lands on the staff and sits there for a number of seconds, looking at Greybeard. It then flutters off, fluttering further and further away until it can no longer be seen.

"Ha, ha!" Greybeard cackles, excited by what he has just done, before looking at Beezle to see if he is impressed with the trick.

"That isn't a trick. That was a nonsense, Greybeard," comments a very disappointed Beezle.

"Young man, how can you not think that what you have just seen is not the most impressive trick ever to have been performed in Everlast?"

"Nothing happened – that's why!" says Beezle impertinently. "Show me some thunder and lightning... show me something really impressive," he continues, challenging Greybeard.

"Beezle, know this, what you have seen is magic in its purest form. It is the kind of magic that the Creators used to create this world and everything you see in it. Nothing is more impressive," booms a very serious-looking Greybeard.

Beezle understands the comments made by Greybeard but remains unimpressed. "Can you show me how to do magic?" asks Beezle, changing his tone.

"The cheek of it! You call my magic 'nonsense' and then you have the nerve to ask me to teach you that very same magic." Greybeard tuts.

"But I have something, I feel it. I could use magic and be good at it, I know it," pleads Beezle.

"You certainly have something. I have never seen anyone provoke a reaction out of my staff before," Greybeard ponders, stroking his beard.

"It talks to me," confides Beezle. "I must be able to hear magic things."

"Yes, I have heard it talk to you," Greybeard says to him quietly, "but my oric is very unsure of you and so am I. Beezle, I will be very honest... you tread between the light and the dark. At the moment you are neither, but I feel you will make decisions that will choose your path for you. The decisions I have seen so far do not bode well, though." Greybeard ponders for a while more. "I cannot risk teaching someone who may cause the world problems, and you certainly might. I am sorry."

Beezle looks disappointed. "Sir, what can I do to change your mind?" he asks, almost begging Greybeard to give him a chance.

Greybeard looks at Beezle. For a moment he wonders what can be done with the boy.

"Well, I could teach you one or two of the basics. You have had your introductory lesson today." Greybeard gives Beezle a wry smile, and Beezle in turn smiles back.

"I'm going to be a wizard," he says to himself.

As the conversation between Greybeard and Beezle has been taking place, Perrywinkle, Igralf and Wattlespalf have also been speaking with each other.

"Yes, I've been around a lot and I've seen many kings and queens. In fact, I have robbed the vast majority of them. I remember that my greatest steal came in the western provinces at Mericusa," Perrywinkle babbles, making himself feel like a bigger man.

"So what did you steal from the King and Queen?" asks Igralf.

"Well, you wouldn't believe it but I was the one who stole Big Blue," boasts Perrywinkle.

It is in the nature of dwarfs to mine treasured gems. Gems taken from the mines are sold on to traders and sometimes directly on to the rich; the rich being lords, ladies and even kings. Many prize a dwarf's fine work highly. It was the dwarfs that had mined the famous Big Blue – the very gem that Perrywinkle is talking about.

"Really? No… the Big Blue? Now that is a gem to be proud of," gasps an impressed Igralf. "How did you manage that?"

"Well, I'd been briefed by my employers as to where the gem was and how to get to it. I rode up to the castle in Mericusa while an event was taking place. There were many lords and ladies who had come to pay tribute to the King and Queen. Many had also come to see the gem and have a good time, if you know what I mean.

"It was dark outside the castle walls, as I remember. The battlements were full of soldiers, what with all the dignitaries present. I found one spot where the defences were lacking, and I took out my grappling hook and threw it over the ramparts. I climbed up and got through a window into one of the guest bedrooms. I stole some clothes from one of the dignitaries, who fortunately enough was of the same stature as myself. I like to think I somehow knew those clothes were waiting for me there. Opening the bedroom door, I walked through it into the corridor and ran down it, avoiding people to the left of me, right of me, ahead of me and behind me. I hid behind curtains, statues and vases until I got to where the gem was being displayed.

"Now, the Big Blue was in a room next to the main banquet hall, so whilst there were ten guards around the gem, I would not be seen by anyone else as they were all eating and making merry in the next room. The gem itself was surrounded by a large iron cage. Whilst that might have been enough to put anyone off stealing it, what the idiots didn't think about was that the gem could fit through the bars of the cage. I mean, come on, how easy could it get?

"Anyway I'd packed some smoke bombs and my homemade goggles, a mask to help me breathe through smoke and my retractable metal pincers. After putting my goggles and mask on, I threw the smoke bombs in all directions in order to confuse and disorientate the guards. I ran in the direction of the cage through the smoke and was able to get a glimpse of the Big Blue every now and again as smoke swirled around it. I extended the pincers towards the gem, closed them around it and retracted them fully so that the gem landed safely in my hands.

"The guards coughed and spluttered wildly. I ran off down the corridors, back into the guest bedroom, grabbed onto the rope attached to my grappling hook and abseiled down the outside of the castle walls. So, Bob's your uncle, Fanny's your aunt – on my horse and out of the province within hours," finishes Connor, grabbing a breath after a delightfully animated explanation of what had happened.

"Now that is a story," wows Igralf.

"So who did you sell the Big Blue to? It hasn't been found yet, has it?" asks Wattlespalf.

"Do you really want to know?" asks Perrywinkle, his voice nearing a whisper, his head looking left and right just to make sure no one else is listening.

"You know we want to know," replies Igralf impatiently.

"Well..." There is a long pause. Igralf and Wattlespalf are getting very excited in anticipation of being told a very big secret.

Perrywinkle eventually whispers in their direction, "I'm not telling you."

Igralf and Wattlespalf look very disappointed. Perrywinkle laughs not for a few seconds but a few minutes. Wattlespalf rubs his finger over the edge of his sword, whilst staring menacingly at Perrywinkle. Perrywinkle soon stops laughing when he notices Wattlespalf's gesture, the regard for his own wit subsiding as he becomes a little bit scared of the dwarf.

"Look, I've been in enough trouble and I'm not prepared to get into anymore by opening my big mouth again." Igralf and Wattlespalf sense Perrywinkle's sincerity and decide not to probe him further. "So, how did you lot get to know Greybeard then?" asks a serious-looking Perrywinkle, changing the subject.

"Well," Igralf begins, "it was around fifty years ago. We met him at the battle of the Ballundo mines in the north-eastern provinces near to where we live. Our mine had got word that the goblins were about to attack the mines and subsequently our cousins had asked us to come and help. Thirty-three of us travelled over to the Ballundo mines. It took us a couple of days to get there. Now, the openings to the mines themselves are set halfway up a very large, very craggy hill – which was fortunate for the dwarfs who lived there as it would make it harder for the little monsters to reach the entrance of the mine. The goblins were camped out at the bottom of the hill awaiting their orders; in total there must have been three hundred or so. We were clearly outnumbered – there were eighty warriors between the two clans at best. Anyway, we hid behind a hillock looking down on the goblin camp. You could see some dwarfs patrolling the top of the hill, making sure these vagabonds weren't trying to get in round the back way. Wattlespalf, who was the fastest runner at the time, went to tell our Ballundo cousins that we were there, ready and waiting to support them. Wattlespalf weaved in and out of the rocks, he crawled and climbed through the grass, always checking to see whether he had been seen by the goblins – but he had not."

"Yes, I was very professional – very good at my work," boasts Wattlespalf, interrupting Igralf.

"Anyway," Igralf continues, "the Ballundo dwarfs, once briefed, readied themselves. At nightfall we would attack – it was highly likely that the beasts were planning the same. Dusk came and we moved from our position, crawling in the long grass towards the goblin camp. Meanwhile, the Ballundo dwarfs, who, incidentally, are small, much smaller than us, began to crawl down the hill as silently and swiftly as they could. Wattlespalf was with them. The long and short of it is a battle ensued, we fought bravely and one by one the blinny fell, but we were still outnumbered. Every dwarf death was like five. Our hammers, swords and axes attacked the diseased little monsters, with their swords, scythes, daggers and pikes coming right back at us. Soon we were down to our last three dozen warriors, our backs to the opening of the mine and surrounded by one hundred and twenty of the blighters."

"Pretty good odds if you ask me," says Wattlespalf, interrupting Igralf again.

"The goblins looked at us with a hatred and an anger so encompassing you could feel it. 'We're gonna slit yer through the middle' and 'we'll eat yer guts' were two of the many terrible things they were saying. The situation was pretty grim. We were able to take on this mob, but we faced the fact that only a few of us would survive. Metres separated us from the goblin horde as they edged closer and closer. Then, out of the darkness, we could see the approach of a bearded man sitting on a grey horse, flanked by two wolves."

"We found out later that the wolves were Stryker and Forester," Wattlespalf interrupts again.

"Yes, I am aware of their ability to shape-shift. It was told to me in a dream," Perrywinkle says.

"A dream?" asks a bemused Igralf.

"Long story," replies Perrywinkle, not wanting to get into the finer points of it.

"And you know the horse Greybeard is riding?" adds Wattlespalf.

"Yes," responds Perrywinkle.

"Well, the horse in that battle is the very same horse he is riding now."

"Really?" says Perrywinkle with a heavy gasp. He is beginning to feel a little sick the more he finds out about this group. Imagine a seventy-year-old horse… impossible.

"Greybeard, Stryker and Forester cut through the blinny throng like a knife would butter. Believe me, for an old man his swordplay is as swift as the greatest sword fighter's, do not be fooled. Anyway, we did our bit and charged at them. After another seventy goblins were cut down, the fifty or so who were left ran away into the wilderness."

"For those little wretches to fight until it was only two to one against dwarfs was quite brave." Wattlespalf butts in.

"After the battle had seen its end we welcomed Greybeard, thanking him for his help. Stryker and Forester were less welcome initially, and we cursed them when we found out they were Otso. Greybeard told us not to judge them on their race's reputation. 'They are good people,' he said and indeed they are. We regret that we shunned those who had come to help, and practically saved our lives. They are now firmly a part of our circle of friends and we would not be without them."

"My story pales in comparison," says Perrywinkle. "They won't try to kill me when the moon rises, will they?" he jokes, pointing at Forester and then Stryker.

"No, we won't kill you. We might nibble on your fingers and toes though," jests Stryker, who has been listening to and revisiting the dwarfs' tale with nostalgia. Perrywinkle gulps.

The morning has turned to early afternoon. The troop has covered many miles and the guesthouse is close. The men begin to sweat. Having descended a few thousand feet or more the air is warmer and more humid. The group stops for a while next to a river by the track. There are large rocks on either side of the river; the water is deep and there are signs that fish live amongst the rocks. The company has time to wash their hands and faces, and remove and pack unnecessary clothing such as cloaks, jumpers, and in the case of Greybeard, sheepskin boots, which are replaced by his favourite sandals. The wizard wiggles his toes, savouring the air that flows around them.

"Forester, hand me your bow and arrows! I'll take you up on the challenge you made earlier," calls Finn. "Have we any string?" Everyone shrugs their shoulders or shakes their heads, wondering why he might need such an item.

Finn looks around the nearby woods. He sees some vines

hanging off a tree on the other side of the river. Finn jumps across a narrow part of the river nearby, and then wanders over to the tree, pulling on a vine until it falls. Looping the vine round his hand and shoulder, he jumps back across the river. Walking over to the quiver holding the arrows, he takes one out and wraps the vine around it. The elf wraps the other end of the vine around his wrist, takes hold of the bow and places the arrow securely against it. Finn pulls back the bow and aims it at the river. Patiently looking at the ripples and bubbles on top of the water, he suddenly releases the bowstring. The arrow enters the water, the vine following swiftly behind. He drops the bow onto the floor and starts to pull on the vine, bringing it onto the bank slowly. The vine tightens and moves from side to side; there is something under the water causing it to move. Disturbances on top of the water become more violent. Finn keeps pulling on the vine, bringing more and more of it onto the bank. Arrow feathers appear from under the water and then, with a sharp tug, Finn pulls out two fish big enough to give four people a meal. Stryker, Igralf and Wattlespalf, who have not yet witnessed Finn's bowmanship, look on in awe of the elf's skill. Forester, who has also not experienced Finn's work before, remains coolly confident in his own abilities.

"I'm impressed," declares Forester. "So this is our contest. Pull the arrow out of the fish and pass it over to me, keep the vine tied to your wrist." Finn does so promptly.

Forester picks up the bow off the floor and places the arrow against its wood, edging closer to Finn. Forester takes longer to place his aim but remains unmoved. Releasing the arrow, it penetrates the water with more force, the vine following and going deeper into the water at a faster speed.

"Finn, pull on the vine and bring them in," says Forester confidently.

"Them?" queries Finn.

"Finn, pull on the vine," repeats Forester.

Finn pulls on the vine but this time he takes longer to bring it in. The tug on the vine this time is heavy.

"I need a little help," puffs Finn, feeling as if Forester has beaten him already.

Gendralf walks over to help Finn, adding his strength

alongside the elf's. With Gendralf's help the vine flows onto the bank quickly and with more pace. The vine again tightens and moves from side to side, the ripples even more pronounced. With a final sharp tug, two very large fish exit the water and fall onto the bank.

Forester walks up to Finn and cups his hands on either side of his face. "Well done, Finn. You truly are a master of the bow. I have not seen anyone other than myself do what you have done. I am pleased and honoured to have found an equal." Forester pats Finn on the back. "I think we are going to have to find you a good bow and a side arm for that matter. Maybe you can show Stryker your sword play tomorrow."

"Finn," Greybeard interrupts, "you can have the honour of presenting the fish to the owner of the guesthouse. She will be very pleased to receive such a gift – she might even cook us a nice fishy meal tonight."

"Yes, yes, of course," Finn obliges.

"Here you go, something for you to put them in," offers Forester, throwing a cloth bag over to Finn.

The men, dwarfs and elves get back on their horses and resume the journey towards their next stop. The sun is starting to fall. It will only be a few hours before it sets. It is hoped by everyone that on this night they will be able to eat heartily and rest in peace. Finn carries the fish in the bag provided by Forester.

Whilst Finn has been 'honoured' by those sitting on the horses beside him, he cannot help but feel that he has got the short straw as the strong smell of fish pervades his every sniff. He notices that the others have kept their distance and sniggers, especially from the dwarfs, are directed towards him at regular intervals.

It is not long before the track splits into two directions. The one going straight ahead follows the route of the main track, and the second, heading towards the right, leads to the guesthouse. The second route is taken. The track is well-trodden and surrounded by trees on both sides; it is also wide, able to accommodate a horse and cart.

Soon, the trees begin to recede and where there were many, there are now few. The path opens out and the first houses of a village can be seen. The guesthouse is situated in the centre of the village; there are not many houses here and the atmosphere is sleepy. Pulling up outside the guesthouse, it is assumed by some that it is not open. Made of brick and wood, the guesthouse is comparatively small against the might of the Old Mill – indeed, it could be considered the size of a cottage and there must only be a few rooms available. The entire roof is made of straw, and plants in pots and a small garden grows nearby, humming with the sound of bumblebees dipping in and out of the flowers collecting pollen. Spiders wait for their food to arrive on webs woven strategically between leaves, flowers, plants and buildings. A potting shed-cum-greenhouse, a composter and a number of tools litter the borders of the land. An enclosed chicken coop takes up a small part of the garden and houses four or five chickens; those in view are scratching, hunting for seeds and clucking away to one another with glee.

The men jump off their horses and ponies, tying them to a post much like the one at the Old Mill. Before they are able to approach the front door of the house, Molly comes out to greet them.

Molly Hepplethwaite is a big woman of mature age who is also quite small in height. Molly enjoys too much of the finer things in life, and spends her days cooking, eating, cleaning and tending to her garden. She always wears an apron over a flowery dress and a cotton hat, just to make sure that the long hair underneath it does not fall on the beds of the guests' bedrooms.

"Hello, Mr. Greybeard," she says, giving him a hug and kiss. "Take it you want rooms for the night? Well, I have plenty, and even if I didn't, I'd always find a room for you." Greybeard blushes. Stryker, Forester, Perrywinkle and the dwarfs nudge each other, which only enhances Greybeard's blushes.

"Yes… yes, erm, rooms and a good meal would be very much appreciated," smiles Greybeard, brushing his hair back with open fingers.

"No problem, Mr. Greybeard. I take it these are your friends." She kisses all of them on either side of the cheek. "Ooh, haven't you got pointed ears?" she says, not noticing that both Finn and Beezle are elves; she is not well read and is not interested in 'outsider' issues.

"Yes, we're… " Beezle starts to say.

"Yes, they're very happy to meet you," Greybeard interjects, shushing Beezle at the same time.

Finn presents the fish to her. Molly looks in the bag, looks at the elf and gives him an extra big kiss on the cheek. "You shouldn't have! Tell you what, I'll prepare you a big meal with these. And as a special treat I'll give you my strawberry tart with cream." Molly ushers the men, who are feeling quite spoilt already, into the house. Inside, the rooms are spotless; there are many ornaments crammed into every crevice, from clocks to vases, patchwork to plants and carved statuettes. She leads everyone upstairs where, at the top, are numerous small rooms.

"Right, you two," she says, pointing at Finn and Beezle. "You can stay in that room." She directs them to the first room on the left. "You three," she points at the dwarfs, "can have this room." Molly points at the second room on the left. "And you two," she points at Stryker and Forester, "can stay in there." Stryker and Forester edge their way to the first room on the right. "And you, Mr. Greybeard, along with your friend, can stay in this room… right next to mine," she says, giving a nervous smile and pointing to the second room on the right. At the end of the hall is the bathroom.

"Thank you, Molly, for making us feel welcome," Greybeard announces, somewhat bashfully.

"Oh, that's alright, Mr. Greybeard… anything for you. Anything. Make yourselves comfortable and I'll see you in an hour or so. In the meantime, I'll get your food ready." At that, everyone opens the doors to the rooms they have been allocated and enters them.

The rooms are very clean and very white, with new bedding in all. All the men, in every room, climb on top of the beds (or floors in the case of the elves – elves love a hard floor to sleep on) to rest their weary feet. After a while, some make moves to empty backpacks or pull out toothbrushes and soap, cleaning teeth and washing faces, some even wash under their armpits. All enjoy the fact that they are not on the back of a horse, exposed to the elements, and instead have a comfortable bed for the night and a hearty meal to look forward to.

Day turns to night, and soon the smell of cooked fish, herbs and vegetables begins to fill the air, floating up the stairs, onto the first floor hallway and then under the doors into the bedrooms. One by one, members of the group walk down the stairs into the kitchen, following the irresistible smell, where Molly is serving the food.

The meal goes down very well. The fish is covered in a white sauce of herbs collected from the garden; there are hints of parsley, dill and a little sage in it. A big plate of vegetables including potatoes, broccoli, carrots and peas, also grown in the garden, is placed in the centre of the table. There is plenty for all, so much so that the dwarfs' bellies are full after only the first course, although they have a second and even a third helping. The pudding of strawberry tart and cream is remarkable, the best dessert this group of creatures has ever tasted, but it is heavy and makes everyone... oh, so sleepy. After the previous two nights' encounters, it is not long before everybody makes their excuses to go to bed.

In the middle of the night, Beezle and Finn are sleeping soundly on a quilt on the floor.

"Beeeeezle, Beeeeezle..." a plethora of whispering voices call out to the little elf, waking him. "Come to me, come to me, come to me," the whispers beckon.

Beezle looks over at Finn, who has not stirred. Beezle sits up, and still half asleep, tries to pinpoint the location of the whispers. They are certainly coming from inside the room. A burning candle, close to its end, sits on top of some drawers in the corner. It gives off just enough light for Beezle to manoeuvre himself around the room and understand exactly where he is. Getting up off the floor, he is sure that the voices are coming from the corner where the backpacks are situated.

"Come to me, I want to see you," whisper the voices. Slowly and quietly, Beezle tiptoes over to the backpacks, a little bewildered as to what he might be getting himself into. "Come to me, I want to speak to you." The voice is coming from Finn's backpack. It must be the rod.

"Are you alright, Beezle?" Finn's voice calls over to him, just as he is about to take the rod out of his brother's backpack. The whispers stop.

"Yes, I'm fine. I was awoken…" Beezle is about to tell Finn what he heard, but changes his mind. "I thought I heard voices. I must have been hearing things." He turns and looks at the backpack, but resists the temptation to go back to it. Beezle lies back down on the quilt. He remains awake for a while, slightly disturbed by what has just happened, but ever so slowly, he falls back to sleep.

CHAPTER 8

THE FIRST LESSON OF MAGIC

Everyone is having breakfast by the time Beezle gets up and wanders downstairs. Molly has prepared a large meal of eggs, freshly laid that morning from the coop, bacon from the farmer up the way, mushrooms from the woods and tomatoes from the potting shed. There is also some freshly made toasted bread, butter and a large mug of nettle tea for everyone.

"Molly, you make a good feast," smiles Greybeard. "I have no doubt you have the best guesthouse in the whole of this land."

Everyone around the table nods their heads in agreement; they have never been treated as well.

"Oh, you're all too kind," replies a slightly embarrassed Molly.

"When we're back in these parts again, we'll definitely pay you a visit," insists Igralf, wanting more of Molly's home-cooked food inside of him.

"You're welcome anytime," is her reply.

Once everybody has finished their breakfasts, they place all the dishes in a neat pile, leave the table, go up to their rooms and get their things. They say their goodbyes, each pecking Molly on the cheek before heading back out onto the track. It will not take them long to get out of the woods, and at that point they will enter the vastness of the eastern plains.

"So what am I going to learn today?" Beezle asks Greybeard, trotting up to him on his dark horse.

"To be honest I haven't yet thought of it. Hmm, let me think… something simple." Greybeard mulls it over for a while. "Ah, today I want you to concentrate on making something move, for example, a tree branch or a stone on the ground. This test will give me a good idea as to whether we can take your learning further. Shall we begin?"

"Yes – I'd like that very much," enthuses Beezle.

"Very good. Now I want you to whisper the words 'grabius movus' under your breath. Keep saying these words over and over again. At the same time, I want you to stretch out your arm. I want you to pick the stone or branch you want to move. Imagine grabbing it with your hand, and once you feel you are able to, wave your arm to shake the branch or pick up the stone and throw it. Do you understand?" Greybeard asks. Beezle nods. "I don't expect you to be able to do this straight away, it may take all day or it may take a week, but you must show restraint and patience or it will never work. To help you on your way, I want you to watch me do it first."

Greybeard begins to chant the words under his breath, then he puts out his arm, chooses a branch on a tall tree and seemingly grabs it and shakes it before letting go, at which point the branch stops shaking.

"Did you see what I did?" asks Greybeard.

"Yes, sir," replies Beezle, getting more excited and even more eager to start.

"Then begin."

Beezle begins to recant the words given to him by Greybeard under his breath, "Grabius movus, grabius movus." He raises his arm, aiming it at a pebble at the side of the track. "Grabius movus," he continues. Beezle grabs the stone and raises his arm but the stone does not rise. "Awh!" he rumbles, disappointed that the stone did not rise.

"Remember – patience, Beezle," the wizard says calmly. The wizard's words cement Beezle's determination, and thrusting his arm out once more, he tries again.

Meanwhile, Perrywinkle is talking to Stryker, trying to gather information about him for his journal. "Stryker, how old are you?"

"Oh, very old. I am ninety-two, and Forester is ninety."

"What, you're ninety-two? Wow, you don't look older than twenty-eight, twenty-nine. I know dwarfs live to about two hundred, so how old should you live to?"

"Honestly, I don't know. Maybe a long, long while yet. I've often wondered… maybe we are immortal, my brother and I, much like Greybeard. Or at least we age at a far slower pace than men like you."

"Hmm, I wish I could live forever, never needing to contemplate death, having an age to do what I would like."

Perrywinkle pauses and contemplates how old he might be before he has to move on from this world.

"Connor, know this, everything must end and whether a life is long or short, rejoice in it, fill your senses, experience all that you can or are able to. You have been given a gift, so love it. Too many wallow in petty desires, much like living forever, or have bitterness for things that might have been or have not become. Some bow out of its challenges and some are overcome by them. One day it will be taken away from you and me both, only the timing differs. Do not regret the life you have led in its last moments. Besides, when I get older and my bones begin to ache, my pain will last far longer than yours – it is something I am not looking forward to," philosophises Stryker.

"It would be nice to see the future to the end of time, though – at least then you can say you saw it," retorts Connor.

"That may well be, but think of those that will follow on from you, do not wish for an end to their time. Instead, offer those in the present the best of your time," replies Stryker.

Perrywinkle thinks upon what has been said for a moment, before his thoughts take him elsewhere.

"Stryker, how did you get to meet Greybeard? I heard about the dwarfs and how they met him, but it sounds like you've known him for a lot longer."

"Yes, we have known him for a long, long time. How did we meet him? Now, that is something I had almost forgotten." Stryker pauses as he searches back through his memories. "We were children – I believe I was seven and Forester was five. Obviously, you're aware of our abilities," utters Stryker, alluding to his and Forester's ability to shape-shift. Perrywinkle nods. "Well, our abilities, or at least our parents' abilities, contributed to getting them killed. You see, when people are seen to be different to others, others can become quite scared of them. They create their own ideas and myths about you without actually knowing any of the real facts about why you are the way you are. Do you understand?"

"I think so," replies Perrywinkle.

"My parents and many of my clan were killed," he continues. "For a long time I thought it was a case of monsters killed by monsters. In reality it was an army of soldiers and mercenaries employed for one purpose, which was to wipe out the shape-shift clans. It came about because the King of Caledon's daughter was murdered by a were-beast. The King was inconsolable, grief eventually turned into anger, and in his anger, the King ordered a slaughter of all shape-shifters in revenge.

Our village was one of the first to be attacked. Unfortunately, we lived very close to the King. The attack came in the day, as it was assumed that our ability to change was triggered by darkness or even by the moon itself, and would therefore make a soldier's task of killing a shape-shifter easier. Whilst the dark played a factor for a lot of the clans, it was not true of ours. We had learned to control the urge both in the day and night. I am a little older than Forester, who remembers nothing of that day. Whilst I don't remember quite enough, I do remember we were playing in the cornfields planted by our clan close to the outskirts of the village. We heard screams and then the crackle of fire. The screams continued, and wanting to see our parents, we ran back through the cornfields. We came back out onto a path leading back into the village. I think I knew they were dead."

"But why did your clan not defend themselves, and change into beasts that could overcome those that attacked?" asks a bewildered Perrywinkle.

"Quite honestly, I don't know. I believe that my clan were peaceful, having taken to farming the land. Maybe they lost their fight, or maybe they believed themselves martyrs. I don't know," reflects Stryker.

"Please, I'm sorry I interrupted," Connor apologises.

"Where were we?"

"How you met Greybeard."

"Ah, yes. Coming up the path, on a wooden cart pulled by a grey horse, was Greybeard. He stopped next to us. 'Get into the cart,' he said, but we didn't want to because he was a stranger. We had been warned about strangers and their dangers, and we also wanted to see our mother and father. 'Get in the cart – you are in grave danger,' he said. We looked back at the flames and saw the soldiers coming. The cart was filled with woven baskets full of apples. It didn't take long for us to get into the back of the cart. 'Lie down,' he said. We did as we were told and he covered us with a blanket. 'Be quiet and do not move. Those soldiers close by are doing terrible things.' We heard him say 'giddy up' to Thundercloud, and at that, the cart began to move faster and faster.

"Greybeard saved us. My brother and I were spared the brutality of the killings. He took us to a couple who became our adopted mother and father – they were also Otso. The couple had a farm close to a village of men; they hid their identity well so as not to provoke suspicion or suffer man's wrath. They treated us like we were their own. We had a good life with them and we were encouraged to understand the ways of the Otso, and for that I am grateful. Greybeard came to see us every now and again to see how we were getting on.

"I believe the King of Caledon regretted his actions years later... he was full of remorse at what he had done. His regrets consumed him, and in the end, he took his own life." Stryker stops talking and looks at Perrywinkle with a solemn grimace.

"Do you notice anything strange?" Greybeard asks, so that everyone can hear him.

"The birds are quiet," answers Forester.

"Yes, I haven't heard them for quite some time," informs Greybeard. "Something's wrong."

Suddenly, there is a creaking sound in one of the trees above, then a snap and a whoosh as a large falling branch drops onto the track directly ahead of the company. All the horses, bar Thundercloud, pull back in shock at this event. 'Neigh, neigh,' they scream, eyes wide open and lips flaring with fright.

The travellers hold their position. Beezle can be heard shouting, "I did it! I did it, Greybeard. I've done what you taught me to do."

Greybeard is not so sure. There is movement ahead.

"Get your weapons ready," Greybeard shouts.

Forester pulls up next to Finn. "Here, take my bow and quiver – we're going to need you." Finn takes them promptly. He straps the quiver to his back, pulls out an arrow and places it against the bow in readiness. The others take out their swords, axes and hammers. Forester, Stryker, Igralf, Gendralf, Wattlespalf and even Perrywinkle jump off their horses and run to the front of the line, producing their weapons in front of them.

Goblins begin to climb down vines and appear from behind the trees. Big ones, little ones, fat ones, thin ones, ones with long legs and short arms, long arms with short legs, big teeth and small noses, small teeth and big noses and more, all come running towards this small group of fearless men.

The blinny, like many other creatures, all come in different shapes and sizes but all share the following traits: their bodies and faces are deformed, they are menacing, vicious and inherently geared towards destruction. Cleanliness, or rather lack of it, is also a common feature. Fingers and toes are covered with overgrown nails. Bits of green, black and yellow caught under them are sometimes picked by teeth when food is scarce. Teeth are rotten, green and brown and black in colour, with breath that could knock out a horse. Noses and ears have long, strong hairs growing out of them. Orifices are full of wax, snot and insects who have made their homes there. Whilst goblins wear clothes, they are often torn and always dirty, full of stains and smells too icky to reveal. Weapons, although they look like those held by men, are not maintained like men would do; axes and swords are often blunt and broken, and arrows are fired without feathers or heads.

How the blinny came to be is sure enough. Once, many, many thousands of years ago, misguided and evil men allied themselves with the first dark beast to soil this world. Fighting alongside the monster, they were defeated by the clans of wizards, men, jotunn, elves and other gracious creatures, who worked together to secure their fates.

Those misguided and evil men who survived the first war were driven underground into the caverns, caves and places hidden away from view, never to see the light of day again. Until, that is, the second dark beast arrived with a promise of escape and domination. The beast had one condition, though. To be released they must be changed, and changed these men were. Exiled for hundreds of years, it was goblins not men who emerged back into the light to serve their new-found saviour. Unhappy that they had been forcibly removed from the world, they sought their revenge upon it.

And so a second war began. Old allegiances were reignited,

and eventually the second dark beast and his minions were defeated. But this time the goblins who survived did not go back into their exile. The blinny bred and spread to all parts of Everlast until they were more than many. So it is that for thousands of years goblins have raided and attacked villages, towns and sometimes even the cities, but without a leader, they were impotent and easy to defeat. Now Warrior has grabbed the goblins' attention with promises that they will dominate Everlast, things are set to change.

"We have been ambushed," shouts the old man. "Beezle, fall to the back of the line."

Beezle does so whilst still reciting the words, his arm outstretched. Time and time again he grabs at stones and branches in the hope of moving them, but again and again he fails.

Stryker, Forester, Perrywinkle and the dwarfs hold the line as blinny begin to jump across the branch in the middle of the track. The men cut and pummel with their swords, axes and hammers, and in response, the goblins fall one by one.

Thundercloud carries Greybeard forward, over the fallen branch, into what is now the goblins' front line. A number of arrows fly from out of the trees, all missing their intended targets. Finn aims Forester's bow with precision, picking out bowmen in the trees before he turns his attention to any little monster getting close enough to those fighting on the front line.

Whilst there is success gained against the goblins at the front of the company, another line approaches from the back unseen. Beezle, who is seemingly out of the battle, notices the throng.

"We're gonna have yer and eat yer," one of the goblins says, licking his lips, whilst another can be heard saying, "The master wants them killed – make them dead, all of them."

Beezle keeps reciting the words. Goblins come ever closer, shaking, twisting and turning their weapons as they try to look as menacing as possible. Beezle stretches out his arm and whispers, "Grabius movus." He grabs a stone and then, finally, picks it up and throws it against the advancing pack. But the stone he has thrown was only a small one, and although he hits a little monster square in its chest, the blow succeeds only in making the beast very angry. Thinking the stone was thrown by hand and not by magic, the angry blinny soldier starts to run as fast as he can towards Beezle, other goblins following behind him. Beezle stretches out his arm again; this time he grabs a bigger stone and throws it at the angry beast. One large stone flies through the air at such a speed that when it hits the angry little monster at the head of the approaching pack it causes him to fall backwards. Like dominoes, goblins fall as one after the other, they are felled by the one in front.

Goblins get up and cry, "Wizard, wizard! Run away, run away!" This time they realise that the large stone was not thrown from Beezle's hand and that magic was to blame.

The real wizard has seen the fight developing and joins Beezle atop Thundercloud. As the goblin pack retreat, Greybeard and Beezle stretch, grab, pull and throw stones at them, enforcing the message that this small band of creatures are not to be messed with. Meanwhile, the others keep swiping, cutting and thrusting their weapons on the front line until, finally, the ambush is quashed. Little monsters lie here, there and everywhere. Those that are alive are somewhat worse for wear, moaning and groaning, holding heads and shoulders, chests and legs. Too few goblins had been sent to greet these seasoned soldiers. Warrior should've sent more.

"I did it, Greybeard. I did it," screams Beezle, excited and proud of his achievement.

"Indeed you did. Well done, young elf," praises Greybeard, ruffling Beezle's hair.

"Is that the best they can do or is this a distraction?" asks Gendralf.

"He is surely playing with us," replies Stryker.

"I think he has quite simply underestimated our strength. Warrior has missed his chance. The beast cannot use his oric to locate us anymore. He will find it hard, if not impossible to reign his terror down on us now," says Greybeard.

Bodies are cleared from the track and taken into the woods. Goblins still alive are tied up and hung from trees. Strung up and swaying from branches, kicking and screaming, the little blighters curse, shouting words in anger, threatening and plotting the downfall of those who have defeated them.

Feet firmly on the ground, Beezle acquires a small sword from the dead hand of one of those most unfortunate. Finn takes a stray bow and quiver off the floor and a suitable sword is also taken.

The exit from the woods is only minutes away. The riders get back onto their horses and resume their journey undeterred.

CHAPTER 9

A VERY BUSY BUGGANE

The riders come to the end of the woodland track. Two stone pillars with a stone plinth on top marks the exit of the woods. The pillars and plinth are old, crumbling and covered in dense, suffocating ivy. Trees in the woods come to an immediate halt where this stone structure stands, exposing open lands ahead. One by one the riders trot between the stone pillars and look out onto the eastern plains. There is a light descent before they will reach the flatlands.

The plains are not really plains anymore; farmers have moved in and cultivated many things, making these plains their own. Greeted by a sea of colour that stretches as far as the eye can see, the creatures feast their eyes upon it. There are purple tones from the lavender used to make perfumes and potpourri, and deep shades of yellow from the rapeseed and sunflowers used to make edible oils. White clouds and patches of brown move slowly against the green backdrops of many fields where sheep and cows graze. Some fields have trees dotted with different shades of red and orange, where the apples and oranges grow. Narrow slivers of blue work their way through the plains where the rivers wind, and large areas of blue where ponds and reservoirs that provide the land with its water dot the landscape. All the colours of this land are neatly separated and contained by stone walling. A few farms can be seen amongst the plethora of colour. The land ahead is flat apart from the odd random hill in the distance; on top of one of the hills the ruins of an old hill fort can barely be seen.

"That is where we need to get to before nightfall," explains Greybeard, pointing to the broken stones of the hill fort.

The sun beats down on the riders' heads. The air is warm and humid with only the slightest hint of a breeze. Sunny blue skies with a smattering of light cloud hover above the plains.

"It should be a pleasant ride," says Perrywinkle.

"Yes, as long as we don't meet up with any more creatures who want us dead," comments Stryker.

"It will be a sweaty ride," grumbles Wattlespalf grumpily taking off his chain mail.

The riders begin their descent down the main track onto the flats of the plains. The track is well-worn but easy to navigate. Greybeard, Stryker, Forester, Igralf, Gendralf and Wattlespalf take in the beauty of the view. Even warriors and those who have experienced the darker things in life still appreciate the more beautiful things in it; after all, this is what they fight for.

Beezle rides behind everyone else. He is still reciting the incantation, stretching out his arm, grabbing and throwing stones like a child with a new toy. Beezle begins to turn the practice into a means of annoying the others. He starts throwing the smallest of stones at them, they in turn believe them to be flies landing on them and then flying off. This proves to be a distraction to the men as they slap their necks, arms and legs every time a stone hits them, but it is a source of great enjoyment for the little elf. Greybeard, who has been noting this, turns around to Beezle and gives him a very stern look as if to say he is not amused. Beezle stops the game he is playing. Greybeard turns back so Beezle cannot see him and laughs to himself, remembering just a little of what it was like to be young.

Perrywinkle takes a book and pen out of his backpack. Opening it, he begins to write. Finn watches Perrywinkle writing lines and verses into his book for a good while.

"What are you writing about?" Finn asks, genuinely intrigued as to what Perrywinkle might be attempting to record.

"Oh, well, erm... all of you I suppose. Greybeard has somewhat tied me into coming on this journey to write about the unfolding events," comments Perrywinkle with a sigh.

"Tied? Does that mean you are here against your will?" asks a concerned Finn.

"Well, kind of... not quite. I owe him a favour you see. He did something for me, gave me a second life as it were. I was saved from a terrible fate – monsters, fire, being eaten and the like. His one and only condition for saving me was that I must agree to do him a favour; either that, or he would give me back to the monsters. Unfortunately for me, the wizard has called his favour in."

"So you're indebted to him and your favour is to write about the here and now?" queries Finn.

"Yes," replies Perrywinkle.

"Do you enjoy writing?"

"I do. It keeps my mind from thinking terrible things and my hands occupied. I have a problem in that I like stealing things – I was a thief you know. Haven't stolen anything for a while, mind… well, maybe an apple here and there."

"Then the favour you are committed to carrying out for the wizard is not such a bad one?"

"I would suppose not, if it were not for the perils we might encounter. I suspect this adventure is going to enhance the chances of me being a dead writer as opposed to a living one… and that wouldn't be very productive at all," explains Perrywinkle, after much thought.

"Let's just hope that will not happen, your death that is. I will be very interested to read your account of this adventure, if I might – when you've finished writing it, of course," quips Finn.

"Very well, I think I can make that happen. So, Finn, whilst I've got you here, do you want to contribute to the writings in my journal?" asks Perrywinkle.

"Yes, tell us about yourself," Greybeard butts in. "I would be very interested to learn about the elves and your way of life."

"Alright then, what do you want know?" responds Finn, excited at what he might be asked.

"Tell us anything you want us to know," replies Perrywinkle, allowing Finn's mind to wander as opposed to putting him on the spot.

"Hmm!" Finn pauses for a while as he searches his mind. "We live in a village called Hem, Beezle and I. It's a small village right at the very centre of Windrush Forest. You probably already know that Windrush has its name due to the winds that rush through it," informs Finn.

"Yes, we are well aware of the winds," comments Greybeard.

"High above the forest floor, we live in tree houses made from the twigs and branches and leaves given to us by the forest. The elves have a strong bond with it, the forest that is, and as such we would never chop a tree down for our own gain. We learnt very early on that the trees are alive with spirits much like ours, and that we must respect them – after all, they came before us. Anyway, our houses sit amongst the strongest branches of the trees. The trees don't mind the weight of our houses or the elves that live in them. In fact, I think they're happy for our company."

"How big are the tree houses then? They can't be that big, surely?" wonders Perrywinkle.

"Oh no, they're not big at all… just big enough for us to have something to sleep in. We have very few rooms, and unlike the houses I've seen so far on this journey, we have very few belongings. We don't even have a bed – instead we prefer to sleep on the floor. We do have a porch, though." Finn smiles, as he remembers the good times he had on his own porch.

"And a chair swing," interrupts Beezle, who has been listening in on the conversation. "It was just about the best and most exciting thing about living in Hem."

"Come on, Beezle. You could have lived somewhere far worse. The porch is where stories are told. Elves love to recount old tales. Every night my father reads us a story, of battles and monsters and magical things." Finn pauses, his eyes glazing over, thinking of happier times. Coming back from his daydream, he continues, "The thing is, we don't really need large houses as we spend the vast majority of our lives outside. There's so much to do amongst the trees, believe it or not. I mean we spend a lot of time at school, learning to read and write, climbing trees and the like. Children help their mothers and fathers prepare food in the communal kitchen. We have a library – I love spending time in the library."

"I like spending time around the pools and rivers. I don't like going to the library or school," interrupts Beezle again. "Tell them about the pools and rivers."

"Alright, I was coming to that!" Finn exclaims, as if his mind is being rushed on by his brother. "Surrounding the village are rivers and waterfalls and pools, which in turn house crags and rocks, and most importantly, fish. Fishermen litter the sides of pools and rivers, catching fish with a rod and line or nets, and if they are particularly skilled, with their bare hands. And elflings… well, we play, swim and fish in the pools as much as we can, whether the weather is warm or not."

"Or we climb the tree vines and rush around the bridges connecting one tree to another," adds Beezle.

An Elven tree house

"Did you ever get visitors to Hem? It sounds quite a secluded place, being at the centre of the forest and all," Greybeard asks.

"Not really is the answer. Hem is well hidden in a remote part of the forest. To get to us was quite treacherous for travellers, I think. You see, some of the trees were quite partial to eating creatures that they didn't like the look of, which I think put creatures off coming to visit. Tree spirits, tree wardens and moss people often ventured close. I know the older elves often chatted with these peoples for ten minutes or so, catching up on any news that might be of interest. We did venture out once in a while, though."

"Where did you go?" asks Perrywinkle, eager to know more.

"We went to the gatherings," Finn says, his eyes lighting up.

"The gatherings?" questions Greybeard. "I think I've read about these elven events in old books. Please tell me about your experiences."

"Well, every five years our village was abandoned for a few weeks and everyone would journey to the gathering place deep in Windrush Forest. Thousands of elves would be there. Here, members of the village would talk to old friends and family, listen to and play music, sing and dance around campfires, trees and tents. There was a lot to eat and a lot to drink from what I remember. Merriment lasted until the late hours, only to begin again early the very next morning. The main attraction and the reason elves attended was to see the King and Queen."

"Ah, the King and Queen. Yes, I remember – I did read about this. Sorry, Finn, I interrupted again. Please go on," apologises the wizard.

"That's alright. Where was I? Oh yes, the King and Queen addressed the crowds at the gathering, speaking of the last five years and the outlook for the elves over the next five years. They also talked about the outside world and the good and bad happening in it. They commanded their subjects' hearts and were beloved by all. It was common knowledge that the King and Queen were very powerful. So powerful that it is said they talked to the Creators themselves. The Queen had the gift of foresight, could predict events to come, and would know the life and fate of any man she touched. And the King is said to have the gift to aid elves who are in danger, whether it be bestowing them with an item for their quest or by planting an instruction in their mind, revealing itself when the elf needed it most."

"Those are very powerful qualities to have," comments Perrywinkle, who is writing everything Finn offers into his journal.

"I met them once, you know," Finn says proudly.

"What, you met the King and Queen?" replies a slightly shocked Greybeard.

"Oh, here we go again," yawns Beezle, bored at the fact that he is going to hear Finn's story for the umpteenth time.

"I did. It was only a couple of years ago, plus three thousand. The Queen, she was really beautiful. She had large blue eyes; I can't remember the rest of her face, funny that. I know she was beautiful though. She was dressed in a long, white, flowing cloak that glittered as if made from the stars themselves. Touching my hand gently, I remember she looked at me for a good few seconds, her blue eyes smiling at me as she did. Releasing my hand, she bent down and kissed me on the forehead. I will always treasure that moment, but that is not the end of it. The Queen turned to the King and whispered something into his ear, I couldn't make out what. He looked concerned – I don't know why."

"What did the King look like?" Greybeard asks, unable to contain his excitement for this story.

"The King looked much like the Queen in that he shone like glitter," replies Finn. "His hair was golden, and I remember that he wore a slim band of silver with a green stone in the middle of it around his head. His eyes were kind and wise. The King picked me up like my father would when I was young. Looking me directly in the eyes for what seemed an age, smiling the most serene smile, he put me down again, before moving on to talk to others. It's strange really. I had no feeling towards my meeting with the King and Queen at the time, but since meeting them I began to have an interest in reading books. It is as if I have been prepared for something against my will now I think about it."

"What do you mean?" asks Greybeard, wanting to understand more.

"Well, I've read hundreds, if not thousands, of books

crammed with legends, stories, histories of other creatures and guides – a lot of guides, about wielding swords and bows and the like. At the time I was more interested in doing the things other elflings wanted to do. You know… swim, go to school, play with friends, fish, climb trees and that sort of thing. It all changed and very quickly at that."

"Hmm! Very interesting," responds the wizard, keeping his thoughts to himself.

"Where else did you go?" Perrywinkle asks, wanting a little bit more from Finn.

"Well, Father used to take us to see the sea. We'd spend weeks away from the village. I love the sea. I often put a seashell to my ear when I feel like getting away. My father taught me how to use a bow and a sword on these trips. Beezle was still a little too young to wield weapons the last time we travelled. Father is a master archer, renowned amongst the elves, and I doubt he ever missed a target. He also knew a lot about maps, and making shelters and how to do this and that. Oh, I do miss him. I hope he's alright," laments Finn.

"He's dead, you idiot," grimaces Beezle, matter-of-factly. Greybeard and Perrywinkle look shocked; even Stryker, Forester and the dwarfs look over their shoulders at Beezle's comment.

"Beezle, how can you say something like that? He's not dead. He could be very much alive in this time. I only saw him a few days ago. I'm sure he's alive – I'm sure of it." Tears come to Finn's eyes; hope survives, if only slight. The realisation that he and Beezle are alone begins to surface.

"Well, you're going to have to get used to it. I already have," mumbles Beezle under his breath.

"That's enough, Beezle. I think we should end this conversation right now," orders the wizard.

The riders end their descent onto the flatlands. Here, the fields begin. The track follows stone walls towards long, wooden gates, which lead on into other fields. The first field contains ripened sweetcorn, which the dwarfs don't hesitate to pick off the taller plants from the luxury of their elevated positions. The dwarfs expose the plump, yellow niblets from behind their green, fibrous shells, before biting into the sweet, crunchy, yellow flesh, savouring its taste.

"Hmm, lovely – I haven't had sweetcorn this good for a long while," Gendralf comments, munching happily away.

All the dwarfs nod in agreement and munch on not one, not two, but three ears of corn before they come to the end of the field and the gate leading into the next.

The next field they come to is covered with vines holding red grapes. The dwarfs take bunches of the grapes and proceed to pop them into their mouths one by one, spitting out the hard seeds once the sweet flesh has been devoured. The dwarfs are very particular about seeds, spitting out each and every one of them. They are scared that if they swallow just one, trees or vines or plants may start to grow inside them.

"Hmm, lovely – I haven't had these for a long while," says Igralf.

Again, the other two dwarfs nod in agreement and munch on two bunches of grapes before they come to the end of the field.

The next field is filled with orange trees covered with big juicy fruits. The dwarfs, still hungry, each take an orange. This time the lure of this fruit is too much for the others to resist. Everyone takes an orange off a tree and peels it before throwing the skin onto the floor and eating them segment by segment.

"Oi," a voice shouts out in the near distance. "What are you swines doin' eatin' my stock?" An old man pops his head round one of the orange trees. His face is weather-beaten, with a large, bulbous nose, big sideburns full of hair that trails down to his chin and large ears covered, to some extent, by a big straw hat.

"Do you lot think I'm made of money, yer buggers? Go on, get orf my land before I come over there and beat you with this long stick 'ere." He pulls his whole body from around the tree and begins to walk towards them, shaking his fist whilst steadying himself with a battered old walking stick.

"Er, sorry, sir. We didn't want to offend. We only took one orange each – we haven't brought baskets and only wanted to fill our stomachs a little," says Igralf.

"One each! One each!" the old man fumes. "Do you know how long it takes for oranges to grow?"

Everyone shrugs their shoulders.

"Ages," the old man informs. "Do you think I do this for the love of it? Do you think I toil away in this beautiful landscape, in the peace and quiet, away from the hustle and bustle of those dirty towns and cities because I love it here?" The old man comes right up to Igralf's horse, waving his stick in Igralf's face.

Again, everyone shrugs their shoulders, gobsmacked and unable to provide an answer for fear of offending him further.

"No, I don't. I hate it here, stuck in this paradise, undisturbed, working for myself, fishing, farming and reading. It's boring!"

"So why don't you sell up and move to the city?" asks Igralf.

"The city, the city! Don't you get me started about the city. Oiks like you hanging around on every corner, stealing out of your own pockets at any given chance, never mind everybody else's. Dirty houses, on dirty streets, with no room, no garden. Outside views of the same kind of house you live in, only made worse because it is your neighbour's house and he's a plonker who doesn't know his right from his left."

"Well, what about a healthy mixture of the two?" suggests Gendralf.

"What, have the worst of both of them? Are you having me on?" shouts the old man, poking his stick into Gendralf's belly. "Go on, be off with yer, and don't show yer faces round 'ere again," he hollers, ushering them off. The riders are glad to get away; the old farmer is more fierce than the goblins and even Greybeard.

"That old man was definitely a glass half-empty person," comments Wattlespalf as he rides off with the others. Everyone agrees, rolling eyes and smirking with just a little embarrassment. All of them feel well and truly told off.

Working their way through a number of other gates and fields, the riders can see the top of the hill fort, which is now only a short distance away. The afternoon is nearly at its end. Jumping off their horses, the riders lead them up the gradual incline of the hill up towards the seemingly abandoned fort. At various parts of the walk up, the riders tie their horses and ponies to random trees, leaving them with plenty of grain and sugar lumps on the floor to keep them going through the night.

It doesn't take them long to reach the top of hill. The hill fort itself appears ancient. Seven standing stones form a circle around the circumference of the hill. Ancient writings are etched into the individual stones. In the centre of the circle is a rock taking up a quarter of the width of the hill top. There appears to be a doorway in the centre of the large rock, housing what seems to be a heavy, unmovable door. Around the doorway, etched into the stone, is some ancient writing, similar to the writings on the standing stones.

Greybeard walks over to the door, and he works his fingers up and down the seal of it, looking for an opening.

"Very curious," Greybeard mumbles under his breath, intrigued by what could be hiding behind it. Perrywinkle walks up to the door and begins to decipher the writings on the doorway.

"Knock three times on your chosen stone to open this door. One chance you get – if wrong you must wait ten years more before your chance arises again," Perrywinkle says slowly, word by word.

"Perrywinkle, I did not know that you were able to decipher old writings," Greybeard says, somewhat bemused.

"You learn something new every day, old man. My previous profession dictated that I learn these things. You can check my interpretation if you want."

"Well, I might just do that... second opinion, clarification and all," says Greybeard, who is a little put out that others know things he thought only he knew.

Connor reads on. "It is a riddle," he reveals. "What is greater than the Creators? What is more evil than evil itself? The poor have it. The rich need it. You will die if you drink it. You are dead if you have breathed it."

Greybeard checks that the interpretation of the symbols on the doorway is correct, taking him some time to do so. It is correct, much to the wizard's dismay.

"Er, well done... well done, Connor. Very impressive," Greybeard concedes.

Everyone starts mumbling to themselves: "What is greater than the Creators? Who is more evil? Poor have it? Rich need it? Die if you drink it? Dead if you breathed it?"

"I think I know," says Wattlespalf.

"Really?" says Greybeard.

"Yes, ale," reveals Wattlespalf.

"And how did you arrive at your answer?" asks Greybeard.

"Well, everyone knows that ale is the greatest thing in the world, much better than the Creators. But it is evil and makes you do the most evil things, like burping, farting and jumping into people's gardens. The poor have plenty of ale to take their minds away from being poor. The rich need it because they are bored of their wealth and always need to satisfy their lust. You will eventually die if you drink enough of it. And I wouldn't advise breathing ale for any great period of time as I'm pretty sure it would kill you."

Everyone, including his brothers, looks at Wattlespalf and sniggers, bewildered as to how his mind interpreted it so.

"I suspect that it is not the correct answer," says Igralf.

"Codswallop and poppycock, Wattlespalf. It would pay for you not to think at all in the future. The poor have plenty of ale because they are poor, indeed. Numbskull!" booms the wizard, unimpressed with Wattlespalf's lack of insight.

Whilst all this has been going on, Perrywinkle has been looking at the writings on the standing stones. There are a number of possible answers to the riddle. "One of the stones gives the right answer and ale is one of the choices," Perrywinkle says. "Well done, Wattlespalf."

"So go on then. Tell us what the potential answers to the riddle are," hurries Igralf.

"Okay, we have the following – ale, no one, disease, poison, space, life… on the seventh stone there is no writing. Nothing has been etched into it. There is no writing on this stone, why is that?" questions Perrywinkle. "Is the last word 'nothing'?" He starts to reel off the lines of the riddle one by one, matching the words on the stones to the phrase.

"What is greater than the Creators? Nothing? No one? Life? Space?

What is more evil than evil itself? Nothing? No one? Disease?

The poor have it. Disease? Life? Ale? No one? Nothing?

The rich need it. Ale? Life? Nothing? No one?

You will die if you drink it. Poison? Nothing? Ale?

You are dead if you have breathed it. Disease? Poison? Nothing?"

Perrywinkle goes through the process again and again; the one word that crops up every time is nothing.

"Nothing is greater than the Creators.

Nothing is more evil than evil itself.

The poor have nothing.

The rich need nothing.

If you drink nothing then you will die.

If you breathe nothing then it is likely you are dead.

This is the stone we have to knock three times against," screams Perrywinkle with confidence.

"I believe you have figured out the riddle. Well done, young man," says a proud Greybeard. Perrywinkle is proving his worth on this adventure. Everyone congratulates him and pats him on the shoulder in recognition.

"Not to spoil this party but what if there is some untold evil behind this door?" warns Stryker. "If we unwittingly unleash something onto this earth that does not belong here, what are we to do?"

"Alright, get your weapons ready for when the door opens," says Greybeard. "Connor, as you figured out the riddle you can have the honour of knocking on the stone." Connor feels privileged and excited, proud that he has shown quality above his station, and gets ready to knock.

"Is everyone ready for me to knock?" asks Connor, his knuckles ready to rap the stone.

Everyone nods.

"Ready?" questions Perrywinkle again.

"Go on then, Connor," shouts Greybeard.

Connor knocks on the stone three times. *Knock, knock, knock*!

Behind the door there is an instant sound of a lock unlocking and very slowly the door begins to open inwards. Rock scrapes against rock, producing a gritty sound as it does so. Fully open, the door reveals a staircase that winds downwards below the surface of the hill. Connor starts to walk over to the others who still hold their weapons in readiness. All of a sudden the men begin to scream; only Greybeard and Finn remain calm but even they are horrified by what they see. Connor takes a step back. Everyone is so terror-stricken that they cannot wield their weapons. In fact, they look as if they cannot move at all. Forester, Gendralf and Wattlespalf stop screaming only to be physically sick at the sight of this monster. Beezle runs and hides behind one of the standing stones. Finn stands still, his initial fright turning to an emotionless stare. Connor is frightened; he is also slightly confused as to why the monster has not yet attacked. Greybeard, after some time, gets over his initial shock and begins to talk to the creature that stands at the open doorway.

"Buggane, what is your name?" he asks gently, his voice slightly shaky.

"Why do you ask? Are you not suitably shocked by my appearance? Are you not going to run away like others have before you?" replies the buggane. His voice is deep, distorted and sad. You see, bugganes are the ugliest creatures in this world – so ugly in fact, that they can send men mad. Fortunately, one look at the face of a buggane is generally enough to make those who gaze upon it run away from it as quickly as is possible. No one has ever documented the ugliness of a buggane, firstly because they are beyond description, and secondly, because no one has looked at one long enough to note it in any great detail. Bugganes are lonely creatures; if any two of this kind were ever to meet they would likely run away from each other in fear. So it is that they keep bags over their heads when socialising and mating. Every buggane's desire is to be in the company of others, to talk about trivial things or the things that mean most to them in life. Very rare is it for these creatures to have company, and if they are lucky enough to have some, their faces are generally covered so as not to scare the company that they keep. But here we have a group of men, dwarfs and elves, quite possibly the bravest in this land at this particular time in Everlast's history, who remain within a reasonable distance of it.

"So, buggane, what is your name?" Greybeard asks again.

"You really want to know?" asks the buggane, touched by Greybeard's insistence.

"Yes, friend," he replies.

"My name is Kevlan," answers the buggane.

"I am Greybeard," replies the wizard.

"You are Greybeard? Oh, I have read so many tales about you... the battles you have been in, the treasures you have uncovered, the people you have saved! You must be very famous in these lands."

"I am known in some circles but not all," he replies humbly. "Let me introduce my friends, this is Stryker."

Stryker waves at the buggane in recognition before promptly being sick again.

"Over there is Forester," Greybeard continues.

"Hello," signals Forester.

"These are the dwarfs, Igralf, Gendralf and Wattlespalf." The dwarfs all wave, their eyes shying away from the buggane's gaze.

"The man behind you is called Connor Perrywinkle. Please don't turn around," Greybeard quickly orders the buggane. "No offence, Kevlan, but this man would probably run a good thousand miles or more if he saw your face. Behind that stone is Beezle the elf," continues Greybeard.

A hand pops itself from behind the standing stone he hides behind and waves. "Very good to meet you," says Beezle.

"And this is the elf, Finn."

Finn walks up to the buggane and shakes his hand. Unfazed, he says, "Pleased to meet you."

"An elf? An elf! I'm sure I have something for you," remembers the buggane, searching his mind for more information. "You haven't been around for a while, have you?" asks Kevlan.

"Not for three thousand years, apparently," answers Finn.

"That's a very long time, isn't it?" says Kevlan, unsure of the meaning of the time he is talking about. Kevlan is more interested in passing it by than living it.

"Yes, a very long time," says Finn.

"Why might you have something for an elf three-thousand years after the race itself has died out?" asks Greybeard.

"Sorry, let me explain myself. Hmm, how do I explain?" ponders Kevlan, putting his distorted finger against his twisted face. "My purpose is... no, no, let me start again." Kevlan stops, takes a deep breath and starts again. "Creatures are brought here by a force of fate to receive information pertinent to the path that they are following, and my purpose is to pass on that information. Many generations of my family have lived here, passing information to heroes and villains over many years. Your group answered the riddle. Nobody gets information unless they

The Buggane

answer the question. Today must be your day, young sir, or at least the turn of somebody in this pack of yours."

"I answered the riddle," informs Perrywinkle, hoping that he might receive some sort of prize from the buggane.

"It doesn't matter who answers the riddle, good sir – it might be someone's fate to answer the riddle in order to reveal the fate of another," confirms Kevlan.

"Oh, I see," replies Perrywinkle, slightly disappointed.

"Where are my manners? Please come down, I have plenty of room, food and refreshment. It is not often I get to host esteemed guests such as yourselves."

"Well, it is getting dark," notes Greybeard, thinking it better to have the warmth of a home than camp outside for the night.

"Refreshment? I think I can handle the night socialising with a hideous monster... just as long as you don't get amorous. I could never live that down," warns Gendralf, pointing his finger at Kevlan.

Kevlan turns round. Everyone is relieved. He is prettier from the back, but not much. Kevlan is a large figure, as tall as Greybeard. His body is big and round with very short legs, but amply-sized arms. The buggane's toes on his large, flat feet have long toe nails, cracked and yellow in colour, and the nails at the end of his fingers are black and bitten. Kevlan's whole body is covered in brown hair, so much so that he does not need to wear clothes. He walks slowly down the staircase into his abode, and the others follow. The staircase is narrow and appears to go on for an age. Close to the bottom of the staircase, a large room becomes visible. The room is lit by hundreds of candles, and the ceilings are very, very high; you could even say it is cavernous. Stone floors are underfoot, and to the right of the staircase rows and rows of bookcases, full of thousands of books, fill the room.

"Have you read all these books?" asks an excited Greybeard, who runs over to the bookcases and starts flicking through the titles on the shelves.

"Oh, not all. About three quarters of them," replies Kevlan nonchalantly.

"That's a well-read buggane," says Wattlespalf.

To the far left of the room there are five huge casks of wine built into the wall. In the centre of the room is a large, thick, dark wood table with twelve equally large, thick, dark wooden chairs around it. At the back of the room is a large four-poster bed, with large pillows and a large duvet; above each bedpost hang curtains which are closed by the buggane at night. Behind the staircase is a stove, numerous drawers and cupboards.

"So how long have you travelled to get here?" asks Kevlan politely.

"It is two days since we left my home in the mountains, though it feels much longer," replies Greybeard.

"Five days, eh?" drones Kevlan, mishearing that it was actually two days. "You must be exhausted. Well, I have plenty of food, so please help yourselves. There are mugs up in the top cupboards and taps in all the casks should you want some wine."

Igralf, Gendralf, Wattlespalf, and even Stryker, Forester and Perrywinkle, rush towards the cupboards, each picking out a mug. The casks are then quickly surrounded.

Kevlan shuffles towards the bookcases. "What year is it?" he asks.

"The year is 11996," shouts Stryker, taking a sip of wine.

Everyone gazes at Kevlan's feet or in his general direction – at the ceiling, at the floor or at a candle, as they daren't look at his face again. The general feeling is he must be mad. How could anyone not know what year it is?

Kevlan shuffles over to a specific row, to a specific shelf and then to a specific book as if he is programmed to know exactly where it is and what it refers to. He takes out a big, dusty book with a big, dusty lock off the shelf. A big bunch of keys hang from a hook at the end of this particular row of books. He takes them off the hook and begins to fumble around, looking for the correct key to unlock this particular book.

"Ah, this is the one," Kevlan says, fitting the key into the lock. He turns it, but it doesn't unlock. The buggane goes through this process very patiently for at least another twenty minutes, until finally one of the keys unlocks the lock.

"I knew it was that one," he says, satisfied of the great mind he has for identifying keys that open locks. He opens the book and dust flies everywhere. Kevlan is not great at dusting books and there are thousands of them in the library, so it is not overly surprising that the dust has accumulated.

"Ahem, we are looking at the year 402, aren't we?" asks Kevlan.

"11996," Stryker reminds.

"10892," Kevlan says, believing that he is repeating after Stryker.

"What, is he deaf as well?" jokes an amused Wattlespalf.

"11996," shouts Stryker very slowly.

"Oh, sorry… 11996," apologises Kevlan. He turns to page two in the book. "Here we are. Strange as it seems, you're the first visitors I've had in ages. Congratulations," he says, as if they might all be eligible for a prize. He reads through the page, mumbling to himself. "Hmm… oh yes, of course. Box thirty-two. I need to collect a box for you – I won't be long."

The buggane shuffles through the rows and rows of bookcases very slowly, Kevlan walks past the last bookcase and he shuffles some more, along the bottom corridor to a locked door. A number of keys sit on a hook beside the door. Kevlan's guests are, by now, all sitting at the large table, drinking, reading and eating. They can hear the buggane fumbling around with the keys again.

"Ah, here we are," he can be heard saying. He repeats himself several times over. Finally, the correct key is found and he unlocks the door. The door opens and shuts with a creak as Kevlan wanders through it. It is a long while before the door opens again, but open it does and out from it wanders Kevlan pushing a box on wheels. Very slowly the box rolls through the library.

"Do you want any help?" Forester asks.

"No, no, I'll be there soon. Thank you for your kind thoughts though."

A while later, the box, pushed by the buggane, appears from behind the bookcases. Kevlan stops a short distance away from the table where the men have been sitting waiting. He walks back over to the dusty book and pulls from it a sealed envelope, he then wanders back over to the box and puts the envelope on top of it.

"So, which one of you is Finn?" Kevlan asks, looking around the room.

"I think he's had too much time on his own. Didn't we introduce ourselves earlier?" whispers Gendralf to the others. Finn puts his hand up slowly.

"Ah, the elf. I knew I had something for you."

"What about me?" asks Beezle rudely. "Don't I get a box? I'm an elf too, you know."

"No… no box for you, young man. Only one box comes out today."

"Well, did you check that dusty book of yours properly? It's obvious that you're slow, and you miss things, and you're ugly and I'm not surprised you're on your own."

"Beezle!" comes the loudest shout you ever did hear. Greybeard stands up. His eyes are full of anger and a white aura surrounds him; what appears to be lightning fizzes inside the white cloud of the aura. "You have taken one step too far, you unmannered, unpleasant, selfish little ingrate. Go to the corner of this room and reflect upon what you have said."

"What if I won't? You can't tell me what to do," Beezle shouts back.

"Then you will not receive any more lessons from me," Greybeard says, as the white aura recedes and he calms down enough not to do anything nasty to him.

Beezle looks dismayed, but turns and walks to the corner of the room, mumbling under his breath: "I'll make you pay for this. Just you wait." Everyone gives each other looks of disappointment; even Finn knows it was right for Greybeard to discipline him.

The buggane looks away and a tear comes to his eye. In his mind he believes Beezle is right. Greybeard interrupts Kevlan's thoughts. "Kevlan, do not believe this immature boy's jibes. He is angry because attention has swayed toward his brother, and so he takes it out on those who are more innocent of thought than he is. From what I have seen you are a kind creature, well-read, and you do your job well. Come sit with us – the opening of the box can wait a while. I'll get you a mug." Kevlan does so. Greybeard pours Kevlan some wine and takes it to him.

"You know what, Kevlan, I was shocked when I first saw you, but I suspect now that you are quite handsome for someone of your race," says Forester, looking Kevlan directly into one of his eyes.

"I second that," says Gendralf. "You have a regal air about you. Are you sure you're not related to royalty?"

"I-I don't think so," stutters a slightly embarrassed Kevlan.

"Hmm, well I would possibly have a look at your family tree," advises Igralf, who is becoming a little tipsy.

"Erm, might I ask you all some questions? I have so many questions to ask. I don't get to speak to people from outside of these walls very often."

"Why?" asks Stryker.

"The world cannot accept me, I scare anyone I meet and they want to have rid of me."

"Believe me when I say I understand what you mean. Have you heard of the Otso?" probes Stryker.

"Yes, are they not evil, killing all in their wake?"

"Funny you should ask but no, they are not and they don't. I am Otso, as is my brother."

"What! You are Otso? Then why are these men with you? Do you know what they are?" asks a slightly distressed Kevlan.

"Yes, yes we do. The Otso are an honourable race, whose character has been besmirched by the writings of those who did not understand the finer points of their character," says Igralf.

"They are not evil, far from it," adds Wattlespalf.

"But my books –" panics Kevlan.

"Kevlan," Greybeard interrupts, "depending on the storyteller, tales have the ability to start and end truthfully. But, in many stories, the storyteller forgets a fact here and there, and the tale loses a piece of the original truth about the people it describes or the events that took place. Other storytellers exaggerate the tale and what was true gradually, or sometimes very quickly, becomes a myth and therefore isn't true at all. This has happened to a number of tribes, the Otso are but one of them. They have been misunderstood as you are misunderstood."

"But my books... what am I to believe?" moans Kevlan.

"Books are exceptional things and they provide all of us with an invaluable amount of information, which must not be underestimated. But you must balance learning with experience to understand more about the world in which you live," lectures Greybeard.

"How do I do this? I cannot leave this place."

"When is the next fated arrival due?" asks Greybeard.

Kevlan gets up and shuffles over to his book, flicking over to the next page.

"They are due in the year 12048," he responds.

"Well, you have fifty-two years to live before this time comes round. How old are you, Kevlan?"

"Hmm, erm... I'm... erm," Kevlan looks up to the ceiling of his abode, trying to focus his mind so that he can concentrate on remembering.

"What I mean is will you live for another fifty-two years?" Greybeard probes.

"Well, I feel well enough at the moment to live a good few years yet," replies the buggane as confidently as he possibly can be.

"Good, good – now we have established that you will live for a while yet, can I ask how you came to be?" asks the wizard, in a matter-of-fact way.

"My father met my mother in the north-eastern provinces..." Kevlan stops, a tear develops in the corner of his eye. A simple set of questions has opened up a whole new world to him. He realises that he has stifled his experience of life and also understands that he needs to leave this place, if only for a while.

"How do I do this?" he asks.

"Be under no illusions, the journey of life is hard. You will suffer times of toil, but you will also gain a great deal of pleasure and satisfaction from your experiences. You must live to appreciate both the good and the bad. The hope is that you will use your learning to make other people's lives more pleasurable. More importantly, teach others of your experiences and knowledge so that they might use them in their lives as well."

"And, what of love? How do I find it? I should need to find it, shouldn't I? I mean, in order to keep this place open to the likes of you and others. How should I respond to it when I do? I would very much like to find it, what with being very lonely and all. Even a companion, one who doesn't mind me, would be sufficient enough."

The room goes quiet. None of these men know of love. Stomachs turn in everyone bar Finn and Beezle, who are too young to have missed out on this experience. For a few seconds the men feel numb and everyone goes silent.

"You, sir, are speaking to the wrong creatures. Whilst you may have chosen a hermit's life, we have chosen one of adventure. I probably speak for all of us by saying that we have sacrificed elements of our lives that have been enjoyed by others," explains a philosophical Greybeard.

"Kevlan, understand this, everyone is flawed and flaws differ between one creature and the next," adds Stryker. "One of our many flaws, my friends and I will admit, is that we are blind to love. There is time for us yet, though, I would hope. Others will take our place in protecting Everlast, and we might be lucky enough to enjoy a different kind of adventure."

"Saying that, there are people you will find who you like and love to be with... and there are others you will not," says Gendralf, continuing in the same vein. "Some love might be unrequited, insofar as you might love someone but they do not feel the same about you, and vice versa. It could be very hard to accept that someone is not of the same mind as yourself, but you must accept it."

"Or find a love potion strong enough to change those feelings," interrupts Wattlespalf.

"Brother, stop your idiotic chatter," Gendralf scorns.

"It sounds very complicated," reflects Kevlan.

"It is, but do not let this put you off; I am sure you will have wondrous tales to tell at the end of your journey, and you might have even found someone to share your life with. I can help you to start your adventure by making you a map that leads to the buggane tribes. I can also make you a charm that will protect you, should you need it," Greybeard informs.

"Oh, please. Many thanks to you all," responds a grateful Kevlan. He slowly shakes hands with the troop. Perrywinkle remains silent as he has been documenting this episode in his journal.

Meanwhile, Finn has picked up the letter from on top of the box, opened it and read its contents.

Dear Finn,

It is a long time ago since we met, and if you are reading this note I would guess it has been a few thousand years. You were the first indication that something terrible was going to happen to our race. That day, at the gathering, when I looked into your eyes I was able to read a little of your life story. Don't worry, I will not give anything away. The fact that our race did not feature in this future chapter of the world in which you are currently adventuring was enough to tell me. Unfortunately, you could not tell me exactly when it was going to happen. The reading gave us a little time to prepare a few elven treasures to help you and your friends in the battles ahead. It is with sad regret that we could not be there to help you. Warrior has not found us upon writing this note, but he gets ever closer. Know that this life, whatever it may bring, good or bad, is the only life you will ever know, so treasure it and those around you.

I spoke to your father after your disappearance, explaining everything I knew. He was very proud of you both. I reassured him that you were in safe hands.

    The items in the box are as follows:
    Medrin the elven bow. Shoot an arrow from this bow and you will never miss.
    Premethian liquid. Drink one drop of this liquid, touch the person whose life you wish to uncover and you will see their story unfold.
    Elven armour. This can withstand many arrows and will deflect many thrusts of a sword.
    Lerwin the sword. This sword will give you a few valuable seconds' grace against your enemy, it tells the most likely outcome of the near future but not necessarily fate. Ask it to tell you and it will.
    Good luck.
    Yours truly,
    Elissa

Finn passes the note to Greybeard, who reads it intently. The elf feels a hint of sadness overcome him as he daydreams of his father, pleased he at least knew his sons were safe.

"Your Queen must have been a fine woman. She considered you highly enough to pass the responsibilities of your race onto you," comments Greybeard, passing the note back to him.

"But there is no race," counters Finn, his head falling with great disappointment.

Greybeard puts his hand on Finn's shoulder. "Finn, you and your brother are the products of your race. Your race lives on through you. You two have a chance to revive it, even if it is just for a brief moment in time. Your actions here will ripple on forever through the ages. You will shape the future of this world, make no mistake."

"If she could tell the future at a touch then why did she not see the poisonings and the deaths in her readings of others?" asks Finn.

"Hmm, that is a very pertinent question, Finn. I suspect a higher, more sinister magic is at play here, one which has hidden itself so as not to be found out. I will need more time to answer that question," replies a perplexed Greybeard.

"Do you think you can get us back to our time?" asks Finn, almost begging the wizard. "If I can change the events leading to our destruction before they even began then I might be able to save my people."

"Finn, I think I can, but I will be honest with you. When Lord told you the fate of your race, he gave you information that you might not be able to take back with you to your time. You hold the key to resurrecting your race at the point it was annihilated. If you were to revive the elves, you may disturb time and space itself and unwittingly destroy Everlast in the process. If I were to find a way to send you back, I might have to erase your memory of this time. This I can do, but you would perish with the rest of your kind."

"We couldn't save them?"

"No, I'm not sure we can. The risk is too great for the future of this world," informs an apologetic Greybeard. "Equally, if you do go back, the events that you influence now might never happen. If you saved this world, it may be unsaved. The consequences either way are great. For now, do as your Queen has asked – treasure your life here, your experiences and the friendships you make. The things you learn over time will help you become a stronger man. I have no doubt you will do what is necessary when time asks of you what it wants. You are a shining light, Finn, and I will think of a way to help you."

Finn contemplates Greybeard's words.

"Thank you, old man."

"Less of the old man!" retorts Greybeard.

"Can I come out from this corner?" asks Beezle, who appears to be very apologetic.

"Oops," Greybeard whispers to Finn, giving him a wry smile, "I didn't really want to keep him there for that long."

"Come on, brother. Come and rejoin us," ushers Finn.

Beezle runs out of the corner and back into the fray. He looks at everybody in turn, asking for their acceptance. Stryker ruffles his hair, before saying, "You really need to learn self-control, young elf. When you do, you will be a better man for it." He smiles as he offers his advice.

"Are you not going to offer your apologies to Kevlan?" Greybeard asks sternly.

"Kevlan, I'm really sorry for what I said. Please forgive me," apologises Beezle.

"I already have," responds Kevlan.

"Go on, Finn, open the box – it would be interesting to see some elven antiquities," urges Wattlespalf.

Finn turns to the wooden box. It is long, narrow and is padlocked.

"Do we have a key?" asks Finn.

"Ah, yes," replies Kevlan, "I tied it to one of the longer hairs on my body so I wouldn't forget." The buggane puts his hands all over his body trying to remember to what hair he tied the key. Eventually he finds it and plucks the hair off his body. Holding the hair between his fingers, he hands it to Finn, who grimaces. "Here you go." Finn doesn't really want to have a buggane hair in his hands.

Finn unlocks and opens the box with a wonder reserved for the most special of times. Inside, on top of some straw packing, is the bow. The bow is made of a light metal and is silver in colour. The curvature and the feel of the bow is smooth. On each end, where the bowstring is tied, is an ornate silver carving of a hare's head. The hare is representative of the bow's ability, which is comparable to the speed and agility this animal possesses. Finn pulls on the bowstring. The string sings – it is a hypnotic sound. As Finn pulls the bowstring back, a bolt of blue energy forms itself into the shape of an arrow. The elf slowly loosens the string of the bow, at which point the energy dissipates. Forester is visibly envious. Finn puts the bow down and unpacks some more of the straw carefully.

The next object to appear is Lerwin the sword. It is

sheathed in the finest black leather with a black leather belt attached. A dragon, made out of the finest silver, fork tongued, smiling menacingly, wings extended and horned tail pointing downwards, emblazons the front of the sheath. You can see the sword's hilt from its sheath. The pommel, grip and cross-guard all give indication that this is a very special sword indeed. The pommel at the top of the sword is shaped like a dragon's head. Worn black leather covers the grip of the sword; this is where the hand will hold it. The cross-guard, separating the grip from the blade, is encrusted with fine, deep green gems, much like the one on the elven king's headband. Finn unsheathes the sword, exposing the blade. The blade shines in the candlelight. It is fine and sharp, the end coming to a perfect point. Ancient writings (not elven) work their way down the blade; they are of a similar print to that of the rod. He looks at it briefly, puts it back in its sheath and places it carefully on the floor.

Finn removes more straw and comes to the elven armour. He pulls it out of the box, holding it by its shoulders. The armour is light in weight, silver in colour and is of a fine fishbone design. It is in the shape of a vest. Finn puts the armour on. It covers him well, from the shoulders to just below the waist. He feels the temptation to ask one of the others to take a swipe at the armour, but for now he resists. The weapons have got the dwarfs' attention, too. All three look closely at each and every item produced from the box, inspecting the work and depth of craftsmanship that has gone into every piece.

Dwarfs are renowned for forging weaponry and magical items which those who are good, evil, misguided or indifferent use as talismans to cause harm and dismay, or promote balance and harmony in the world. Needless to say, both good and evil protect these weapons and powerful magical items in order to make sure that the balance does not swing towards one side or the other. If they had not produced these magical items at all then perhaps, only perhaps, the battles and destruction of past ages and ages to come may have been, or might be, avoided. Finn appears to have a few of those weapons forged by dwarfs in his possession, and this is why the dwarfs are particularly interested in them.

"One of our clans must have had a part to play in the production of these items," Gendralf says, looking at the bow and sword on the floor. He puts his face close to Finn as he peruses the vest. Igralf and Wattlespalf do the same.

"Lovely work." says Igralf. "You don't happen to have a magnifying glass, do you?" He directs his question towards Kevlan.

"Well, actually, yes. I have it in the back room. I'll go and get it." Kevlan turns round.

"No, no, that will not be necessary, Kevlan," insists Igralf, changing his mind quickly at the prospect of having to wait an age to receive the magnifying glass in his hands.

Finn works his hands and arms way down to the bottom of the box. He moves his hand all around it trying to find the Premethian liquid. He happens upon a small bottle and takes it out. The liquid inside is clear with a hint of blue. The small, clear bottle it is kept in has a dropper at the top of it. Being the smallest, most delicate of the items and the one most easily lost, Finn walks over to his backpack and puts the bottle inside one of its pockets in order to keep it safe.

Soon the interest in Finn's gifts dies down. The group retire to the table, drink a little bit more, laugh and talk, while Greybeard puts together the charm he had promised for Kevlan. The charm will automatically pacify anyone wishing to cause the buggane harm.

"Here you go," says the wizard as he passes the charm and a rough map of how to find the buggane clans to Kevlan.

"Oh, thank you, thank you. You have been so kind." Kevlan is eternally grateful.

It is not long before the buggane's guests tire and make their way to their beds on the floor. Kevlan, too, shuffles off to his own bed, drawing the curtains around it before falling asleep.

The men awake at what can only be presumed to be morning. Kevlan is up and about. He has used Finn's box as a trunk and filled it with his favourite belongings, including a couple of books for the journey ahead.

"How are you going to get that to the top of the stairs?" asks Wattlespalf.

"Oh, I'm not going up the stairs – I'm going through the back door," Kevlan responds.

"What, there is a back door to this place?" replies an astonished Wattlespalf.

"Yes, it is where I take deliveries of food, books and all the essential things I need," explains Kevlan. "The horses and cart are waiting for me outside. I cannot thank you all enough. I hope we meet again, but for now, I bid you all farewell." Kevlan shakes everybody's hands, the men avoiding looking at him one last time. "When you are ready, make your way back up the stairs and simply knock on the door at the top. It will open and let you out." Kevlan begins to make his way to the back door very, very slowly.

A swift amount of movement takes place as the men reload themselves of their gear and weaponry. With some excitement and trepidation, Finn puts on his armour, wraps the belt holding his sword around his waist and puts the bow on his shoulder. He gives the bow and quiver he took from the blinny to Beezle. The younger brother looks up at Finn, noticing that he appears more grown up than he has ever done before. The little elf smiles at his brother. Underneath his smiling surface, Beezle has mixed emotions for Finn – seething envy as well as a strange sense of pride. 'I'm the special one,' he thinks to himself. 'So why is it that my brother is the one getting all the attention?' Beezle controls his feelings; he knows that he is close to being shunned by Greybeard and he wants to learn more of the magical arts.

"Are we ready?" Stryker asks of the others.

Everyone nods, and with that, they begin to make their way up the winding stone stairs. Stryker leads the line. At the top of the stairs, Stryker knocks on the door. The door opens and the group make their way back outside; the day is fine and bright. As the door closes itself, the writings on the doorway and the standing stones can be visibly seen changing into new words. Perrywinkle looks briefly at the doorway.

"The riddle has changed, ready for the next visitor," he reveals, astounded by what he has just seen.

Greybeard looks eastward from the top of the hill, in the direction of the next stage of the journey ahead. The view reveals a route working its way to a road which leads south. Further east, carrying on along the eastern road, a tower surrounded by a wall pokes upwards towards the sky. It is the site of Milias, one of the great cities of this world. To the northeast, large walls of rock dominate the horizon. If you travel many, many miles further, through the gorges and tracks, you will arrive at the mines where some of the dwarfs dwell. To the southeast, where the travellers head and Warrior awaits, there is not much to be seen as a mist covers the horizon.

Greybeard turns round to face the others. "Come on – if we have a good day's ride we can hit the road to the south and maybe a bit further."

"Let's get back on those horses," rouses Forester.

CHAPTER 10

A NEW FRIEND?

The company make their way back down the hill. The horses are sufficiently rested and chomping at the bit to get moving. Walking down the hill, the horses are picked up one by one and mounted. Setting off through the fields again, as a pack, the men follow a narrow road. The first field they come to is filled with apple trees; the apples are ripe and ready to be picked.

"So what will I learn today?" asks Beezle.

"I want you to do pretty much the same as you did yesterday, but I want you to change the words, and as such, the action achieved. So today you will choose an item that you wish to come to you. The item must be small, though. Something too large is likely to do you damage, should you not perform the trick perfectly."

"It wouldn't be a bad thing," whispers Igralf to his brothers, provoking giggles and sniggers.

"Hold out your arm – your fingers should be stretched out to reveal your palm. Utter the words 'grabius come' over and over again until the object flies towards your palm. Remember that you must maintain your concentration to direct the object – if you do not, there will be consequences. As it hits your palm, close your fingers over the object. Now watch me before attempting it yourself." Greybeard puts out his hand. He has spied an apple he wants hanging from a tree. He mumbles the words under his breath. "Grabius come, grabius come." The apple flies off the tree, hitting his palm with a slap. He closes his fingers quickly, turns to Beezle and takes a bite out of the apple.

"This will be too easy," boasts Beezle. He turns around, looks at the apple trees, puts out his hand, fingers stretched, and mumbles the words. The apple flies off the tree, and Beezle laughs cockily. But the apple does not fly to Beezle's hand – in fact, it completely misses his hand and hits him in the face.

"Ow," Beezle cries, rubbing his cheek.

"That will teach you not to lose your concentration midway through an act," sniggers Greybeard. Beezle can hear the others sniggering behind him. The little elf turns round and screws his face up, showing that he is not amused. The giggling stops. Beezle tries again and this time the apple nearly hits Igralf. The others are no longer amused as they begin to dodge apple after apple, which are flying with regularity off the trees. It is not long before he masters the trick though, and after five or six successful attempts at catching the apples, he becomes tired of it.

"Teach me something else, Greybeard," he orders.

"Today's lesson has ended. If I were you I would practise for the rest of the day."

"But I could learn more."

"I'm sure you could, but you will practise what you have already learnt and nothing else for rest of the day," Greybeard tells him firmly. Beezle falls into a sulk but controls his anger as he wants to have the opportunity to learn more.

"The world is a beautiful place," comments Perrywinkle, ignoring the constant distractions provided by Beezle. He takes a deep breath through his nose. "I mean, can you smell the flowers, the apples and the grass? Can you feel that sun beating down on your back? Clouds changing size and shape? Can you see the beauty in trees? The fruits and the flowers adding to their form?" Perrywinkle takes an apple off a nearby tree. "Can you feel the smooth skin of this apple?" He takes a bite out of it. "And what about the taste? Bitter and sweet in the same moment."

"What is your point?" asks a bewildered Gendralf, thinking that Perrywinkle has gone slightly doolally.

"I'm just saying that this is a remarkable world. The Creators must have been inspired. It does make you wonder why they brought evil and annoying things into the very same world. I mean evil and annoying things do make life less pleasurable," philosophises Perrywinkle.

"I suppose the world needs balance, Perrywinkle. Maybe the Creators wanted to make this place a little more interesting. Maybe they wanted to give us all this only to provide constant reminders that they could just as easily take it away, in the hope that we will appreciate it more. It is just a shame that most creatures do not, or at least not all of the time."

Perrywinkle goes silent, mulling over Gendralf's words. "You know that last thing you said, it makes perfect sense. Can I add it to my journal?"

"Of course… I too have a talent for what you are doing, sonny," boasts Gendralf.

The fields and the stone walls come to an end, and the track opens out. On either side of them are overgrown fields with wild flowers and long, straw-coloured grasses. From atop their horses, the riders can see many miles ahead on all sides. The horses gather speed; there are no obstacles here and the path is wide. Grey, white, brown, yellow, red and black flashes dart in and out of each other's paths. The horses are playful. Their manes and tails sway as they move faster and faster through the countryside. The horses have been waiting for this. The sound of their hooves thudding against the hardened ground produces a beat, enthralling not only the horses but their riders as well. Clouds of dust form behind them as they rush onward. The countryside flies past on either side of the riders, colours of the flowers and the straw grasses melting into one another as if lost in an artist's painting. The riders' eyes are partially closed, the winds generated by the speed of the horses drying them. Their hair and beards float and sway in the wind trap they have created. The long road leading south, heading towards their destiny, appears in the distance.

Further ahead is the dark tower Greybeard saw from the hilltop. It is the residence of the King of Milias. Thick walls surround the tower, and indeed, the city that spreads out around it. The walls are there to protect them; they have seen fighting before. Large boulders can be seen on the outside of the wall, stones making up the wall have been damaged. The stone walls are dinted, some dints are large and some are small. There is a large, thick, wooden gate, which is open; it is a sign that it is peaceful here at this time, but there is movement on the battlements. Workers are fixing the walls and reinforcing them. Many soldiers stand atop the battlements, guarding all points.

'Something has prompted the King into action. The news of Warrior must be spreading,' Greybeard thinks to himself.

The riders will not be going into the city. They make a right turn onto the southern path and they do not stop. Track turns to a road made of large flags of stone. The flags are smooth. The beating of the hooves turns to a distinct clippity-clop as metal shoes hit the hard stone. The road is wide; all eight riders can sit together on it side by side. On either side, the views for the immediate future will remain the same with fields of straw, grass and wild flowers dominating.

"Put your hoods up," Greybeard orders Finn and Beezle, anticipating what is to come.

The riders continue onward. As they travel down the road, they begin to see more and more people travelling in the opposite direction to themselves. Many people have horses, donkeys and carts filled with their belongings, while others walk alongside with nothing but a backpack on their back. People of all ages travel north to the city of Milias; in this mix are families of at least three generations. Greybeard stops beside one of these families with a horse and cart – they appear dirty and tired.

"Can I ask why so many people are travelling this way?" he asks a young man and a woman holding a baby, who are riding atop a cart pulled by an old horse.

"Death, sir," reveals the woman. "The goblins, they are fiercer than they have ever been. They are killing everyone in our villages and burning them down whilst they do it."

"How far are they behind you?"

"We think maybe less than a week or two. We were warned early to leave our village by a messenger."

"Thank you for the information." Greybeard rides off and joins the others. "The situation is grave. We have much to do and little time. It appears that they have started to move more quickly."

"So what do we do next?" asks Stryker.

"See our old friend, Pengwellen the dragon," replies Greybeard.

"Are you sure we should be making that journey? Last time we nearly killed him – he's not going to be pleased to see us," pleads a hesitant Stryker.

"He'll be fine. It was a long time ago. He has probably forgotten the incident by now. Besides, Lord foretold it," reassures Greybeard.

"So where do we find Pengwellen?" asks Finn, who has been listening in on this conversation.

"See that mountain in the very, very far distance, peering out from over the horizon, there on the left?" points Stryker. "That is King's Mountain. Pengwellen and his like live there, within its caves and caverns."

Riding on, the men stop at a few stalls at the side of the road, buying bread, meat and cheese. After a few hours' ride, the horses are urged to move off the road and inland to some trees that offer a little cover from the elements and other things less pleasant. The sun is starting to set. Grasshoppers begin to play their violins, prompting others to come out of their sun-fuelled slumbers. Noises can be heard in long grass. Mice, snakes, insects and owls wake, picking up where they left off, playing their games of life and death.

A fire is lit. Lying beside the fire, the company chew on their food – even the most basic of meals is a welcome one. They settle down for the night using their backpacks as pillows – that is, except for Finn and Beezle, who are happy to lay their heads on the ground. As night draws in, everyone is soon sleeping soundly.

Beezle is awoken again this night by the whispers coming from Finn's backpack. It is the rod and it is talking to him.

"Come to me," it beckons him.

Beezle gets up, walks over to Finn's backpack, and takes the rod out of it. The gems in the rod light the immediate area but no one sleeping is disturbed, and Greybeard's oric is not alerted to it. Beezle walks away from the tree where he and Finn rest, into the long grass, holding the rod with both hands. The moon is full and shines much light on Beezle and the rod.

"You are the one," whispers the rod. "We want you to be our master, the red oric and I. You are the one. You will help us fulfil our purpose. You are special," it whispers, ploughing Beezle with compliments.

"Special? Yes, I am special, and I am very glad you know it," replies Beezle.

"Yes, you are… very special. You are meant to be with us. You are our master. We can help you."

"Be with you? Help me? Well, I can help you – I am being taught to be a great wizard you know," says Beezle, telling white lies.

"We know. You can become very powerful... the most powerful wizard in the world with our help. We will teach you more than Greybeard ever could. Join us and we can help each other fulfil all of our dreams."

"How?" Beezle asks.

"Beezle! Beezle, wake up. We need to get a move on," shouts Finn, shaking Beezle's shoulder. Beezle wakes with a start. Finn is looking down on him. "Beezle, come on. We need to get a move on. We've got a long day ahead of us."

Beezle looks at Finn's backpack, which is now on his back. 'It was just a dream,' he thinks.

"Yes, coming. Sorry, I was deep in sleep," apologises Beezle.

"Yes, you were," Finn replies with a smile.

CHAPTER 11

HORROR AT THE STONE CIRCLE

A village is on fire. Individual houses burn brightly. Waves of heat and smoke bellow upwards towards the sky. Crackles, snaps, spits, pops and fizzes of burning wood and straw drown out all other sounds. The smoke and fire can be seen from miles around. The people who can see it in nearby villages and towns know that they are most probably next to experience this fate. Many villagers pack their belongings, putting them on their horses and carts. Those who do not have a horse and cart pack only a backpack, and knowing that their progress will be slow, set off walking as quickly as they can. Everybody wants to be anywhere but here.

People cry as they leave family homes and villages; many were born in these houses, and they know that it is likely that they will return to nothing if or when these attacks subside. Those who stay are resigned to their fate. Some set about putting up defences and sharpening their weapons, while others sit silently on a chair in their home, waiting. Everyone is different in how they deal with the inevitability but their deepest feelings are the same.

In the burning village, lifeless bodies litter the floor. Arrows stand up in the chests, legs and backs of the dead. Screams can be heard on the outskirts of the village. Blinny chase the remaining men, women and children through green, grassy clearings, hoping to catch them before they reach the woods. Like cats playing with mice they torment their prey before doing unspeakable things to them. Goblins laugh and scream with sadistic pleasure. No one who lives here will survive the attack on their home.

Numerous goblins do all manner of horrible, but for them, extremely enjoyable jobs. They cannot control themselves. A goblin's fury is never really satisfied. Some are running in and out of houses looking for odd pieces of gold and jewellery to steal. Some are cooking their victims in the blazing fires to quell their hunger. Others are satisfying their blood lust further by killing animals in pens; the meat on these beasts satisfies empty stomachs but it doesn't taste quite like a man – nothing does. Most of them are being destructive: chopping, sawing and slicing through fences and buildings, making sure that the village is well and truly flattened before they leave. Goblins scream, shout, gurgle and grunt as they carry out their work. They have not been this happy for a long time.

Once content that they have completed their daily chores, the goblins begin the journey back to their leader. Idolising this Warrior fellow, they feel as if he has freed them once again; their hope is rejuvenated, and the world they have sought is finally within their grasp. The goblins, who have caused so much despair in this place, are just one small group of many. Only one hundred make up this pack. Hundreds more are, at the same time, finishing off their attacks of other villages in the area. Goblin hordes walk back from their day's plunder, joining with other packs as they filter into the woods leading back to the camp. Warrior is only a matter of miles away, waiting for them; a vast army of thousands waits also, for bigger things to come.

Why so many of these little monsters? You might ask. Greybeard earlier reported that the army was only small. But time has passed since the wizard received his information and Warrior was clever. Greybeard will be surprised when he realises his task. Goblin messengers trekked forth a good while ago, at Warrior's behest, to all corners of this land. Messengers spread the word to the clans and tribes, urging them to come and help their race. "This is the last battle. Finally you will get your wish. Man will be wiped out and the world will finally be yours," the messengers proclaimed. Goblins had heard this all before; so many times their clans have fought to overturn their woe but they have always been thwarted. Many clansmen dismissed the messengers' calls to arms. Some were apathetic towards the call and decided instead to eat the messengers. But others, they saw it as a grand opportunity, an invitation to go out and cause havoc, mayhem and destruction. Some saw this as a chance to relive past triumphs and re-assert the fear that they once held whilst the tribes of men were still working towards dominance. And so it is that hundreds, nay – thousands upon thousands of goblins from all corners of this world are hoping to congregate in support of Warrior and his vision. Who knows, this might be their time, their chance to make this world a better place – one which is dark, fearful and grave.

For those who have already gathered in the south, the work has already begun; beasts of many clans are happily destroying the villages of the creatures they call enemy. The destruction has been relentless and they are glad of it.

Blinny from the most recent raid have joined with their brothers and cousins on the path back towards Warrior. Goblins hobble, wobble, limp and walk past birdless trees on a track that leads to an open encampment. Clansmen have had a pleasurable time today, and at this juncture wipe their swords, axes, pikes and clubs clean of blood with their tongues. The more civilised blinny squeeze the red stains from their weapons onto their fingers before putting those fingers into their mouths and savouring the blood of their victims on their taste buds.

"A tasty treat, this man's blood," says one goblin.

"Yeah, sweet, gooey and messy," another laughs, blood dribbling down his chin.

"Ooh, they taste so nice when they're cooked," another giggles, nibbling on a finger attached to the severed hand of a cooked man.

"I agree. Can't wait till tomorrow to cook some more. Where d'ya think they're gonna send us?" asks another.

"Won't be far, won't be far. There are a lot of villages in this area," says the nibbler.

"But they're getting scarce now. Time to move on methinks," comments another goblin.

"Can't wait to hit the city – loads of men. We'll feast for months," enthuses the nibbling goblin gleefully.

A larger goblin walking behind the nibbler taps him on the shoulder. "Give us a bite on that hand," he orders, chattering his sharp, dirty teeth.

"Yer should've got yer own when yer had the chance," retorts the nibbler, taking another bite, this time out of the palm of the hand.

"Here, give it us," responds the larger goblin, putting his dagger against the nibbler's throat.

The nibbler gulps his meat and starts to pass the hand over to the larger goblin, but as he does so, he reaches for his sheathed dagger, pulls it out and sticks it into the larger blinny's stomach, slicing across his girth. The larger goblin's eyes open wide. "Oh no, what've yer done?"

"Ha, ha, ha," the nibbler laughs. "That'll teach yer not to mess with me." Waving his dagger, he puffs out his chest in the other's direction triumphantly. The larger goblin pulls away from the nibbler, stops walking and holds his stomach as guts begin to slide and slither from out of the gaping wound created.

Blinny of all sorts look at the larger one and lick their lips. He falls to the ground in pain; he is very much alive but he won't be for long. Turning on the larger goblin, a crowd gathers around him, smelling him as they would food. Blinny dive onto the larger one, ripping and pulling and eating and burping. The feeding frenzy lasts only a few minutes, crowds dissolving when there is nothing left to take. All that is left of the large goblin, when everything is over and done with, is a pile of empty clothing sitting amongst sinew, bone and a big pool of green blood.

Believe it or not, an order prevails in the world of goblins; much like men, they have seniors who maintain or direct action to a set of rules that are understood by all. In this particular instance, the rules have been broken, although they often are. A general, followed closely by his lieutenants, beats his way through the hordes with a stick to the scene of this murder.

"Ay, ay, what's goin' on here then?" the general asks as he makes his way through the throng.

The goblin general is tall and more rotund than the rest of them; he is fed well. His name is General Glum. Most of the goblins for whom Glum is responsible are slight in stature and sinewy with it. His face is missing an ear and nose – these were things he lost in a battle with a renowned pikeman years earlier. The pikeman did not live for long, though, once Glum had got his hands on him. General Glum's chubby face is distorted; his mouth is large and wide, and skin peels off all parts of his face as well as his hands. Glum wears a studded, brown leather jacket over rusted chain mail, which sits over a tattered brown shirt on his back. A metal helmet, covered with round metal studs, sits on his head. Heavy, black leather pants are held up by heavy, black belts. Numerous other belts, across his chest, hold a sword, a small, sharp axe and a sheathed little dagger. On his feet are large, worn, black leather boots. In his hand is a long, thin stick used for whipping and beating naughty things.

"Nothing happenin' here, sir," shouts one goblin.

"All good here," adds another.

"Only a small kerfuffle – nothin' to look at really," informs another. The general can sense the goblins' lies, but then goblins lie all the time so he already expects them to do this. Wandering closer to the scene of the crime, he notices green splatterings of blood on clothes and dripping from mouths. And then he stumbles upon the pile of empty clothes surrounded by stinking bones and blood on the ground. The general is horrified by what has unfolded, but that is not to say that when he was younger he had not partaken in the same sort of event, because this particular general had.

"You barbaric scum! What possessed yer to do what yer've just done, eh?" Glum screams at the soldiers standing around, who look up into the air and at the trees, feigning innocence. "I think it would be wise to teach you men a lesson. The master wouldn't approve of what yer've done. Yer minds need to be dissuaded from doin' it again. Anyone covered in blood, beat 'em, all of 'em," the general orders his lieutenants.

"Yes, sir, with pleasure. Ooh, I can't wait to show you lot what for. Not often I get the pleasure of doing this," one of his lieutenants hisses.

Glum and his lieutenants beat the blinny who still stand around the carcass viciously with whips and small clubs. The blinny take the whips and knocks to their bodies without prejudice – it could even be said that some of them enjoy it.

"We are not barbarians and we do not eat our own," shouts the general. Every word spoken is accompanied with the whip of a stick to one or another goblin's head or body. "Now get movin' before you make us late for our dinner," he says, pointing the long stick back down the path in the direction of Warrior.

The pack moves forward. None are ashamed, none carry guilt for the act that they have just been party to, but their lust to kill another has subsided... for now. General Glum and his lieutenants walk back to the front of the line, pushing and shoving little monsters left, right and centre until once again they lead the way back down the track.

"It was quite good that beating. Got the itches out of me back," says one of the goblins as the general and his men walk away.

"Yeah and I kept me meat – they didn't find that, I made sure of it. Hmm, lovely man meat – there isn't a finer delicacy to be had," adds another.

The blinny laugh and joke about the multitude of ways they have killed men, women and children from the villages, giving tips and tricks to each other to better their methods for the next raid. The little monsters hope that they will be chosen for tomorrow's raid even though it will mean working in the daytime. When it is dark, goblins are naturally more active. It has taken some time for these blinny to get used to working in the day, although they are called upon to work during the night every now and again, when they most enjoy it. In contrast to the darkness of night, they despise the day, the sun often making them not want to do very much at all.

"Oi, Bobbucket," one scruffy goblin bellows, resting his thin, wiry arms on a small goblin's shoulder.

"Yes, Pompucket," the small goblin answers.

"You enjoy yer day today? A lotta killin' was done. Never gets better than that does it?" questions the thin, wiry goblin called Pompucket. He and Bobbucket belong to the Ucket clan and are very much related.

"Oh, yes. As always I got a great satisfaction out of killing and maiming others," replies Bobbucket, with the most well-pronounced of voices. As blinny go, this one is very smart in appearance, with a brown-breasted jacket complete with matching trousers and shiny, brown shoes. A belt around his waist holds a dagger and a sword, and in his hand he holds a little wooden shield. In fact, you would swear that he was Perrywinkle's brother, were it not for the hideous contortions of his face. Much like many of his brothers and cousins, the goblin has a pointed nose, chin and ears, his eyes are dark and wild, and his skin is lumpy and scaly. These and many more things make him not a very nice thing to look at, but in his favour, his teeth are well-placed, white and shiny, and his hair is neat and tidy – neither does he produce that horrendous smell goblins are well known for.

"What d'yer say, yer little groveller?" questions a perplexed Pompucket, before giving out a big, loud laugh and a big slap against Bobbucket's back. "Can't understand a word yer say, Bobbucket. Always been funny this one, but before any of yer think about harmin' this little fella, think about me and me mates first, because we wouldn't let anyone touch another one of our clan." A roar rings out from the thin, wiry goblin and numerous others as they identify themselves as being part of the same goblin tribe, this tribe obviously being the Uckets. Bobbucket also tries to give out a roar but it turns out to be more of a whimper.

It is not before time that the goblins leave the tracks of the woods as it opens out onto the fields of the southern plains. The lush, green fields of the plains stretch outwards for miles and miles. Rolling hills sit amongst the fields. The sun shines its wondrous rays of light through patchy clouds blown onwards by a light breeze. Dark green shades of the grass sheltered by clouds share the same space as the light green shades of grass that nestle in sunlight. The view, once so filled with beauty, is spoiled by the sight of the goblin camp. The area they cover is vast, what with thousands of these deformed monsters having made it their temporary home.

Large flags fly in the light breeze. The flags are tied to poles that sit firmly in the soft earth and are emblazoned with the insignia of the individual clans. Some are covered in stripes of colour and others have the portraits of legendary goblin leaders, pictures of hanged men, severed hands or weaponry, such as a sword. The flags separate the clans from each other, and they also tell goblins where their particular clan is situated.

"Ere, Bobbucket. Find out where our clan is will yer? Yer pretty good at findin' these things," praises Pompucket. Bobbucket looks around, and as Pompucket predicted, after only a few seconds he locates the clan's flag. The Ucket flag has the bloodied head of a black boar emblazoned on a yellow background. Bobbucket looks up at his thin, wiry protector and points in the direction of the clan flag, announcing at the same time, "There it is."

"Well done, Bobbucket. Knew yer'd find it. Come on you lot, let's go and get some dinner from the best cook in the world."

Bobbucket's tribe walk through the fields, passing other goblin clansmen as they do so. Foot soldiers, cavalrymen, archers and drummers all inhabit the same space here. Most wear garments of leather covered with metal studs, and if they are lucky enough, they will also have a basic, ill-fitting metal bowl for a helmet. Goblin armour is not particularly effective. Those who do possess chain mail have procured it from dead men killed in battle – generally the chain mail is rusted or cut and is therefore not much use at all. Swords are, more often than not, jagged at the edges and have lost their ability to slice effectively. You see, blinny are unskilled in the arts of the blacksmith, or architecture, mining or science, or even reading and writing for that matter. But what they lack in armoury and intelligence, they more than make up for in numbers. Blinny breed like no other race in this world, although it is not really known how they do this as goblin women are rarely seen.

A few dozen barghest grunt and growl loudly through the small metal cages they are held in. There is only one to a cage; two sharing the same confined space are likely to kill each other and that would not be good for business, especially the business of war. As Bobbucket and his clansmen pass these beasts, the barghest bare their sharp, pointed teeth at them.

As the barghest growl, those passing by retaliate by banging their swords against the bars of cages. Red, piggy-eyed, coarse black-furred barghest grunt and growl louder as the passing goblins patronise and torment them. Getting angrier, thick white foam drips down from the barghests' jaws. They are the most vicious of creatures – don't ever forget that. They would kill their offspring to have your meat.

Barghest are, in actual fact, giant boar bred with giant wolves for that extra little bit of wild ferocity. Barghest look much like boars as they have large pot bellies, short pink snouts, short, pointed tusks on either side of their jaws and short, round tails. What makes them different is that they have long, muscular legs, paws with short, thick claws and mouths full of long, sharp teeth. Barghest are tall, but not as tall as a good sized pony, stocky, and very strong in stature. Damage instigated by these beasts can come from teeth that grab and pull at flesh, claws that slash and shred, and tusks that can impale a man and carry him for miles upon them.

Whilst men ride horses, blinny prefer to ride these beasts into battle. Barghest do a lot of the harm to those that are hunted before goblins need get involved. Bred in significant numbers for this purpose, at birth metal rings stamped with the names of their owners are put through these beasts' noses. Blinny tie ropes or chains to the rings in order to control them better when riding. Barghest learn when they are very young that a quick pull on the ropes is enough to control them, as the pain felt round their noses is too much for them to take. Barghest remember many things, not least the cruelty asserted by blinny. These beasts would be more than happy to kill their owners, given the chance. When they are not doing the job that they have been bred to do, a number of wooden carts with wooden wheels carrying cages and other provisions are pulled by the barghest, helping the cause even outside of battles that they love so much.

"Are you sure the cages will hold them? They're very scary, and by the looks of them very strong as well," Bobbucket shouts out to a goblin standing close by to the cages, who appears to be preparing meat for the beasts.

"Hold em? Course they'll hold em. Doesn't stop them from swiping at little goblins who get too close to them, though. They've had a couple of arms and heads off, these buggers have. Beware of them at all times, I say," answers the goblin.

Moving on from the barghest, Bobbucket notices dozens of rats darting around the goblin camp looking for food. Food is easy to come by here as blinny are not tidy. In fact, rats follow them more or less wherever they go. Morsels of food can be found everywhere in this camp, and if the worst came to the worst, then the rats could always nibble on goblin scabs or corns on the bottoms of their feet.

"Disgusting – a smart goblin like myself should not be exposed to these horrors," Bobbucket protests. He is sickened further; the smell in the camp is unbearable. The little goblin turns his nose up at the other little monsters who generally do not wash and do not mind where they leave their filth.

Arriving at the bloody boar-headed flag, Pompucket, Bobbucket and the rest of the clan surround a big, fat goblin cook, who is stirring up some tasty gruel in a decent-sized cauldron, sitting atop a small fire.

"Ha, Cook, yer stinkin' mess of a goblin, have yer been working yer magic on our food?" asks Pompucket of the big, fat goblin.

"Yer food is as lovely as it ought to be. What about yerselfs – did yer have a good day today killin' men and the like? Hope yer didn't eat too many of them so yer can't fit this tasty concoction into yer bellies. Nothin' but the best for my boys," replies the cook, priding himself on his abilities.

"Ay, we had a great day, and no, we didn't eat any men today – worse luck. Feeling peckish for some though, now yer talk about it. I was savin' myself for yer gunk. Maybe tomorrow, though, eh?" responds Pompucket with a rotten-toothed smile.

Suddenly there is a slight rumbling of the ground.

"Oh, here we go again," moans Pompucket. "Bloody show-offs comin' round to show us how good they are." In this melee of blinny, barghest and rats is another race – ogres belonging to goblins who caught them as youngsters are now treated like pets, which are paraded around proudly by their owners. Getting nearer to the Ucket clan, the ground rumbles more and more.

Ogres are horrifically ugly and give off a nasty smell (especially when they fart) much like the blinny who share the same space as them. Only a foot or two taller than a very tall man and solidly built, they have big, round heads full of hair on top of and on their faces. Big yellow teeth and big, flat noses adorn the faces of these creatures. Large stomachs, long arms and long legs are other notable characteristics of this race. Chained to their goblin owners, the ogres carry big, heavy clubs as weapons. Whilst ogres have weapons, they are not particularly interested in fighting or battles, but they love their owners without prejudice, even if those owners regularly beat and whip them mercilessly. Ogres seek only to protect their owners from harm; their large size and ferocity is useful when faced with violence – which generally comes from those defending themselves against being attacked.

To the far right of the camp, a pathway lined by standing stones makes its way through the fields towards a stone circle. The stone circle has seen the happiest of times. Men and women bound together by love have become one here, their love formally recognised by villagers from all around. Babies have been named, and boys and girls have experienced their rites of passage to adulthood here. This has been the scene of many festivals and much merriment has been enjoyed. It has also seen moments of sadness as whole villages paid their respects to their immediate descendants, and in the same breath celebrated the passing of others, giving them back to the Creators of this world. History has been created and experienced within this circle – it once represented the circle of life itself. It is certain that the people from the area loved this place. The stone circle and its views were so loved that practically every day, no matter what the weather, men, women and children came together to play, talk and reminisce about what was and what might be. No one ever imagined that the horrors camped here would dominate, defecate and soil this place, and no one ever thought the stone circle would house terror.

But terror now dominates, and standing in the centre of the large stone circle is Warrior. Giant in stature, he is as high as the tallest of the stones in the circle; he must be eight feet tall or more. Dark, grey armour, with long and short metal spikes protruding outwards from head to foot, protects his body.

Standing in front of him is his broadsword. The pommel of the sword, above the grip where the hand holds it, houses a large blue gem which has been cut into the shape of a ball. The blue gem is very precious and goblins can often be seen coveting it. Much bloodshed would be the result if the blinny got a chance to take it from Warrior, but they dare not.

The cross-guard of the sword harbours the red oric, which gleams in its place. The arms of Warrior face forwards in front of him, his hands caressing the pommel and grip of the large, broadsword gently. The long, wide blade runs downwards to its end, the point of it touching the soft ground within the circle delicately, so as not to penetrate it. Warrior's sword is so large that the red oric sitting in it is dwarfed by its size, but the power it possesses can never be underestimated. When used properly by the most accomplished wizards, its power could outstrip even Greybeard's.

"Pompucket, look at the master. He has done a terrible thing.

143

Have you seen him?" screams Bobbucket, feeling a little sickened by what he sees.

Pompucket looks over towards the stone circle. "I've never seen anythin' so beautiful. Isn't he lovely?" A cheer rings out from his clan, who are all in full agreement with Pompucket's statement.

If Warrior was not horrific enough to look at already, the pale, lifeless face of what was a bearded man adorns the front of Warrior's faceplate, making him truly monstrous. It is the face of a knight who had fought Warrior bravely today.

"Yer missed a treat, young goblins. A knight paid the master a visit when yer were gone, hopin' to defeat him. Came on his own he did, on his own two feet. Challenged the master, but in the end he lost, badly. Took the master a good while to beat him though – suspect that's why he took his face from his head," reveals the cook. "Once the knight was defeated, Warrior cut the face from the man carefully so as not to spoil the skin – like a good butcher, much like me, if I don't say so myself," boasts the cook.

The face has been tied onto the helmet like a mask. Warrior believes he has done this in honour of the defeated knight. In addition, a necklace of skulls that once belonged to heroes, knights, men and kings who stood up to or fought valiantly against his wrath sit proudly against his chest. The skulls act as a warning: do not resist, run – run as fast and as far away as you can, because if I get close then this will be your fate. The appearance of Warrior is so horrific that no man should want to meet him anyway, and those who do are often so terrified that they are defeated in mind before a blow is struck.

No one knows what lies behind the armour; no one has even had a glimpse of Warrior's eyes. It is assumed that the figure of a man is encased in its eerie confines. What lies within his mind cannot be fathomed. Whatever is behind the armour, no matter what form it takes, can only ever be called monster.

Sitting in the stone circle with Warrior are the five long-armed, large-handed animals that Greybeard talked of earlier. These animals have no name given to them by men because they have never been seen in this world before. Like dogs and ogres, they love their owner, who is good to them, so for the purposes of this tale we will call them 'pets'.

These pets will kill and rip, squeeze and shred at the utterance of a word. The brutality of these animals is like no other. They are not like goblins, though, and they do not kill and maim out of enjoyment – they do it because they are asked. Pets are dark in colour; their skin is hairless and leathery, so much so that a sword cannot penetrate their hides. Their smooth, flat faces have no visible evidence of eyes, a nose or ears. Only a small, round mouth filled with pointed, sharp teeth adorns their large round heads. The pets arms are much, much longer than their legs, and their stature and stance is much like that of a monkey, but they are bigger, much bigger. They walk and run on all fours when travelling and are quick when they do so. Pets are also very agile, able to climb trees and cling to walls with ease.

"And his beasts, did they show what they are capable of?" asks Pompucket of the cook.

"Nah, the master didn't let them near the knight, but like always, they wanted to do somin' terrible I say," answers the cook.

"It'll happen soon enough, I promise yer that. Can't wait to see them… bet yer they're lovely to watch and deadly, very deadly. Just like me, eh?" Pompucket says quietly and thoughtfully. "Anyway, lads, shall we break the ale out? It's about time we did some relaxin'."

Day draws closer to its end. Goblins smoke pipes and sup ale to while away the more boring hours. They cannot hold their ale; some would even say that they are worse than men. Ale and smoking makes them dizzy, sick and raucous to the point where they are easily provoked, using its effects as an excuse to fight.

It is noisy in the camp, and goblins' voices boom out as they become ever more drunk and talk to each other ever more loudly. Goblins like to make themselves heard. Some throw insults at each other whilst puffing out their chests in order to prove, once and for all, that they are better than the one they are berating. Others boast about their prowess on the battlefield, recounting tall tales of how they took on an army of men and defeated it.

A few blinny cooks dish out gruel into bowls and hand them out to the foot soldiers. Goblins eat the gruel quickly, using their hands and tongues to get the food out of the bowl and into their stomachs sooner. Generals, lieutenants, captains and sergeants roam around the camp trying to maintain order, but blinny are notoriously difficult to control and soon there is a fight, a drunken fight that will quickly get out of hand.

Two of the drunken little monsters quarrel over a bowl of food. One of them eats his gruel too quickly, and still hungry, he attempts to grab the bowl from a goblin sitting right next to him.

"Give us it – I believe that food belongs to me now," orders a muscular, bullying sort of goblin, picking on a smaller, skinnier variety.

"No, it's my gruel. Yer've had yours. Yer shouldn't have eaten it so fast as to want more," replies the bullied goblin.

"I said give us it, you weaselly little ingrate. Yer don't need this much food anyway – yer belly isn't big enough for it," the bullying goblin patronises, pulling the bowl away from the bullied goblin's fingers. Naturally, the one who has had his bowl stolen wants it back because he is hungry, and so a fight breaks out between them. Two fighters soon become four, and four fighters soon become twenty. The officers in the goblin ranks, noticing the fracas, try to restore order.

On the outskirts of the camp, in the stone circle, Warrior has been silently watching the events unfold and he is displeased. Taking one of his hands away from the pommel, he sheathes his sword with the other hand slowly. Turning to his pets around him, he looks at them one by one, and they in turn look back at him, knowing he is about to issue an order and they are relishing it.

"Take one goblin each and squeeze them until they are dead," he says to his pets. Warrior's voice displays deep emotionless tones as he points towards the fighting goblin pack. The pets look at the blinny and immediately run around the stones of the circle towards the fighting pack very quickly on all fours.

Warrior disappears into thin air. He reappears within seconds at the very centre of the fight. Looking down on the goblin who started it in the first place, he picks him up with one gauntleted hand round his neck. Goblins fall quiet everywhere, though the silence is short-lived and is soon replaced by cheers. The blinny sense blood is about to be spilt and they revel in it. Warrior's other hand takes hold of the little monster's leg and he is held horizontally above his head for everyone to see.

The bullying goblin can see the blue skies and clouds above

him. He has an inkling that this will be his last vision in life, and oh, what a let down it is. The goblin rolls his eyes and closes them. Warrior, in one slow movement, starts to bend his victim backwards. As he slowly crushes the vertebrae in the bullying goblin's back, he responds with blood curdling screams; the pain is exquisite.

Bobbucket, who has been watching from a distance, turns away. The little goblin doesn't want to see the horror unfold. Pompucket, on the other hand, flicks and flares his tongue whooping with glee. And then, with one swift move, the life of the bullying goblin is over. The body is dumped on the lush, green floor to the delight and entertainment of the others.

But the show of strength is not over yet. Whilst Warrior had dealt with the bullying goblin, the pets had run to the fighters and each selected a goblin, grabbing them around the waist with both hands. Pompucket was right to predict that they would be unleashed sooner rather than later. Squeezing blinny waists with their large hands, the pets begin to crack and break bones inside goblin bodies. Unable to breathe as organs from around their waist push up against their lungs, blood begins to trickle out of mouths and noses, and faces go a deep green in colour as goblin blood finds that it has nowhere to go other than out.

"Stop," Warrior shouts over to his pets; he has had a change of mind. They look to their leader with a growl. Warrior's beasts begrudgingly drop these lucky blinny who cower, regain their breath and crawl away, glad that they will live another day.

Disappearing from the scene of the fight, the spiky armoured monster reappears again seconds later in the centre of the stone circle. Unsheathing his sword, he caresses the pommel and grips it with both hands. The pets run back to the circle and take up their seated positions by their beloved owner once more, nuzzling their faces against his polished armour. The goblins now know that if they ever enter into a fight in front of Warrior again, the punishment will be severe.

Dusk approaches and fires are lit around the camp; there is no cloud cover tonight and the air will become cold. General Glum approaches Warrior, along with his lieutenants, to deliberate over what they are to do next. Unfolding a table in front of Warrior,

Warrior's sword and red oric

one lieutenant produces a map. The map has many marks, detailing villages that have already been destroyed and those that are yet to be visited.

"You have done well," praises Warrior, turning his bearded-faced mask towards General Glum.

"Yes, we have done everything you've asked of us, sire. The morale in the camp is good. Your direction is wise and there are but a few villages and small towns left to conquer in this province before the work here is done. We hear that most men have left their homes and travel north to the cities for protection. You have truly prompted much fear in them as you planned," hisses Glum.

"Show me the new map. We need to plan our next movements," Warrior orders.

One of the lieutenants holds a roll of parchment. It is a new map full of places to visit and conquer. He unfurls it and holds it down on the table with two round metal weights.

Warrior looks at the new map for a while. After a few minutes, he presses his finger down firmly on it about a third of the way up. Warrior's finger presses close to the town of Paledon, which leads to the southern city of Fricas. Fricas is the first great city Warrior will attack. They will be close to Paledon in the next day or two, and it is anticipated that they will attack Fricas within a day or two more.

"Tomorrow we will leave this place and head for Paledon," he tells General Glum. "Choose whomever you will to complete the work on the villages left in this area. The rest can walk with us to a new camp."

CHAPTER 12

AN 'OTHER' WORLD

Hours later, in the darkness of night, goblins have gone to sleep and dream wonderfully terrible dreams. Warrior has reverted back to his motionless position in the stone circle – until now, that is. Moving for the first time since perusing the maps, Warrior appears to knock three times against thin air, and suddenly, taking only one step forward, is gone. The spiky-armoured monster has disappeared, or he is at least invisible would be your immediate thought. But, unbeknownst to the likes of you and I, beyond the fabric of this world there is another.

Warrior has entered another dimension, a world very different to the one we are used to, where dark red skies are ever present. Standing on red sands, Warrior looks all about him. Breathing in sulphurous air, Warrior relishes it – this is home. Behind him, the world he has just left carries on, seen through a doorway that looks back from this other world onto the one he has just left. The doorway is both an entrance and exit between the two worlds, between where Warrior stands and where he once stood. Look through the door into our world, imagine where you want to go in it and within a flash you will be there; this is how Warrior is able to move between one point and another without being seen. Simply knock on the door three times and you will be able to walk through it to get back into our world. Turn your back on the door and you will face the dark recesses of this other world. Think of moving through it and you will.

Warrior turns his back on our world and takes a few steps forward. The door follows him, the image back into our world unchanging as the stones of the circle remain firmly fixed behind him. If Warrior travelled a thousand miles in this other world, the door behind him would follow him, still holding the same image of the last place he stood before passing through.

"Caladan Castle," Warrior utters – this is to where he wants to travel.

A voice can be heard in the distance.

"Warrior, Warrior, Warrior," it says. Warrior travels at an unimaginable speed through this dark world, but he does not move from the spot he is standing. Dirt, rocks, boulders, hills, mountains, deserts, burning volcanoes and dark, dark rivers all shoot past him as he travels through this other worldly landscape. The scenery is beautiful here but eerie, imposing and even frightening. This world appears devoid of trees, flowers and grass. There are no blue skies, here they are red, but there is no burning sun. Thick grey cloud, produced by the many volcanoes that pass by, rises high up into the air covering every pore of the world above. Lightning bolts throw themselves down to earth with regular aplomb, lighting the skies momentarily. A wide beam of green light shines outward from the horizon and a shape develops: it is that of a castle. It must be Caladan. Each time the word 'Warrior' is said, the voice gets louder and the castle gets ever closer.

"Warrior," the voice booms; it is clear and gentle. It is a voice that could belong to a man. The world stops running, and Caladan stands in front of Warrior. The wide green beam focuses itself on the monster, his armour lighting up in its radiance.

Caladan Castle stands tall on a hill, surrounded by a moat, but this moat is not filled with water; in its place an open pit falls for miles and miles, though no one knows what lies at the bottom of this deep, long drop. The drawbridge is up at this time, it is made of a smooth stone that has been cut by masons into the shape of an arch. The gatehouse and thick castle walls branching off from the drawbridge weave their way around the main area of the castle. Parapets designed to protect soldiers run atop the castle walls, but there don't appear to be any soldiers here at all.

The main castle has a bailey on each corner, away from the main outer wall, and a second castle wall connects each of the baileys to one another. Parapets line the top of the baileys. From where Warrior stands, you can barely see the baileys which would normally house the carpenters, masons, candlemakers and serfs, but there don't appear to be any people here apart from the one voice. At the centre of the castle complex is the keep – it is tall and imposing, towering above the baileys and castle walls that surround it. The green beam of light shines down from the parapets on top of the keep; the gentle but loud voice comes from behind it.

Hundreds of animals the same race as Warrior's pets seep out of holes and crannies, until they crawl all around the castle like spiders, grimacing and gurgling warily at Warrior.

"Why have you come to me?" asks the gentle voice from beyond the green light.

"I have unexpected news and I need your guidance. My oric has alerted me to elves," replies Warrior.

"Elves?" the voice is alarmed upon hearing this. The green light shakes a little as if it is taken aback by Warrior's words.

"I have seen them, my oric has shown me."

"But they were all killed. You assured me of that," the gentle voice responds, displaying a little anger and frustration.

"Two elflings appear to have survived the slaughter. From what I have learned, they travelled to the time in which we presently work not long before the slaughter took place," reveals Warrior.

"The timeline... could it have fractured when you entered it?" the voice asks itself. "Who are they with? Where are they now?"

"They travel with a number of creatures including men and dwarfs, only nine strong. A wizard appears to lead them. My oric found his and infiltrated it before alerting me to their presence," replies Warrior. "The name Greybeard was mentioned – I have not heard of him before."

"Greybeard!" the voice responds coarsely. There is silence for a moment. "It is imperative that they are killed, all of them," commands the voice. "Nine will soon become many. Greybeard is a wizard with much guile and influence. There must be no elves and no Greybeard alive in Everlast by the time you have completed your task. We might not achieve our final aim if but one of them survives."

"I had anticipated you would say this. Draugar were summoned and a company of goblins were sent to attack this small band, but they were easily avoided and easily defeated. Greybeard knows that I have spied on them, and he has blocked my sight. I do not know where they are now to hinder them further, and I do not know if they come in my direction to confront me," informs Warrior.

Warrior

"If Greybeard truly is on the move then it is more than likely that he aims to pay you a visit. You must break his spell. Know that Greybeard is a great wizard, though you are more than capable of defeating him. But do not underestimate him because this wizard is more dangerous than most," hisses the voice, ceasing to be gentle anymore. "Be as quick as you can carrying out your task, and make no mistakes as we can ill afford them."

Warrior bows his head with respect for the voice. He turns around to face the door, knocks three times and walks through it, back into the stone circle. Still dark, he resumes his position and waits for the night to turn to day.

The goblins wake early the next morning. All around the camp they can be seen stretching and yawning. Pompucket is one of the first to wake. "Come on, get up yer lazy blaggards." Pompucket enjoys kicking those who are still asleep, and those being kicked grunt and groan lazily in response before lifting themselves off the ground.

The weather is good today, for the likes of you and me that is, but not for these little monsters; they hate the warm sun. Warrior and his pets wait at the edge of the woods. Pompucket and Bobbucket walk forth along with the rest of their clan, away from the camp in the direction of the trees. The army must walk through them and head northwards to get to the outskirts of Paledon. The walk will be long.

Other goblin clans travelling down the main roads and tracks from all parts of this world are expected to join Warrior's cause; if that happens this army will be nigh on invincible.

Four companies chosen to carry out the last of the attacks in this area split from the main group and head east and west over rolling hills.

Warrior and his pets take the lead through the woods; cavalry, foot soldiers, archers and drummers drumming follow on behind.

CHAPTER 13

SAY SORRY TO THE NICE DRAGON

Grey clouds hide the sun from this world today. There is going to be rain over the course of the day, and maybe even some thunder and lightning. Men, women and children sleeping in tents, under sheets and in carts are lining the sides of the southern road; they are refugees, hoping to reach a safe place away from the destruction that is taking place behind them. Hundreds, if not thousands, have made their way north to avoid the conflict. The creatures travelling in the opposite direction are hoping to quell the unrest, but it is becoming increasingly apparent that the situation is going to be more difficult than first imagined. The solution is easy: get the red oric out of the sword using the rod. The hard part is getting close enough to the sword to do it as hordes of goblins, ogres and unnamed assailants try to stop the attempt.

Men, women and children travelling northwards marvel at the elves riding in the opposite direction. Just a glance at the two boys sparks expectation and hope in those who view them – their hoods are down.

"The elves are back," some people can be heard saying. "They are here to save us." Crowds walk alongside the elves, staring up at them as they sit on their horses, touching and squeezing their legs and hands.

"I touched an elf, and he was as real as you or I," one woman can be heard saying. "Praise the Creators for their mercy," cries another.

Finn feels uncomfortable with all the attention. He has never seen this type of behaviour before or been surrounded by this amount of people, all with eyes on him. 'This is not real,' he thinks. To be hailed and treated, just by their presence, as if they will single-handedly defeat a strong foe is desperate at best. Beezle, meanwhile, is enjoying his new-found fame, even if it is founded on the suffering of others, as it satisfies his desire to feel special. He waves to the gathering crowd. Greybeard – and the others, for that matter – look displeased.

"We will save you, don't worry," Beezle says, taking hold of people's hands and smiling at them insincerely.

"Beezle, put your hand down. This is not the time or place," orders Greybeard.

"But we give people hope," retorts Beezle.

"Beezle, please do what I say," asks Greybeard. The little elf pulls his hand away reluctantly.

One by one the riders order their horses to move faster; the crowd is stifling their progress and it is getting bigger by the minute. Soon the horses are running at a great speed. People at the sides of the road can only catch a glimpse of the elves now, and they can be seen gawping all down the road, pointing at the riders after they have passed. The men come to a track leading off the main road to King's Mountain. King's Mountain dominates the immediate landscape, and today the riders have a good view of it.

The peak of the mountain, much like those in the Falcon Gorge range, sits above the clouds, hills and trees partially hiding it. It is called King's Mountain as it is the largest mountain in this land. The mountain stands alone, unlike those in the Falcon Gorge range where there are many. Like a solitary snow-encrusted pyramid, filled with caves and caverns large enough to accommodate the largest of beasts, it suited the dragons to take it as their own… too bad for the mountaineers and climbers who would love the opportunity to scale it, test their wits and conquer it, the dragons would eat them without the slightest thought. Only once the riders have climbed many hills will they get a full view of the mountain and the cave openings where the dragons dwell.

The horses follow a narrow line leading the way ahead. No carts or large groups of people have been this way for a long time, and the track is now hidden and overgrown. Wooden warning signs are everywhere: 'Travel at your own peril', 'Beware the dragons' and 'Danger! Don't go down this track or you will be eaten', they say. It is well known that dragons like eating people. The vast majority of travellers who have the option to follow the track are generally wise and choose not to. The ride is pleasant enough, although the rain has finally been released by the clouds. A few droplets fall like individual tears onto the heads, hands and faces of the party, but the droplets soon turn to showers as if the clouds themselves cry uncontrollably. Our riders carry on through this unperturbed; in fact, the warm rain is welcome as some lap up the droplets running down their faces. Up and over hills the riders go; hours pass and many more showers fall before they reach the last hill that looks down on the foot of the mountain. The view is awesome.

At the bottom of this hill, the land becomes rocky; deep grey tones of stones are mixed in with light grey tones, blacks and off-whites. The rocky ground stretches out for at least a mile or two before it reaches the foot of the mountain where the dragons dwell. Halfway between the bottom of the hill and the mountain is a wide river which appears to be relatively deep. The mountain itself has many cave openings dotted around it, and in and out of those cave openings dragons come and go. The dragons come in a spectrum of colours: reds, yellows, greens, blues, browns and more, and they are all around. King's Mountain is one of the dragon cities – now only three exist.

Dragons, for those who don't know, are very large. Fully grown dragons are at least twenty metres or more, from the tip of their nose to the point at the end of their tail. They generally walk on four short legs which have large claws at the end of their toes. Their heads are long and they have big, sharp teeth. Inside their mouths they can have a forked tongue or a tongue like a man – although a lot, lot bigger. Their nostrils are often flared. Their eyes are either black as night, or have a yellow-green iris and a black slit of a pupil running down the centre. Their bodies are scaly and some can have horns from the crown of their skull to the very ends of their tail, but most do not.

Dragons possess different qualities and are designed to be most comfortable in differing terrains, so for example, a land dragon may possess the ability to breathe fire. Usually these creatures have larger feet and talons, which enables them to move rocks and boulders and dig far into the ground. The dragons of the air have wings and the ability to breathe fire. Water dragons are more slender than their air and land cousins – they have webbed feet and are able to swim at phenomenal speeds, having gills which allow them to stay under the water for an age. Finally, there are snow dragons, who have white fur all over their bodies. They do not have wings but they can fly and breathe ice instead of fire. The claws on snow dragons have been replaced with pads on the ends of their wide, woolly feet, allowing them to walk undeterred in the snowiest of conditions.

At this particular city, no dragons are in view, quite possibly because of the rains – dragons hate rain (except water dragons, of course) as it douses the fire in their bellies.

"All of you, beware the dragons from now on – they are all about and everywhere," warns Greybeard.

"Why would you say that? There is nothing, not anything around for miles… at least, not that I can see," retorts Beezle, trying to be clever.

"Do you feel the strong breeze blowing down on you, little elf?" asks Greybeard.

"Yes I do. It is a breeze, a wind. Winds are everywhere," replies Beezle.

"Do you feel its beat? Do you not think it strange that the winds have a rhythm to them? It is not a wind of a normal sort, my young friend. Those are the wings of a dragon producing it."

"Yes, okay. If you say so," says Beezle sarcastically, waving away the wizard's comments.

"Well, it is – this is not a story I am telling," the old man replies gruffly.

"It is a dragon," interjects Stryker, "and you would do well to heed the warning."

Winds flow down on the men from above. The wizard is right – dragons are flying above the clouds. Every beat of their wings produces a strong wind, making the leaves in the trees rustle and the hairs on a man's head sway from side to side wildly. When there are many dragons flying they can make winds so strong that, it is said, buildings can fall. The cloud cover currently protects our friends. Dragons cannot see through them, and as such, cannot see the men to attack, but these men must be careful as dragons can see very, very well. Only one of them knows these men and he may leave them alone. Those who do not will most likely see them as a threat or as a nutritious meal not to be missed.

It is well known that dragons and men do not get on; both have encroached upon each other's lands since time began, often with devastating consequences. Men have bred and become many, whilst in stark contrast, dragons have become fewer and fewer. It takes an age for a dragon to breed, and unfortunately for them, their quarrels with men have led to fewer births as opposed to deaths, which have been many. Dragons now realise that battles with men are not productive and they have retired to their cities where men now leave them be. Their lives are mainly peaceful and dragons wile away the days, months and years undisturbed, but they still hanker for the flesh of men and will often prey cheekily on unsuspecting travellers who have strayed into their path. They are careful to take those who will not be missed too much, though. You see, goblins, ogres, draugar, erkling and the likes of Warrior and his beasts lay claim to many a man's death, so it is not often man will now blame a dragon for their woes.

And here we have a group of men, dwarfs and elves standing on dragon territory; there is no better excuse for a dragon to claim a meal, and because of this, the men will have to tread carefully. The horses are taken back down the hill and tied up in a sheltered valley where dragons will not easily be able to see them. Returning back to the top of the hill, the group begins their descent. They are cautious, hiding behind rocks and trees – all that is, except for Beezle.

"Anyway, I'm not afraid of dragons. I will use my magic to ward them off. They are no match for me," Beezle boasts.

"Have you actually ever seen a dragon?" asks Wattlespalf.

"Hmm, of course I have," Beezle says, knowing that he has not; he has never seen a dragon, not even in a book.

"What do they look like then?" probes the dwarf further.

"Well, they are quite big, bigger than a man…" replies Beezle trying to imagine what it is they might be.

"Will you two be quiet! Wattlespalf, you should know better. Beezle, you should get it into your head that dragons are very dangerous, and that they would love to taste the flesh of an elf. Your kind will be considered a very rare delicacy. They would pay to eat you, and I have half a mind to sell you to them," warns the wizard. "Now please be silent until we are safe."

Beezle presses his lips shut and falls into a sulk.

The majority of the men know that at some point they will be seen, heard or smelled by the dragons. Dragons have very keen senses, and have the uncanny knack of knowing who they are smelling or hearing, be it man, dwarf or beast. The point of this exercise is to get as close to the mountain as possible before a dragon identifies that they are near. One at a time, the company moves between one hiding place and another. Signals are given by those who notice, indicating that there is danger from a dragon looking in the direction of the group. When the signal is given everyone stops and stands very, very still like statues.

Eventually, the group reaches the bottom of the hill and hides behind a tall, wide boulder next to some trees. A two mile walk to the foot of the mountain and into the caves awaits the company. They can see five young dragons playing together; they are wrestling each other to the ground, grabbing each other's tails and legs with their teeth.

"Come on, let's go into the hills and play hide and seek," says a little (only two or three times the size of a man) red air dragon. Ah, I have forgotten to mention that dragons can talk in the language of men when they feel like it. More disturbing is that they like to converse with other creatures, often showing off their extensive vocabularies before they eat them. Greybeard and the others gasp; if the young dragons catch any one of these creatures' scents then their position is likely to be exposed.

"Yes, let's go into the hills. We haven't been there for days," says a young, blue land dragon.

"No flying then," adds a yellow water dragon, "I'm not chasing you up hills when you lot can cheat and fly there."

"Promise we won't," says a green air dragon.

The dragons come closer and closer to our companions' position. The little red dragon puts his nose into the air and asks, "Can you smell something funny?"

"No, what can you smell?" comes the reply from the green dragon.

"Don't know, haven't smelt it before. Smells quite nice, though – a bit like a cow, only better."

The group hold their breath because these young beasts are getting too close for comfort. The little red dragon walks towards them and stops at the edge of the boulder, unable to get this wondrous, strange smell out of his mind. The smell is stronger now and he wants to investigate further. The others also pick up the scent and join the little red dragon's investigation. Our companions crouch down on the floor, pressing their bodies against the boulder. They are still and silent. All the dragons are sniffing, trying to get their heads above and around the boulder but the trees are getting in the way. Dragon noses sit on top of the rock inhaling deeply, close to heads which are only centimetres away. All of a sudden there is a roar in the distance; the children are being called home as it is time for lunch. Suitably distracted, the young ones turn their heads back towards the mountain.

"Hmm, lunchtime," they cry excitedly. All of them run back as fast as they can, past the rocks and boulders, through the river and back towards the caves. Their parents are waiting with all manner of foods, be it fish from the river or unsuspecting cattle from a farmer's field. Sighs of relief ring out from behind the boulder. The fact is that the young dragons would likely have been no match for these men but they could raise an alarm, and that would be the end of it. What is notable is that these dragons could not identify the smell of the creatures hidden, indicating that they had not yet tasted their flesh and that is very curious.

Everyone looks at each other as they ponder their next move. Young dragons can still be seen in the distance, rushing back to the caves. Bigger dragons within eyesight of this group look up at the clouds and set off back towards their caves in the mountain. It starts to rain again.

The route towards the caves is now clear, and the companions can make a move away from the boulder. Knees are hurting from maintaining a crouching position, so getting up and stretching legs is both painful and satisfying. Peering over the rock, the next available hiding place is a short distance away, where a huge boulder large enough to conceal the men is suitably positioned.

"That was close. It is a good thing that they were only young. It would have been an unfortunate thing to be revealed by them," whispers Igralf, stretching his legs.

"What? They were small ones?" gawps Beezle.

"Now you know why we walk carefully, young elf," comments Forester. "Think about the dragon you have seen and multiply it by ten, then you will get a good idea of the size of them."

"Ten times the size?" gulps Perrywinkle. "Might I be able to go back to tending the horses? I'm sure I would like to very much."

"No, you cannot. You will be better for the experience you are about to have. It is not every day you get to meet dragons. You will remember it for the rest of your life," Greybeard says resolutely.

"How long am I going live, though? A minute, two, ten?" whimpers Perrywinkle.

"Don't worry, Connor. The closer we get, the better off we will be," assures the wizard.

"That's what I am worried about."

"Shall we run?" asks Stryker.

"Yes, let's. The rains are clearing our path – fortune shines on us. Come quickly before the dragons come back to eat us," growls Greybeard.

The rain unfolds from being just a few specks to become a heavy shower. Seizing the opportunity, the men run one by one towards the boulder. In the open, the men feel a little exposed and nervous, but as long as the rain pours, the dragons will be hesitant to come out of their homes. The crouching, running and hiding behind boulders and bushes on the path towards the base of the mountain continues. Soon the group reach the halfway point behind a prickly bush close to the river.

From this point onwards the men will have no place to hide. It is here that they will have to make their request to see Pengwellen quickly. The heavy rain showers stop suddenly, the cloud cover opens up a little, and a dragon can be seen flying in the sundrenched blue skies above. Greybeard leads the line of men through the river. It is not that deep after all, although the water sits just above the waists of the dwarfs and Beezle. The river is almost stagnant; there is no current at present, and this helps the group speed through it. Halfway across the river, the company can feel winds beating down on them.

Wattlespalf stops, turns round and looks up. To his horror a dragon, horned from neck to tail, yellow in colour bar spots of red all over its body, beats his wings above the dwarf. The others, not suspecting anything, have continued to plough on through the river. Wattlespalf is exposed, away from the rest of the pack. He calls out, "Dragon!" just as the beast above him forces out a huge line of flame that shrouds the dwarf.

"No!" come the prolonged screams from his brothers, who turn in time to see Wattlespalf engulfed in flames. The dragon's fire stops, and Wattlespalf is gone. The beast turns his attentions away from where Wattlespalf stood to the rest of the pack. Hovering above the men, he gives a shrill cry to alert others. Dragon heads appear from out of the caves almost immediately, and others flying above the clouds surge down below them. These men are trapped.

"Come on, lizards. I will fight you," challenges Gendralf.

"Taking a dwarf from behind, you coward. Come and face me," continues Igralf. Both brandish their weapons and swing them towards the murderous beast.

"Pengwellen – we are here to see Pengwellen," shouts Greybeard, trying to calm the situation.

Many dragons start to surround and circle the group. Hissing loudly, they extend their long necks towards the company so that their noses are within inches of them. The group watch the dragons intently. Weapons are raised as they wait to defend themselves against their breath.

"Pengwellen, we are here to see Pengwellen!" shouts Greybeard again. None of the dragons are listening. One dragon breathes a small plume of fire towards the men. This time Greybeard puts forth his staff; the oric lights and produces an invisible shield that deflects the fire from the group. All of a sudden these beasts pull back. They did not know they were in the presence of a wizard and this startles them. Wizards are capable of doing far more terrible things than even they themselves can do.

As the dragons pull back from the group there is a large splash. Jumping out of the water, close to the beast who tried to kill him, is a badly singed Wattlespalf. The hair not protected by the helmet on top of his head and his face has been burnt so badly that this dwarf is now clean-shaven and with a basin haircut. Wattlespalf quickly produces his sword from the water, points it up in the air, and strikes down on one of the dragon's talons. The blade of the sword cuts through the talon cleanly and it falls into the water, but before it can glide to the bottom of the river, Wattlespalf grabs it.

"I'm keeping this for what you tried to do to me, you numbskull," he shouts at the dragon, who is crying with pain and shock. No lasting harm will be done to the dragon as talons grow back quite quickly, much like fingernails that have been cut or chewed. "That will teach you to go breathing fire on a dwarf!" Wattlespalf walks through the river over to his friends, who are relieved that he is alive. He receives a pat on the back from his brothers and beaming smiles from the others, who are in part amused by his lack of beard and can't wait to see his new styled hair on top of his head.

"Pengwellen, we are here to see Pengwellen," shouts Greybeard a final time.

"Who calls my name?" a large, bellowing voice shouts out from inside a cave a little way up the mountain.

"You know who it is, you old lummox," replies Greybeard. "Call your minions off and let us through. We need to have a talk, you and I."

"Why should I let you through, you blundering old fool? I don't suppose you remember that you and your bumbling friends nearly killed me in our last encounter?" booms Pengwellen.

"Well, actually, we did talk about it," says Greybeard a little sheepishly.

"What makes you think I shouldn't set my 'minions' on you this very second? I'm sure they'd be very happy to dine on you." Dragons around the party begin to lick their lips.

"Oh well, if you don't want to meet the elves then we'll leave right – "

"Elves?" interrupts Pengwellen. "Well, why didn't you say so earlier?" Pengwellen's tone changes.

Pengwellen talks to his kind in dragon speak, which takes the form of shrill cries and clicks. One by one the dragons slope off into caves and back into the clouds, and the men are eventually left alone. It is then that they notice a chill working its way from their toes upwards; everyone is beginning to feel very cold, having stood in the river for more than a good while.

"Come up, come up," beckons Pengwellen. He breathes a

plume of fire from the cave he has claimed as his residence so the men know to where they should walk.

"It is a long walk up there. He could have at least got a dragon to take us up," moans a slightly disgruntled Forester.

"He is not going to afford us that pleasure. He will be as difficult as he possibly can," comments Greybeard.

"He's a miserable old bugger," adds Forester.

"So what did happen between you and him then?" asks a curious Finn.

"Well, it's a little complicated," says Forester. "To cut a long story short, we asked for Pengwellen's help in a matter in which we had been caught up and nearly killed him in the process," says Forester.

"But how? I understand that there was an incident but how did it arise?" Finn probes further.

"Go on, tell them the story. I love this story. Go on," urges Wattlespalf.

Forester, who looks embarrassed, looks at an equally embarrassed Greybeard, who looks at an equally embarrassed Stryker.

"Alright then," capitulates Forester. "It was a while ago. Ogres and goblins had been raiding and burning villages together. For the intelligence they were expected to have, they were quite canny in the way they conducted business and made it look like a dragon was behind it. The raids were done in the way that dragons would normally carry out a raid. Villages were attacked at night when it was dark – when villagers recounting tales by the fire couldn't distinguish the shadows and shapes in the air from one thing or the other. It would begin with fire raining down on a village. 'But ogres and goblins cannot fly,' I hear you say," acknowledges Forester, anticipating the questions that will be directed towards him. Finn's open mouth, which was ready to ask the very question Forester has just anticipated, closes quickly.

"Tell them about the lanterns. Oh, it's very clever, the lanterns bit," interrupts Wattlespalf.

"Yes, yes, I was coming to that. Patience, Wattlespalf. The blinny and ogres did know how to make flying paper lanterns, though, and used them to great effect. Goblins hung open bottles filled with spirits off candlelit lanterns, which floated and flickered like stars high up in the night sky. The monsters flew a number of these lanterns over a village. Goblin bowmen waited until the most opportune moment before shooting them down. When the arrow hit the lantern and the lit candle fell onto the spirit in the bottle, flames were created. The flaming bottle invariably smashed upon hitting a hard surface, behaving like a bolt of fire, or spilled as it fell, creating lines of flame much like dragon's breath. The fire raining down from the sky mimicked the dragons and thus the villagers believed they were under attack from them.

"Now, when that breath of flame caught the walls, floors and roofs of the houses in the village it spread quickly as the fiery liquid seeped into every nook and cranny it could find. The villagers' first instinct was to save their children and run from the danger they faced. So the villagers would, more often than not, disperse to the outskirts of the village. The further they ran the better – as long as they ran in the opposite direction to the goblins and ogres, that is."

"Tragic this bit. It always brings a tear to my eye," says Wattlespalf, his eyes already welling up. Forester looks at the dwarf angrily at first, then upon seeing his eyes, pats him on the shoulder in support.

"The ogres and goblins moved in; strength in numbers overawed those who were left. Those who stayed were easily killed by a club or a sword, and thrown into the fire or taken to places where they would not be found. Looting took place – this is the reason why this elaborate plan was created in the first place. Dragons love to collect gold, silver, gems and old items, magical or otherwise, and so do goblins. The deception was both despicable and genius in the same instant."

"But you were going to show them, weren't you? You had a plan, didn't you?" interrupts Wattlespalf once again.

"Yes we did, old friend. From the sidelines, behind trees and bushes, we experienced the devastation these murderous thieves had instigated, but we were not strong enough to help. We knew that we needed an army of men to help us dispel the threat to these villages. A nearby army would not listen to the vagabonds talking sense to them, though. The generals were convinced it was dragons who were responsible for the mayhem.

We did convince them in the end that it may be a rogue dragon, fearless and fearsome, capable of causing this amount of destruction all by himself. It was suggested to them that Pengwellen might have been the culprit, having seen him only days before.

"Pengwellen, unlike most other dragons, was a friend to men… or at least the right sort of men. He had been around for a long, long time and had become wise to both the good and bad in this world. He recognised the struggles and the movements of those purposefully involved in the maintenance of balance in this world. Pengwellen, at this time, was good friends with Greybeard and to some extent myself and Stryker, although only by association. Travelling back to where he resided at that particular moment, we asked whether he could help."

"So he did help you then?" asks Finn, who has immersed himself in the story so far.

"Yes, he did, but it all got a bit complicated. You see, the armies of the south, misguided by the information we gave them, began to march upon King's Mountain in response to the attacks. But the army was still behind the raiders, who were moving northwards. Goblins and ogres were unaware that they had been seen and were being tracked by us. Anyway, Pengwellen was persuaded to help; after all, he was now involved in a larger cause to save his kind.

"The plan was to make the army follow Pengwellen to the attacks being carried out by the real raiders and plunderers of these villages. It was hoped the armies, after some more gentle persuasion, would attack the real culprits. Utilising Pengwellen, we led the army to within reach of the goblins and ogres who were camping outside of a village on the borders between the southern and eastern territories. Stryker, Greybeard and I turned up to talk to the generals once more. We pointed out to the army that Pengwellen would attack a village that night. The army agreed to follow us.

"Night was falling. The raiders began to move towards a village, as did Pengwellen, who flew above it leading the army closer and closer to the real aggressors. The blinny lit the lanterns as they always did and directed them towards the night sky. Positions were taken by bowmen. Ogres and foot soldiers hid on the outskirts of the village waiting for their moment. Following Pengwellen's flight our army stumbled across the murderous goblins and ogres. Engaging these callous thieves in battle, the goblins and ogres were easily defeated.

"What we did not know is another, much smaller company had been travelling alongside the main army with whom we had been in contact. Having trekked to the northern side of the village, they had followed Pengwellen's route in the skies above more carefully. Pengwellen hid away from the village in thick woods thinking his job had now been done, but this wily set of soldiers had unwittingly trapped him where he lay. No one would ever have known but he gave out a cry so loud that men, goblins and ogres alike cowered in its ferocity. When we were able to uncover our ears we ran towards the woods where he was situated. We arrived in time to see him pegged down by dozens of ropes. Soldiers had scaled the top of his body and head, positioning themselves onto his back, pointing swords down on him ready to thrust through his skin. Pengwellen was resolute that he was going to die. I speak for all when I say that this was a very sad situation, and we were guilty as we had instigated it."

"This is the best bit," enthuses Wattlespalf, punching the air with his fists.

"Acting quickly, Stryker and I turned into lions and over-powered the soldiers. We jumped first beside and then onto Pengwellen, swiping claws in front of the soldiers' faces. Soldiers fell, one by one, unharmed onto the floor. Greybeard then thrust his staff forward, striking those still left with a small but painful bolt of lightning upon their bottoms. Thinking we were done, we missed one soldier who, in his moment of bravery, thrust his sword down into Pengwellen's body, close to his tail. The shrill bellow that came from him was blood-curdling – you could feel his pain. The last soldier was overpowered. Others had already run away. Greybeard produced a potion and quickly administered it into the wound. The potion would save Pengwellen, but he was angry for having been put in this position. Removing the ropes around him, he limped away, cursing us all. If we saw him again, we knew we would be dead. But it was a long, long time ago and now, for reasons of fate, we endanger our lives by stepping into the dragon's den once more," Forester ends his epic tale, drained from reliving it.

"Well done, Forester. That was a tale well told," says Greybeard, clapping lightly.

"Yes," adds Igralf, "I have never heard it so vividly before."

"And that, Finn and Beezle, is why Pengwellen hates Greybeard, Stryker and Forester's guts," remarks Wattlespalf.

Everyone gawps at Wattlespalf, his honest but uncouth outburst bringing home the reality of the situation they currently find themselves in.

"He doesn't hate our guts, Wattlespalf. He's just a little cross with us. Admittedly, he's potentially cross enough to kill us all, but all the same," retorts Stryker.

"I just hope that he has calmed down since that day or we really are in trouble," warns Forester.

"What do you mean 'in trouble'?" asks Wattlespalf ironically. "Have you not seen my hair and my beard? We're already in trouble, or at least I am. Not that you lot care."

Up and up and step by step the group climb. The path leading up to the cave is steep and the stone the company are standing on is worn and slippery, but they eventually make it to the cave where Pengwellen waits for them. The opening to the cave gives you a good idea as to the size of this dragon. Inside is a huge cavern, high, wide and long like a great hall; it is imposing to all who step inside it. Light is flickering from around a corner towards the back of the cave, which hides a main chamber, and more importantly, Pengwellen.

"Come on in, then," orders Pengwellen's booming voice.

The group enters the mouth of the cave; rain water drips from the ceiling, *drip, drip, drip* echoing all around. The dwarfs, elves and Perrywinkle step forward in trepidation, their hearts beating loudly. Greybeard, Stryker and Forester walk ahead towards the flickering light, seemingly unfazed. The dwarfs look closely at the cavern rock; to their surprise small gems twinkle from the ceilings and walls. It reminds them of their mines in the northeast; memories flicker through their minds, and for a brief moment, they are homesick. Perrywinkle, too, is attracted to the gems. He gets out a penknife and tries to force a small gem out from the cavern wall quickly so as not to fall too far behind the others. The companions walk around the corner into full view of the light, and directly ahead, there he is – a big blue dragon with big blue wings lying on the floor, reading a book on a big brown rug in his big cavernous lair.

Pengwellen is not dissimilar to the descriptions of his kind that have already been given, but in the sentences that follow, the finer points of Pengwellen's appearance will be divulged. This old dragon is the largest of his species. The largest of dragons grow to thirty metres or thereabouts, but Pengwellen is forty metres long, making him by far the biggest there is.

This dragon is blue and scaly all over, except for a soft underbelly that is a much, much lighter blue than the rest of him. His head is the size of the wizard, and his eyes are green with a black slit of a pupil running down it. Starting on the bridge of his nose, small horns protrude out like thorns, right to the very tip of his long, strong tail. On one of the thorn-like horns, he rests his spectacles, so that his eyes are less strained from reading. The jaws of this big old beast are full of long and short thick teeth, and on his upper jaw are nostrils wide and round. His ears… well, dragons have them more or less where a man might have them but they do not stick out like a man's do; a dragon's ears are discreet, being only a small round hole in the side of the head.

A long neck, able to twist and turn, is long enough to enable this dragon to bite his tail and do numerous other things besides. At the end of his neck is an oval-shaped body; it is large and bulbous, testament to the weight this dragon has gained by eating much and doing little to stem its growth. On top of the body, either side of it, is a wing; when fully open these wings span the length of Pengwellen's body, from head to tail and more. Pengwellen's four legs, two at the front and two at the back, are short and sturdy, though long enough to let his fat belly clear the floor, but only just. At the end of his feet are claws, much like an eagle's, with thick black talons, versatile enough to flick the pages of a book, yet brutal enough to do damage to the most armoured of creatures.

Pengwellen appears, at first glance, to be a civilised sort of dragon. Large paintings depicting dragons in battle, dragons in the countryside, dragons flying in the air and portraits of dragons past adorn the walls of this lair. He has many treasures and artefacts made of gold, silver and gems collected from his past exploits, which sit happily on many small ledges jutting out from the walls. Perrywinkle, forgetting himself and his fear, rushes up to one of the ledges and starts perusing the treasures.

"Mr. Pengwellen, you have things that have been lost for ages," comments Perrywinkle, almost behaving like a child in a sweet shop. Pengwellen responds only by grumbling at Perrywinkle and what he perceives to be his greed. Whilst Perrywinkle may be considered greedy for these kinds of things, he is also well-versed in antiquities. Given the chance, Pengwellen could learn a couple of things from this little man.

The cavern is dry and bright, a large chandelier with hundreds of lit candles hangs down from the ceiling. The light provided by the candles hits the gems on the ceiling, which as a consequence, twinkle brightly like stars. The air in the cavern is warm as dragons give off a lot of heat, and the friends who now face this dragon can feel themselves becoming warmer.

"Very nice, cosy place... very nice indeed," comments Igralf, rubbing his hands and looking all around with glee.

"Yes, reminds me very much of home," adds Gendralf.

Wattlespalf is only concerned with grooming himself as he pulls the last remaining hairs of his once proud beard out from his chin.

"Has anyone got a brush?" he asks. Needless to say, no one has got a brush.

Pengwellen is reading a large book. Greybeard, Stryker and Forester walk forward. Pengwellen gives out a large yawn to show his disinterest in the men.

"So, wizard, you have come to see your old friend at last. You look a lot older than I remember," the old dragon sighs.

"I'm not that much older, surely. It has not been that long since I last saw you, considering the timelines we travel," retorts Greybeard.

"No, you're definitely much older – too much ale and fine food I would warrant."

"Indeed. Well, nice to see you as well, lummox. Your belly has expanded since I last saw you," remarks the wizard, angry at the jibes put forward his way.

Pengwellen reading a book

"Silence," booms Pengwellen. "It is not you I wish to see, anyway. You are troublesome, meddlesome and many other things besides."

Greybeard is instantly silenced. He looks to the ground. The others flinch and wonder what might happen next; unfortunate happenings could certainly be in the offing.

"You two elves, come closer so I can see you better," Pengwellen commands, a little more gently than he had spoken before. Finn and Beezle walk forward relatively confidently; the dragon wants to see them and by his tone he doesn't sound like he is particularly interested in eating them. Pengwellen peers over his spectacles, spending a little time looking at them. It has been an age since he has seen one and he wants to reacquaint himself with their form.

"So, little elves, are you enjoying your time in this age?" he asks them. It is rather a strange question to ask, as if he has prior knowledge of everything that has happened over the past few days.

"Yes, a very good time indeed," gushes Beezle. "Very exciting." Finn doesn't speak.

"And what about you, young elf?" the dragon asks, looking directly at Finn.

"Well, I miss my homeland and I am told that I may not be able to return to it, but I have been made to feel welcome here and I enjoy these men's company. How did you know we had come through –" Finn is interrupted.

"Time?" answers Pengwellen. He extends his neck and presses his nose against Finn, blowing out air through his nostrils. The wind created blows Finn's hair back and his eyes are forced to close. "Well, it is not hard to understand that you could not realistically be here unless you were brought here by something unusual," he continues, his tone slightly patronising.

"It is not for you to humble our young friends. They are in a strange place, experiencing strange events in a strange time. You could afford them some humility, you old bugger," Greybeard retaliates sternly. Pengwellen looks at Greybeard and begins to laugh. Greybeard in turn laughs back nervously – and quite rightly, because at any point Pengwellen's huge head could turn and quite easily devour this wizard.

"You are right, old man. My age has made me intolerable. I am indeed… oh, what is that word? Ah yes, grumpy."

"So we're okay then, you and us?" asks Forester.

"Okay? Whatever do you mean? Oh, the incident. Well I would be within my rights to remain a little cross with you, but the wounds I sustained healed quickly enough," Pengwellen tips his backside revealing the scar left from his encounter. "In the end it was only my pride that was hurt."

"We are deeply sorry for getting you involved in such a foolish plan, and we really are eternally grateful for the part you played," grovels Greybeard. "In the end you saved many lives. I just wish those you saved understood your sacrifice as much as we do."

"Stop being sycophantic, wizard, and know that you owe me many favours," scorns the dragon. "Unfortunately for me, I know that you are coming to ask for another."

"Well, yes. Actually we are here to do that," Greybeard mutters.

Pengwellen refocuses his eyes back onto the elves. "I met your King and Queen, you know. They'd just come from the eastern plains." Finn looks excited that they might receive some valuable information from Pengwellen. Beezle, on the other hand, rolls his eyes as if sick of hearing about the elves and Finn's insistence of finding a way back to their own time. Pengwellen spies Finn's weaponry. "I suspect you have just come from there yourselves. Have you been to see the buggane?"

"But how can you know that?" asks Finn.

"I know many things and much more besides. So, Finn, are you a warrior? Are you going to help my esteemed friends?" probes Pengwellen, changing the subject.

"I didn't tell you my name," responds Finn. "How did you know?"

"We talked at great length, your Queen, your King and I," reveals Pengwellen, to Finn's delight.

"You didn't tell me this," huffs Greybeard, a little disappointed having known the dragon for hundreds of years. Pengwellen turns to him and he looks cross.

"It wasn't right to tell you. If you'd known what I knew years ago, you would not have got this far already. You may not have even found the boys. You are following a path of destiny, and you

174

cannot afford to disrupt that," scorns Pengwellen firmly. Greybeard is taken aback but realises that there is sense in the old dragon's words.

Beezle gives a wry smile in response to Pengwellen's telling off of Greybeard. The old man may be wise but he is certainly not the wisest. 'Just wait until I take the rod... then we'll see,' he thinks to himself.

"What do you think they said?" Pengwellen asks the elves.

"I think the Queen told you about the life I am going to lead," says Finn. "Everybody else we have met appears to know something about me that I do not."

"Yes, you're quite right, she probably did, but as I've already mentioned, you cannot disrupt destiny. Your life is written and you need know nothing of it from me. But I will tell you this, you need to prepare yourself for a battle both in mind and with sword. I suggest that you learn some tricks from these men standing beside you."

"I suspect they told you nothing about me," utters Beezle. "I never met our King or Queen."

"It is true that she was unsure of your role in all of this, but the general feeling was that you are very important."

"What, me? Important?" says Beezle, acting as if surprised. He isn't going to tell them about what the rod has told him.

"Yes, quite so," replies Pengwellen. "What can you do to help defeat this Warrior?"

"I have already begun to learn from Greybeard," he says proudly. "I can do magic."

"So you have the makings of a wizard?" asks the dragon.

"Yes, the boy displays a talent for the magical arts, but he has not learned – and will not learn – too much from me until he begins to behave well, like others do," interrupts Greybeard. "As we are talking about what everyone can offer to this battle, Finn met with Lord in the Whispering woods. Lord prompted us to travel here to see you, as he said you would be able to help us in our quest. Do you know to what he was referring?"

"Help? I have already helped you. I have passed on advice to Finn. He must learn a little of what it is to be a warrior," replies a nonchalant Pengwellen.

"Pengwellen, we do not have time to play games. Do you

know what Lord meant?" the old man asks gruffly.

The dragon looks at Greybeard and then looks away, a little ashamed of his petulance. Beezle frowns. 'Maybe they are as wise as each other after all,' he thinks.

"Yes, I have a role to play, and yes, I will help," sighs Pengwellen. "I also have an item for you. Stryker. You see the horn in the corner over there?" Pengwellen points to a horn sitting on a ledge in the corner of the room to his left. "Go over and get it – I'll entrust it to you as you are a man who has a lot of puff." The horn is as you would expect, ivory in colour and conical in shape. It also has carvings of dragons etched into its hard exterior. The carvings depict dragons in battle against goblins and men. It looks like the dragons are winning the battle quite comfortably as men and goblins are piled high upon one another, burning.

"This horn is called Temper. It has a magic about it," explains Pengwellen. "No matter how far away you are, blow on this horn and we will hear it. I expect you to call us the day before battle, and we will come."

"Of course, thank you, friend," says Stryker, picking it up off the shelf carefully.

"Is that the very horn you stole from the trolls at the Battle of the Horn?" asks Finn, recognising Pengwellen's likeness to the big blue dragon in the book he read back at Greybeard's cave.

"How do you know about the Battle of the Horn?" replies Pengwellen.

"Oh, I know a thing or two, as well you know," answers Finn.

"Hmm, well now you ask, no – that isn't the horn from the battle. If you look behind me, in the middle of that ledge over there, that's the one in which you should be interested," he says pointing at it with his talon.

Finn looks at it. "Yes, that's the one from the battle I saw. Have you ever thought about giving it back to the men you stole it from?" asks Finn, in a 'maybe you should do' tone of voice.

"No, I haven't and you would do well not to judge, elfling," replies an annoyed old dragon, looking Finn directly in the eye before turning away, distracted by another thought.

"Before I forget, Lord also gave us an item… a rod. It will apparently sway the final battle in our favour by neutralising

Warrior's threat. It has ancient writings on it. Would you be good enough to look at it to see if you understand it better than I?" Greybeard asks.

"I will, if you show it to me," gestures the old dragon.

"Oh, erm, yes. Finn, please remove the rod from your backpack and show it, the writing side up, to our esteemed host," urges the wizard.

Finn does as he is asked. Walking slowly up to Pengwellen, he holds aloft the rod right up to the dragon's face. Beezle's face lights up. The gems in it twinkle under the candle light. The rod hums, but only Beezle can hear it. Unnoticed by anyone, he tries to hide his desire and growing hunger to hold and have it for himself.

"Yes, intriguing – very peculiar – curious," mumbles Pengwellen. "The writings on the rod indicate..." Everyone gasps, expecting the old dragon's answer. "Nothing to me. No, I can't say I understand the words written on it. I am not really an expert on the old languages. But, oh... no, erm... I ate him a good while ago. Sorry, the fellow I did know who would have been able to help was far too tempting a meal. He was rather large, you see."

"Finn, put the rod away, and keep it safe once more," Greybeard grumbles, disappointed by the old dragon's answer.

Finn once again does as he is asked. Beezle's face drops as Finn puts the rod back in his backpack, wanting to observe its beauty and hear its call for longer than he has been able to on this occasion.

"Well, what can I say? Not very helpful at all. In fact, you are a creature who conspires against fate," continues Greybeard.

Pengwellen is not listening to the wizard. Greybeard can see sadness in the dragon's eyes. Stryker and Forester notice this also. Pengwellen may not be willing to reveal the fates of others, but he appears to have revealed his own. This will be Pengwellen's last battle. You see, Pengwellen did speak at good length with the King and Queen of the elves. She revealed to him everything she knew about Finn and Beezle, Greybeard, Stryker, Forester, the dwarfs, Perrywinkle and the impending battle with Warrior in the south. She also spoke to Pengwellen about his place in all this, and whilst she did not know his fate at the time, the dragon asked her to do a reading. She accepted his request. Putting her hands on his face, she smiled as she always did. The Queen never revealed anything to anyone she touched. She had become skilled at concealing her emotion so as not to distress the creature she was reading, but the dragon pressed her to tell him. For three thousand years he has been waiting for this meeting with the elves. He has dreaded this moment and now his stomach turns because within days he will be dead.

This solemn moment is interrupted by Finn. "Sir, you say you spoke to the King and Queen at length. Do you know where they went, and whether they survived or not?"

"Three thousand years is a long time and my memory has faded a little. I know that they were heading south towards your homeland in Windrush Forest. I don't know if they ever made it – there were many blinny around that part of the world. But – and this is important – there were never any rumours stating that they had been captured or killed," the dragon replies. "The whole incident was very unfortunate. The genocide of your race was done very stealthily. Only a handful of creatures knew it was happening, and most only found out when the event had reached its final conclusion."

"So it is possible that they live?" asks a hopeful Finn.

"It is possible, Finn, but it is strange that they have not been seen or heard of all these years. Although, Everlast is large and there are many places to hide and be undisturbed. If they did survive, then it may well be that there is a thriving population. The King and Queen did not travel alone, you know."

"Did you hear that, Beezle? The King and Queen could actually be alive. There is hope."

"Wonderful," says Beezle, unimpressed. Beezle does not want his race to have lived at all. We know he did not fit into the tribe he lost only days ago. The little elf feels a loathing for his home and his people in the forest. He is now happy exploring the world, meeting new creatures and having adventures... and he does not want it to end.

"Finn, do not live your life believing what you have just said as you might be disappointed. Your race may well have perished. Furthermore, the controlled genocide of your people was done for a reason with much planning. Your Queen was enchanted by someone or something, and cursed by an elaborate spell that altered the visions and futures of those she read. Instead of seeing those elves poisoned or cut by goblins, she saw a different story for everyone she touched – a false future in different times and different places. The spell did not take into account that you would travel through time, though. The one who cast their magic had not considered this possibility. It was only upon reading you, Finn, that she knew something was wrong. But unaware of the spell or of how to break it, she was unable to fathom the where, when and how any of it would take place. I suspect the reason your race was targeted is because whoever is behind Warrior and his armies is threatened by the elves. They obviously know something we do not but one thing is clear, now that you two are here it is imperative that you remain alive."

"The oric does not belong to him," adds Greybeard. "Somebody else is playing out this game through others, including ourselves. We are but pieces in it. Whatever happens in this time will affect the future of this world, and I think whoever is trying to mould time to his liking has already changed history. Pengwellen, is it possible that the elves should not have fallen? And if the world were to have run its course undisturbed, is it possible that they would be walking among us now in this time?"

"Greybeard, you are very wise and yes, you are right. We might not be here talking to each other now. If the world had run its original course undisturbed, it is conceivable that you may never have even been born because a world full of elves might have dictated it."

"So by sending us home, knowing what we know, we may actually put the world to rights?" asks Finn.

"Exactly, but it is one of many possibilities. The world may well have run its course," warns the dragon.

Hope runs through every inch of Finn. The others know that their quest has now taken a more uncertain twist. Now they know that if they are successful in their quest and the world is changed, they will most probably not be the creatures that they are now. The lives they have already lived, the experiences that they have built over their years on this world, will not be remembered by them or anybody else. Worse still, they might have never been born and will not experience any life whatsoever in the new world they might be party to creating. But they remain resolute – they could die at any time anyway, so why not die making the world what it once was and what it should be?

"I think it is time we get back to the horses," says Greybeard. "Perrywinkle, empty your pockets and put those items back." Perrywinkle looks at Greybeard and blushes; once a thief always a thief, it appears. The lure of the gold on show was too much for him to resist. Perrywinkle empties numerous items out of his pockets and puts them back where they belong.

"If I understand this correctly," utters Perrywinkle, trying to deflect his embarrassment by beginning another conversation, "I may not be here to write this story if we change the events of this world. Does that mean I can go home? I'm obviously, potentially, not needed now."

"No you cannot, vagabond. You are coming with us and that is the end of it," orders Greybeard.

"Well, if I'm destined to die I might as well embrace it," responds Perrywinkle, who now feels that he can be a little braver and worry a lot less. The fact is that no matter what he does, fate will deal its hand over the course of the next few days and he will have no answer to it.

Greybeard walks up to Pengwellen. He puts his arms round the dragon's face as Pengwellen is far too big to hug.

"Dear friend, it looks like we all have a deeper purpose than we could have ever understood. Thank you for allowing me to see," says Greybeard, as Stryker and Forester both pat Pengwellen on his scaly blue shoulder.

"Come on, I'll walk with you some way to your horses. Where did you leave them by the way?" questions Pengwellen.

"In a secluded valley behind the hills," replies Stryker.

"Oh, well, I apologise now on behalf of any of my clan if they have made a meal of them."

"Hmm," grunts Greybeard. "If that is the case then you will be flying us to our next destination."

The company walks towards the outside of the cavern. Pengwellen rises up off the floor and stretches his comparatively short legs and his long tail. He then unfurls his long, wide blue wings on the top of his back and stretches them out whilst producing a big yawn, exposing a mouth full of long sharp teeth. After this process of stretching various parts of his body, he is ready to walk. Pengwellen keeps his head down as he makes his first steps forward, so as not to bump it on the ceiling. He catches up to the advancing men within three or four steps, such is his size. Pengwellen is careful not to step on any of the creatures by accident, as that would obviously be a tragedy and could sway an outcome one way or another – unless, of course, it is written. It is not long before everyone is out of Pengwellen's cave and down at the foot of the mountain.

"So, where is your next destination?" asks Pengwellen.

"I thought you would already know that, dragon," replies Greybeard.

"I might, but I am bound not to tell you," responds the dragon with a smile.

"Finn was told by Lord that the jotunn, as well as you, might help us."

"The jotunn, eh? A very formidable opponent, but it is such a long time since they have gone into battle. They may not have the heart for it. If you can get them on side and they do have warriors with the same skills and temperament of old, you may have half a chance of defeating this Warrior," advises Pengwellen.

"Well," explains Greybeard, "the hope is that Warrior has not already approached them for their services. Indeed, they may have already chosen to flee their town in order to save themselves from battle."

The company walk on; the route back to the hills is easier now, as they are able to walk straight ahead and clamber over large rocks in the river so as to avoid getting wet again. They are still a little damp from the last visit they paid to it. Dragons peer out from the inside of their caves, watching the oldest of them talking to the visiting creatures. All are a little bewildered as to why he has not eaten them, but they trust him. As well as being the oldest he is also the wisest, and has looked after all of them for a long, long time. Eventually, they come to the hills. It is time to say goodbye.

"Remember, call us the day before you go into battle if you are given the chance to prepare. If not, call us and we will come to your aid as quickly as we can fly."

Everyone thanks Pengwellen for his kindness, and he in turn wishes them well for the journey ahead. The men climb to the top of the hill and return to their horses, who are all content in their place of hiding. It is late in the afternoon. The men mount their steeds and set off back along the track. Soon a clearing that leads back onto the southern road comes into view. It leads a little bit further south than the track they originally came in on.

Travelling down the southern road, it is plain to see that more and more people are heading northwards. The men know that they will have to come off the road in the next day or two, taking the back roads to get to their chosen destinations. The chances are that advance parties of enemy foot soldiers will be on the move northwards, seeking to gain territory. For now it is too dangerous for Greybeard, Stryker, Forester, the dwarfs, Perrywinkle, Finn and Beezle to engage any sizeable army. They need to recruit some bodies or at least use their wits to get to Warrior without engaging any of his army at all.

Clouds still hover above the men, and showers pelt down from time to time only to be replaced by sun moments later. So it is that the horses travel ever more quickly down the road. Trees, villages, hills, rocks and people all blur as the horses pass. Travelling for hours, the riders cover many miles, stopping only to pick up food from the ever present food stalls. Stall owners are the only ones, it appears, benefiting from the mass exodus of people running away from the fighting.

Afternoon turns to evening and evening turns to darkness. The group stops off and rests in a deserted barn just off the main road to avoid the rains. The barn is filled with bales of hay, which are warm and soft. After a small meal, the men take up residence in different parts of the barn to sleep. The horses munch on the hay whilst the company rest. Tomorrow it is hoped that they will see the jotunn. After this visit has been paid, they can then begin to head straight towards Warrior and his army.

Beezle has stuck close to Finn; they are sleeping next to each other in the far corner of the building, at the top of the hay piles. Tonight he wants to see the rod again; he has been thinking about it all day, ever since it was revealed to Pengwellen. The elf waits for everyone to go to sleep. He has made his bed right next to both his and Finn's backpack, where he is within easy reach of the rod.

Beezle is laying on his side, his face pointing away from Finn; he looks longingly towards Finn's backpack and what is hidden inside of it. The little elf turns his head over his shoulder quietly every now and again, checking to see whether his brother is asleep. When convinced he is able to make his move, Beezle releases the buckle of Finn's backpack and lifts the front flap which covers the main compartment. Reaching inside he takes hold of the rod, pulls it out and tries to look at it in the darkness. He cannot see much, and sensing this, the rod speaks to Beezle's mind.

"Put out your first finger and whisper the words, 'Finger illuminatis'," it orders, giving Beezle his first lesson.

Beezle does this ever so quietly so as not to wake anyone from their sleep. After reciting these words only once, his finger gives off a small amount of light. He immediately covers his body, head, hands and the rod with his cloak.

"Wow," he whispers, pointing at the rod with his lit finger. He looks closely at the writings and the gems on the rod. Whilst they look impressive enough, he is more interested in what it will do for him as opposed to how it looks.

"I can teach you so much more, so much more. Will you join us?" it hisses. Beezle looks at it in awe... he wants its power.

"Yes, when can I have you?" he whispers back to it.

"Soon, very soon. I will help you, when the time comes."

Beezle is excited by this prospect. His desire, for tonight at least, has been satisfied.

"How do you turn this light off?" Beezle asks.

"Finger extinguishus," comes the answer.

Beezle says the words and the light at the end of his finger fizzles out.

"Thank you, rod. I will put you away now," he says graciously. He puts the rod back into the backpack, closes the flap, re-straps the buckle and makes himself comfortable before falling soundly asleep.

CHAPTER 14

A LEISURELY SWIM

The River Ancholme, a river wide and deep in places, runs from the far northwest to the equally far southeast of this land. Galloping up towards the river, our riders are greeted by a large, wooden bridge which runs the width of the River Ancholme. This bridge is old but sturdy and it creaks wildly as the riders cross. The river is so wide that it takes the riders a while to cross it, though the horses do take their time trotting, slowly and steadily.

"It is time to steer away from this road. Here, our journey will become increasingly more difficult and dangerous," comments Greybread.

"More difficult and dangerous? I don't like the sound of that. I presumed it was dangerous already," Perrywinkle gulps.

A short track leads down underneath the arch of the bridge to a path that follows the river. The jotunn town stands proudly next to the River Ancholme; at present it is but a speck in the distance. The town is miles away, but the tunny (as jotunn people are known) architecture and masonry can be seen even here, as it was the tunny who built this bridge what seems such a long time ago. Jotunn are the true giants of this world; they are muscular in stature, and in previous ages they were the most feared warriors in Everlast. Almost single-handedly, these giants quelled goblin uprisings and played their part in defeating the unnamed evils that have soured these soils.

Many small boats head northward; some will have passed the tunny town to get to this point. Beautifully-crafted vessels floating by come in all colours. The hulls on all these boats is generally the same shape as any other, and they are long enough to accommodate four or five people. Some of the boats have masts and sails, and some do not; those that do have small triangular-shaped flags called jibs running their way down ropes which secure the mast safely to the main frame of the boat. Children wave from the boats as they pass by and in response the men, dwarfs and even the elves (although they find it a strange custom) smile and wave back at them.

The waters are tranquil; one or two of the boats have fishing rods poking off their side. A spinner hook is attached to the end of the fishing line, and as the boat moves in the water, the hook spins and spins. The metal of the spinner hook catches the light as it spins, reflecting this light deep into the water. The hope of the owner of the hook is that a large enough fish will want to eat the spinner and become caught on it. If a large enough fish does take the bait, it will present the owner of the hook with a nice big treat for his supper.

Without a wind, parents and children alike row the boats against the slow current of the river. There is a silent desperation in the faces of the men and women, who hide their real feelings and emotions from their children so as not to alarm them. But children are very perceptive, seeing through their parents' reassuring smiles, and they too feel a little bit afraid.

It seems that, as well as carts and good old-fashioned feet, other forms of travel are being utilised to get away from this province. The advantage to having a boat is quite simply this: goblins do not like water, cannot swim and are afraid of what lurks underneath the surface. The disadvantage is that in a boat there is nowhere to hide. Whilst goblins are not the greatest of archers, it is better to be hidden behind a tree on the other side of the river as opposed to being exposed on the open water.

Close to the banks of the river and near the riders trotting along it are long, green-stalked, brown-headed reeds. Clumps of them line the river. Birds dart in and out of the reeds, where their nests are situated. Fledglings are being brought up on juicy worms and caterpillars, found by their parents who roam the banks searching for food. River rats use their tails to glide elegantly in the water, making their way from one side of the river to the other, carrying food for their young as well.

Stryker gets off his horse and dips his hand in the water; it is reasonably warm. "This is the fifth day of travelling and the third day since I last had a bath. I am starting to smell, and on that note, I think I might go for a swim," Stryker announces, looking at Forester mischievously.

"A great idea! I too could do with a bath," comes the reply

from Forester as he jumps down from his horse, sniffing under both his armpits.

"What about the rest of you?" asks Stryker, taking a bar of soap out of his backpack, which is tied to the saddle of his horse.

"Only a few minutes. We have much to do," says a slightly grumpy Greybeard.

"Come on, Greybeard," shouts Forester, who has dived into the water. "A clean mind and body is a healthy mind and body. I'm sure you have told us this on numerous occasions," lectures Forester playfully.

"Yes, yes, a few minutes more then," he replies.

Forester takes his clothes off underneath the water and shouts out politely, "Igralf, throw us some soap over. There is a bar in my backpack." Igralf gets off his horse, roots around Forester's backpack blindly and finds the soap.

"Here you are. Catch!" Igralf, throws the soap over to Forester. Forester catches the soap and, dipping it in and out of the water, begins to rub it onto his clothes, before rubbing the clothes together. Foam is soon produced on the materials as the fabrics get a good clean. Rinsing his clothes off and wringing them dry, he throws them onto the bank before washing himself.

"Forester, that's a great idea. I could do with giving my clothes a good wash as well," says Perrywinkle, watching from the sidelines. Taking off his shoes, socks, trousers, suit top and shirt he throws everything into the water.

"Yes, I could also do with a bath," says Finn, taking off his chain mail. He quickly dives into the water fully clothed. He doesn't reappear for a long while; so long in fact that the others get a little worried waiting. And then, Finn jumps out of the water, does a forward roll and dives back in.

"Where did he learn that?" asks an astounded Wattlespalf.

"Swimming and climbing trees, that is what everybody loves to do where we live," responds Beezle, diving smoothly into the water.

Greybeard joins them, fully clothed, with a bar of soap in his hands. He leaves his staff nearby on the bank of the river and wades in. The dwarfs finally make it into the water. Dwarfs are not the best swimmers and they are uncomfortable with this situation although, in reality, they are perfectly safe.

"Carefully," says Gendralf, steadying himself at every step.

"Oooh, I don't like this," adds a shaky Wattlespalf.

"Come on, nearly there… nearly there," reassures Igralf.

"There aren't any ram sharks in here, are there?" asks Wattlespalf with trepidation.

"Oh, you never know where they might be. All I know is that there are plenty roaming these waters," teases Forester. "Nibble on your toes and legs they will."

"I'm getting out," cries Wattlespalf, wading back through the heavy water towards the bank. Igralf and Gendralf follow in mild terror.

"There are no ram sharks here," calms Greybeard, somewhat spoiling Forester's fun. The dwarfs stop their advance back onto the riverbank, unimpressed by Forester's jesting. They remind themselves that they are fearless dwarfs, and wander back into the water until they are waist deep. The dwarfs have a clothed wash, plucking up the courage to dip their heads under the water, until even they would admit it is an extremely refreshing thing to do. The swimming, washing and cleaning goes on for some minutes. All the horses and ponies stand and watch, somewhat bewildered by the childish behaviour of their owners. 'Strange creatures,' they think. 'Not anywhere near as civilised as ourselves.'

After a while, everyone gets out of the water bar Stryker and Forester, who come close to the side of the riverbank.

"Put the clothes on the horses for us will you, so they dry. We'll meet you further up the river," says Forester.

"But they could never swim fast enough – we will be waiting ages for them to catch up," retorts Beezle.

"You forget, young elfling, that these are no ordinary men," rumbles Gendralf.

Stryker and Forester wade back into the water. Waving to their companions they dive underneath the clean, clear blue waters of the river. Under the water Stryker and Forester the men are nowhere to be seen. If it had been anybody else then they would have assumed that this pair of swimmers had been eaten by a very big fish. Stryker and Forester have instead transformed into otters, and they are enjoying the pleasure of darting through the water at a good pace. Ducking and weaving in and out of the pondweed, over rocks, chasing smaller fish and pulling on the hooks of the fishermen on the boats, Stryker and Forester get into much mischief. It is a happy sight to see these two brothers expressing their ability to shape-shift. Shape-shifting loosens the muscles, the bones and the mind. Otso have a natural desire to do it. If they weren't so exposed to narrow-minded men almost all of the time, then the brothers would do it more often. As it is they are and they don't, so at best this is a wonderful, magical treat.

Meanwhile, the dwarfs lead Stryker and Forester's horses along the path. Everyone is still wet but it is quite hot today and the clothes are drying quickly on their backs. The dwarfs cover their heads and necks with towels, so as not to burn; they can feel themselves going red already. All along the river, boats are moored up with people embarking and disembarking from them. As always there is a throng of gawps and glares aimed at the elves but most are too preoccupied to pay any direct attention to them. Narrow streams coming from villages in the distance run into the river. Most of the streams are barely noticeable as they are covered by the reeds and grasses from their mouths to the villages. A few narrow wooden bridges cross over the water from time to time, and sometimes the path moves inland a little when the banks become too steep or too loose. All in all, the journey is a relaxed one.

Underneath the water Stryker and Forester are also travelling at a great speed. They have angered a gulp fish (on purpose) and it has decided to chase them. Outwitting this large, bulbous beast is the endgame. The gulp fish is named because of its legendary ability to eat its prey in just one gulp. Whether you are man or beast the gulp fish can accommodate you. This big, fat, brown fish is unusually fast in the water. Long, sharp teeth front its hefty body and its big white, blue and black eyes are able to see many metres ahead, not to mention that it can smell you from a mile off. Stryker and Forester weave their slender forms in and around the gulp fish. Playing games only makes this fish more determined to make its mark upon them, but we should not get worried too soon; Stryker and Forester are more than able to take it on.

To the sudden surprise of the two otters, another gulp fish, and another and another join the chase for their meat. Stryker and Forester look over their shoulders to view this, now not so fun, sight behind them. Nonetheless they carry on moving forward, back, left and right trying to shake their stalkers, whilst testing the resolve and wit of the other brother. Brothers being brothers, they are determined to outdo each other, but these are dangerous games and someone could get hurt. At the same time, four gulp fish would provide a hearty meal for all tonight and the next day and the next. Gulp fish are a delightful meal when filled with herbs and butter and toasted over an open fire. Stryker and Forester lick their lips as both of them visualise gulp fish fillets sitting on large plates. They both head to the surface, as a breath or two is needed. With heads above water brief words are spoken.

"Head towards the bank," says Stryker. "When I throw it up into the air slap the fish onto it." As Stryker makes clear his words to Forester, a gulp fish jumps up from behind them, opening his big, wide mouth and trying to swallow one of the otters in front. Stryker and Forester scarper back underneath the water.

The gulp fish chase the otters, and the otters make swift turns and chase the gulp fish. Stryker grabs the tail of one of the fish. Swimming as hard and fast as he can, he drags it to the surface. He then flings it up into the open air above the water. At the same time Forester shoots out of the water, propelled by his large webbed hands and feet. Forester twists around in mid-air so that his tail whips the gulp fish in the direction of land. The slap is a good one, and a flailing gulp fish lands on the banks of the river in the path of the approaching horses.

Greybeard, the dwarfs, the elves and Perrywinkle trot towards it. The gulp fish, sensing that water is around and about, tries to make an escape but is swiftly speared by a sword. The sword does not belong to Greybeard or Finn or the dwarfs, though. Surprisingly it is Perrywinkle who has asked his pony to gallop faster and is the quickest to react. Perrywinkle quickly falls behind the rest of the pack, jumping off his pony to finish the gulp fish off. It will take time to load it onto his pony as the fish is at least two-thirds the size of Perrywinkle. What we must remember is that he is one of the smallest of all the creatures present, and the size of the fish must be quantified as such.

"I always knew there was something more to that boy," mutters a proud Greybeard, enjoying Perrywinkle's sublime skill of both sword and horsemanship. The hunt is on. The pack above know that they will have to work in unison with the otters below the water in order to seize these fish, if indeed there are anymore to be had. Watching the ripples and the bubbles on top of the water, the men, dwarfs and elves follow with interest.

Underneath the water, three gulp fish remain. Forester sees a bridge to his side; the riders following above will cross over the bridge back onto the main path very soon. Underneath the bridge is one of the streams that break from this river and lead to one of the villages inland. Forester has an idea; he splits from Stryker and heads towards the bridge. One of the gulp fish breaks away from the other two, snapping at Forester's tail. Forester slows his pace, instead using his wits, keeping the fish within distance and fooling it into replicating his every move.

The bridge draws nearer and Forester heads to the surface, the fish following only centimetres behind, still snapping at Forester. Gathering pace, Forester flies gracefully out of the water and over the full width of the bridge, from the river through to the stream on the other side of it. The big, bulky fish opens its mouth wide in the hope of an easy meal. Jumping out of the water, much like the otter it chases, the gulp fish begins to make its way seamlessly across the bridge. Finn is not far from it. He takes Medrin the bow from off his shoulder, and pulling back the string, reveals the blue, pencil thin, arrow-like energy. Releasing the bowstring, the blue arrow flies with purpose and pierces the fish as it flaps in mid-air, dropping onto the bridge it had almost crossed. All this is done within a second of the sighting. Medrin stuns the riders; it even stuns Finn for a second or two. The elven bow is a very dangerous weapon indeed.

Two gulp fish chase Stryker. Shadows of the two fish bear down on Stryker, who is now starting to tire of this game. Forester is too far behind his brother to help distract the fish away from him. Stryker heads towards the bank, and the gulp fish predictably follow. He finds a spot where the shoreline gradually gets shallower and shallower, leading those who take this route out of the water onto the land. This otter has an idea – a simple idea, granted, but it will ensure his survival and hopefully a fish. The fat, sharp-toothed fish are getting closer to the otter and he is running out of energy. The fish nibbles on his tail, he is close to the shallow banking, which runs upwards to dryer climes. One of the gulp fish has opened its mouth wide and it surrounds the lower half of Stryker's body, as Stryker makes one last push to the shore. His feet touch the bank and he begins to run as fast as he possibly can out of the water. One gulp fish has built up such a speed that it cannot stop. Its big, hefty body follows the otter and slides up the bank, out of the water. Gendralf is waiting with his axe and promptly throws it at the fish from his horse. The axe flies through the air, turning a number of times in a clockwise movement before landing in the belly of the floundering fish. Stryker breathes heavily, he is exhausted. Amongst those heavy breaths is one big sigh of relief.

"Can someone get me a towel?" Stryker the otter asks, laying himself down onto the ground.

One gulp fish remains. The fish is nowhere to be seen; it has quite possibly accepted defeat and trundled off towards its original hiding place. Forester's head peers out of the water – he is searching for Stryker.

"Where is he?" he asks himself. Looking over to the bank the others can be seen with the fish. Igralf has spotted Forester, although quite rightly he is unsure whether he is looking at a talking otter called Forester or just an otter.

"Is that you, Forester?" Igralf calls out to Forester.

"Yes, it's me. Where is Stryker?" Forester asks, whilst waving at Igralf.

"He's on the bank with us." Stryker has got his towel and changed back into his normal form. Still out of breath he waves at Forester.

"Is he alright?" asks Forester.

"He'll be fine," responds Igralf.

Forester lies casually on his back as he paddles into shore, unaware that one gulp fish remains. Igralf spots a large shadow underneath the water and it is heading in the direction of Forester.

"Gulp fish, gulp fish!" Igralf shouts. But Forester cannot hear Igralf's warning as his ears are immersed in the water. The others run to the bank and start waving their arms, shouting and screaming over to Forester but he is oblivious. The gulp fish swims underneath the otter, circling him for a little while before shooting upwards with its mouth open, swallowing Forester whole in one big gulp. Back on the shore the others shake their heads at the event that has just taken place.

"What a buffoon," sighs Stryker, still covered head to toe in his towel.

"Do you think he's alive?" asks Igralf calmly, looking out into the water.

"Probably... we'll find out in a few seconds," responds Stryker, who is only a little bit concerned for his brother.

"So what do you think will happen next?" asks a curious Perrywinkle of Wattlespalf.

"Dunno, but I have a pretty good idea," replies Wattlespalf.

"Bugger," says Forester in the dark recesses of the fish's belly. He is still very much alive but he feels a tingle on his skin – it is the belly acids of the gulp fish, the fish is beginning to digest him, slowly. Forester knows that there is only one thing he can do. Changing swiftly, his brown paws become dark, grey, leathery feet. Forester loses his whiskers and develops a long, pointed horn in the middle of his forehead that looks like a huge thorn on a rosebush. The horn is so long that it stretches the body and the skin of the gulp fish. Forester's slender otter body grows and grows into a large grey, leathery mass. Small ears pop out on top of Forester's head. His nose and mouth grow in unison to support his long, thick horn. The otter's tail shortens itself and curls round. His legs become proportionately smaller than the otter's long limbs, enabling Forester to sustain a new large, bulging belly. Forester grows and grows and the gulp fish stretches and stretches until the thing growing inside it cannot be contained any longer.

Pop goes the fish!

Bits of fish splatter all across the water. There, standing in the middle of it all with a piece of fish strewn across his horns and face, is a poppapocerous, or Forester for short. The poppapocerous is much like its cousin the rhinoceros but much larger. Everyone on the bank starts laughing wildly as the poppapocerous tries to blow the fish off its horn from the side of its mouth. Eventually, giving up on the tactic of blowing, the poppapocerous sinks below the surface of the water and shakes its head, until the remnants of the fish wash away.

People in boats either side of the huge beast scream and shout in fear. Poppapocerous are known for tipping boats. Bows and spears quickly appear in peoples' hands and they begin to aim them at Forester from the sides of boats. Forester very quickly ducks back under the water, hoping to avoid any conflict, and swims towards the bank whilst changing back equally as fast into Forester the man.

As Forester gets back onto the bank, Gendralf provides him with a towel to cover his nakedness. Soon, boats filled with frightened and curious passengers approach the party.

"Did you see where the poppapocerous went?" asks one man of the group on the bank.

"He went under the water and headed in your direction," replies Greybeard. "He must have slid past you."

"Looks like you were lucky to get out alive. He must have been very close to you," the man on the boat says, directing his comments towards Forester.

"Too close," replies Forester with a hint of smile.

"Are those elves?" asks the man, turning his attention to Finn and Beezle. Everyone stumbles a little over their words.

"No, no… they were born this way. It runs in the family. They look like elves but actually they are men," babbles a quick-thinking Perrywinkle.

"Poor boys. Haven't thought about putting them in a circus then? I could pay you a good price," offers the man.

"How much?" asks Perrywinkle.

"Never, these are family members! I promised their mother and father I would look after them," responds Greybeard, giving Perrywinkle a slightly annoyed look.

"I was only joking," Perrywinkle mouths back.

"What's a circus?" questions Beezle, butting in.

"Anyway, must be off," says Greybeard. "Hope your journey is a good one."

"Not likely with all these goblins and poppapocerouses running around," grumbles the man despondently as his boat begins to sail further away down the river.

Stryker and Forester walk towards their horses and pull their now only slightly damp clothes off their saddles. They dress quickly so as not to waste any more time. Gulp fish drape off Perrywinkle, Gendralf and Finn's horses' backs. For now the fish smell fresh but the sun is blazing, the air is warm and the flies are slowly but surely making their way towards them.

Setting off again down the river, the riders pass by a number of once thriving villages that now look empty and lifeless. Fields of corn, wheat, grapes and orange groves are devoid of any movement. Everything appears abandoned. The tales of the goblin hordes have frightened men away from their homes; it is hoped by all that the jotunn have remained firmly in theirs.

Further and further down the path they travel, the villages that were once aplenty back up this road have thinned out until there are no more. Lack of settlements in this part of the province is not unusual; the jotunn were feared many years ago and men purposefully made sure that new settlements steered clear of this race. Much like the dragons, elves and dwarfs, jotunn live lives away from the hustle and bustle of the larger towns and cities. It is unlikely that you would see one of these creatures ever in your lifetime. Greybeard's hope is that the tunny do not have sufficient knowledge of the attacks, and that they are thriving. He must gauge how capable and responsive they are to helping him and the others confront the threat that draws ever nearer.

Jotunn monuments dominate the immediate views on the path they now travel. Tunny work well with stone; strength, height and an artistic eye for detail enables jotunn to produce great monuments that compare favourably to those of men who are renowned for these crafts. Standing stone monuments of kings and warriors in different poses line the path to the city. A strikingly detailed statue of a helmeted warrior lunging forward, his sword angled downward, points at a group of horrified blinny. A king standing tall, high up on a plinth, points his axe upwards to the sky, his head looking up into the cosmos. A long mural, running for a good twenty metres and at least ten metres high, depicts a number of tunny warriors with spears pointing towards a vast army of goblins, ogres and one of the unnamed. These are jotunn legends and tales brought to life in chiselled stone. Many more stone structures stand alongside those highlighted. Anyone travelling down

The path to the Jotunn town

this road is likely to be overawed, if not scared, of what lies in front of them.

At the end of this straight road is the entrance to the tunny town. A dark stone wall as tall as the sky and miles wide hides what lies behind it. Sturdy wooden doors as tall as the tallest trees mark the way into the town but they are closed. If there was a knock at these doors would anyone hear? The wall confirms to those travelling towards the town that the tunny might not be welcoming.

"Can we turn back?" asks a rattled Perrywinkle, the colour of his face white.

"We cannot," replies Greybeard confidently.

"But…" Perrywinkle grimaces, pointing to the sky above the wall.

"But nothing," interrupts Greybeard forcefully.

"But…" Perrywinkle continues.

"Perrywinkle, be quiet. The jotunn will do us no harm," grumbles Greybeard.

But Greybeard has not seen the arrow as big as a horse heading towards them. The other riders have seen it and directed their horses away from the main path into the long, heavy grasses of unkempt fields. Thundercloud has also seen the arrow and quickly changes direction, almost throwing Greybeard off the back of him, but Greybeard holds on with eyes wide open in surprise.

The arrow lands just to the side of Greybeard with a thud that shakes the ground around it. The riders spread out further as more arrows fly towards them. Heavy grasses covering open fields slow their advance; Finn, Perrywinkle and Gendralf are slowed further as the gulp fish have weighed the horses down and they are getting steadily more tired.

The ground shakes violently as time after time arrows pierce the ground one by one. Hearts beat quickly, terror takes a hold over everyone, but no one turns back. Pantus' horses are admirable; they are truly bred from kings, as in and out of danger the horses ride. The riders do not control this moment – it is the horses who confidently lead this pack. Arrows stop raining down on the riders. Someone from behind the wall must have ordered a refrain. A sound from behind the doors rings out; it has been unlocked. Doors creak as someone or something pulls them open. What will come out to greet the riders now? If hearts were already beating hard they beat even faster now as throats push up into mouths. The expectation of all is that darkness is inevitable, and the battle is potentially over. Last looks are given, eyes drop and deep breaths are taken. The doors open fully and five giants run forward with purpose.

CHAPTER 15

GIANT TOWN

Five giants running determinedly stop and stand in front of the riders.

"Hullo," smiles one of the giants. As first impressions go these jotunn boys are dressed smartly, not like soldiers at all. Gleaming shirts, trousers and a waistcoat adorn each of these young men; their shoes are shiny and new. The boys are clean cut, their hair neat and tidy. There is a playful air about them and they are curious and excited to see these small toy soldiers looking up at them. In reality, the men are not the size of toy soldiers but they are not far off. Look at them now against the size of these giants and you would say they must be the size of a child, maybe even a toddler who has just begun to walk.

"Hello," says Greybeard. The other riders look at each other, a bit perplexed at how jotunn arrows have just been raining down on them only a minute ago and now they are in the company of sniggering young men. The warriors they have been looking forward to meeting are nowhere to be seen. In hindsight, it is probably a good thing that there are no soldiers at all at these gates because the riders might already be dead.

"So," pipes up the curly-haired tunny, "not often – not often at all do we get such esteemed guests coming to visit our small town." Emphasis is put on the 'small', at which point the young tunny men burst out laughing.

"Young rapscallions, I'll have you know that I am Greybeard, and I fought with your... "

"Greybeard?" interrupts a blond-haired tunny, cringing at the very name. 'Greybeard' is whispered between the others quietly; legends have obviously been made of this wizard in tunny folklore.

"Sorry, Greybeard. We didn't mean to put the lives of you and your friends in danger. That's not what we meant to do at all," whimpers a young giant with ginger hair. The tales about Greybeard must have been very fierce. "Please don't turn me into a frog," pleads the ginger-haired lad, trying to cover himself with his hands.

"Hmm... well, you have made me very angry," booms Greybeard, playing on the opinions they have of him. "What shall I do with these giant rascals who fired upon us, wanting us dead? You were the ones firing those arrows upon us, weren't you?" the wizard asks, just to make sure that he has the right culprits.

"Yes, we..." replies the ginger-haired jotunn, at which point the others push and prod him, hoping that he will keep his big mouth shut.

"So, you really did mean us harm. You need to be punished for your actions. You are already aware, no doubt, that conspiring to kill a great wizard brings the harshest of sentences. So, men, what shall we do with them?" the old man asks, turning to the other riders for ideas.

"Oh, maybe you could save him the embarrassment of being turned into a frog and turn him into a beautiful pig instead," says Igralf.

"No. Please!" the ginger-haired giant screams, getting on his knees in the process, hands clasped, and begging to be forgiven.

Greybeard gets off his horse and struts up and down the line of the five young men, and pointing to a blond-haired giant, he asks, "And what about this one?"

"I'd like to see him turned into a mouse – then he will know what it is to be small. Oh, and for good measure I want him to be followed by a hungry cat for the rest of, what will hopefully be, a very short life," teases Gendralf.

"A mouse! I couldn't possibly be turned into a mouse. I am allergic to cats. Please, not a mouse! It would be intolerable," pleads the blond-haired giant.

"A mouse it is then," laughs Greybeard with menace.

The jotunn giant who made the discourteous comment about the group standing before him being 'small' is the next to be tackled. He is a curly-haired giant with a face full of pimples and poppable spots. "This one?" asks Greybeard, pointing towards him.

"Definitely a gulp fish, and the reason for this is because you have a big mouth, literally," says Perrywinkle. The curly-haired giant's eyes roll; he is close to fainting at the shock of this revelation.

Two giants are left to be judged. They are brown-haired, blue-eyed twins who have been a little too well fed.

"I suggest these two boys share the same fate as we are merciful," hollers Greybeard. "Any ideas?"

Everyone thinks for a little while.

"Two jam puddings, ripe and ready to eat," Stryker suggests, licking his lips. "I could do with something tasty to eat."

"That sounds delightful," enthuses Greybeard, as the twin giants cry and plead for their lives not to change. The wizard lifts his staff in the air and his oric lights up, producing the brightest of lights. The giants close their eyes, sweat runs down their faces and all cry and whimper. A long pause ensues and finally Greybeard, rather than turning them into the creatures or desserts suggested, hits each and every one on the knee with his long, hard staff.

"Ow," says one.

"Ouch," says another.

"Ow," comes another cry.

"Ouch," and "Ow," come the last two cries.

"Let that be a lesson to all of you," bellows Greybeard, winking to his companions over his shoulder.

"Ha! Now who's laughing," Beezle shouts, giggling uncontrollably. The young jotunn giants hop left, right and centre, the ground shaking ever so slightly round each and every one of them. After a good rubbing of the knees, the giants regain their composure and begin to thank Greybeard for his mercy.

"This is not what I expected at all," says Stryker to Forester. "They are all fools."

"Hopefully we will find better inside the walls of this town," responds Forester.

"You lot, I expect you to guide us round this town of yours. Now please be kind enough to show us the way before I am tempted to do some real harm," commands Greybeard. Greybeard gets back on his horse. The tunny giants hobble back slowly through the large wooden gates, but 'slowly' for giants is quite a pace for creatures of normal size, and so it is that the riders follow at a canter.

Behind the wall, a host of voices can be heard. It sounds busy and hearts beat in anticipation of the world they are about to see. Through the gates there is a long arched passage – or a short arched passage, if you are a giant reading this. At the end of this seemingly long passage, the town becomes immediately visible.

A long, wide courtyard full of colour is the first thing you see. The town is much like any other in this land except it is a lot, lot bigger. Carts full of normal-sized fruits, vegetables, meats, chickens, fish and grains dominate the square. There are no such things as giant chickens or cows in Everlast; everybody knows that kind of thing is the stuff of fairytales. Stalls selling luxury goods such as fragranced soaps, candles, clothing, fine woven materials, pots, pans and so much more also fill the square.

Men and women rush around all over the courtyard, buying or exchanging goods. Jotunn appetites require a lot of feeding. Eggs are bought in hundreds not dozens, apples are bought in sacks as opposed to bags, gulp fish that can feed five to six normal-sized men make a meal for only one or two tunny and a cow will only just feed a family. Painted ladies in long, flowing dresses and fine-coloured leather shoes smell fragrances and look wild-eyed at the most luxurious silks. The jotunn are all so busy that no one has taken any notice of the riders at the entrance to the town.

More satisfying and awe-inspiring is the sight of the huge houses and shops in the near distance. Shops and houses look like any other in this land but they are as big as the tallest towers in the great cities of men. Going up a step here would require the men to almost climb it. A sweet shop sells goodies such as sarsaparilla tablets, pear drops, apple fizzes and chocolates the size of an open palm. Toys hang in the window of another shop with some dolls, puppets and teddy bears in it standing half as tall as Greybeard. The riders themselves look remarkably like toys – dwarfs like big lolloping teddy bears, elves like hanging wooden puppets and men like sturdy action dolls all sitting on adequately-sized rocking horses.

Tailors can be seen in the window of another shop quickly measuring a customer with the longest tape measure, which measures in feet not inches. Big trombones, trumpets and drums blare out melodic tunes from inside a music shop. In the front window, violins, lutes and flutes hang down from the ceiling beckoning tunny to look inside. A bric-a-brac shop contains many things old and new. Large windows at the front of the shop reveal a whole host of art, furniture, books, antiques, homeware and clothes which are recycled again and again, having given many families much pleasure and usage over many years.

The companions look on, all of them in awe of the sights in front of them. No one expected this bustling town – no one really knew what to expect. No one had ever seen a tunny never mind dozens happily working their way around a market with bags and bags of shopping.

"Wow," gawps Beezle, his mouth wide open and eyes displaying wonderment. "This is without doubt the best thing I have ever seen." Beezle and the others' senses are bristling, hairs stand up on their arms and goose pimples tickle all over.

"I've got to agree, brother. This really is something wholly magical," comments Finn.

Perrywinkle is inspired; he has got his journal out and is writing at a frantic pace, taking in everything around him.

Greybeard shouts up towards the young jotunn men, "You, the blond-haired one – do you have a king or a leader that I might visit? I need to talk to them urgently."

The blond-haired jotunn kneels down next to Greybeard. "King, no. Leader… erm, yes. We have a leader, kind of."

"What do you mean kind of?" asks a slightly disappointed Greybeard. How can this town function without a leader? And who will make the decision that will need to be made when the time comes to answer the gravest of questions?

"Well, we have someone here who, when asked a question or given an idea, tells us whether or not the question or idea is a good one," replies the blond-haired giant.

"Someone who answers questions for a living is your leader?" Greybeard booms, before pondering upon what the blond-haired giant has said. "Hmm," Greybeard grunts after a while. "Do they tell you what to do?"

"No one tells us what to do. We just use our common sense, and when things get complicated we ask for an opinion," responds the blond-haired giant, a little bewildered by the questions being asked.

"And what of rules? You must have a set of rules that you live by."

"What do you mean?" the blond-haired giant asks.

"Well, don't you have rules that say do not steal or do not kill?" asks Greybeard.

"Everyone knows that. Isn't that just common sense?"

"So what do you do when common sense does not prevail, for example, when someone steals or murders?"

"No one here has stolen or murdered anyone as far as I know."

Greybeard is shocked by this revelation. Tunny people were vicious once, feared by everybody. How this race has changed. Dwarfs and men are easily called into a fight; some even enjoy the sight, smell and sound of it. Goblins, well we all know about them. Dragons instigate it and wizards, well, they tolerate it. Elves haven't been around for a long time, but even Finn and Beezle know how to use a weapon – and Finn is not afraid to use his to protect others. But the jotunn, once most feared, are they really so placid now that they would not say boo to a goose? They do have defences. These silly boys who guide Greybeard now, they know how to use them and are not afraid to use them, even if it is in some misguided form of jest.

"Where are your warriors?" Greybeard asks the blond-haired giant.

"We do not need them," he replies.

"But we do train," says the ginger-haired boy, interrupting. "The old man maintains that we must keep the old ways alive, and so we are encouraged to spend time practising. A good proportion of the town know how to fight."

"We must respect old and new," adds the blond-haired giant. "We respect you, Greybeard, because the tales have told us that you respected us and helped us when we needed you."

Greybeard bows his head humbly. He now understands a little more about how the tunny lead their lives. Respect for others around them allows them to live their lives in peace. There is an element of self-control in these people, but as the ages have passed and generations have led by example, it has become easier to instil those ideas into the young... as if they have always been.

"Take us to your leader, young jotunn. I need to speak to him."

"He is not a he, he is a she," replies the blond-haired giant.

"Take me to her then, and stop playing with your words," says Greybeard, correcting himself.

"Sorry, sir, follow me," he replies, cowering at the wizard's grumpy tones.

The middle of the courtyard boasts a large, round fountain. Water shoots upwards through the stone mouth of a fish in its centre. Gravity pulls the water back down into a pool full of coins and charms thrown in along with a wish. The tunny walk slowly towards the fountain across a cobbled path. The cobbles appear like paving slabs to the riders. One of the twins throws a coin into the water as he walks past it. A jotunn coin is the size of a small pebble, and as it hits the water there is a large plop, but this is not the plop of a normal coin. Water splashes upwards and over the side of the fountain. The splash of water drops downwards until finally it lands on Perrywinkle, wetting him and his pony right through from head to toe. Perrywinkle looks like a drowned rat, which provokes some heavy laughs from companions and giants alike. Fortunately, only moments earlier, he had put his most precious journal away, so that at least escaped a real soaking. Perrywinkle gives a reluctant smile, gathering himself after his initial shock.

"Okay, okay, but don't tell anyone back home," he says, wiping himself and his pony down with a towel passed to him by Stryker (who feels a little sorry for him). Perrywinkle passes it back with a dignified "Thank you". The tunny boys clear a path for the companions; they stand in positions at the front, back and sides of the riders so as to protect them from the hustle and bustle of the crowds.

Some children are small enough to have noticed the riders. A little girl with pigtails, who is a little taller than Greybeard, tries to stroke Igralf's pony as it passes by.

"Mama," she says excitedly. She looks up at her mother and points at the little white pony and the even smaller dwarf sitting on top of it. The little girl's mother looks down, and upon seeing the riders at her feet screams the loudest of screams. Not many jotunn have seen men before, so her shock is understandable. It is, however, unfortunate that someone who is obviously more easily startled than others has seen these companions first. Everyone in the square stops and slowly a crowd gathers around the tunny boys who protect the riders. The blond-haired boy announces that they are in the company of the esteemed and very learned Greybeard.

'Hoo's' and 'haa's' follow. Pokes and prods are endured by all except Greybeard, who they consider above the others. Women mention how cute they look, and others comment that they would make nice pets. Children gather in droves to have their first experience of men, dwarfs and elves. The elves feel a little bit more comfortable with the attention than the others. All the riders here are a novelty and they receive no more and no less attention than they do. It appears that the story of the elves is either largely forgotten or has not been told at all to these giants. Indeed, whilst the crowd marvels at the riders, the riders are still marvelling at the jotunn, a mutual curiosity of each other being very much apparent. A boy of about seven who is nearly twice as tall as Greybeard pulls on Beezle's ear.

"That's an awfully pointy ear you've got," says the boy.

"All the better to hear you," roars Beezle.

"They're silly," he says, almost pulling Beezle off his horse.

Beezle grimaces. "I wouldn't do that if I were you."

"Or else? What are you going to do about it?" says the boy, sticking out his tongue at Beezle whilst continuing to pull and prod him further.

Beezle puts his arm out casually, opens his palm, aims at an apple on one of the carts nearby and recites the magic words, "Grabius come." The apple flies towards Beezle, but instead of guiding it towards his palm he flicks it towards the boy. The apple subsequently hits the little boy on the back of the head.

"Ow," the curious little boy cries.

"That's what will happen," laughs Beezle.

"Wow. Are you a wizard?" asks the boy, rubbing the back of his head, excited at the prospect he might have just been on the receiving end of one.

"Yes I am," replies Beezle, revelling in his new-found status with this child. "So beware, you will hear lots about me when I am older... as I will be considered great." The dwarfs look at

Beezle and their eyes roll, unimpressed with his claims and boasts.

"Beezle, do not use your powers to hurt children," grumbles Greybeard.

"Sir, do not worry. It didn't hurt too much. I'm just glad to have met a real wizard," says the boy, standing up for Beezle.

"He is not a real wizard by any stretch of the imagination. He knows only a few tricks at present," replies Greybeard. "That reminds me, Beezle, you have not asked for a lesson today. This is very unlike you."

"Ah, patience," responds a quick-minded Beezle, glancing very briefly at Finn's backpack. "I think I have mastered it."

"You very well might have." A surprised Greybeard grins. "I'll teach you something later, and if not later then tomorrow,"

"Please, that would be very much appreciated," responds Beezle.

"Hmm, yes. Very good," says Greybeard quietly in response.

"Shall we move onward to the wise woman?" Stryker asks, trying to prompt a way out of the crowd.

"Yes, we cannot waste our time gawping at giants, and I'm sure they have got better things to do than gawp at us," adds Greybeard. "You, the ginger-haired one," he shouts. "Can you get us moving again?"

"Yes, sir, without question," he replies. "Come on, nothing to see here," he adds, shoo-ing and ushering the crowd away.

"Before we go, give these fish to the fishmonger over there. I want him to fillet and bone them. We will come back later to pick them up," says the wizard.

The twins and the curly-haired boy each take a fish off the backs of Perrywinkle, Finn and Gendralf's horses. The gulp fish are taken to the fishmonger, who is more than pleased to fillet fish for such important guests. The horses are also relieved to have the extra weight removed, you can almost hear them sighing with pleasure. The riders, with the help of the giants, fumble their way through the crowd. Children follow behind, hand-in-hand, skipping on the cobbles.

"Little men, little men, going to see our lady. Little men, little men, look like little babies," they sing, playfully taunting the riders.

Greybeard puts his staff over his shoulder and asks his oric to give the children a surprise. A bolt of light emerges from the oric and shoots high up into the air. There is a loud bang and confetti of all shapes and colours floats down onto the children. The children scream with delight as they try to catch the confetti in their hands. Some of it lands in their hair and on their faces. Some of the children stand underneath it and try to blow it back up into the air. Needless to say the distraction is enough for the riders and the young tunny men to lose the children. Passing huge red brick and light stone houses with huge wooden front doors and huge wooden windows, they slowly ride through part of the living area of the town.

It seems like the riders have travelled for miles when they get to a green field with a park. A slide, swings and roundabout, as well as a frame for climbing on, sits at the edge of this park. It is surrounded by bushy oak trees and plenty of benches to sit on. A couple of families sit around, taking in the afternoon sun, having picnics out of huge hampers filled with food and drink.

On one side of the field, a group of young men and women dressed in battle armour are practising hand-to-hand combat. A teacher stands in front, guiding them on how to perfect the move taught. The young men and women copy, eager to please him. The teacher is much older than his pupils; he looks much the same age as Greybeard, his hair is short and slightly balding, and his round face is covered with a short beard. Despite his age, he still has a strong, stocky physique; the muscles on his arms and legs bulge, his torso slightly flabby but not overly so. He wears only a short, cream tunic and shorts, and his feet are bare (maybe he likes the feel of the grass under them). He doesn't wear the battle dress of his pupils. Behind the teacher, propped up on a grass verge, are sheathed swords and shields similar to those depicted in the murals and statues situated on the paths outside the town walls. The swords are truly enormous, standing taller than Stryker and Forester; the shields, too, almost stand as tall as the men.

"Please, I'd like to watch for a moment. This is more like it," Greybeard calls out to his young tunny guides, and everyone stops.

The movement of the youths is serene and slow, the purpose is to perfect the move not to execute it at speed. Careful consideration is given to the height of the enemy; it is not jotunn these young men train to fight, they think of blinny and other nasty things. Greybeard wanders over to the teacher and asks to speak with him; the teacher gestures for his young tunny pupils to continue on without him. From a distance, the others can see the teacher's eyes widen; he smiles enthusiastically, nodding his head at Greybeard's every word. The teacher looks over at Stryker, Forester, the dwarfs and the elves before putting his hands together as if the wizard has given him a gift from the Creators themselves. The conversation ends. Greybeard rides back towards his friends, who have been watching the wizard's chat with the teacher from their horses with curiosity.

"Friends, I would like you to train with the tunny." It is almost an order given, but there is purpose in his words. "I want you to teach, and more importantly, gauge how well these men might help us in our cause. I truly believe from Lord's word that they are meant to come with us – unless, of course, there is something here that we are meant to find. If there is a hint that they are not the warriors they should be then we must not endanger them. In addition, I want you to work with Finn as Pengwellen hinted. We are aware of his skills with a bow, but we need to make sure his movement and swordplay are of such a standard that he is able to protect himself and others."

"We will," reassures Igralf. "Besides, it would be interesting to see how these men fight, and I have a feeling that Finn will not need too much instruction."

"Are you ready for the challenge?" asks Forester, looking back at Finn.

"I think I want to be," replies Finn, unsure what he is getting himself into.

"I will go and see the leader. She is likely to guide us further," informs Greybeard.

"I hope you have good words with her," replies Stryker.

"Train well," says Greybeard, winking at the group encouragingly. Greybeard looks at the young jotunn giants. "Curly, take me to see your wise woman."

"Who, me?" cowers the curly-haired giant, playing with one of the spots on his face.

"Yes, you," Greybeard answers, looking at him sternly. "The

rest of you I want over there with your teacher. You are going to learn a few tricks."

"Yes, sir," says the blond-haired giant.

"Thank you," add relieved twins in unison.

"He's not going to turn us into frogs, is he?" asks the ginger-haired tunny who has not been listening at all.

"No, but I might if you do not get over there right now," threatens Greybeard.

The young jotunn run towards the teacher so quickly and clumsily it makes the riders smile. If the warriors in front are of the same ilk as these numbskulls then they may as well leave now.

"Good luck," smiles Greybeard. "You, take us to your leader!" he commands the curly-haired giant. The giant is so alarmed by Greybeard's command that he is fast to respond and leaves Greybeard behind. Thundercloud, who has been listening to the conversation intently (horses in general understand most things men say), follows the curly-haired giant with vigour.

"Goodbyeeeee," Greybeard can be heard shouting as he flies off into the distance. Eventually, Thundercloud catches up with Curly. Giants, when they get into their stride, walk much faster than horses can canter and Thundercloud is quite old, as we already know. Curly walks at a fast pace and Greybeard, for all his shouting and screaming for the giant to slow down, is not heard. Curly is slightly deaf, or at least deaf enough not to hear Greybeard when he feels like it. In actual fact, he can hear Greybeard quite clearly, but he is scared of his reputation. All he wants to do now is make sure he leads this wizard to the wise woman as quickly as he can.

You see, as Greybeard has already made quite clear, the storyteller can exaggerate facts or even lie in a tale to make a story more interesting or even more magical. Storytellers do this to entertain or provoke a bigger reaction from the listener. Ages have passed since Greybeard made himself known to this race. His presence was felt in the last of the wars in which the tunny were involved before exiling themselves to this place. Greybeard appeared and disappeared hundreds and hundreds of years ago, and in that time many, many generations of jotunn have passed on into another life. Generations have told tales of Greybeard time and time again.

The wizard's tale is particularly special because of his inclination to perform magic or feats of magical significance. Children, who have been told these tales, will generally stare open-mouthed at the storyteller when his tale is told, as tales of magic take them to a realm that others don't. Magical realms in tunny tales over the years must have become more and more astonishing and more frightening. This is most probably why Greybeard is both feared and loved in equal measure.

Many questions have been raised on the advice of storytellers and none have ever been answered about this wizard, such as... has Greybeard actually turned men into frogs? And has he flown hundreds of miles into the night air to touch the stars? Or has he, with one incantation, made at least one army disappear? Greybeard will not say but is this because he is too humble to become the showman and prove these claims, or is it because he enjoys his fame and does not want anyone to believe any less? Maybe, just maybe, we will find out and maybe we won't. One thing, which is without doubt very true, is that he has always been in the right place at the right time, and he has helped save many lives belonging to all races. He has even been known to save goblins on the odd occasion.

"We're here," reveals the curly-haired giant, stopping at the front of a big red door with two large steps leading up to it.

"Young man, what is this woman called?" asks Greybeard.

"I dunno," says the curly-haired giant shrugging his shoulders.

"Go on then, off with you. If you have any sense you'll go back to the park and learn something useful," patronises Greybeard. "Oh, and thank you for bringing me here. It is very much appreciated, even if you do not care to remember the name of your leader," he says, changing his tone.

"Yes, sir, that's quite alright. Thanks for not turning me into a gulp fish," he replies gratefully.

The curly-haired giant runs off in the direction in which he came. He doesn't look back. Greybeard climbs down from Thundercloud, onto the top step leading up to the door. Having to climb up what seems like small walls in a wizard's garb is not very easy, so Thundercloud's help is more than welcome. Staff in hand, Greybeard knocks three times on the huge red door.

Footsteps soon approach and the door opens. As expected, a giant woman answers it. Battleaxe describes the woman who answers the door best. She is of a good age, and her wrinkled face looks as if it has a permanent scowl of dissatisfaction and disappointment in anybody and everybody she meets. Her greasy black hair is rolled around wooden curlers. She wears a large sheep's wool cardigan over a conservative blouse that covers her neck, and a long grey skirt covering her ankles; the ensemble is finished off with thick black socks and slippers. If she is wise then she is also firm. The woman looks left and right and tuts several times, failing to spot that Greybeard is standing right in front of her.

"Hello," Greybeard shouts, but he is not heard by the woman.

"Incorrigible tykes always causing mischief," she curses, slamming the door in Greybeard's face. The force of the air created in slamming the door nearly knocks the old man off the step he is standing on. Steadying himself just in time, Greybeard tries again. *Knock, knock, knock,* he raps on the door with his staff. The door opens again. The jotunn woman looks about, but before the wizard can say a word, the door is slammed in his face once more. Dull sounds can be heard from behind the door.

"I tell you, it's getting worse. If it was up to me I'd have them over my knee," drones the woman, talking to someone else. Greybeard is getting a little impatient, too. He mumbles to himself as he makes yet another attempt to get the attention of the wise woman at the front door; maybe he should rap her ankles with his staff.

"That'll do it," he says to himself.

He knocks again. The door immediately flings itself fully open as if the battleaxe had been anticipating the 'prank' to continue. Greybeard can see into the hallway. The tunny woman curls her wrist and shakes it.

"Whoever it is," she shouts down the street, "will feel my fist next time."

But Greybeard is not listening to this burst of anger because there in the hallway is a middle-aged woman. She is not a giant, she is born of man, and she is staring back at Greybeard silently. The giant woman puts her hand against the edge of the door and promptly slams it shut.

Greybeard's shoulders slump, silently he turns to his horse.

"Ridiculous." Thundercloud neighs in agreement with his friend.

Slowly, the door opens for a fourth time, silently behind him.

"Come in," an apologetic voice says. It is that of the small woman who was standing in the hallway. Greybeard turns around and stops, as her face is now only inches away from his own.

"Erm, hello," he says, touching the hairs on the back of his head nervously, before taking a step to his left and climbing up into the house. The giant woman, who stands behind the smaller woman, closes the door behind Greybeard.

"Are you alright to be left with this man? He looks very strange," asks the jotunn woman sternly.

"Humph, strange?" the wizard whispers, he cannot be heard by the two women standing close by.

"Yes, Celia, I will be fine," replies the smaller woman.

"I'll be upstairs if you need me." Celia walks up the wooden stairs situated on the far right of the hallway. She disappears onto the landing and presumably walks into one of the bedrooms.

"She is irreplaceable," says the woman, looking up the stairs as Celia disappears. "I saw you in the window. It is not everyday I get to see a man my height – well, closer to my height. You are Greybeard, aren't you?" she continues, looking up and down at the very tall wizard.

"Yes, I am. How did you know?" Greybeard replies, a little surprised by her knowledge of him.

The woman is pretty, her hair is strawberry blonde in tone and her green eyes are large. Greybeard cannot help but look into her eyes; they are hypnotic. The wizard drags his eyes away only to be instantly recaptured by hers. She is slim and her body is covered with a deep green dress that is so long it flows on the floor behind her.

"I was told in a dream that you would come, but that was a long, long time ago. So long I'd forgotten that it ever happened. It was quite vivid as I remember," the woman says, turning around. She walks through the hallway towards the first room on the left, which happens to be the lounge.

"Believe it or not, there are creatures in this world who have known that I was coming to visit them for over three thousand years," quips a pragmatic Greybeard light-heartedly, referring to Pengwellen.

"That is a long time," says the woman, unsurprised and not amused by him.

As they walk through the hallway and into the lounge, Greybeard notices immediately that the furniture in it is designed to accommodate a normal-sized man (or woman in this case). This woman has man-sized sofas, bookcases, clocks, drawers, tables and chairs; everything she needs is in this room. The woman settles at a wooden table with two wooden chairs siting either side of it. The other chair has been empty ever since it was made, waiting in expectation of a visitor. That expected visitor has always been Greybeard.

"Please sit down," offers the woman.

The wizard sits on the chair 'made' for him. The room is full of paintings and books of all sizes, some obviously made for or bought by the smaller woman who sits opposite him now. The walls are covered in paper full of red, blue and yellow flowers. Great care has been given to the placement of vases, houseplants, ornaments and furniture, which makes this room homely and bright. Varnish on the furniture and mirrors on the walls reflect the light coming through the windows; at this moment the room shines.

"What is your name?" Greybeard asks politely. "No one has actually been good enough to reveal it. Although I might add that I did not ask them, bar one silly boy, for that particular piece of information."

"Sorry, where were my manners? I am Parva," she replies, holding out her hand over the table. Greybeard shakes it gently.

"Pleased to meet you," Greybeard says, letting go of her hand.

"Pleased to meet you," responds Parva. "A drink?"

"A drink?" replies a confused Greybeard, as if this comment is something of a clue.

"Do you want a drink? And if so, what would you like to drink?" asks the woman.

"Yes, tea would be lovely, if you have it," Greybeard stutters, thinking about how foolish he might look.

Parva's room

"Tea it is then." Parva leaves the room for a little while and comes back holding a tray with a nice big pot of tea and a plate full of big biscuits with big chunks of chocolate embedded in them.

"So, where were we?" asks Parva, pouring tea from the pot into Greybeard's cup.

"I suppose we were getting to the question of why I am here," replies Greybeard.

"So, why are you here?" asks Parva.

"A very good question. I need your help or at least the help of your people," confesses Greybeard.

"Why do you need our help?" asks the woman.

"Have you heard of the warrior who is making his way slowly northwards?"

"No, I haven't heard this," she replies, a little disturbed.

"Parva, Warrior is changing the world. How can you not have heard of his wrath?"

"Greybeard, can you not see that this is understandable? These people have not left this place for hundreds of years, and I have been here many years myself. In that time there have been no visitors. Nobody wants to come into this place – I don't blame them, either. It is a daunting and scary place to those who don't know, especially with the reputation these people have."

"And the huge arrows raining down on us," Greybeard interrupts.

"Huge arrows? Oh, don't tell me," Parva holds her head in her hands. She looks through her fingers at Greybeard. "Babbling fools those boys are! Not a great welcoming party then?"

"No, not the best of welcomes, but I have had worse, believe you me," replies Greybeard, taking a big biscuit off the plate; it is the size of his face. Snapping a bit off it, he dips it into his tea.

"So, how did you come to be here, and why have you remained here?" Greybeard asks, intrigued as to how Parva is going to answer.

"Where do I start? There are no leaders here, and there hasn't been for generations. In the early years, after battling for so long, the tunny sought an unrivalled peace. Leaderships and councils were dissolved. Without anyone to order the tunny to do things and organise them, they slowly and surely forgot their passion and

215

their work ethic. Over time they also lost their way. How did I come to be here? Well, let's just say I was paying a visit," Parva says, revealing nothing. "When I arrived, buildings were crumbling, fruit and vegetable farming was beginning to fail, litter was strewn along the streets, rats and other nasty things inhabited the town, and fields and parks were overgrown. Disorganised and unable to contemplate how best to maintain a town that was falling into ruin, the tunny needed strong guidance. I arrived at the right time to give them some – it just took a bit longer for things to sort themselves out than I anticipated."

"So how did you do it? The jotunn town appears like any other, if not better maintained than most."

"Well, I initially gained a reputation through Celia. She was talking about friends who had problems and I listened to her. I gave her some advice to pass on to her friends. She presented it as advice from another friend, which was right. She did not reveal that it was from a daughter of man as that may have provoked a 'reaction'. Giants believed themselves better than men. Others came to Celia asking for advice – some asked questions about relationships, some asked for practical advice. All manner of questions flew in our direction. At first it was fun to have answers to all of these problems, and we used our burgeoning reputations to get the tunny to do jobs for us around the town as payment for our advice. Slowly but surely, the work around the town has been done, the tunny have been liberated once more and people are once again taking pride in everything they do. The questions don't come as often now; it seems that we have been very positive and the tunny have begun to take responsibility for themselves and their town."

"Does that mean you are relinquishing your role as leader?" asks the wizard.

"I am not a leader. I never have been, though it does mean that my job here is done. You have arrived on the cusp of my retirement. I don't want to live my life giving out advice, however enjoyable it might have been in the past. Celia and I have done enough of that already. Besides, the tunny can do it for themselves now and so they should. The jotunn know better than they once did," she admits.

"Hmm, quite. You are a very honourable woman. I am in awe of what you have achieved here."

"Thank you, but your pride in me is not necessary," comes Parva's humble reply.

"The warrior is very dangerous, you know," Greybeard informs her, changing the subject. His tone becomes more serious. "He has an army of goblins who have killed many in the south. Villages the length and breadth of the southeast have been and are being burned to the ground at this very moment."

"And their movement dictates that they will end up here at some juncture," Parva interrupts, anticipating Greybeard's next words. She is alarmed and her eyes widen as she imagines this place being besieged.

"Do not worry yet," Greybeard reassures Parva. "We have a solution – good men and the help of dragons. But we have been led here because we were told you could help us further. There is an element of fate that dictates why I sit here before you now. You may well hold the key to our victory."

"But we have no magical weapons, and no obvious books with answers that would help you in your quest. We have nothing to offer you," Parva insists.

"You have warriors. My men are with them now – they are gauging their abilities. If the tunny have been passionate enough about learning the old ways as they seem to be, then they might be passionate enough to become the warriors their predecessors were."

"But they are still children and have not seen battle. I cannot advise them to leave this place. I cannot see them to their death," protests a protective Parva. She drinks her tea quickly and rubs her hands in a disconcerted manner.

"You said that they should make their own decisions. Sometimes children need to grow up and find their own way," urges Greybeard, trying to persuade her.

"But not like this… surely it has to be gentle. They must first understand this world, not go to war with it," Parva replies, almost pleading with him.

"If it were any other time then I would agree. But this world demands that people must battle for their place and the places of others, at this time," shouts Greybeard in frustration.

"Then I say they should not leave these walls, and if the time comes they must make their stand here," she says, pointing at

Greybeard, her mouth quivering with anger.

Greybeard leans over the table, slightly towards Parva, and takes hold of her pointing finger and then her hand. "Parva, I am not going to push you to make a decision you will regret."

"Thank you, Greybeard," she says, calming down. "It may be that they will make their own decision this time, but I personally cannot allow this." The comment is apologetic but final.

"Can I ask one favour of you?'" asks Greybeard. Parva nods. "Will you come to the fields to watch your warriors with my men?"

Parva looks annoyed at Greybeard's request. "Greybeard, I am not coming to the park to be swayed by you. I will not change my mind. Now I'd like you to leave," she says resolutely.

"I'm sorry," apologises the old man. "It might well have been my intention to sway you, but the situation is grave and I believe we need the help of your people."

"Please leave," says Parva, effectively telling the problem she is faced with to go away.

Greybeard gets up and leaves the table. "Thank you for seeing me. You make a good cup of tea."

Parva leaves the table and rushes over to the staircase in the hallway before calling for Celia. "Celia, could you come downstairs and open the door for our guest?"

Celia comes down the stairs, hearing the distress in Parva's voice. She opens the door and Greybeard leaves, looking back one more time at Parva, who looks away. The door shuts quickly behind him. Greybeard, humbled by his failure, gets back on Thundercloud, who has been waiting patiently. Asking his horse to move forward, he canters back towards his men.

CHAPTER 16

WE NEED AN ARMY

While Greybeard is at Parva's residence, Stryker, Forester and the dwarfs dismount their horses and tie them loosely to a tree, close to the edge of the park. Walking coolly in a line towards the teacher and his pupils, these men and dwarfs are full of confidence. In their mind's eye they are warriors here to teach those ahead of them some tricks. Young tunny men and women watch the warriors approaching them and smile excitedly. It is not often they get the chance to meet battle-worn soldiers who must be able to teach them much. Jotunn men and women part ranks as Stryker, Forester and the dwarfs walk in between them. Finn, Beezle and Perrywinkle walk behind them, less sure of themselves; they are a little overawed by the giants. The tunny warriors are in full battle armour and there is more than a passing resemblance to the statues of the warriors that line the road into the town. Imagine if the tunny in front possess the same prowess as the warriors of old? It doesn't bear thinking about.

Rounded helmets made of a smooth bronze cover not only the skull but the nape of the neck and bridge of the nose as well. On top of the helmet is a black mane, much like a horse's. Shoulders, stomachs, chests, elbows, knees, shins and feet are protected with armoured plates. Tunny legs are particularly well protected – for obvious reasons. Behind the armour, all wear cream tunics, which cover the body to just above the knee, and shorts underneath the tunic to hide things other people shouldn't see.

"I don't think they should be too over confident. These warriors look pretty menacing and look at the size of them!" gasps Perrywinkle, directing his comments towards Finn and Beezle.

"I'm sure they'll be alright. Surely it's just posturing on their part. They must know these giants will pose some sort of threat, even in games of war," replies Finn.

"They're only here to teach. It's not as if they're going to have an all-out war with the tunny. I cannot believe you two are taking this so seriously," comments Beezle, unimpressed by Finn and Perrywinkle.

The jotunn teacher greets Stryker, Forester and the dwarfs warmly. A handshake would have been right and proper, but tunny hands are the size of a man's arm.

"Thank you for coming here to see us," smiles the teacher, stumbling over his words, his voice gentle and kind. He is very excited, as if this is a moment he has craved for years and years.

"So, who might you be?" asks Stryker.

"You can call me Teacher," he replies.

"Yes, we know you're a teacher. What do we call you?" asks Stryker again impatiently, obviously not satisfied with the first answer given.

"Teacher," replies Teacher.

"Hmm, Teacher it is then. Greybeard has asked us to teach you how to fight properly," Stryker huffs.

"You are mistaken… we are here to teach you. He believes you are a bit rusty and in need of some battle practice," interrupts Teacher.

"Hang on a minute." Stryker raises his voice. "Greybeard told us that we were here to…" Stryker breaks off from his sentence, turning back towards Forester and the dwarfs. "The old goat, he's playing mind games again."

"Don't worry, old friend. These young jotunn have absolutely no chance of beating us. Look at them, they're kids. They'll never beat us. Not in a million years," assures Igralf.

"Too right – shall we give them a whipping?" adds Gendralf bullishly.

Stryker turns back to Teacher. "Are you sure that these young whippersnappers can handle themselves appropriately?"

"Without a doubt, they have been taught the ways of the jotunn. I take it that you have never been party to our arts," Teacher says, patronising the little men in front of him.

"Well no, actually we haven't been party to your form of battle, but I can pretty much guarantee that you have not seen ours either," says Stryker, patronising Teacher back.

"Ah, a healthy rivalry. I like your tone, little man," replies Teacher, emphasising 'little'.

"We'll give him little," grumbles Stryker, a bit miffed.

"Indeed," say the rest.

"We'll make it easy for you, select three of my pupils to match you," offers Teacher.

"Three? Make it seven and pick your best. We don't want any of your stragglers either," replies Stryker, looking back at the others, who all nod as if to infer seven is not nearly enough.

Teacher points at seven individuals in turn. Four are young men and three are young women.

"What! You want us to fight girls? Are you sure?" Stryker asks.

"They're making a mockery of us," interrupts Igralf.

Confidence is brimming in this camp, arrogance is rampant, too. Teacher is not impressed with the behaviour of the warriors in front of him, having high opinions of themselves and a disregard for young women who they don't know anything about. Teacher gestures to his warriors to pick up their swords and shields, the tunny warriors do so dutifully.

"By what rules do we play?" asks Stryker.

"Swords remain sheathed and no excessive contact. If you are touched by a sheathed sword on the body or head you leave the field of battle," responds Teacher.

"This does seem a little unfair," retorts Stryker, "as we cannot reach the bodies, never mind the heads of your soldiers. What about legs and arms?"

"Legs and arms are usually exempt from this game. The game is not about disabling, it is about getting an outright kill."

"Accounting for our lack of height, may I add one more rule then?" Stryker asks.

"Please explain," replies Teacher.

"If we strike the legs of your warrior, he or she must kneel and fight on the spot where they have fallen."

"Agreed," Teacher responds. "Did you hear that?" he asks his students who all nod positively, indicating that they have.

In the middle of the park, where it is open and undisturbed, four jotunn warriors line up side by side. The other three line up behind them.

"Watch and learn," Stryker tells Perrywinkle and Beezle.

"Finn, I want you to stand with us, so that we might see what you are able to achieve."

The ramshackle group of over-confident men and dwarfs are joined by Finn, who looks nervous but maintains his composure. Gendralf walks away from the group to his horse. Pulling a cotton sheet out of his backpack, he covers and ties it to the head of the axe before walking back to the line.

A large gap separates the jotunn from their foes. The distance gives an element of time to both groups, enabling them to prepare against any onslaught. Preparation is key, but our heroes appear almost nonchalant in their approach. Perrywinkle and Beezle watch from the sidelines in anticipation of the 'battle' that is about to ensue.

"Are you ready?" asks Teacher of Stryker.

"Yes, of course we are ready," Stryker replies in a terse tone, whilst looking down the line.

"Then begin," orders Teacher.

Immediately, a deafening roar coming directly from tunny mouths dominates the air. The men are taken aback, eyes widen and confusion reigns. Stryker, Forester and the dwarfs did not expect this and they step back. Weapons flailing, they try to cover their ears from the sound that envelops them. The jotunn stretch their sword arms far to the side whilst their shield arms point forward. They then bring the pommel of their weapon back sharply, bashing it against the shield metal which vibrates on impact, giving out a deafening 'clang'. The ear drums of the jotunn's opponents ring violently. Stryker, Forester, the dwarfs and Finn step back a number of times, clearly in disarray. Teacher and the other pupils left on the sidelines are delighted at the impact the warriors have already had on their guests. The jotunn move one step forward, continuing to beat the pommels of swords against shields, quickly following up with a roar from deep inside their bellies. All their opponents can do is take one more backwards step. Stryker looks down the line and everybody else looks back. The eyes of these men tell a tale and they realise that they have underestimated their 'foe'.

"They're very good, aren't they?" shouts Perrywinkle over the noise towards Beezle.

"Say it again," replies Beezle, deafened by the noise.

"They're very good, aren't they?" shouts Perrywinkle, even louder.

"What?" screams Beezle.

"Never mind," gestures Perrywinkle, looking back at the 'battlefield'.

The tunny are getting closer; soon they will be upon their opponents. Stryker runs in front of the others waving his arms wildly to gain their attention. The others look at him as if he is mad. Standing in front of Igralf, he mouths one word: 'Clobber'. Igralf understands and runs towards the advancing jotunn. He stops halfway between the two groups of soldiers, and with one swing, he strikes his hammer down hard onto the ground. The impact from the hammer blow shakes the ground. Earth reverberates and cracks. A noise, more deafening than the tunny roars and beating on shields, replaces all these sounds.

Waves of grass, soil and dust ripple across the field. Jotunn fall to the ground one by one as they are caught up in it. Jotunn giants topple, and as they do so, the ground shakes even more. Teacher and the sidelined jotunn warriors on the sidelines gasp and gawp in disbelief. Stryker, Forester, the dwarfs and Finn seize the opportunity to move forward.

The jotunn quickly regain their balance, jumping back up onto their feet. But Finn is fast. Like a cheetah, he has targeted the tunny nearest to him who is still in the process of getting back up. Finn jumps onto the knee of the jotunn warrior, grabs onto his armour and makes a second jump quickly onto the back of his 'foe'. Finn's sheathed sword directs itself underneath the warrior's helmet and, in a flash, one warrior is already 'dead'. Finn jumps down off the jotunn's back. One tunny warrior leaves the field and now there are only six with which to contend. Perrywinkle claps in appreciation of the 'kill'. Stryker, Forester and the dwarfs have noticed the skill Finn has displayed and they are impressed.

In a moment, the jotunn regain their posture, form and balance. The tunny formation, at the loss of one of their compatriots, goes to four in front and two behind. Stryker and the dwarfs engage the front line whilst Finn and Forester take on the two warriors at the back.

A jotunn sword flings forward, but fails to make a hit against Stryker. Pulling back the sword, the tunny warrior swings it from right to left hoping to make contact with the long-haired, unshaven man in front. Stryker leans backwards and then to the side to avoid the swing. Men, dwarfs and elf cannot get anywhere near to the jotunn warriors. Every time they make a run or lunge at them, a shield blocks or a sword attacks, prompting the men to engage in a moment's retreat. Finn, with his ability to jump high and jump wide, tries to perplex his giant opponent with quick movements left and right and up in the air, but to no avail. Jotunn reflexes are not as slow and laboured as you would imagine them to be. The giants are invariably thinking about every move ahead of time. They are clever enough to defend, whilst catching out their 'enemies' with a penetrating attack in the same instant. Stryker calls the men back to a safe position away from the tunny; there needs to be a change in style of attack. Calling a timeout, all of them huddle together.

"I suggest we seek not to take on one each but all of us attack just one target, and whittle them down one by one."

"Agreed, though I suggest half of us go for one, whilst the other half protect the flanks from the others," suggests Igralf. The attack formation is a clever one. The thinking behind it is to restrict the jotunn from utilising all six warriors on the battlefield, putting pressure onto one individual.

"Good idea. Forester, Wattlespalf and Igralf, you take the flanks and protect Finn, Gendralf and myself from the others moving in," orders Stryker. "Ready?" Stryker calls out to the jotunn.

"Ready," replies one of the jotunn.

"We'll take that one first," orders Stryker, pointing at a young woman.

The men rush towards the female jotunn warrior, seeing her as a potential weak link. Judging her by her gender, they immediately get a shock as she swipes her sword close to the ground, making Stryker jump high up in the air and the dwarfs fall heavily onto the hard earth. The swipe is followed with a forceful thrust forward of her shield which hits Stryker mid-air, sending him flying and then crashing to the floor with a thud. Her sword flies down towards Stryker in order to finish him off, but Gendralf's axe knocks the point of her sword away just before she can claim victory.

Forester, Igralf and Wattlespalf prevent the other three warriors on the jotunn front line from closing and coming to the assistance of the singled-out female. Two jotunn warriors at the back are effectively useless as they are unable to join the fight. And then, as she is distracted by Stryker and Gendralf, Finn finds his chance to rush underneath the jotunn soldier's attack. Unfurling his sword, he brandishes it against the legs of the warrior. She is disabled and kneels down, accepting her fate. The jotunn warriors call a timeout, much to Stryker's chagrin. The attack, this time at least, has worked.

"Well done, Finn. You are definitely a warrior in the making. Talking of warriors, we have been fighting them for a good while now and we have taken only one and disabled another. How do we beat them? By now a goblin army would have fallen," asks a frustrated Gendralf. "Their reach is so long that we can't get close enough to them to do any serious damage."

"I agree. I fear the only way to bring these warriors to heel is with a barrage of arrows. Even then I can imagine an arrow piercing their skin will feel like a pin prick as opposed to a deathly blow," adds Igralf.

"Look, we're playing games here. We have been asked to test them. There is no contest," says Stryker. "What do you all think? Can these men and women fight on a battlefield?"

"Stryker, we cannot compare what we are doing here to a battlefield scenario." Forester is concerned. "They are not looking at death here. Imagine if they were to see their comrades being felled one by one."

"Every warrior needs to experience bloodshed. Our eyes have all had to endure a first kill, be it with our own sword or watching someone else do it," responds Wattlespalf.

"I suppose you're right. They are frightening when they move. I think goblins would be beside themselves with fear if they saw these men and women approaching. You've got to give them their due," concedes Forester.

"Are you ready?" shouts over one of the jotunn.

"Are we ready?" asks Stryker, turning around, hoping to test these warriors some more.

"Hang on, Finn. What about Lerwin the sword? It allows you to see the near future and you haven't tested it yet. Why don't you try it out on the jotunn for good measure?" asks Gendralf, knowing that this breaks a number of rules and boundaries.

"But that would be cheating. I believe my weapons will do

what the Queen's note says they will do. I think it would be better to use their skills when I need them most rather than on a whim," Finn replies, a little cross at Gendralf's suggestion.

"Just reviewing our options," Gendralf replies, holding his hand up apologetically.

Meanwhile, Beezle and Perrywinkle have lain down in the sun and are looking upwards at the sky.

"Can you see that man walking his dog?" asks Perrywinkle pointing at a cloud formation to his left.

Beezle looks for a while, letting his eyes dream a little and replies, "Oh yes, it's quite a big dog, isn't it?"

"Yes, it is," responds Perrywinkle.

Swords clink and clash in the background, but Beezle and Perrywinkle are content to ignore it.

"Ooh, can you see the crab with his big pincers over there?" asks an excited Beezle pointing directly above. "I've seen them by the seaside. We used to explore the seashore quite a lot, myself, my father and Finn." This game is new to him and it fires up his interest and tickles his imagination.

"Yes, I can. You wouldn't want those pincers nipping you," replies Perrywinkle. "What about the apple with an arrow in it over there?"

"Wow, yes! This is such a good game, Perrywinkle. What about the one which looks like the rod in my brother's backpack or… the monster's face over there or… the man with a sword in his head over there?" he continues, pointing at images all around.

"You're beginning to see some pretty strange things, Beezle," Perrywinkle winces. He is a little taken aback by the little elf's imagination. This game was meant to be fun, not horrific.

"Clouds are brilliant, aren't they?" enthuses Beezle, ignoring Perrywinkle's words. He does not answer. Both lie on the ground for a while, looking up into the clouds. It is hypnotic, and it is not long before both of them become sleepy and decide to take a nap.

Greybeard returns from his meeting with Parva. A crowd has gathered on the sidelines of the park, watching their warriors intently as they battle against other creatures of note. Thundercloud winds his way around the bodies in the crowd.

Greybeard appears downbeat but maintains a happy face as

he trots up to Teacher. Getting off his horse, he stands next to the giant and looks upon the contest. He sees that the jotunn, men, dwarfs and Finn are equally matched in this encounter.

Teacher appears to be more intent on watching Greybeard's men as their skill is technically good, and there have been some good tips and tricks to be stolen. What is noticeable is that the tunny are tiring; the tactic now being used by the men and dwarfs is not to expend energy. They must wait, be patient and let the jotunn work harder than they do.

Greybeard turns to Teacher. "Your warriors are very good. How long is it since they began their fight?"

"Oh, about an hour!" exclaims Teacher proudly.

"An hour... that is a very long time. They must have an abundance of energy to have outlasted my men," replies Greybeard graciously. "Shall we call them off now? I think they have done more than enough battling for today."

"Yes, I think it would be wise. They'll all sleep tonight, I dare say," responds Teacher. Teacher whistles with his fingers loudly. The battle stops. Beezle and Perrywinkle wake with a stir. Teacher gestures for everyone to come back in. The exercise has finished.

"You have taught them well, Teacher." Greybeard claps, secretly hoping he can gain this army's support after Parva's refusal.

"Thank you, Greybeard. It means a lot to me that someone so esteemed as yourself would make that comment." Teacher takes Greybeard's words as testament to his success with these pupils. It has been his life's work to teach, and he has practically taught everyone within this town's walls the arts of battle.

Lots of patting of backs and legs, depending on what height you are, is happening in the distance. Smiles and laughter are exchanged between the two groups of soldiers. You can see conversations and relationships are in the process of developing, driven by a mutual respect for each other. Greybeard tries to seize on this moment of mutual admiration by striking up a conversation with Teacher, revealing his real needs and intentions. Greybeard's hope is that Teacher is untouched by Parva's influence. After all, she does not want to be an influence to these people any longer, preferring instead that they find their own paths.

"Teacher, I have come to your town for a reason. I am in search of warriors and fate, it appears, has brought me here to you."

"Why would you ever need to find warriors? Is it not peaceful outside these walls?" asks Teacher.

"No, it most certainly is not. There is a goblin uprising and it threatens to become a lot bigger than it ought to be. My problem is this – I do not have the men to quell the uprising and I need your help," Greybeard reveals. Jotunn warriors listen in on the conversation, curious and alarmed by the content of Greybeard's last statement.

"And what does Parva say?" asks Teacher.

"Parva does not want any part of it. She will not advise your warriors to partake in this quest," replies a despondent Greybeard.

"Then we cannot help you," Teacher responds bluntly.

"This is a decision for you and your warriors, not Parva. She is not your leader and she wants you to make this important decision for yourselves," comments Greybeard. "The tunny were once great warriors and feared throughout Everlast. Tales of your feats are still remembered all over this land. The warriors that stand before me now have been taught well and I am sure that they can help in our cause."

"Whilst I want to help you, Greybeard, and would relish the chance to go into battle, I cannot. I will listen only to Parva. If she does not want it then we will not go."

"She does not, but think hard, Teacher – these goblins and their leader will not stop. They will arrive at your doors someday, and by that time there may not be anybody left to help you and your kind."

"I would come and help you," pipes up one jotunn warrior in the crowd who has been listening in.

"I would, too," shouts another at the back of the throng.

"This is what we have been trained for."

"Ay, the cause is a good one."

Soon there is a chorus of approval from those who want to go out and help these small men in this matter. Greybeard's party all smile – there is hope after all. It is a sign that the young tunny want to push their boundaries and that they want things to change. These young men and women are eager to make these important decisions, governing their own actions rather than relying on another. Maybe Parva was right, people are beginning to make their own decisions, but maybe it was the younger generations she was referring to.

"Please," Greybeard calls out to everyone, "do not think this is a game. Your very lives are at stake if you help us. It is likely that some of you will perish, and at the very least, you will see things, terrible things that you have never seen before. At the very worst you may have to do terrible things yourself – and you must be prepared to kill another creature in order to protect your life and the lives of your comrades."

"You are talking out of turn, old man," seethes Teacher. "None of you will be leaving with these men," he orders, pointing into the crowd of young men and women. "I will see Parva. Whatever she advises will determine the direction we follow."

Looking through the crowd and back up the cobbled path from where he came, Greybeard is sure he can see Parva and Celia watching. He is distracted momentarily by a passing jotunn who blocks his view. The giant passes, and the spot where he thought Parva and Celia were standing is empty.

"Must have been my mind playing tricks," Greybeard mumbles, rubbing his eyes.

Teacher walks off towards Parva's house. He huffs a little as he is not used to his pupils questioning his judgment, or Parva's for that matter. Greybeard's men have clearly been a bad influence, and the havoc already caused erupted only hours after they first arrived. But there is something stirring inside Teacher. Having never left this town, barely walking a few steps outside the walls, he has always dreamed of getting out, visiting other places and other peoples in this world. Maybe he could come on this adventure and fight, if it were allowed to happen. He was a good fighter when he was young, and he's still young enough to raise a sword. Maybe he could be the general of this army? As he walks closer and closer to Parva's home, he becomes more and more convinced that he wants to join Greybeard and his men.

Knocking on the door to Celia and Parva's house, Teacher feels as if he has a battle of his own to overcome: he will try to gain Parva's blessing to go to war. The door is answered by Celia, and as always, he is invited in. Teacher is one of only a few jotunn who have consulted personally with Parva, knowing what she is and what she looks like. She tends to remain behind a screen in one of the upper rooms when talking to other members of this large community, and as such, she is considered somewhat of an enigma. Celia plays her part, too. Parva's talent has rubbed off on her, and they both bounce ideas off one another now when the question or idea being asked is a complicated one.

"Hello, Celia," Teacher gives her a peck on each cheek.

"Hello," replies Celia. "It's been a long while since we have seen you grace this house."

"Oh, I've been busy doing one thing or another. I'm wary that the years are rolling by just that little bit too quickly of late," the old man in Teacher grumbles.

"So you've been graced by dear Greybeard's presence, then. I presume that is why you are here?" the voice of Parva utters from behind Celia.

"Yes, yes, erm, it has been a very interesting day – it has opened my eyes to many things, and to be quite frank, I was a little rude to him before I left the fields to come here," he reflects. "I must remember to apologise when I get back."

"I, too, was a little coarse with him. Please give him my apologies as well," she says. "So, Teacher, I suppose you are here for a piece of advice?"

"I am, madam."

"And what is your question?"

"My question is this – do you think we should support Greybeard in his quest and go to battle against the evil of which he talks?"

"The question you ask is a very complicated one. Neither I nor Celia will answer it. Instead, I am going to ask you a very important question in response and take this as my advice. What do you think you should do?"

Teacher ponders for a while. "I would very much like to go, Parva. I have dreamt of it since I was young… leaving this place and lending my skills to other creatures, that is. But I have never acted upon my dreams, and as time gets short, I believe I must take my chance."

"Well done. You have quite clearly made your decision," reveals a smiling Parva. Celia smiles too, although there is a tear waiting in her eye. She regards Teacher as a close friend and fears that if he leaves, he might never come back.

"One more question, Teacher. We saw in the park that your pupils were keen to join Greybeard's men. You are their teacher, so how will you choose what is best for them?" asks Celia.

Teacher goes quiet. 'Choose for others?' he thinks. 'How can I choose to take people to their deaths? I have taught and trained them from when they were very young. Greybeard told them what they were up against, this must dissuade some. I know them... and their strengths and their weaknesses. I can find out who wants to join, and I can sort out who is capable.' His mind asks many questions and eventually it gives him an answer.

"Give them the facts. Let them choose and be responsible for their choices, but protect them as far as I can. Most of them have already made their minds up anyway."

"Teacher, you are beginning to find your way," comments Celia. "Now go and become responsible for your future, and teach them to become responsible for theirs."

Teacher bends down and kisses Parva on the cheek. He hugs Celia. Opening the front door, he looks back, waves and heads outside onto the cobbled paths. Celia closes the door behind him. She turns to Parva and grins, still with tears in her eyes.

"Do you think we have done the right thing?" she asks Parva.

"Only time will tell," she replies.

Teacher walks with a spring in his step back up towards the park where everyone waits for him. He feels that a weight has been lifted from his shoulders. Not wanting to give anything away, he strolls towards the warriors. The crowd that watched the fighting earlier on has dispersed; only a few children remain and they are playing on the swings, slide and climbing frame. Soldiers from both sides wait anxiously to find out what the final decision might be. Some sit or lie on the ground in quiet solitude. Some sharpen swords or practise moves in their own area of space. Some talk amongst each other, asking questions of the dwarfs and men about what life is like on the outside.

Stryker is teaching Finn. Whilst Finn fights well, he lacks agility in his wrists, which is hindering his swordplay. Stryker is teaching him how to position himself to get maximum power and poise from the sword he is wielding, but the necessary changes that Finn must work on are minor.

"So, how did the young elf do?" asks Greybeard, walking towards Stryker and Finn.

"Oh, he's very good – Finn is very good indeed. He gave all of us a run for our money," replies a very complimentary Stryker.

"Really, why doesn't that surprise me?" smiles Greybeard. "Good, well we needn't worry about you now. Your brother is a different matter, eh?"

"Yes, sir. I'm pleased that I've been able to impress. I surprised myself. I've never been in a situation like that before, a battle that is."

"It will stand you in good stead, young elf. Dangerous times lie ahead," warns Greybeard.

Everyone's attention is suddenly caught by Teacher returning from his visit to Parva, and those who weren't already standing get to their feet. Teacher stops on the sidelines in front of the nervous jotunn, men, dwarfs and elves in front of him. Pausing for some time, he searches his mind to find the right words to express himself well.

"Did everybody hear Greybeard before I left? This is not a game. You are likely to see terrible things and you will be called upon to perform terrible acts, which will include taking lives. Once you have seen this, you will be changed – some will be affected badly by it. You must be prepared for every possibility, including your own death." Teacher stops.

Greybeard's head bows and his shoulders slump, believing that Teacher is in the process of dismantling his words. The wizard is just waiting for that particular word to be uttered so as to confirm it and that word is…'No'.

"You are potentially going to sacrifice your lives for people you do not know and who quite possibly do not care about you," he continues. Greybeard's ears prick up; could it be that there is a twist to this tale? "But there is a possibility that by marching out to help save these creatures, you may also have a hand in saving our people. It may be equally true that if we need help in times not far from now, we might be remembered for our sacrifices and friends will hopefully come to help us."

"I will make sure of it," Greybeard mutters to himself.

"I am going to give you one night to decide your fate. Many of you have done so already. Tomorrow morning as the sun rises, if it pleases our guests, we will set out against the foe."

Greybeard nods. "Thank you, Teacher."

"I expect you to pack lightly. Come in full battle dress and make sure your swords are sharp and your shields are ready. Have a good night's rest." Teacher ends his speech here. There is much cheering and it can be heard all around the town. Warriors walk and talk amongst themselves as they leave the park, excited at the adventure lying ahead. Teacher stays behind.

"Have you got anywhere to stay for the night?" asks Teacher of Greybeard.

"No, we will be quite happy here, and I think more comfortable if the size of your houses is anything to go by. We have scaled enough mountains on this journey already," Greybeard replies jovially.

"Ha! I understand. I will see you tomorrow," responds Teacher. He begins to walk off, but then stops and turns back round to face the wizard. "Oh, erm… Parva and I would like to apologise for being so rude to you earlier on. She told me to tell you."

"Don't apologise – it is understandable that my request came as a shock. It is not every day that you are asked to go to war. My words can also be a little insensitive at times."

Teacher waves awkwardly, nodding his head at the same time as he leaves the park. The blond and curly-haired boys approach soon after Teacher's departure with what appears to be a hamper, a big bottle of wine and a keg of ale. As you would imagine, all the items are oversized and more than ample.

"We thought you might forget about the fillets of gulp fish."

"Forget about food! Never," interrupts Wattlespalf.

"Anyway, we went to collect them for you and it turns out that the market traders had put together a few things for you to eat." The blond-haired boy puts the hamper on the floor, opening its large heavy lid.

Inside the hamper is a feast of food. Bread, butter, cheese, ham, tomatoes, cucumbers, lettuce, apples and a big cake are all pulled out one by one. Other things are packed in there as well, such as children's mugs, just right for men of this size, along with toy knives, forks, spoons and bowls made out of wood. At the very bottom of the hamper is a large brown pot and in that pot is the gulp fish, which have been cooked with herbs, spices, vegetables, cream and a bit of bacon. They smell absolutely delicious.

"This is very, very kind of you. Can you give everybody a big 'thank you' from us all? I suspect we will not get the chance to do it ourselves before we leave. We're leaving very early in the morning," Greybeard asks of the blond and curly-haired young men.

"We will, but you might be quite surprised," replies the curly-haired boy with a snigger, before running off quickly towards the houses. Greybeard is intrigued as to why he would say something so cryptic.

The men, dwarfs and elves sit around eating food from the picnic whilst drinking ale and wine. The sun sets behind the town walls and everyone is upbeat, as the day has seen a lot done and a lot achieved. As the sky darkens, the men can see silhouettes of giants from behind the curtains in their homes. Some are clearly packing; others are being hugged by people they love, whilst some argue with those who love them. As lights are put out in the houses, the creatures sitting in the park know that it is time to go to sleep. The air is still humid and warm, and it is comfortable enough to sleep without the luxury of a soft duvet; lying on the ground never felt so good.

A few hours pass in the night before Greybeard wakes with a jolt; he can hear his oric talking to him. Warrior is calling. He gets up and wanders away from the field. No one wakes up to see him leave, and no one knows where he has gone. The wizard does not return until the early light of morning before anybody is awake.

CHAPTER 17

DEATH OF A TOWN

An old woman sits in a rocking chair on a balcony, overlooking the town of Paledon. Her long, flowing white dress, decorated with small yellow and red flowers, hangs off the rocking chair, almost covering her brown sandaled feet. The view she has is a good one as this woman's residence is the tallest in town. An open square surrounds the house; the old woman's house is the centre point of it. From the balcony, unhindered views of the houses on the outer edges of the square, as well as the countryside beyond this town, can be seen. Streets which should be full of people at this time of day are empty as everyone has run away from Paledon to the city of Fricas. The few people who remain also look out, much like the old woman, from their balconies or from the flat-topped roofs of their houses. No resistance to Warrior or the goblins will be put up in this town. Struggling bodies carried out of homes, or at best, men and women brandishing old swords, is all that can be hoped for here. In the distance, plumes of smoke rise upwards towards the blue skies above; these plumes each represent a village under attack – or worse, destroyed.

The old woman's husband is downstairs making tea and preparing a few slices of cake. Having wavy grey hair and a clean-shaven appearance, he is determined to keep his standards high even though he has no one to impress. So it is that he wears his finest brown suit and a crisp white shirt underneath it, finished off with a shining pair of brown leather shoes. Both the old man and old woman have resolved to treat themselves before the monsters arrive in town. Rather than feel forsaken, they hope to ride out this storm tucked safely away in the walls of the house. You see, some houses have been made to be special, and this one has a secret corridor hidden in the library behind one of the bookcases – it has been built for these kinds of moments. The dark and undecorated corridor runs round the whole house, on all levels. Spiders have found their way into this dark place and hundreds of cobwebs dominate the walls and ceilings of it.

The house is one of the tallest in town because it is the official residence of the local mayor; official residences tend to be grand and domineering, you know. The old man and woman are the mayor and mayoress; this is why they will not leave, as they feel duty-bound to remain here, much like captains of sinking ships. Their whole lives have been entwined with this quiet little town that stands in the shadow of the city of Fricas. Paledon has stood here proudly for years, although over the next day or so its existence will be callously ended.

Birds of all colours and sizes fly out of the woods from the direction of the blinny approach, through the town and away from it as fast as they possibly can. Whatever is coming must be terrifying. On the edges of this town, the old woman rocking in her rocking chair can see and hear the rampaging hordes from her balcony. Blinny come out from the trees and along paths. Upon seeing these horrors she whimpers, taking in deep breaths to calm herself down.

The road to Paledon passed without incident as villages were swept aside with little or no resistance. The expected armies never materialised, pleasing Warrior; the impact of his tactics has obviously paid huge dividends. No army means no hope, or at least hope is reliant on the might of cities, where men are captive with nowhere else to go. It has taken only a day to reach Paledon and it is only just starting to go dark. The goblin army is somewhat bare at present, as legions still make their way to this town after a hard day's work, but they will all be here soon.

For today at least the bloodshed and burning have stopped. Whilst Warrior's goblins celebrate, he will try his hand at breaking the wizard's spell upon his oric. Tomorrow, Paledon will be razed to the ground and the march on Fricas will begin, before moving further north towards Milias in the east.

The old man sits on the balcony with his wife and watches the sunset, possibly for the last time. They cannot avert their eyes from the fires lighting up at the edge of the town, knowing it is surrounded by a darker force. Blinny drink and dance round fires, very much aware that there will be no army to greet them this night.

The mayor drinks his tea and eats his cake, savouring the taste

Goblins making merry around the fire

of both whilst listening to the raucous noise coming from the blinny camp.

"That is an invading army, for sure," the mayor comments calmly. "I have never seen an army of that size in all my time here on this land."

"How do you think the city will fair? Surely an army of that size is more than a match for those poor souls hidden behind the city walls," asks the mayoress.

"You might well be right, dear. There are too few men to guard it and too many monsters invading it. They might have a chance if the walls hold out – if the walls or the gates fall, it will not bode well," answers the mayor.

"And what of us? When do you think they will come to take us?"

"I don't know, dear. By the sound of it, the goblins are making merry. It is unlikely they will attack as a unit tonight, but some may stray into the town if they are curious enough."

He glides his hand over the table that separates him from his wife and touches her hand lovingly. Smiling at each other, quietly they both sigh at what was and what might be.

"Shall we retire into the walls, dear?" asks the mayoress.

"I think it might be a good idea. It's getting dark now," replies the mayor.

"Come on, then – up you get," orders the mayoress with a bittersweet playfulness, enacting days gone by. Both get up out of their seats and walk into the library, which is adjacent to the balcony. Opening a secret door (masquerading as a bookcase full of books), a secret passage is revealed where the old man and woman will sleep tonight. Walking slowly through it, they close the door behind them. Even tonight, both are wary that little monsters might approach them in their sleep.

Warrior has left the site of the goblin camp on the outskirts of Paledon. He needs some peace and quiet away from his goblin army, which is being raucous and crude.

Pompucket and Bobbucket are enjoying drinking ale. They and their clan dance and sing as best a goblin can (that is, not very well at all). Pets guard the camp; they will wait patiently for their master to return.

Warrior needs to break the spell that has been put on his oric, blinding it from the movements of Greybeard and his small band of men. The master who hides behind the green light has ordered it and Warrior dare not defy his wishes. Finding a fallen tree that sits in a position where the town can be overlooked, Warrior unsheathes his sword and sits on its trunk. He points the blade of his sword to the ground between his legs. Looking forward into the cross-guard of the sword, he consults the red oric sitting in the centre of it and tries to break through the wall Greybeard has raised against him. Light shines out from the red oric as it tries hard, under the guidance of Warrior, to shatter the darkness placed upon it, but to no avail. Warrior's emotionless stare, hidden by the rotting face of another, belies his true feelings of frustration and anger at both himself and his foe. When they finally meet, he and Greybeard, Warrior dreams of ripping him apart and removing his face; this will be his ultimate gesture. He tries again and mumbles words this time, as he seeks to give more of himself to the red oric, which responds by burning ever more brightly.

The goblins in the distance have stopped dancing. Deformed faces turn away a little, protecting their eyes from a blinding brightness even though it shines from a distance away. Indeed, those left in Paledon who have not yet retired to their hiding places look out from their roofs, balconies and windows wondering what manner of power they see.

The pressure intensifies in Warrior's mind; he feels pain in his head and body, and energy saps from every pore as he puts more and more effort into breaking Greybeard's hold against him. The red oric fizzes, buzzes and then gives out a scream, which gets louder and louder until the light and sound coming from it stops. For only a second does the silence last, ending in a huge bang which reverberates outward for miles and miles. The bang is so loud that the blinny are knocked off their feet, houses in Paledon shudder and people lying in their beds in the city of Fricas wake with a jolt. Warrior has felt the worst of it, though. He has been propelled through the air for a few metres or so, and being flung against a stray branch, his armour is pierced. The damage is ever so slight, but now a small hole the size of a pea can clearly be seen on the back of Warrior's right shoulder. Meanwhile, Warrior's sword stands upright in the same spot, unmoved, as if nothing had ever happened.

Warrior can see movement in the red oric. He gets up and walks to his sword before staring into the oric, wondering if he has broken Greybeard's spell. True enough, he can see Greybeard looking back at him.

"Ha, ha, ha." Warrior laughs. "I have beaten the old wizard and his trick."

What happens next surprises Warrior, for it is not he who has broken the old man's spell, it is the old man himself who has allowed this meeting to take place. Whilst Warrior can see Greybeard's face looking back at him sternly, Greybeard can also see him and he has words for this monster.

"You – monster! I know you can hear me," shouts Greybeard, his calls aimed at Warrior.

Warrior takes a step backwards, startled that it is he who has been infiltrated. Greybeard holds back a slight sense of fear for this armoured beast; the view of the decomposing mask enough for him to feel sickened.

"Do you know how much harm you have caused Everlast? You have taken the elves from us and now you exact punishment on men, but know this… I am coming for you and have no doubt that you will be defeated at the hands of my army," spits the wizard.

"It is you who will fall. You and your armies are no match for me and mine," Warrior's dulcet tones threaten.

Greybeard looks back unimpressed. This old man has wrestled with his thoughts as to whether he should tell Warrior about the rod. Could doubt seep its way into the mind of Warrior if he were told, exposing a weakness? Or would it reinforce his wariness and therefore strengthen his guard against attack? By not telling him, will Finn have the element of surprise needed to catch Warrior out? Does he know of it and does he know his power would be greater with it? Examining the questions and subsequent answers he tells himself to keep any talk of it quiet for now. But there is one thing he will reveal, which may or may not plant a seed, prompting Warrior to examine himself.

"I know your weakness," reveals Greybeard. "Oh and don't expect your full complement of men, I have seen to that. Everlast at this time is more resilient than you could know, and it is already fighting against you where you cannot see it. Beware, Warrior, I'm coming to get you and yours."

The old man had anticipated Warrior's call to arms, and the messengers that would be sent to all corners of this land to draft goblin soldiers. Greybeard, from his home on Crescent Moon Mountain, had sent dozens of white doves to all the kingdoms of all the creatures in all this land. He implored those that received his note to engage the goblin packs that wandered their lands before it was too late. Kings and queens all over read with interest the messages they received. Some consulted their wizards, and some consulted their advisors, and some were so resolute in their commitment that they sought no advice at all. Soldiers and armies from most, if not all, these kingdoms in the north, east and west in particular responded fast and sure, finding and beating down the blinny and their ogre pets with no mercy. Not all goblins were caught, of course, but many were. Now Warrior, acknowledging Greybeard's words, knows that his army can never be at full strength. Greybeard's face disappears out of Warrior's sight as his red oric appears to switch off. The wizard has re-installed his spell and Warrior will not be able to break it.

Warrior stands, seemingly unmoved and silent in front of his sword. Greybeard has indeed plunged him into deep thought. His pets and General Glum arrive to see that their king has not been harmed.

"We heard the bang and we saw you fall, sire," says Glum.

"Leave me. I am not hurt," Warrior's deep voice orders.

"But sir... "

"Leave me," Warrior shouts, keeping his pierced armour out of the sight of his general. Any realisation that Warrior is not indestructible may prompt a backlash from his army. Everything that has been achieved thus far might unfold in an instant. General Glum immediately runs back towards the goblin army none the wiser. Pets are allowed to stay.

Warrior turns to his oric. "Heal my armour." This is no sooner said than done. One stream of liquid red light slowly curves and sways its way towards Warrior's shoulder. Reaching his armour, the red liquid stream of light fastens itself onto the metal where the wound has been sustained. It then turns to metal, quickly filling the hole in the armour and returning it to its previous condition, before releasing itself, curving and swaying back to its point of origin. Warrior stretches his arm, hands and fingers. Touching the plate that was damaged on the back of his shoulder, he caresses it gently before sitting back on the trunk, putting his hands on his knees.

The rotten-faced monster remains seated until morning. Pets lie at his feet. A beautiful red sun peers over the horizon. The sun lights anything and everything that can be seen in the near and far distance, from Paledon to Fricas and beyond. Warrior stands up quickly, startling his pets. They growl grumpily as they are awoken. A resolute Warrior begins to take large steps back towards the goblin encampment outside of Paledon. This is the last day this town will stand, and Warrior is determined that he will play his part in its destruction. Goblins awaken all over the camp, excited by the day that lies ahead, unaware of Warrior's failings last night. Dreaming of Fricas' downfall, they agree that the burning of Paledon will be a good start to the proceedings.

General Glum waits on the edge of the camp, watching Warrior approach; pets follow behind.

"Sir, what would you have us do? We await your command," asks the tall, chubby general.

Warrior says nothing, raises his sword and points it into the town casually. A red orb-like bolt, the size of a melon, flies out from the sword and into the houses closest to him. The bolt hits the house, shattering first the front wall and then several walls behind, eventually leaving a hole through not one, not two, but three houses. Warrior can see through these three houses onto the street behind. The blinny have not seen this power before, as Warrior has tended to direct this army but not engage his enemies. Now the goblins know a little more of what he is capable of, they are sure that they have not seen nearly enough.

Warrior gestures his sword towards the city with the words, "Burn it."

Immediately, Glum orders that archers line up and face towards the town. Dipping bandaged arrows into buckets of flammable liquids carried by small, runt-like goblins, archers light arrow after arrow. Hundreds of burning arrows are held aloft, waiting on the command to let fly. The order comes, and in a flash, waves and waves of fire climb up and then beat down upon the houses of Paledon, onto roofs, through windows and into walls. The impact of the fire is instant as well-aired buildings full of cloth, paper and wood enrage the flames, which multiply quickly, engulfing everything. Men and women are flushed out of their homes as smoke and fire bellows out, making them breathless and hot. After the initial attacks from the fire-breathing arrows, foot soldiers and pikemen flood into the town, killing unarmed men and women escaping from the fires.

Drummers drum, giving the blinny a beat to work to. A constant, rhythmic rallying call is menacing and ultimately deadly. The goblin army wreaks its destruction against houses and the remaining townsfolk, dancing and whistling to the beat of the drums as they do so.

Half of the army will attack from the edges of this town, following the paths and the open fields around it. After all, thousands upon thousands of monsters piling into a small town would only stifle the speed of this attack. Cavalry and carts pulled by barghest shadow those attacking from the outskirts.

"Bobbucket, follow me! Let's have some fun. If we're gonna get some men then we need to be quick," enthuses Pompucket.

"Yes, of course. I'll be right there behind you – go and enjoy yourself," replies Bobbucket, hoping to fall behind so that he can avoid doing anything nasty and horrid.

"What d'yer say, Bobbucket? Didn't understand yer ramblings. Come on, follow me. I'll teach yer how to skin one of 'em," urges Pompucket. The crowd heaves and hos, pushing the clans and the individuals within them apart. Bobbucket is separated from his clan and all the better, he thinks, as he can get away with not doing any fighting at all.

A skinny man with sword held high holds his shirt against his mouth as he tries to deflect the smoke from his lungs. This man has no chance, but he chooses to fight honourably and to the end. A group of a dozen goblins rush towards him – one of them is Pompucket.

"Come on, you measly waste of meat. Not much of you to go round, is there?" Pompucket roars. The man swings his sword to the left and the right, beating away the attacks from pikes, but as the blinny get close, he is pierced by one. Bending over in pain,

Pompucket's sword hacks its way through the man's skin on his back again and again.

Pompucket screams, "'Ere, have it, have another... 'ere have more. Go on, die, will you?" Blood spills and splatters around the skinny man. Goblins sniff the warm blood in the air. A wide-eyed Pompucket licks the man's blood from his blade in appreciation. It is then that the frenzy begins and the man becomes breakfast.

Watching the destruction from their balcony are the old man and woman. This house has not yet been touched but fires rage on in front of them. The archers who caused the damage are moving forward for a second attack, which will no doubt engulf this house. Heads turn as they see old friends fall violently to the ground. It is not the world that they are used to, and their hearts beat in disgust and dismay at the events unfolding.

"It is time to go," says the old woman, tears welling up in her eyes.

"Come on, my love. Let us retreat into the walls then," replies the old man, putting his arm round her whilst holding a sword in his other hand for protection.

"We're not going to survive this, are we?" she says, terrified.

"We just need to hide for long enough. If we can get into the cellar as they leave this place, we can make it," reassures the old man.

The morning sun has been replaced with clouds – rain is coming. Sensing this, Warrior pushes his way to the front of the goblin army, followed by Glum and his lieutenants.

"Destroy everything in front of you, apart from this building," he orders, pointing towards the mayoral residence. "We will need it for a little while." The archers ready themselves ahead of the rest of the army, and carry out their second attack against this town. Everything is consumed with fire apart from the building hiding the mayor and mayoress. Thick, grey clouds rally and rain begins to fall lightly.

Warrior walks towards the mayoral building with his pets, Glum and lieutenants in tow. The building is much bigger than the others, but the same in design. Clean, straight, red tiles sit comfortably on the pointed roof, overlapping one another. The shell of the building is made of a white limestone; the stones used to build this place are large, wide and smoothly cut. The building is four floors high and two rooms wide. Balconies surrounded by flowers and grape vines line the second and third floors. The fourth floor, in contrast to the others, has one room covered and another that is treated as an open-air roof terrace, where the mayor and mayoress would often entertain when important guests came to visit. Two strong, wooden doors with strong, cast-iron locks are well-oiled and dark in colour. The front doors open inwards, leading through to the first room of the house. Wooden window flaps open out, settling flat against the stone walls, allowing light to filter into the rooms. When closed, the window flaps keep the flies, attracted to the candlelight, out of the house in the evening.

Goblins and ogres pile forward, causing more destruction. Pompucket, having finished his deadly assault and subsequent meal of one member of this town, searches through houses untouched by fiery arrows for more. Bobbucket, in contrast, remains right at the back of the line away from the action. He dips in and out of deserted streets, trying to keep out of trouble – and more importantly, a good distance from his brethren.

Warrior wanders around the ground floor of the mayoral house, touching nothing but looking at everything. The ceilings are high, which is all the better; Warrior can move round freely in this place. This floor of the building is designated for official mayoral business. A waiting room is the first area that greets Warrior. Rows of neatly-placed wooden chairs fill the room. These chairs had once found themselves regularly filled by the men and women who waited for the mayor to see them. In the waiting room, the people he would see ranged from those with disputes over land and cattle to suspected criminals and members of the wider council. An ornate door, with deer, cattle, rabbits, dragons, eagles, horses, trees and men hand-carved onto it, separates the waiting room from the mayoral office.

Warrior opens the ornately-decorated door; the immediate view inside is one of panelled wood on the walls. A large, wooden desk is filled with parchment, feathered pens and different coloured inks. The Paledon flag stands tall and proud behind the desk – it is a black and white chequered flag with a bull in its centre and a sun with a smiling face in the abdomen of that said bull. Shelves filled with thick old books stick out from the panelled walls, and a suit of armour stands tall against the wall next to the door leading into this room. Next to the armour, a painting depicts the current mayor when he was younger, suited in the exact same armour. Warrior notices that the sword accompanying the suit of armour is missing; he wonders if the mayor took his sword when he left this town... or whether he is still here, waiting.

Behind the walls on the second floor, the old man and woman move slowly along the hidden corridor so as not to make any sound. The mayor carries his sword beside him, just in case they are found. Warrior's pets, unlike their master, have gone up the stairs and are sniffing out anyone who might be hidden from view. Putting their noses into the air they pick up a scent – they are excited and intrigued by it. Up and down the floors, in and out of rooms, the pets run frantically, trying to make sense of the smell. Any door that is closed they strike down with their long-fingered hands. In the hidden corridor, behind the walls, the mayor and mayoress can hear the banging and clanging upstairs. Disturbed by this, they are scared that if they are found terrible, terrible things will happen to them.

"Map carrier, unfurl the map," Warrior asks the map-carrying lieutenant.

"Yes, sire. Where do you want it?" asks the lieutenant.

Warrior remains silent. The lieutenant understands that he has upset Warrior with his seeming lack of intelligence. Quickly making his way to the mayoral desk, parchments, pens and inks are unceremoniously swept off it, and the map is unfolded and secured in its place. Marks denoting the villages visited and burned already fill the map. Warrior looks down upon the map at Paledon's position on it, and searches out the available routes to the walls of Fricas. It reveals a river to the left of Paledon, running up to the western side of the city. At the right-hand side of it is a stretch of wooded land leading up to and behind the north-eastern walls of the city. The wooded land hides a valley, which in theory, a small goblin army could travel along quickly. On the other side of the valley is Windrush Forest, where our two elves were born and raised. Apart from the river and the woods, either side of the city there are only flat plains between

246

Paledon and Fricas; these open lands mean that any hope of a surprise attack is lost.

Warrior's pets have identified the scent of the old man and woman, and have been sent mad with the lust for blood. In the library, wild rampant pets run at the bookcase and walls which hide the corridor and stairs behind. Talons, at the end of long fingers, screech and scrape against the walls as the pets try to dig into the brick. The old man and woman descend the stairs onto the ground floor quietly. They can hear the commotion upstairs; the old woman shrieks the quietest of shrieks so as not to alert anyone to her fear.

"What the hell is that up there? Sounds like bloody big rats," the mayor whispers.

"Whatever they are, they know we are here," responds the mayoress in the quietest of tones. Tears well up in her eyes. Her husband, who follows behind, feels his heart beating faster and faster. Feeling sick to the stomach, sweat beads down his forehead. Warrior's pets have pummelled the walls and bookcase, exposing the stone behind the painted plaster. The stone walls are thick, though – so thick that they have no chance of breaking through it.

The pets stop their destruction. Unable to break into the hidden corridor, they focus their attentions on the old man's heavy heartbeat. Slowly they adjust their hearing, homing in on the whereabouts of this heavy beating heart, and wander out of the library, over books, plaster and pieces of wood that litter the floor. Pressing earless heads against the wall, the pets wander down the staircase to the third floor, where they can hear the heartbeat more strongly. The old man's heartbeat, however, begins to slow down to a normal pace as the terror exacted from the banging upstairs dies down. The sound that emanated from his chest grows faint. Pets on the staircase press their earless heads harder against the wall, and frustration sets in as the heartbeat they have followed subsides. Noses push up into the air again – where is the scent? The pets are unable to grasp the smell of man anymore, as smoke from the houses outside has taken its place. Disgruntled that they have not made their kill, the pets head towards the ground floor, back to their master in the mayoral office.

Warrior has considered the path to Fricas and has made a decision.

"I want the majority of this goblin army of yours to travel to Fricas from the open plains, attacking the southern walls," Warrior tells General Glum, plotting the route on the map with his gauntleted hand. "How many goblin men do we have?"

"Thousands upon thousands," replies Glum.

"Specific numbers," retorts Warrior.

"We are looking at six to seven thousand soldiers," replies the general.

"Where are the rest of the soldiers we were expecting?" Warrior grumbles, questioning Glum and his lieutenants, although he knows the answer. The goblins stand open-mouthed; they do not know and could only lie – a lie that Warrior would be able to see through and so they remain quiet.

"Never mind," Warrior continues angrily. "You," he says, pointing to a wiry lieutenant with a pointed nose, ears and chin. "You will take one thousand soldiers and travel the path to the east, behind the trees, and attack the north-eastern walls of the city." This is a good move, Warrior thinks, as it is likely that these walls will be lightly guarded. Seeing Warrior's army of thousands, Fricasian generals will surely pile their resources forward to greet them at the southern walls, leaving other areas more than exposed. "You will wait until I give you a signal before you make your move. Only when the north-eastern wall falls will you rush the city. Head towards the keep and make sure any and all resistance is quelled before you get there."

"But how will the north-eastern wall fall if we do not have the tools to do it?" asks the lieutenant.

"It will fall, and you will rush the city," Warrior repeats himself. His tone is such that he will not tolerate the question being asked again. "Your thousand men will be chosen for you when the assault upon this town has been ended."

"Yes, sire," bows the wiry lieutenant.

The pets wander into the mayoral office on all fours, agitated by their lack of success in finding the source of the scent they smelled. Warrior greets them one by one with a pat on the head as they pass by him.

Inside the confines of the hidden corridor, the old man and

woman have stopped at a door leading into the cellar. They are wise not to open this door, because the pets will pick up their scent once more through the small gaps in the floorboards separating the cellar from the ground floor of the building.

Rain has stopped pattering down on the windowsills. Warrior turns his attention to the burning town outside. He looks through the open windows on the same side as the front door. Crackling sounds generated by burning houses soothe Warrior's senses. The burning is beautiful, particularly because there are no goblin soldiers to spoil the view.

"Open the windows behind me," Warrior commands General Glum. Glum moves quickly to please his King, opening a number of the closed windows. What is revealed is a hellish scene, full of fire and decay; goblin soldiers can be seen eating the remains of the last available victims who had abandoned their smoke-filled houses. Warrior turns to view this carnage, sniffing the air victoriously, his earlier doubts forgotten. Warrior has been made for these days. He has no memories of childhood, of parents or of love. He knows only of his teacher and of the lessons he was taught, which were terrible and unforgiving.

Warrior walks out of the mayoral office, back into the waiting room and out through the front doors of the building, closely followed by his pets and his goblin generals. Now out of the mayoral building, he looks at it from the cobbled roads.

"This building should not stand any longer," he comments. The general and his lieutenants run behind it, rounding up archers.

"Follow us, a building must be burned," they cry. Within a matter of minutes, goblin archers have surrounded the mayoral building and await orders from their seniors. Dipping their clothed arrows in deadly liquids, arrows are lit and strings of bows are pulled back towards the bowmen's stinking, sharp-toothed mouths in readiness.

Warrior gestures for the burning to begin and arrows fly into the building on all four levels. The archers' arrows touch books, curtains, parchment, wooden shelving, furniture and bedding. It takes only seconds for the building to fill with flames and smoke. Flames escape through every opening as the air through windows and doors feeds the fire, encouraging the flames to become more violent and destructive. Smoke filters onto the top floor of the hidden corridor and begins to make its way slowly down the stairs. The old man and woman can feel the heat rising as the sealed corridor begins to act as an oven would; it cannot be long before they will need to move.

For only a few minutes do Warrior, his pets and army watch the flagship building in this town burn. More needs to be accomplished and time is of the essence – the rest of the town must be flattened and there is the small matter of a march to Fricas waiting. It is not long before they have disappeared into the final third of this town; two thirds of it now burns and the job is nearly done.

The old man and woman, still hiding in the corridor, sweat profusely – the heat is unbearable. The old man puts his sword down on the stairs and tries to open the door into the cellar, but the sweltering heat has already swollen the door and is in the process of melting the locks. Removing his suit jacket, he covers his hands with it in the hope he can protect them from the searing heat of the door handles. The mayor wrestles with the locks and handles, pushing himself aggressively against the bulk of the door, burning his shoulder as he does so.

"It will not open," he screams. The air is being burned by heat and stifled by smoke, and both the old man and woman find it increasingly hard to breathe. The mayor of Paledon changes tack, and taking hold of his sword, he chops at the wood of the door. Small pieces chip off on impact – this may take time, but by weakening the wood there is a chance of breaking through it. Minutes pass, and a hole in the door has been created. Sweat drips off the old man as he defies his age; the life of his wife is important to him and he will not let her perish. As it is, she is close to becoming unconscious as she sways on the steps above him, breathless and overheated. The old man kicks the weakened door until finally the wood cracks and splinters. Breaking through, the mayor ushers his wife through the broken door into the cellar.

Small flames beat down through the gaps in the cellar ceiling, but worse, the house is beginning to collapse upon itself. Running as fast as their legs will allow, the mayor and mayoress head towards the cellar doors leading onto the street above. The stairs head upwards towards the two cellar doors, which open onto the street. The cellar doors are generally locked from both the inside and outside by a wooden latch. It is already known by the mayor that the outside latch is locked, and he curses his lack of foresight. He unlocks the latch on the inside and tries to push the doors outwards with his back. A gap in the doors is created. Utilising the gap, he thrusts his sword through to the street side of the building. Frantically he tries to unlock the outside latch. The mayoress stands behind him, still weak, crying as her husband works hard for their survival. The creaking above turns to a crash as half of the cellar ceiling collapses under the pressure of the four floors above falling down onto it. An abundance of red, orange and yellow flickering flames flow onto the cellar floor, spreading quickly and ferociously.

"Help us!" screams a terrified mayoress.

"Help us, anyone!" screams her husband, convinced that this is the end.

All of a sudden the latch unlocks. On hearing this, the mayor pushes his back hard up against the cellar doors, and as he does so, light breaks through the ever-widening gap. The mayor stumbles exhausted onto the street, and holding his wife's hand, he pulls her to safety. Both the mayor and mayoress fall to the ground, and lie face down on the cobbled road outside the crumbling, heat-filled walls of their once proud home. The mayoress catches something out of the corner of her eye.

"Please don't let it be a goblin," she pleads quietly. Turning her head to face the apparition, she sees her saviour and there, walking out of sight up the street, is indeed what appears to be a goblin: it is Bobbucket. The mayoress sighs a breath of relief; the goblin has gone. It is just hoped that he is not in the process of alerting the others, but then if he was, why did he save them in the first place?

The mayor and mayoress regain their breath and begin to move once more. Only a short distance away from where they lie, they can hear horses pulled by a cart stopping and starting with a purpose. Slow to rise, the mayor and mayoress use the walls of the burning house to lift themselves off the ground. Stumbling forward, holding onto each other, they make their way cautiously in the direction of the square.

"If they are not goblins we must warn them," the old woman tells her husband.

"Of course we will, dear," replies the mayor, "but be silent. We may not be out of danger yet." The old woman clenches her husband's arm, walking behind him as he looks round the corner of the building into the open square. To the old man's horror, he sees something he thought he would never see in his lifetime. What he can see before him is not Warrior, a goblin or an ogre. Seated in the cart that stops and starts intermittently is Ankou.

Ankou is the henchman of death itself, collecting the souls of the dead departed. Wearing a long black leather coat over a black tunic and pants, along with a black, wide-brimmed hat that hides his pale, thin, gaunt face, he will take them on this cart into the next world. His ice-white, bony hands hold the reins to two horses. One is old, its brown face withered, the pupils in its eyes pale, its black mane lank and its body showing off ribs and bone – this horse appears close to death. The other, a black horse, is young, tall and youthful, its black coat shines and its muscles ripple outwards; this horse comforts the other, and quite probably pulls the cart for the both of them. The horses pull this cart every minute of every day, as Ankou's work is never done. Since Warrior has appeared, Ankou has been busier than normal, so much so that he has been slow to keep up with the demands for his service. What lies ahead, who knows, but Ankou is happy in his work and will fulfil what is required of him until the end of days.

Before the mayor's eyes, neighbours who were alive only an hour ago now leave their lifeless bodies on the floor and walk towards the back of this rickety old cart. Waiting for these souls are two skeletal figures, who help these men and women climb onto it. Men and women seat themselves on benches positioned on either side of the cart. Looking in the mayor's direction, they somehow know that he can see them and happily they wave goodbye to him. Raising his hand nervously, he waves back. Ankou's cart moves slowly forward. The two skeletal figures walk behind the cart on their naked, white-boned feet until they meet the next set of souls waiting to be taken. Rickety cart wheels creak on every turn, and horses' hooves click and clack against the hard, cobbled floors. Ankou's cart disappears behind buildings that are in the way of the mayor's view. For a good while, creaking cart wheels and horses' hooves can be heard stopping and starting, until the cart travels far enough away not to be heard any longer.

"Why did you not warn them?" asks the old woman.

"You don't want to know," replies the old man, his face as white as the ghosts he has just seen.

Goblins and ogres regroup a few hundred metres outside the now uninhabitable town; no one could ever rebuild this place. Attention turns to Fricas, its majestic form beams down upon the army, its size awe-worthy.

The plains in front of the city stretch all the way down to Paledon. The yellow-green grasses of the plains are generally kept short due to the amount of traffic that makes its way up and down this hill. Walking up to the city as an advancing army leaves them at a disadvantage; the incline is long enough and steep enough to tire out the strongest of legs. But advance this army will. Warrior takes the lead, followed by his general, cavalry, pikemen, foot soldiers and dozens of carts carrying anything and everything else. The one lieutenant who will take the route behind the thin stretch of wooded land close to Windrush Forest has had his thousand men selected for him. Pompucket is one of them. Bobbucket, for reasons that will become more apparent later on in this tale, has been spared a continuation of his journey in tow of Pompucket. It might even be written that fate has decided Bobbucket's path.

The goblin lieutenant walking with one thousand men points in the direction of the wooded valley, gesturing for his small army to march forward, away from the town of Paledon. The chosen cavalry, pikemen and foot soldiers, understanding the lieutenant's orders, walk on. Both armies will likely travel through the night, setting up camp close to the walls of Fricas in the morning and resting well before storming the city tomorrow night.

The old man and woman walk the streets of their burning town, calling out to others who may have survived the attack, but at this moment no one calls back. The scene they are faced with is apocalyptic: buildings crumble, houses that once had floors, furniture, flowers and plants are hollow shells of their former selves. Bodies of the dead block the roads and streets.

"How could they have done this?" cries the mayoress uncontrollably as she is hugged close by her husband, who also has streams of tears running down his face.

"It is barbarism. Uncontrollable rage has been let loose and this is its result. Curse the goblins... and curse Warrior for what he has done," he says, crying inconsolably.

"And how can you let this happen?" his wife questions, looking up at the skies and addressing the Creators. "You created us all, so why have you let them do what they have?" she shouts, raising an angry fist.

The mayor and mayoress are distracted from their anger. Listening hard, the sound of sobbing children invades their ears. Quickly, they run around a corner following the sobs and cries. In front of them, one house appears to have been largely missed by the blinny. It burns brightly on the upper floor, but it is still intact – just. Peering through a window, the old man pinpoints where the sobbing comes from. A plain, varnished, dark wood cabinet, long in width, standing on plain wooden legs in the living area of this house, hides the children. Outside, the bodies of a man and woman lie face down in the street.

"Why didn't they leave?" he asks, bewildered, especially as they had small children to care for. It is careless at best. The front door is open, so the mayor and mayoress walk up the steps onto the ground floor of the small house.

"Young children, we are friends. We have come here to save you," the mayoress calls softly, making it clear that they will not harm them as the blinny might. The mayor opens the doors of the cabinet slowly, so as not to surprise them. Inside it, to his horror, are two half-breed goblin children huddled together. One is dressed in the clothes of a little girl and the other in the clothes of a little boy. The boy and girl are only three or four years old at most. They are different to children of men insofar as their features, like ears, noses, fingers and nails, are longer. Unlike goblins, their skin is smooth and not hideously deformed with bumps, swellings, coarse or peeling skin. Both also have big blue eyes, not the dark, emotionless pools that most blinny do.

The old man and woman gasp in horror at the children, thinking them abominations. The mayor raises his sword, making it ready to strike down upon them.

"What are you doing? These are innocent children," screams his wife, pulling his sword arm down and away from the children. The half-breed children cower and whimper, grabbing onto each other even more tightly.

"What are you doing here in this cupboard? Answer me!" the mayor orders angrily, a red mist still upon him.

"Mummy and Daddy told us to hide and not to come out until they told us to," sobs the little girl.

"And who are your mummy and daddy?" asks the mayoress more kindly.

The little girl points directly ahead at two painted pictures, one either side of a window that looks out onto the street. "That's Mummy and Daddy," replies the little half-breed girl. Mummy and Daddy are the man and woman lying out in front of the house.

"We cannot leave them here," the old woman tells her husband.

The mayor's head looks down at the floor. How can he be expected to take in two half-breed goblin children after the events of today? No time whatsoever has passed to grieve the loss of his friends, and of course, his beloved town. He might gain some semblance of revenge and satisfaction by killing these two children. Pondering the unspeakable, intense thoughts enter his mind. These thoughts are not created by his mind alone – a higher voice speaks to him now. The entity in his head tells him to care for these children as happiness and satisfaction will come to him and his wife by doing this. He doesn't question the voice. All his life he has been bombarded by messages and direction; it has always done well by him. A creak and then a snap on the floor above is a signal that they should leave this house, quickly.

"Come on, out, both of you," commands the old man. Both the half-breed boy and girl clamber out of the cupboard. The old man takes hold of the boy's hand and the old woman takes hold of the girl's.

"Cover his eyes," the old woman says to her husband, covering the eyes of the little girl as they head to the front door. Knowing why his wife has said this, he puts his hands over the eyes of the boy. The old woman, in her wisdom, has made sure that the children do not see their dead parents, as the trauma would no doubt be too much for them to take. Walking quickly out of the front door, there is another snap and another. Down the porch stairs, past the bodies, up the street and around the corner they walk before removing their hands away from the children's eyes. Behind them they can hear a succession of snaps and a creaking roar before the house crumbles like the others around it have done. At the end of the road the mayor, mayoress and the two half-breed children can see the goblin army a fair way away in the distance, heading towards Fricas.

"I just hope that they are defeated soon," says the old man.

"I do, too. For all our sakes," adds the old woman.

The nightmare the mayor and mayoress have endured has ended. They have lost their home but they have found two children who are far more precious. Little do they know how precious these two children really are, but that is for another tale.

CHAPTER 18

MARCHING THROUGH EMPTY LANDS

It is a rumbling of the ground and a chatter of voices that disturbs the men from their slumber this morning. Five days and five nights have passed since Greybeard locked the front door to his house in the cave. The sun is not yet up, although it is getting light. Eyes slowly open to see what the kerfuffle is. To everyone's surprise, scores and scores of men and women line the streets next to the park, all of them smart in their full battle dress. Shields straddle backs, swords sit at sides and some even have bows and arrows. Teacher walks over to the men, dwarfs and elves as they slowly get up and stretch their limbs. They are overwhelmed by this response – tears even well up in Greybeard's eyes, but not a drop will run down his face.

"So this is what the curly-haired boy meant," Greybeard says to himself.

All jotunn walks of life are represented. Young men and women are joined by Teacher's pupils of old. Farmers, bakers, butchers, home-makers, builders, painters and more have all made the decision to come. It is overwhelming to see such commitment to a cause that was not theirs only a day ago. It is quite plain to see that the majority of the men and women are glad to have been given the chance to make this decision themselves.

"So, what do we do now?" asks Teacher.

"We march," says Greybeard, smiling happily. Lord's advice had been good and right. "We need to head towards Fricas. Do you know of any back roads that lead there, Teacher?" Greybeard asks, almost anticipating a 'no'. Obviously the town's residents have not ventured outside for such a long time that the old tracks may have disappeared.

"Yes, yes, I've often looked out beyond these walls towards Fricas. You can see the city on a good day from the top of the wall – there is a path leading all the way there, although it is a little overgrown now," a self-assured Teacher tells Greybeard.

"We'll follow you then," Greybeard replies. The wizard turns around to his friends, who have climbed on their horses and are waiting for him. "Time to get a move on, I think," he orders, walking towards Thundercloud.

"Yes, old man. Time for you to get a move on," patronises Igralf.

"Yes, quite," he replies. Greybeard fumbles around tying his staff onto his horse's saddle and takes his time mounting Thundercloud. After only a short while, although long enough for his men to get a little impatient with the wizard, Greybeard is ready. "It must be nerves," says Greybeard quietly to the others. "Shall we get a move on?" he continues, setting off on Thundercloud in the direction of the front gates.

"Fall into line," Teacher shouts loudly to his warriors. The warriors do not take long to fulfil Teacher's order, standing two soldiers wide and many lines back. Within seconds, they have assumed their position within the formation, standing tall and silent, eyes ahead and still. "March forward," orders Teacher. The warriors do so dutifully, following Greybeard through the town whilst Stryker, Forester, the dwarfs, elves and Perrywinkle take up the rear.

Perrywinkle has taken out his journal again; at every opportunity he pours his thoughts into it. He has been silent these many days. In deep thought, he wonders how he will portray the characters in the tale, and how best to do justice to the events that have unfolded in front of his eyes. When we first met Perrywinkle at the Old Mill, he was afraid of the world, and at that particular time, Greybeard as well. Connor Perrywinkle is now at ease with the often grumpy old man and feels he understands him just a little better than he did before. Perrywinkle is also comfortable with this world of magic, hidden secrets, shape-shifters, jotunn, dragons, dwarfs and elves. Like most people, he'd had his preconceptions of what the world was like – enough to frighten most people, and him more than many others. He has learned that you needn't be scared, and that there is good and bad in everything. The magical world will not encroach upon you unless you want or encourage it. The only creatures to be scared of now are the ones to be confronted, yet Connor has a sense of ease about it. He would not be without these creatures around him; better these creatures than anybody else.

"How long do you think it will be before we get to Fricas?" asks Perrywinkle.

"A couple of days. It depends on what we stumble upon on our way there," informs Forester.

"What do you mean by 'stumble upon'?" Perrywinkle replies.

"Oh, goblins and ogres… and maybe even Warrior. Who knows what devastation awaits? He may have already attacked Fricas and be headed in this direction. What we experience over the next few days we cannot plan for," Forester says, giving an honest answer about the current situation.

"We'll scout, of course. I don't think we'll need to worry about meeting anything nasty today," assures a calm Stryker. Perrywinkle shivers at the thought. Maybe he is a little scared of what might happen after all. The army quickly marches on to the market square. Thundercloud stops just before the archway leading to the main gates, which in turn leads out of this town. Stepping to one side, Greybeard's horse allows two giants to walk down the arched corridor to open them. No crowds line the streets or town square and no families are gathered to wave these men and women off. It is very early, but one suspects that farewells have already been made, or that some of the warriors left without saying goodbye so as to avoid being questioned by their loved ones.

Nonetheless, those travelling now are happy to be here and battle is not the only thing on their minds. Travel and the opportunity to see new things outweighs everything, and they cannot wait to experience life outside of these walls.

Creaking as they part, the gates open out slowly. A beam of sunlight peers through the gap in the doors, which gets wider and wider as they open more and more. A new dawn for this day and a new dawn for the jotunn becomes ever more apparent as they walk out in single file through the open doors. Once everybody is outside of the town, Teacher orders the army to stop. Everybody stops, still in formation, bar Greybeard's band of men, of course, who all pile out in a somewhat scruffy fashion.

"Turn eyes left," commands Teacher. Everyone turns to face him. "We are going to head in this direction." He points into the distance towards Fricas. "You may break your formation as we head through the fields, but keep your wits about you… and your eyes and ears open."

"Yes, sir," shouts the army in unison.

"Walk on," orders Teacher.

"They're very good, aren't they?" comments Wattlespalf, leaning over to Gendralf.

"Very professional," replies Gendralf.

Nerves are now showing in the faces of the tunny. The first few steps away from the town walls are the most difficult, as if a comfortable blanket has been taken away from them and they are now naked to the elements. The initial nerves don't last long, though, and are soon replaced with excitement. Travelling through long, unkempt grasses, the men, dwarfs and elves are partially hidden in them. In comparison, the grasses come no further than the thighs of the jotunn. Grass and insects whip and tickle faces, and the men, dwarfs and elves are covered in spiders, beetles and ants. Grass that flicks in their faces and gets in their mouths is a hindrance. Poor horses and ponies wading through the grass must not be very happy at all, but it doesn't stop them from eating some of the drier grasses they pass by. A number of the young tunny warriors notice the group of smaller creatures and the trouble they are having, and kindly offer to walk in front of them, treading the grass down as they go. This makes the journey a lot easier and much more comfortable for all involved.

Greybeard remembers his promise to Beezle that he will teach him a lesson today. It also crosses his mind that Beezle might be able to help a little. At the very least, he must be able to defend himself should a goblin or an ogre get close enough to him. Greybeard trots up next to the little elf and says, "So, young whippersnapper. Are you ready to learn a trick or two today?"

"Oh yes, that would be excellent. It gets quite boring travelling on a horse, having only your own mind to entertain you," he replies.

"Well, this should test you. I'm going to teach you a few things over the next two days that will enable you to defend yourself and others. The first piece of magic is simple. All I want you to do is produce a light at the very tip of your finger."

"But I am already able…" Beezle interrupts but then stops.

260

'Oh no,' he thinks. 'Have I given everything away? Think quickly.' His mind searches frantically for an answer.

"You already know what?" asks a curious Greybeard.

"That I am already able to perform a trick like this easily. Show me and I'll do it first time," Beezle composes himself.

"Well, young man, don't go thinking it's going to be that easy. You may well be gifted but magic is a complicated thing," replies Greybeard. "Anyway, getting back to it, I want you to put out the first finger on your right hand and recite these two words, 'Finger Illuminatis'." Beezle looks at Greybeard blankly. "Well, go on then," prompts the wizard.

Beezle puts out his finger and recites the words, "Finger illuminatis." His finger lights first time as he had promised. "See, this is too easy," says Beezle, looking pleased with himself.

Everyone close by and further away looks on in amazement at Beezle's feat. Finn is especially proud of his brother and he smiles at the sense of achievement he sees in Beezle's eyes. Greybeard has a potential star of wizardry here; even some of the better wizards have taken longer to action this move.

"How do you turn this light off?" Beezle asks, knowing the answer.

"Say, 'Finger extinguishus'," replies Greybeard.

Beezle says the words and the light at the end of his finger fizzles out.

"I am very impressed, young pupil." Greybeard revels in Beezle's achievements, bestowing praise upon him.

Finn trots up and pats Beezle on the back. "Well done, brother."

"We're not done there, Beezle. This is just the first part of the trick. What you will learn now is how to use that illumination on the end of your finger to produce a shot of lightning," informs the old man. "Beezle, illuminate your finger again," he orders.

Beezle puts out his first finger and recites the words, "Finger illuminatis." Immediately his finger lights and he awaits Greybeard's next instruction. Beezle is excited; if he can produce lightning from his finger then he can quite possibly do some real damage. He has to keep his destructive instincts at bay, though. Who knows what Greybeard will reveal over the course of the next two days. Not that this matters, because another voice in his head tells him that once the rod is in his possession then it will teach him and he won't need anybody else anymore.

"Beezle!" Greybeard's gruff voice calls out. "Stop looking at your finger and listen."

Beezle pulls out of his trance. 'How did that happen?' he thinks, directing his attention back onto Greybeard. "Oh, sorry, Greybeard. I really don't know where I went then."

"Fine, just don't wander off too often – this is delicate stuff, you know. Back to the job in hand. This is important, Beezle. I want you to put out your arm with your finger pointing forward. I want you to aim for…" Greybeard looks around the immediate area. There in front is a rock pointing upwards out of the long grass. "That rock over there. Concentrate all your energies on your finger and the rock. When you are ready, all I want you to do is say, 'Strike!'" Beezle looks between his finger and the rock, rock and finger, finger and rock.

"Strike!" he shouts. His finger sparks, but there is no lightning. "Strike!" he shouts again – another spark but no lightning. Jotunn, dwarfs, men and Finn all look on in anticipation, while Greybeard has got his hands over his ears. "Strike!" shouts Beezle once more. This time there is a shot of lightning so strong that it fizzes loudly as it flies through the air. Beezle, at the same time, flies backwards off his dark horse, the bounce of the long grass cushioning his fall. Making contact with the rock, the lightning blast from Beezle's finger cuts through it like an arrow through paper, the blast leaving a neat, circular hole so that you are able to see from one side of it to the other.

All creatures clap and cheer Beezle's effort, especially the jotunn who have not seen wizardry like this before. But some of the creatures feel that the elfling's power is growing too quickly, and that if he wanted to, he could cause them great harm.

The little elf gets up and brushes himself down as he is greeted by smiles and laughter. Beezle smiles back and his eyes light up because, at this very moment, he feels accepted by the others.

His finger is still lit. Holding back his urge to fire another blast, he says, "Finger extinguishus." The light at the end of his finger fizzles out once more. Greybeard is pleased that Beezle has resisted the temptation; responsibility appears to be having a good effect on his behaviour.

Getting back on his horse, Greybeard, who is sitting next to Beezle's black pony, declares, "And this is the end of the lesson for today. Better you avoid falling off your pony again." Beezle nods in agreement. 'This adventure just keeps getting better and better,' he thinks.

All creatures make their way to the end of the long grasses where they come to a fence covered by trees and hedgerows. The fence marks the end of the jotunn boundary and the beginning of the fricasian province. Immediately beyond the fence, through the hedgerows and trees lining the borders, is farmland. The jotunn warriors can see over the hedgerows, the path forward is clear and well-trodden – there will be no getting lost now.

Only scarecrows work here at this time; farmers and labourers are nowhere to be seen, but vegetables and fruits look well-cared for. Maybe those who work the land are having breakfast; after all, the morning is still very young. No gate between jotunn and the fricasian province exists to let these men through. The tunny can stride over the fence and hedgerows. The rest will have to figure a way around it as the hedgerows are too high and they follow the fence for many, many miles.

Stryker has an idea. "Gendralf, could we use your axe to make a way through?"

"Good idea, friend," replies the dwarf, getting off his pony.

Gendralf unties the axe from his saddle and removes the sheet which covers the blade. The dwarf looks down the line of the fence, through the fence and under the hedgerows. He hums a tune as he rattles the fence to see how sturdy it is and knocks on the wood to see how hollow it might be. Maybe woodworm have made the wooden fence weak over time, and therefore easier to cut.

It is all a bit convoluted and time-consuming, but the men and the jotunn (well, most of them) wait patiently. Some of the more athletic tunny men and women have jumped over the fence onto the other side and are now scouting out the area, although they remain close to the main army. Gendralf is finally ready, having positioned himself next to a fence post. He raises his axe above his head and drops it with some power so it cuts through four vertical fence rails attached to the fencepost. The strange thing about this cut is that it makes no sound. The axe quite simply goes through each fence rail like a knife through butter. The jotunn look on amazed.

"How can an axe not make a sound?" they chatter. Unfazed by the talk behind him, Gendralf then cuts through the four fence rails of the next fence post down the line. This time, as the rail is cut, it falls to the ground with a clatter. With all four fence rails on the floor and nothing in his way, Gendralf is now free to start work on the hedgerow. With a few swift cuts through branches and twigs, Gendralf appears to have done nothing to the hedgerow – not one twig and not one branch appears to have snapped. Everyone is puzzled. 'Why is Gendralf smiling as if his work is done, and why should we be impressed?' they think. The dwarf pushes against the hedgerow with the flat palm of one hand, and as he does so, the part of the hedgerow that he has cut falls forward into the farm fields in one big piece.

"That was a fine set of cuts," claps Stryker, impressed and somewhat taken aback.

"Yes, not bad at all, was it?" replies Gendralf, admiring his work.

Two jotunn pull the piece of hedgerow away from the new opening created by Gendralf. Jotunn who had not jumped over the fence along with the rest, pile forward through the hole in the hedgerow and start to follow the well-trodden path towards Fricas.

Tunny who have been scouting the immediate area have found nothing. No one at all can be seen in the near or far distance. Only rabbits can be seen, working hard at munching on lettuces and carrots. It is strange to find things deserted, hearing nothing other than silence itself. Even the birds aren't singing, although they can clearly be seen in the trees or popping in and out of the hedgerows.

The well-trodden path leads through fields full of fruit and vegetables, as well as the farms where the farmers who tend to these fields live.

"I wonder if the farmers have left as well?" ponders Forester.

"I can't see it," replies Stryker. "The cows will need milking, the pigs will need feeding and the eggs will need to be removed from the henhouses. I just can't imagine them leaving."

"Thing is, what can they do? If they leave the animals then it is likely that the animals will die. If they stay then the blinny are likely to kill all the animals and also the farmer," says Forester.

"Now you put it like that," replies Stryker, agreeing with his brother's assessment of the situation. "We'll just have to wait and see. The nearest farm cannot be too far away."

Finn talks to a young tunny woman who is walking next to his horse; other jotunn listen into the conversation intently. The young woman, a little older than Finn, carries a bow and arrow as well as a sword. She has olive-coloured skin and is a little darker than the rest of her clan. Her dark skin is complemented by long, straight black hair that flows down her back from underneath her helmet and piercing blue eyes.

"So you are an elf and you travelled through time to get here?" the young jotunn woman asks Finn, confirming information the conversation has yielded so far.

"Yes, it is strange really, by travelling here we've actually saved ourselves from a terrible fate. Yet the potential is that we may meet a similarly terrible fate here in the next few days," he says.

"Does that make you think the outcome to this battle will be terrible?" the young tunny woman asks.

"I really do not know, but I'm pleased to have Greybeard, Stryker, Forester, the three dwarfs and your brethren here with me. I don't know what to expect, but I think that there are going to be a lot of goblins that we will need to overcome. And Warrior, I just can't imagine what kind of monster he is going to be," replies Finn.

"Are you scared? Should we be scared?" she asks.

"I should think that when the blinny see you, then they will be more frightened of you than you are of them. Anyway, why have you come on this journey?"

"Oh many reasons. I want to have experiences outside of the city. I want to say that I protected my people. I do not want to have any regrets by not living life as I see fit. Or turn round in years to come and say I wanted to do this and that, but I didn't and for that I am sorry. Imagine how bad it would feel to say sorry to yourself, especially if it was something you had always dreamed of doing," she remarks.

"What is your name?" asks Finn.

"Meena."

"Well, Meena, that is quite a list you have. It is quite a special one, too. You are obviously here for reasons you feel passionate about," compliments Finn. "So what will the future hold for you when the battle is over?"

"I haven't yet thought about that… warrior-like things? There are probably many paths and so much more that I can do. What about you?" Meena asks Finn.

"The idea is to get myself and my brother back to our own time. But if this were not to happen, then I can see myself wanting to explore this land or work closely with Greybeard and the others." He tries to search his mind for other ideas but he cannot think straight enough to give a stronger answer. "It is a hard question, isn't it?" he says, smiling at Meena. "What can you see up there?"

"Why don't you come up and have a look? You can put your legs around my neck," Meena offers.

"Hmm, alright then. Maybe for just a minute." Finn jumps off his horse, and Meena picks him up off the ground and puts him onto the nape of her neck. He looks like a toddler being carried by a parent; the situation is quite odd. Stryker, Forester and the dwarfs all point at this odd couple as Finn puts his arms gently around Meena's neck.

"What a view you've got up here! You can see for miles and miles," wows an awestruck Finn.

Meena points into the distance. "Can you see Fricas over there?"

Finn looks and indeed, in the distance, high up in the hills, a large area of land appears to be covered in stone, but it is too far to get any real detail of what is or isn't there. Certainly he cannot see any goblin hordes attacking this large area of land. In fact, the goblin hordes will not be able to see the approaching army of jotunn, men, dwarfs and elves as they approach Fricas from the opposite side of the hill. It is therefore likely that Warrior and the blinny do not know that there is an army assembled, but those in the city of Fricas might. Fricas has been strategically placed high up on that hill. From this city you can see all around, and as such, approaching armies can never surprise the men who live there. The question is whether they know that Greybeard's army are approaching from a north-easterly direction to help them, not harm them?

Finn looks down on the others. "I can see the city of Fricas up here. It looks huge."

"Very good – how far away are we from the city?" shouts Wattlespalf. "I need a lemonade; my mouth is very dry," he continues.

"It is a long way away. It must be at least another day or two before we'll get there," says Finn.

"Bugger," curses Wattlespalf. "Well, if the city is too far away can we stop at the nearest farm? If indeed the farmers have left the area, then they won't mind if we take a tipple or two from their houses to keep us going, will they?"

"Wattlespalf, I really do think that you're losing your moral sensibilities. Going into strangers' houses and stealing from them is very bad, isn't it? Besides, you have plenty of water to keep you going," says Igralf.

"Water does not satisfy my tastebuds, and it wouldn't hurt to take a peek should we get the chance," replies Wattlespalf.

"Well, I suppose if you're putting it that way then we could peer around a corner or two," responds Igralf with a mischievous smile.

"Meena, it's probably best that I get down now. I don't want to give you neck ache."

"Yes, you're probably right. You're very heavy," laughs Meena, and she stops walking. Finn's horse, who has been following beside Meena since Finn got on her back, also stops. She puts Finn down on the saddle of his horse, and they continue to walk along the route together.

"Do you think love is blossoming between those two?" Forester whispers over to Stryker playfully.

"He is surely too young for her, and she is surely far too tall for him," replies Stryker.

"It makes a strange combination, doesn't it? An elf and a jotunn together," comments Forester, blowing kisses as he does so.

"Well, he hasn't got elven ladies around to talk to. At least she is a little closer to his age than we are. It's all very innocent," considers Stryker.

Forester, inspired by the idea of Finn and Meena, has been set off on thoughts of coupling unlikely creatures together. "An elf and a jotunn giant... their offspring could be called elfants. What about a goblin and a gulp fish? They could call their children gobulps. Or a buggane and a dwarf, they would produce a buggarf. Or a man and a dragon, that would make a dragman."

"You really are quite bizarre sometimes. Who'd have thought you were my brother?" tuts Stryker.

"Only having a bit of fun," retorts Forester with a mischievous grin.

Perrywinkle has been writing all of this down. Smells, sounds, conversations and characters are all listed and detailed in his journal. Greybeard trots over to Perrywinkle with the intention of talking with him for a while.

"You have been quiet for these past few days, Perrywinkle. Are you alright?" asks a slightly concerned Greybeard.

"There has been quite a bit to take in, sir. What with elves coming back to life, draugar and goblins attacking us, a buggane living in a post office holding messages from the dead, dragons threatening to eat us, men turning into otters and giants wrestling with their ability to make decisions," comes Perrywinkle's reply. It could be seen as sarcastic if it were not for the fact that it is true and well summarised.

"Quite true, Perrywinkle," Greybeard says with a chuckle. "What a tale you have to tell, and you've got more to come. May I have a look in your journal? I'm interested to see what you have written so far."

Perrywinkle passes his journal over to Greybeard, and the old man takes it gratefully. He flicks through the pages of the journal very slowly, taking in everything that has been written. Greybeard's eyes tell the story he is reading as they show sadness and glee, embarrassment and pride. In the journal, as well as writings, are a few ink drawings. The drawings depict everyone who started on this journey, as well as a few of the places that have been visited over the course of the last few days.

"I didn't know you could draw as well, Perrywinkle," comments an impressed Greybeard.

"Oh yes, sir. I have an eye for art. If I ever got the chance, I would always spend some time in the castles or buildings of high esteem to take in the artwork. Don't tell anyone, but I stole one or two paintings for myself on my travels. I stole those paintings when I was active in my former life as a thief, of course."

"Of course," says Greybeard, shaking his head with a 'that is not very good' expression on his face.

"In the meantime, I've painted a couple of pictures myself, which sit in my house at Kardarnath."

"Hmm, well depending on the outcome of what lies in wait for us, I may come to visit and take a look at those paintings. And if things change dramatically for this world, as they might well do, then I would hope that in your altered guise you still carry the same talent for drawing and writing that you do now." He winks encouragingly. Greybeard carries on reading Perrywinkle's journal in silence, right to the very last page, which at present is around two thirds full.

"These are fine observations, Connor," praises Greybeard, looking at Perrywinkle proudly. "The words you have written will lead you to your final conclusion in only a matter of days. I want you to find a good position on the sidelines where you are safe, and if not, then I want you far enough away from the action so as not to be harmed. The words you have already written will make more sense in those hours. Your words may be well observed, but it is the crafting of these words that will bring greatness or failure to the tale you tell. I think hindsight will also play its part, should you survive it. Do you think you have your story?" asks Greybeard.

Perrywinkle does not know if Greybeard wants a definite answer from him or whether he is asking for an opinion. He does know that he feels pressure from the question he has been asked. Perrywinkle does finally give an answer, and although he is anticipating that Greybeard will be disappointed with it, it is an honest one.

"I do have a story, sir, but it changes daily and it will change again until I have the truth... but it will be a particular truth, my truth," responds Perrywinkle.

"What do you mean?" probes Greybeard, wanting just a tad more information from him.

"I want to give an honest description of everything I see, but I only know my characters, my places, my conversations and my relationships from what I have seen, what I have heard and what I believe to be the underlying messages that are unseen by others.

When I have thought about it, I will be better placed to piece everything together to give the tale you want. I do know this, the things I have seen, heard and been a part of have the makings of a very good yarn indeed. I just hope I am the right person to tell it," Perrywinkle explains.

"I think you might well be," replies Greybeard.

"Then again, if everything goes to plan all my ramblings will be instantly forgotten, even futile," Perrywinkle says, reminding Greybeard.

"Just keep doing what you are doing. This may be the prelude to greater tales."

"Greybeard, what about you? You are the most enigmatic of all, and as you have asked me to recount this tale, are you not able to tell me something more about yourself?"

"What do you want to know?"

Perrywinkle pauses for a few seconds. If you had the opportunity to ask one of the greatest living characters in recent history a question, what would you ask? He searches his mind for the question. Greybeard waits patiently. All of a sudden it pops into his head and the question makes sense.

"What makes you Greybeard?"

"Hmm, how did I become who I am?" Greybeard ponders. "You want a back story to my character?"

"Yes," replies Perrywinkle.

"Why?" asks the old man.

"Because you are an important character and no doubt people would like to know. Where were you born? Who were you born to? Did you want to be a wizard when you were younger? Who taught you your magic? What do you stand for? Why do you stand for it? And how did it come about?"

"Yes, yes," interrupts Greybeard. "I understand what you mean. I will tell you three things. My beard was not always grey, I was not always called Greybeard and I have lived for close to two thousand years."

"What does that tell me?" a frustrated Perrywinkle says.

"It tells you that you need to do some reading," replies the self-satisfied old man.

"You don't make things easy, do you?" grumbles Perrywinkle.

"Life is not easy, Perrywinkle. It has a habit of making things hard for you, but if you overcome your obstacles then the potential is that it will make you a better and wiser man," philosophises Greybeard.

"Fine." Perrywinkle is short with Greybeard. He grasps the wizard's words and his elusiveness but the old man could have made it a little bit easier for him.

Travelling on this road is far from languid. While conversations develop and drift away, the horses and ponies trot along in harmony with giant strides. As the pace is set by others, the mounted travellers talk, side by side, while hair and clothing flies in the winds behind them. The words are easy, and there are no misunderstandings between the men here. As ever, fields and trees pass with regularity, and fast as this journey may seem, for those travelling the end cannot come sooner. The riders' confidence is high as they try to keep up with the giant warriors who run on ahead of them.

The first farm on the main path, only a third of the way between the jotunn town and Fricas, appears on the horizon. Nothing out of the ordinary differentiates this farm from the next, apart from an ensuing army travelling through it. Other farms have been spared, or should we say not blessed by this resolute band of creatures passing by. As it is, the farmer who farms this land is surprisingly in residence, although his labourers are not. He greets the army with a pitchfork at the edge of his homestead, although he is sure that the army trespassing on his land are not the foes the goblins would be. Quite rightly, though, this farmer is unsure of how much less of a threat this intimidating army is. Arriving in front of him, the army slows down.

"I am no match for you and neither do I want to be," the resigned farmer shouts out to the creatures invading the quiet of his farm from behind a long gate, leading to the houses and barns. "Leave the land and I will not react. I may not be able to take you all, but I can certainly take one of you, and there are many other farmers round here who would do the same."

The young tunny raise their weapons. Anyone and everyone on this journey could be the enemy. Teacher, recognising the lack of threat, shouts out orders for his men to stand down immediately. Without hesitation, the giants halt and weapons are lowered and sheathed. Teacher moves to the forefront of the line to talk to the farmer.

"We are not here to hurt you," calms Teacher, moving cautiously towards the gate. Greybeard and the others are just feet behind him.

"Then what are you doing here? I know of Jotunn and I know you like to fight," the farmer announces, raising his pitchfork higher.

"Have you have heard of the goblin hordes marching on Fricas?" asks Teacher.

"I have, and they are not welcome either. What are the blinny to do with you?" the farmer probes Teacher, searching for more reassuring news.

"We have left our confines and are travelling to Fricas to help make sure that they get no further," Teacher says, palms open, gesturing that he is to be trusted.

"And why would you, jotunn, come to the aid of Fricas?" asks the farmer, who is wily and curious. He sees the other creatures behind and he has also seen the elves. The farmer may be slow in lifestyle, but he is not slow in mind and understands the significance of their presence, though he shows no surprise.

"Greybeard and his men came to us. He told us of the nightmare that waits. We took it upon us to relieve ourselves of our self-inflicted exile, launching whole-heartedly into battle once more to save your kind," Teacher explains. The farmer looks blankly at Teacher for a few seconds.

"Well, that is good enough for me," he says, convinced by Teacher's sincerity. He immediately lowers his pitchfork and opens the gate to let the army through. Greybeard smiles; this farmer is very much enlightened, he thinks. To have someone open up their world to the giants with little fight and only well-chosen words bodes well for the future. Greybeard hopes that the tunny have also recognised this fact. The sight of a man so honourable should give them hope for when they meet other men, who will be less honourable and less accepting.

"Take whatever fruit and vegetables you need to keep your bellies ready for battle," the farmer says, knowing little of jotunn appetites.

"I think that you may regret those words," Forester says to the farmer with a knowing chuckle.

The jotunn warriors pass through the farmer's gate, and every one of them says, "Thank you, sir," as they travel through it. Greybeard, Stryker, Forester, Finn, Perrywinkle and the dwarfs pat his back and nod, smiling as they pass through. Beezle does not know what to do and so does nothing. The farmer reciprocates the gestures given to him by holding his open-palmed hand up above his head and waving slowly as they disappear down a dip in the road leading away from the farm.

The path from the gate is more civilised than the one previously travelled. Stone chippings replace hardened soil. It is a sign that this farmer trades well with the city and that a proper road is needed to facilitate what would normally be regular trade. Farmers unable to trade face an uncertain future. Without labourers, a good proportion of the un-harvested fruit and vegetables will go rotten – indeed, the process has already begun. Without money from the fruit and vegetables, the farmer will be unable to invest in tools, horses and materials so that the farm is maintained; though the farmer will be able to eat, unlike his cousins in the city. As the army travels along the path, they pick fruit and vegetables at the farmer's behest from the fields and hedgerows. Appetites are satisfied and some of the food is packed for later, just in case the battle is long.

Fields and hedgerows are replaced by wooded areas, steep climbs and descents, gorges, waterfalls and rivers. Open fields filled with corn and wheat either side of them are surrounded by green-grassed hills covered with tall, evergreen trees. Windmills with roads running from their bases dot the landscape, and the windmill sails still turn as if the grain is still being crushed, but no one works within them.

In and out of the hills ahead, the far distance reveals Fricas in all its glory. This is the city these warriors might yet have a chance to save. Hope lasts only because of the realisation that the city is not smouldering and no smoke can be seen rising from it. Goblins do not like daylight, but the light produced by fire is a different thing; it evokes their deepest passions, purifying the evils of races they feel they have cleansed. Still, a day separates these men from the city, but they can see it clearly now and the hope is that they can reach it in time.

Weapons are itching to go into battle; the tension can be felt amongst the men and dwarfs in particular. The immediate feeling of these men is that time is now precious and they must keep travelling, but the young army in tow will need their sleep. Urgency has to be curtailed in favour of responsibility.

Dusk approaches and red skies fill the horizon. The journey, for today, is at an end. The travelling army stops close to a wood, but it is set some way back so that arrows have no chance of piercing soldiers in their slumber. Prior to this night, the travelling group was able to rest in relative peace, knowing that the goblin hordes were nowhere near to provide any threat. Although one eye has always been looking over the shoulder, tonight the camp will be properly guarded. Some members of this army will play their part in making sure that there is no breach, and if there is, they will raise an alarm.

CHAPTER 19

THE WORST NIGHT EVER

Goblins travelling behind the trees, treading the deep valley floor, are not having a good time at all. The beginning of the trek was not so bad and they were in good spirits. Destructive urges had been heightened by the possibility of felling Fricas but had been temporarily satisfied with the fall of Paledon. The valley looked friendly enough when they entered it. A long, straight, wide path made of a flattened, red-coloured earth, with steep climbs of white rock on either side of it, greeted the goblin army. Surrounded by trees on both its banks, the valley looked innocent and unthreatening. The most unpleasant thing for the goblins at this point had been an abundance of pink, red, blue and yellow tinted flowers growing out of the rocks and the edges of the woods and forest.

Blinny don't much like flowers – flowers bring with them emotions unrelated to the destruction and death they love to cause so much. At any given opportunity, the flowers are ripped out of the rocks by eager hands, or cut with flashing swords and trampled on until dust and dirt hides what they once were.

A few goblins make the climb up the steep valley banks to the edges of the trees above. Here they have a good view of the road ahead and they can see dozens of over-fed rabbits lolloping and playing around. Diving in and out of holes on the steep banks and forest edges the rabbits play.

"Here, I wouldn't mind getting my hands on one o' those rabbits," sneers Pompucket. Other hungry little monsters lick the drool away from their lips, longing for a rabbit's meat. Archers hoping to catch them out, get their bows ready and aim at the creatures. Releasing arrows in the direction of the rabbits, goblins miss their intended targets time and time again. Goblin archers, as already mentioned, do not have a great aim and not one single rabbit is killed or maimed. And so they begin to feel even hungrier.

Some monsters switch their strategy, waiting by rabbit holes, hands at the ready for a head to pop out, but blinny and ogres smell rotten and the rabbits smelling them can't be fooled that easily. Others take to sticking pikes down holes as they attempt to spear the rabbits, but the holes are too long and too twisting for any of them to reach. The rest of the blinny and ogres run, hands in front of them, trying to catch stray bunnies. One of them is Pompucket, who shouts at the rabbits angrily, "Come here, yer little buggers. It's a privilege to be eaten by me, don't you know?" But the rabbits don't believe Pompucket's claim, and so they decide to outrun and out-hop him instead. All in all, rabbit catching is harder than it first seemed, and with copious amounts of energy used trying to chase and capture this vermin, bellies rumble and turn.

And now, as day turns slowly to night, this should be the happiest part of the day, but for this army it will soon turn out to be the worst. The goblins must keep walking through the night if they are to reach Fricas by the morning. Comforted by night, it must be said that these goblin men cannot wait to relax their dark eyes; the sun has stifled and strained them for a long time already. They do things better at night. In fact, they were brought up as little gobs with the rays of the moon forming the background to their lives, and they cannot wait to revisit the pleasure of darkness once more. It has been a long time since they have been active in the presence of the moon; Warrior has made sure of that in his wisdom. Tonight they will not enjoy the darkness, though – they will hate it more than the day itself, and after tonight, some will never want to go back to it.

A mist develops, shrouding the valley floor to the tips of the trees above. It turns quickly into a blinding fog, and soon the goblins cannot see further than the first few lines of blinny in front of them. Mists do not scare these monsters but when the sounds begin, feelings change. In the forest above, twigs break and strange howls fill the air.

"What was that? Where did it come from? Somin's not right," come the cries from the goblin throng.

"Ha, it's probably nothin' – an old wolf or a dyin' cat," Pompucket says, trying to shrug off the fear he feels inside.

"Yeah, yer probably right," come the replies to Pompucket's

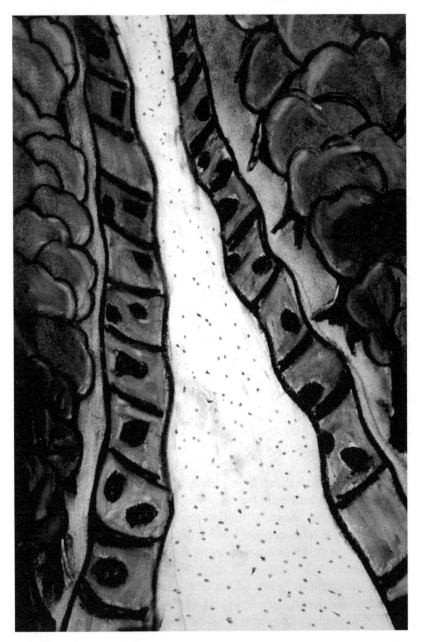

The valley

explanation. And then their fears are realised further as the strange sounds get nearer and nearer, and louder and louder. The goblins turn their heads left and right, trying to get sight of anything that does not appear natural, but the fog persists and their eyesight becomes distorted.

Owls hoot and birds scream, adding to the tension felt by the army travelling through the valley. Shuffling feet can be heard above the goblins on the grassy verges at the edge of Windrush Forest. The valley paths crack and snap with the sound of things moving around behind. Goblin hearts beat faster than they have done in a while; they breathe heavily with fear, and some even whimper and shake uncontrollably. Pushing against their compatriots, those at the back scramble to hide themselves in the crowd in front.

"It doesn't sound right, doesn't sound right at all," Pompucket whispers to himself. Although pushed and pulled by the crowd, little does he realise that he is safer than some of his cousins, for he is in the centre of it.

Right at the very back of this armed pack, fears are realised as cold, icy hands come out of the mists, landing on goblin shoulders and over goblin mouths. Silently, scores of goblins are pulled backwards into the dense fog. They are taken without a whisper until the deathly screams of one can be heard by others who are also being stalked. Goblin heads turn, surprised that they are at the back of the line, sure that this was not the case only moments ago. Hearing the moans and groans of their compatriots, it quickly dawns on them that they are the next in line to be taken.

Screaming for their lives, they raise an alarm that causes pandemonium amongst the others. Like headless chickens, they run around and about, trying to find a way out of this place – there isn't one. The goblins have strayed too far up the path and are too far from an exit to get away from the beasts who want to harm them.

The lieutenant, who walks at the very front of the line, screams out, "Ready yer weapons and be ready for an onslaught. Send in the ogres. They above all others should lose their lives in protection of goblin folk."

Ogres' chains are released by the hands of their owners. Let loose, they climb the walls of the valley with relative ease, disappearing into the fog. Goblins hear ogres sniffing out those who dare to attack their masters. Eerie deep-toned rumblings bellow out of ogre mouths and ogre feet pound on the floor above as they ready themselves for battle. Heavy footsteps are heard running along the grass verges and the beginnings of the woods into Windrush. Chilling gurgles suddenly sound out behind the curtains of mist, along with the ogres' deep bellowing screams. The heavy footsteps continue. Could the ogres have caught the monsters? Goblins begin to cheer, thinking that their pets have served their masters well once more. The lieutenant, thinking better, remains quiet, listening carefully in the direction of the screams and footsteps.

"Be quiet, all of yer," the lieutenant shouts, and then another sound pierces the air as metal hits metal. The goblins stop cheering, everyone falling silent again in the same instant.

Heavy footsteps cease and heavy bodies fall with a thump onto the grassy floor. A cacophony of thuds, like balls bouncing and rolling, is complemented by clanging and clinking chains dropping onto the hard ground. The goblins look at each other, perplexed and confused by what has happened. Chains can be heard rising from the ground and shaking violently from behind the smoke and clouds covering the valley. Dozens of bloody chains, once around necks, fly onto the waiting army from above, closely followed by ogres' heads. One lands at Pompucket's feet.

"Bugger and damnation. What demons stalk these woods?" screams Pompucket, looking down at the ogre's head. He is overcome by heavy breaths, panicked and sickened in equal measure.

The goblins scream and shout in terror. Something sick and unrelenting walks this place, and it has wiped out the ogres who walked with this army in only a matter of minutes.

"Bowmen, fire your arrows in the direction of the forest where our enemies dwell," the wiry lieutenant commands. The blinny do so gladly. Arrow after arrow is pulled out of quivers and fired into Windrush.

"Hold your fire!" shouts the general after a minute's bombardment. The bowmen stop shooting and everyone remains silent; only heavy breathing, brought about by anxiety, can clearly be heard. Whatever attacked the army must be dead, as nothing could have survived the attack. No sign is given to disprove the possibility and no one can see through the fog to be sure. Dread seeps through all the blinny, who know it might still be out there, waiting to pounce again. The silence lasts for a good few minutes; no twigs snap and no hollers or howls fill the air. Eventually, the goblin lieutenant orders that the army resumes their march.

"Keep yer wits about yer, as I suspect we have not seen the last of it," he orders.

Twitchy goblin soldiers begin to walk forwards then turn and glance backwards, eyes looking out for movement, any movement. Hours pass, the mist is not lifting, and the army walks a good distance borne out of trepidation and fear. As the minutes and hours pass, tension subsides. Maybe what was there has now gone, never to bother them again.

In the early hours of the morning, the silence is disrupted as something whooshes above the goblin army from Windrush Forest into the valley. More and more whooshing winds pass by, ending abruptly, prompting a scream or a fall to the ground. Pompucket ducks and dives, left and right, as whooshes fly close by him.

"What the…? What is this? What are these things flying round my head at bloody great speeds?" cries Pompucket. Arrows are being fired, that's what. Instinctively, Pompucket and other goblins rush towards the Windrush side of the valley, trying to avoid the arrows as they do so. All can see carnage through the thick mists, as a hundred goblins or more lie on the ground pierced by arrows. Looking at the fallen, those that are close enough to be seen that is, the goblins realise that the arrows are their own.

"Here, this arrow in the back of me, mate, it's an arrow me mate fired earlier at the monster in the forest. I'd recognise his arrows anywhere. Ironic, really," informs one goblin.

"Ay, it was probably coming back to teach him a lesson for missin' it," shouts out another, trying to lighten the air.

"Here's another one – I fired that one myself. Why has it come back to haunt him instead of me?" asks a goblin bowman, pointing at an arrow embedded in the skull of another lying at his feet.

"I don't think it's come back to haunt him. I think the monsters are using our weapons against us," responds Pompucket. "Methinks we're in trouble, all of us."

Whoever or whatever has attacked them appears to have collected the arrows fired earlier and fired them right back at the goblins in an act of defiance, or maybe even as a show of strength.

Night cannot turn to day quick enough now. The army sobs, wondering what other attacks will befall them tonight. One thing is true enough, they feel powerless to do anything about it. Walking in single file against the valley wall, heads turn once more, looking upwards and around in fear that death is not far away.

Indeed, death is not far away at all as something follows the goblins silently on the grass banks above them; they are many in number and they carry swords. Wandering further up the valley wall, these creatures line up shoulder to shoulder, grasping their swords in both hands, central to their chests. It is hard to make out what they are as the mist covers their faces.

The goblins do not suspect that their attackers are so close, never mind only the point of sword away. As the goblins cower, hugging the valley wall for protection, the figures above wait patiently until the right moment. When the time comes, swords held up high thrust down on the goblin army, piercing skulls, necks, collarbones and chests. High and low, up and down, swords move to a beat until nothing below presses or catches on the blades anymore. Pompucket is seemingly blessed, because as goblins fall all around him, he is untouched by any of it.

Watching left and right, Pompucket falls to the ground and crawls, muttering the words, "The horror and the carnage! Don't let me die. I'm still too young to die now."

Screaming, terrified blinny who have survived this merciless attack from above run, hobble and limp further into the mist, sure that they will be next. Pompucket picks himself up off the floor and runs as fast as he can. Others dart in front and around him; no one wants to be caught out at the rear of the pack.

Soon the mists begin to lift. The goblin lieutenant and his

goblin army have run as far as their legs and lungs would allow. Looking back on the valley as the mists dissipate and disappear, the real extent of the carnage is revealed. Goblin soldiers lie all around, with arrows protruding from backs, fronts, heads and tails. What is noticeable is the lack of weaponry with the lifeless bodies. Whoever or whatever has killed these men has also had the nerve to take their weapons from them as well.

"What are these beasts?" the goblin lieutenant asks. Soldiers shrug shoulders and twiddle thumbs in response. But how could anyone have known what had awaited them? "Come out and fight us now the air is clear, you cowards," the lieutenant shouts in the direction of Windrush. There is no response.

One or two goblin stragglers hobble and limp over the dead. Bottom lips quiver; the goblins are disturbed and disgusted with the way that their brethren have been dispatched. Goblins may be sadistic, but when it is not them or their counterparts inflicting the pain, then a hint of something more human engulfs them and they do not like it.

Hints of night turning to day are welcomed by the demoralised army stuck in a valley of murderous ghosts. No sun peers through yet, but the dark blue skies are slowly getting lighter, with red and yellow hues growing outwards from the horizon. Goblins can see the keep of Fricas peering through the trees; it is only a short distance away from the wooded area. Soon they will be at this valley's end, able to rest and regroup.

Elsewhere, Warrior and his army finally make it to the city walls, but they are far enough away to avoid any surprise attacks from arrows or the like. Bobbucket lollops around happily at the back of the throng, fumbling with his sword and shield. Taking in deep, cool breaths of air, the little goblin looks up at the moon and stars wondering who lives there, imagining wonderful, magical things.

"I wish I could be there as opposed to here," dreams Bobbucket.

Other goblins and ogres fall to the ground, lying or sitting on the short, well-trodden grasses of the plains. Cavalrymen lock barghest in cages brought down from carts using strong rope nooses attached to long metal poles. Cooks start fires underneath great cauldrons full of gruel. Flags are thrust into the ground.

Ogres sit next to their masters, heads in hands, eyes closed, as sleep is uppermost in goblin and ogre minds. Soon the sun will be out, the available hours need to be utilised well and sleep will leave all refreshed and ready for battle. Warrior, surrounded by his pets at the front of the army, stands silently. Sword in front and hands firmly fixed on the pommel, he assesses the battlements, the defences and how best to bring them down.

Fricas sits on the tallest of hills, and that very same hill stretches for miles and miles across. On the river side of the city, the hill ends abruptly with a steep drop to the river below. The city walls can clearly be seen to start a mile or more down from the very peak of the hill. The walls are thick; stone found on the site of the hill mixes well with imported stone brought to this place via the river. It took seventy years to build this city, and thousands worked tirelessly on it so that its residents could send a message to the world stating, 'We are strong'.

The keep stands proudly at the top of the hill, close to the side where the river flows. It is large and tall and its stone walls are the same thickness as the outer walls of the city, making it almost impenetrable, at least to the conventional weapons of this time. The sheer height of the keep on top of the steep hill means that the views from it are unsurpassed. The keep is where the King resides, and it is only accessible through a series of gate and walls, filtering upward from the city's beginnings. The keep, and therefore the King is difficult to reach – especially if the people do not want you to get there.

Hundreds, if not thousands, of houses line the protective walls, sheltering a large population. Houses range from the grand to the basic, as all types and classes of people work and live relatively soundly to keep this city great. Large areas of parkland, market squares, libraries and reservoirs of water are dotted strategically, so as to give the best possible amenities to the widest number of citizens. Statues depicting old heroes, battles and memorials rival those of the jotunn in craftsmanship, reminding visitors and invaders alike that this is not a city you would want to trouble. Towers and spires point up towards the sky; the building of these was necessary as the city grew bigger and bigger. Towers house many people, providing them with a place to work or a place to call home.

If Fricas falls, then the message given to those kingdoms not affected by the fighting is that death will not be long averted under Warrior's wrath. Given the rate of destruction so far caused by Warrior, only a year or so can pass before the marginalisation of man is apparent. The future may well dictate that men will survive only in small packs. Hiding in the most desolate of places, never to be seen again could be man's ultimate fate, much like the goblins all those years ago. But the army, however blood-driven, has not been tested yet, and to all intents, neither has Warrior. Theoretically, Fricas cannot survive the vast army bearing down on them. The army at Fricas has a thousand men at most, and although the walls are thick and the citizens will help where they can, a miracle is needed to beat this throng.

As rays of sun break through the horizon, hundreds of soldiers lined up on the parapets look out onto the army before them. Soldiers are protected by well-maintained chain mail and plain steel-plated helmets that catch the light of the moon and the flickering light from torches. Blue cloaks keep the soldiers warm on cold, chilly nights whilst also identifying them as fricasian. It is noticeable that there are no mothers, children, or older men and women roaming the city. A last minute evacuation was ordered by the King. Those lucky enough have escaped the city via the river, and have been carried by many boats heading eastward towards Milias.

"It's not the blinny that are the problem," one soldier observes. All know that this race has a knack of fighting only until it suits them to run away; numbers mean nothing against skill.

"But have you seen that Warrior fella? Now that is a big problem. I mean, it is not that he is bigger than big, it's not the armour, or the sword he carries that I'm afraid of," comments another soldier, his face describing the horrors he sees in his mind's eye. "He's two a penny in these parts. But the skulls, the skulls around his neck – they're the kings and warriors he has defeated, aren't they? I hear some of them were great heroes, and if heroes can't kill him, what can?"

"And what about his face. That isn't his own, you know. Isn't that Sir Gerwain? How can he wear a face of another, and how did he manage to get it? This is not the behaviour of a sane man. He is either insane or not a man at all, I'm sure of that," adds another.

"We're going to die, aren't we? There are too many of them, and even if there were too few it wouldn't matter because we would be overcome by their leader anyway. How do I get out of here? Surely there is an escape route. The women and children have been set free. Oh, how I wish I were one of them now," a soldier cries out, driven mad by what he can see before him.

"There is nowhere to go; it is here that we must stand. If we are to die here today, then at least we must resolve to take as many of these little monsters with us as we can before Ankou comes for us," rallies another.

The wooded valley is peaceful and bright. Goblins feast on a few of their brethren from behind a hill at the far edge of the valley. The army have made sure that they are far enough away from Windrush Forest to defend an attack, but close enough to Fricas to carry out Warrior's orders when the signal comes. After a head count, not inclusive of heads that are no longer connected to the bodies of their owners, it turns out that a little under two thirds of the goblin army were killed last night by their unknown assailants. The talk here is of revenge, but not one goblin dares go anywhere near the forest. Half of them believe that they were attacked by ghosts, and that is a very powerful thing to say. Goosebumps and shivers are felt all over this small camp at the very mention of the word 'ghost'.

"I just hope we don't stay here well into the night," says one goblin.

"Methinks the night was the plan," replies another.

"Let's hope it changes fast," adds another. "There is no way I want another night like that comin' to haunt us."

"Don't let them come in the day," replies another. "Not much worse can happen than that happenin' last night."

A voice comes from out of the crowd, it is Pompucket. "At least we are alive, able to do nasty deeds for one more day. They left us some tasty meat for our mornin's delight as well. And I'm hungry, what with all the runnin' and hidin' we've done."

The goblins push themselves to go to sleep after their early morning breakfast; some keeping one eye open just in case the monster that attacked them in the night comes back for them in the day. It has been a long night for these goblin men, and whilst heads spin with fatigue now, a good rest will do them no end of good.

CHAPTER 20

A SHAPE-SHIFTER'S FLIGHT

There is only one fire tonight. Normally many fires would blaze, in some way to show the strength of the army waiting to attack. But this army is at a disadvantage; it is small and attention should not be drawn to it. The jotunn understand the caution, as do all the other creatures. Realisation of how serious and life-threatening this quest is touches everyone; stomachs turn to the point of sickness, and minds focus to the point of aching. Banter is replaced with solemn conversation about mothers and fathers, swordplay and strategy, life and death, but no one dwells on it as sleep is critical.

As the majority of the creatures sleep, Stryker and Forester take up positions away from the camp. They hide their clothes behind trees, close to the entrance of the wooded area separating the camp from the fricasian territories. Tonight Stryker and Forester's shifted forms resemble those of owls; they are wise in their choice as owls understand this terrain and time of day better than other creatures. With keen eyesight the owls fly in different directions and cover the area surrounding the camp. If anyone or anything is to try and ambush this army as they sleep then they will have to pass by either Stryker or Forester. And so while the minutes and hours pass, Stryker and Forester remain alert, although their eyes feel heavier and heavier, tiring by the minute. The flying guardians of this camp search in and out of trees, behind stones and in the natural dips of the hills, scouring for any form of activity – be it the snap of a twig, the whisper of a voice or a shadow moving in the moonlight. No activity at all is registered by either of them, but the night has plenty left in it before their job is done.

Stryker rests in a tree at the exit to the fricasian side of the woods. He has shifted back into human form and is chewing on a twig, admiring the view of a peaceful and secure-looking Fricas. Fricas flickers with light, as the flames from various fires and candles in houses and buildings wave this way and that against a light breeze. His eyes blink as he tries to keep them open, the dark helping him on his way towards unconsciousness. Stryker yawns, content and comfortable in the tree. He is just about to nod off when there is a sound. The clatter of metal cuts through the silence of night. Stryker sits up in the tree open-mouthed, the twig hanging off his lip.

"It is time to shift once more," he whispers to himself and within seconds he is back in the form of the owl. From behind a dip in the woods, the metal clatter assumes a shape as the heads of soldiers appear. Moving forward, it is revealed that they are cavalrymen sitting atop large armoured horses.

The eagle-eyed soldiers keeping lookout on the parapets of the castle at Fricas had indeed seen Greybeard's army approaching. By the look of it, they are hoping to defeat the jotunn before they get close to the city walls. Behind the cavalrymen are foot soldiers, many hold pikes with sharpened daggers on their long, thin poles. Pikemen will be useful, as their reach against giants will be better than those wielding swords.

Stryker has seen enough – this army outnumbers Greybeard's two to one already and his feeling is that it has more men besides. Opening his large, wide wings, Stryker flies off his perch and back into the breezes that will help carry him. He chooses to fly upwards, high up into the darkened skies, his large frame silhouetting against the moon and stars. Stryker can see the army filtering into the woods and it will not be long before they reach the tunny camp.

Sharp eyes pick out Forester in the distance. Alerting Forester via a series of cries and hollers, Stryker is soon joined by his brother who immediately sees the threat below. Both of them fly together to the tree where their clothes hide. Shifting back into their human form, they dress more quickly than they have ever done before. Tucking shirts into pants and fastening their belts, Stryker and Forester run towards the camp, which is only a minute away from the edge of the woods, shouting in order to raise the alarm. Men and women quickly wake all over the camp, calmly falling into groups. It surprises Stryker and Forester, but out of all the figures in the camp only they appear panicked by the thought of an army bearing down on them. Greybeard wakes with a start.

"What is all this fuss?" he asks grumpily, having been woken well before he was ready. Taking hold of his staff, Greybeard turns his head in the direction of the cries coming from Stryker and Forester. They are close as the darkened shapes of the brothers can be seen approaching at a good speed.

"An army of men approaches. An army of men approaches," Stryker shouts, repeating himself over and over as he runs to Greybeard. "The army, it will be in the middle of the woods by now. There are many soldiers... both on horseback and not," he says, catching his breath between words.

"They must have seen us and travelled from Fricas to greet us," mutters Greybeard, with a tinge of excitement.

"What shall we do?" asks Stryker.

"Well, we do not want to fight them. I suppose that it is up to me to confront them before they come close enough to make an attack," advises Greybeard giving a big yawn, confident he can appease those making their way to the camp.

"Yes, that does sound like a good idea," replies Stryker, with a sigh. "Seeing as you are looking after this issue now, can I get a little bit of sleep?"

"You deserve it, I suppose," smiles Greybeard.

"Good, I'll see you in the morning then," Stryker announces, wandering off somewhere quiet, Forester following behind him.

Greybeard begins to walk away from the camp on his own, using his staff as a guide.

"We would like to come with you, keep you company, fight with you should we need to," offers Igralf, running up to the wizard with Gendralf, Wattlespalf and Finn in tow.

"Yes, of course. That would be very much appreciated – your company, I mean," replies Greybeard, accepting the dwarf's invitation. There is a purpose in his words, as he knows he may need them to prove their cause. Greybeard is well known in the realms of all creatures other than men, his tales are not regularly told by this kind as part of their folklore.

Wizards are treated with relative disdain insofar as they are often regarded as troublemakers or possible debasers of power in men. The latter is quite possibly true, as wizards generally try to disrupt the centres of power within kingdoms that are ruled by unwise or evil men. In equal measure, the unnamed have oft been seen as being of wizard class. Indeed, Warrior has been thrust into this classification already, and a second wizard entering the battle may only serve to further the suspicions of the army who approach through the woods at this moment. As for being a troublemaker, well, Greybeard would refute this passionately, claiming his intentions are always honourable, mostly. But dwarfs, dwarfs have been friends of men for a long, long time. If Greybeard's testimony is not enough, then the dwarfs will surely sway the verdict.

"I may need you," Greybeard tells the dwarfs as he walks towards the woods.

"Good! It is always nice to feel needed," says Igralf.

"Who would have thought that of all the armies, of all the creatures I have met, it is men who I might need to persuade the most. I hadn't even considered this moment," reflects Greybeard.

"Old man, our cause is just. I hope we meet a man who is equally just and able to see that we are honest or we may be in for a long night," replies Igralf solemnly.

"It would be a sad thing to go into battle with the men we intend to save," adds Gendralf.

"Don't worry, Greybeard. You have a good honest face and, besides, you are an old man. They won't find you intimidating one bit," informs Wattlespalf, offering his take on the situation.

Mischievous smiles and tickled ribs come from Wattlespalf's words, but no one ridicules him; instead the words are taken in their right context and meaning.

"Friend, you have a good way with words and your honesty is very uplifting. I should not even worry. Of course not," Greybeard's tone is lighter now, realising his age has taken some of the indestructibility and vigour of youth away from him.

"Finn, I did not want to do this, but you are now the bait. The army you are about to meet may or may not know of your kind. But if they do, then you, by your very presence, will make sure that our quest is very special in nature," the old man reveals. "You must remain near, but for your own safety you must stay a little way behind us, away from immediate danger. We will call you when we need you." Finn agrees to Greybeard's request and stands at the edge of the woods. Greybeard and the dwarfs press forward through the trees with better thoughts and spirits.

Exiled and dead races are on the cusp of joining together with the world of men to overthrow a common foe, once again. Battles of ages past have been glorious. After the battles that have gone before, for a while at least, the creatures were brought together in peaceful collaboration. Greybeard is excited. He has seen races live well with each other only to slowly lose touch and eventually segregate themselves from other creatures' worlds once more. Maybe this new age of collaboration can reignite the flame, and with some help, forge a new society, one that will last. The wizard wants to make sure of this. A new world excites and perturbs him at the same time, because he is also guilty of removing himself from the imaginations of creatures in this land. If he is an instigator of this new-found peace, where elves help dwarfs and men help jotunn, then he too must bring himself to the forefront and become a champion of it.

The wizard walks ahead of the dwarfs in the woods. The darkness is blinding. Dare he ask his oric to light? This would give away their position right away. Would he endanger his and the dwarfs' lives by lighting the way? Of course he would, but not without cause. But if he and the dwarfs were not hidden would this army treat them as travellers and not as foes? Possibly, but their cause would surely win out should the worst happen. These questions and many more race through his mind and so he must make a decision or two. But before he can, a twang can be heard, and within a second an arrow whizzes past the old man, close to his head. Greybeard is immediately shaken by this and asks that his oric light straight away, which it does.

"Wait," Greybeard shouts out ahead of him.

"Hold your arrows," a voice orders in the near distance. "Who goes there?" it asks forcefully.

"My name is Greybeard, and I travel with three dwarfs," he replies.

"What are you doing in these woods at this time of night?" asks the voice.

"We come to talk to you. We think that you may be marching our way with misgivings and misunderstandings," replies Greybeard.

"And what makes you think that we misunderstand you?" the voice shouts.

"A goblin army approaches from the south and you are under siege. We have acquired an army of jotunn, dwarfs, shape-shifters and elves to help combat the threat of the goblins and their leader," Greybeard reveals to the voice.

There is a silence, apart from whispers that cannot be made out.

"The elves are dead, and the jotunn wild and dangerous. The shape-shifters are murderous scum, and you... who are you, Greybeard? Answer quickly or feel the full force of our armoury."

"I am a wizard. One who may be known to you or not, but my intentions are humble and honest. The jotunn who wait in our camp have come for the goblins, not for your kingdom. The elves are but two, and whilst it is hard for me to explain why they are here, they are here. I have no doubt that these elves are important and that they will play a good part in the battles ahead," states Greybeard, answering quickly and honestly.

Silence and whispering ensues again; this is a good sign because it means that the army in front is cautious. The arrow that passed Greybeard's head must have been a warning shot as none have been fired since.

"Why should we trust you? The world is in turmoil and you could be just another band of murderers and vagabonds. Know this... you are very close to being fired upon again – and this time we will not miss – so it is in your best interests to answer quickly," the voice commands.

"I have no answer to that except that, in these times, creatures must band together to prevent a larger evil, as has been done in the past. It is in the best interests of all races, whether considered good, bad or indifferent, that the goblins and those promising them domination do not get what they want. Everlast will not survive under their wrath."

"Can I be used as testimony?" a voice calls out. It is Finn.

"Finn, get behind me," Greybeard shouts angrily, trying to protect him.

"Please, give me your staff," Finn asks Greybeard. Greybeard obliges reluctantly, passing his bright-lighted staff to him. The wizard knows why Finn has asked for it. He will become visible to the army in front, revealing his elven form and confirming Greybeard's honesty. But if Finn were to be fired upon the staff would not protect him, as this elf has no magic in him to control it, or at least not a magic the wizard's oric understands. Finn walks past Greybeard towards the unseen army that is still shrouded in darkness. Gasps can be heard in the near distance; as predicted, the army can see Finn. Finn walks forward determinedly, stopping a short distance from them.

"I am one of the elves of whom Greybeard speaks. Warrior murdered all of my people, and through some strange twist of fate I have been brought here from the past to this time – maybe even for this very cause," shouts Finn, accepting that these may be his last words.

Whispers from the army covered in darkness turn to shouts.

"This cannot be!" shouts one voice.

"He is an abomination!" comes another.

"There stands something more evil than what awaits us back at the city," adds another.

Another twang comes from the bow of one of the men in the distance. An arrow can be heard piercing the air, and a second later Finn falls to the ground.

"Stop!" booms the commanding voice to his army.

Greybeard and the dwarfs run towards Finn. More arrows fly, missing the running pack.

"Stop!" orders the voice again. This time, the sound of a horse cantering and the clicking of metal against wood indicates that a superior is taking action against his bowmen.

Greybeard and the dwarfs reach Finn. His still body is face down on the ground.

"Where has he been hit?" asks a frantic Gendralf, dropping to his knees.

"I don't know – I can't see," an equally upset Igralf replies.

Greybeard is panicking. "I forgot my backpack. I don't have the dangleberry potion to hand. We cannot afford to lose this elf. Oh, Finn, what have they done?"

"Turn him round slowly. Maybe we can find the wound and stem any bleeding," orders Igralf.

Wattlespalf and Gendralf turn Finn onto his side. They look closely at his head and upper body, but they cannot see any wound.

"Lay him on his back. We may get a better view," advises Greybeard.

The wizard and the dwarfs look all over, but they cannot see an arrow embedded in him or a wound. Other than a tear on Finn's tunic, near the lower part of his shoulder and unprotected by his armour, there is nothing to indicate that he is hurt.

Finn opens his eyes and winks; he has faked an injury to buy them some time and favour.

"Very unlike you, you bugger. Oh, you had me worried," whispers Greybeard to Finn, controlling his joy, sighs ringing out from the rest.

The sound of a horse's gallop approaches, the ground rumbling underneath it. All look up, anticipating who might be coming to greet them; no doubt an apology will also be made. The gallop soon changes into a trot as the horse slows down. Greybeard's oric is still shining, lighting up the immediate area.

Whilst those tending to Finn cannot see the horse approaching, the horseman looking back at them can certainly see them. Out of the darkness, a huge, muscular horse, heavily armoured, appears. Thick front legs, sizeable hooves and stocky shoulders are revealed by the oric's glow, and it is not difficult to see that this is a horse of war. The expectation is that the soldier who remains cloaked in darkness will complement his horse. As he walks into the light, though, it becomes very apparent that nothing could be further from the truth. The warrior is a small man, only a little taller than Perrywinkle. Greybeard gets up off his knees and stands to greet him. He towers above the approaching soldier. The man is decorated with a fine chainmail tunic which stretches across his shoulders and chest down to his waist. He does not wear a helmet, and his face is that of a young, slim man, his brown, tousled hair falls to his shoulders. It is obvious he prides himself on his cleanliness and has lived a privileged life.

"Sir, I am Laureate, Captain of the fricasian army," he says, announcing himself to Greybeard. "I sincerely apologise for the arrows fired in your direction. My men are a little tetchy as you might well expect. Is the elf alright? I heard the commotion. Please say that we have not killed him, as this would truly be an injustice."

"Your men are indeed tetchy and blundering. You nearly did kill this precious elf, and us for that matter. But he and we are fine and there is no harm done. I just hope your men have not targeted more arrows our way as they are likely to fire upon you as well," Greybeard patronises.

"Again, I reiterate my apologies. Can I see the elf?" Laureate asks, wanting a closer examination of what had appeared in front of him and his men before Finn was unceremoniously fired upon by his bowmen.

"Of course," Greybeard stands to one side revealing Finn, who remains in a seated position on the floor of the woods.

"By the grace of the Creators." Laureate gawps, putting his face close to Finn's. Laureate pulls on Finn's ears and taps on his shoulders and knees. He pokes, prods and pinches all over, making sure that this elf is real.

"Can-you-say-something-to-me?" Laureate asks Finn, saying every word very slowly.

"Hello-I-am-an-elf," responds Finn, feeling a little patronised, saying every word very slowly in response to Laureate.

Laureate gasps dramatically. Finn and the dwarfs roll their eyes a little – Laureate's awe is a bit too much.

"Sir, I am convinced. How would you have me serve you?" he says, finally bringing the examination to a close.

"Take your men back to the edge of the woods nearest Fricas, and wait for us there until morning," Greybeard orders politely. "Oh, and thank you, Laureate. I promise you, we will repay your faith in us."

"No problem, no problem at all. This is a very special time and an elf is a very special thing. I just hope that the elves have been sent for a good reason. I will await your arrival later this morning," Laureate says, bowing his head towards the group. Turning quickly, he heads back towards his horse, mounts his steed and disappears into the darkness.

"Right, you lot, back to the camp. You too, Perrywinkle." Perrywinkle appears from behind a tree. "How did you…"

"Just know that I did," interrupts Greybeard, picking up his staff.

CHAPTER 21

THE HORN IS BLOWN

It is the eighth day since the companions set out against Warrior. Spirits are high because today it is likely that Greybeard's newly-founded army will reach the walls of Fricas and the battle will begin.

Greybeard and the rest have left the camp and are working their way through the woods. Lines of tunny soliders find the woods hard to navigate; in many instances they are as tall as the smaller trees and this brings many dangers. The giants cannot see the branches and twigs below them, and although they tread slowly, most come close to tripping up as ankles and shins catch on hard, unmoving wood. If a giant were to fall on any creature of a smaller size below them, the creature in question would be well and truly squashed. Jotunn are nowhere near the height of the tallest trees and this poses another problem: branches, twigs and leaves obstruct their views, with faces, necks and chests slapped numerous times by the more flexible of woods. It is, at best, annoying for the jotunn, at worst, a perilous jaunt that they must endure.

Twigs and branches fall close to the men, dwarfs and elves. It is decided that they must get as far away as possible from the jotunn in order to avoid any unnecessary dangers posed by the giant army.

Greybeard and the others soon emerge from out of the trees and are greeted by Laureate and his army. Laureate's soldiers are well-armed and well-prepared. Archers, cavalry, pikemen and foot soldiers are all separated into their different divisions. Body armour and shields emblazoned with lions shine, while swords and pikes glint in the sun. Bows are made from the finest woods; horses are strong and well looked after. Fricas, it appears, is awash with wealth and has invested its currency wisely in its protectors. This army comprises two hundred men and maybe a few more; for the size of the city it is a relatively small congregation, but this is only one division of the army and it had been decided by those who rule it that only these men were needed to defeat Greybeard's men. It is obvious that those who rule did not know with whom they were dealing.

A shaven-headed fricasian King stands on top of his keep, looking out at Warrior from the parapets. Seeing views of his land filled by aggressors – and more importantly, Warrior – he is instantly afraid. Age has made him more fearful. When this King was younger his prowess was not legendary, but he was heard of as he tried to emulate the victories and honours of other more famous kings, although this was not to be. Battles had not raged quite so much as they had done in previous ages. Whilst not a peaceful land, the scale of battles in past years had been small in comparison.

"Oh, I would love to be a part of this, but my muscles, bones and indeed, my strength of mind are not what they were. Why risk my life and the lives of others by stepping onto the field of battle? Everlast is over with – surely it would be better to get away than grace the fields as a corpse. But what then of my reputation? Should I relinquish it on the whim of one foolish moment? No, I should revel in it. Whatever the result, it is a battle for which one will be remembered. It is a shame I am not younger and more capable of doing things that I can only attempt now."

Walking the length of his parapets, he looks for Laureate and his army. The sun's rays are fast rising, blinding the King who raises his hand above his brow, cutting the sun out from his immediate view. Over the fields, the King's eyes focus on trees and large stones at the bottom of the hill away from the city. Laureate is a good distance away and the King's search appears to be in vain, until there in a small wood, a giant's head can be seen and giant arms push back the branches of the trees.

"It is the jotunn. They are still alive," he mumbles. A frustrated King stamps his feet on the ground.

"Move your army back," commands Greybeard. "The jotunn are not far behind, and they are likely to crush you if you remain in the same spot."

"Move back," Laureate orders his men, heeding Greybeard's advice.

The tops of trees can be seen moving behind Greybeard,

black-mane topped helmets oft pierce through them. Laureate's men move back further in fear and awe of what will appear from the woods shortly.

Teacher is the first to emerge out of the woods, closely followed by the other tunny, who are more than pleased to leave them. Leaves, twigs and insects are brushed off tunics, out of hair, picked out of shoes and armour. Laureate's army look closer to the skies as they watch these monsters multiply to become many. The jotunn form their ranks and the fricasian army cheer for their new-found friends. Giants stand proud, smiling at this rapturous reception, humbled that they are considered so highly by another race they have not mingled with for hundreds of years.

"Dear jotunn, it is a pleasure to receive you. We hope graciously that with your help we can defeat Warrior's marauding army and send it back from where it came," announces Laureate.

"With such a welcome, I sincerely hope that we can do you the greatest of service," replies Teacher.

"And we hope we can repay the service you bring," enthuses Laureate.

"Less of the platitudes and dramatics – we have work to do," grumbles Greybeard.

Fricas dominates the landscape ahead. This army (much like Warrior's army) has a steep climb ahead of it, and whilst Laureate's forces travelled for less than a day to get to these woods, it may take much longer to return. As the army travels towards Fricas, Greybeard pulls up alongside Laureate, who leads his men from the front.

"Laureate, I've been meaning to ask… where were the goblins positioned when you left Fricas yesterday?"

"They were at the edges of Paledon town from what we could see. The town will be no more by now, as there were few people left to defend it. It is possible that the goblin armies are already outside the city walls and will attack soon. I fear that our battle has arrived," replies Laureate, sounding slightly sombre.

"From Paledon, how would Warrior best reach Fricas?" Greybeard asks, sweeping aside Laureate's previous comments for less emotional chatter.

"Well, the most obvious route is from the plains at the southern end of the city. They could of course flank the east and west of it," replies Laureate.

"Are there any vantage points that this army can use to gain an advantage against the city?"

"What do you mean?" asks Laureate, uncomfortable about where this line of questioning is headed.

"Are there any places this army could hide? Woods? Dips in the view? Secret entrances to the city? Anything that they could exploit?" Greybeard asks, imploring Laureate to search his mind.

"There is a wooded area to the left of the city as we see it now. The woods lead from the outskirts of Paledon to the north-eastern walls in front of us. The river to the right of the city weaves in and out and around the hills, the view is obscured from time to time. I suppose they could travel along it undetected. Saying that, all they would gain is an impossible and impractical climb up to the top of the cliffs," Laureate advises.

"Tell me more about the wooded area," Greybeard asks, probing Laureate further.

"The trees straddle the plains all the way up from Paledon. Between the wooded area and Windrush Forest there is a shallow valley, which acts as a corridor. It is an unremarkable route, easy to navigate and would be advantageous to any army who travelled it but for the rumours." Laureate stops in his tracks.

"What rumours?" asks a curious Greybeard, his ears pricking up at the very mention of Windrush.

"It is said that there are rumblings and rustlings in the forests, and that there are ghosts afoot. Anyone who has travelled through the valley, be it traders or poachers, have not travelled this route again. They say that they were watched – that the trees were alive and that they did not feel welcome. We haven't felt the need to wander that way for many, many years but this is partly because we do not want to," he explains.

"Windrush, eh?" responds Greybeard, pondering over what has been said. "I wonder…" he asks himself, thinking of elves and other such things. "And your armies, do they defend from inside the city?"

"We did not see fit to move beyond the walls of the city as it must be protected at all costs. Our army is a fraction of the size of the one that approaches, it would be a mistake to expose ourselves to them," replies Laureate.

"How many protect the north-eastern walls?" the old man says.

"The majority will defend the southern walls. Only a few will man the battlements elsewhere, raising an alarm should a threat pose itself," replies Laureate with a lump in his throat, understanding why he has been interrogated so.

"I think it is imperative that we head for the north-eastern wall then, don't you?" comments Greybeard. Laureate nods. "We need to move quickly; can your men move any faster?"

"The cavalry, yes, but I doubt that those on foot can."

"Your cavalry needs to make haste. I will go back to my men and follow shortly," commands Greybeard. Laureate agrees, calling his cavalry to attention, gesturing that they travel at a fast pace towards Fricas. After receiving their instruction, the horsemen break away from the main pack.

Greybeard turns Thundercloud around and heads back towards his companions. He passes row after row of young tunny men and women as he does so. The wizard reminds himself that many of the faces he has ingrained into his mind will not be here in a day or two to speak of their exploits. It is a sad moment for him, especially as some are just coming of age and have barely lived.

Unbeknownst to Laureate and Greybeard, the fricasian King has been watching events unfold with satisfaction. "This is good news." The King smiles at his servants, grabbing their shoulders and shaking them. "It appears we have got some help, they follow Laureate to aid us in our fight. Tell the soldiers all is not lost," he says enthusiastically to his servants, who run quickly down the stairs leaving the King alone on top of the keep. The King walks back to the southern facing parapet and looks down at Warrior. "We might just survive a little longer than you expect us to," whispers the King in Warrior's direction.

Greybeard trots over to Stryker, Forester and the dwarfs announcing, "I think I know how Warrior is going to bring down the walls of Fricas."

"Tell us," says Stryker, prompting the wizard to reveal his thoughts.

"Stryker, I think we need to blow Pengwellen's horn. I've been told that Warrior and the goblins may already be at the city walls, and if not, I suspect that they are within distance now. We should not hesitate any longer," he warns.

Stryker reaches into his backpack and pulls out Temper, the horn. He looks at it for only a few seconds before pressing the end of it against his lips. He blows hard, but no sound comes out of it.

"Is that it? Have I done it correctly? No sound came from it – can that be right?" Stryker shrugs his shoulders, confused.

"Erm, well I don't know," Greybeard says, scratching his head. "Blow it again for good measure."

Stryker presses the horn against his lips again and blows the biggest blow he could have ever achieved, but still there is no sound. Stryker looks at everybody in turn and shrugs his shoulders.

"Are you sure you're doing it right?" asks Wattlespalf with one eyebrow raised.

"Here, let me try," says Igralf, who has blown many horns in his time.

Stryker willingly passes the horn to Igralf, who hopes to show Stryker up a little. He wipes the horn of Stryker's spittle and presses it against his lips, looking at the others with confidence. Igralf huffs and puffs and pushes out a long, hard breath into the end of the horn. But still there is no sound.

"Well, he didn't tell us that bit, did he?" comments a puzzled Igralf, referring to how Temper should be blown.

"All of you make haste. Blow the horn as you might, but do it at a speed. Time is short," hurries a disgruntled Greybeard. "I will follow you from behind. Take the tunny with you, they will be faster than any of us. You may need them sooner rather than later. Beezle, you stay with me. You have one more lesson to learn before you will be set loose. And Perrywinkle, I want you to stay behind as well."

Forester, the dwarfs and Finn snap their reins and kick their heels, prompting the horses they ride upon to go faster and faster. Beezle and Perrywinkle stay behind as ordered, following behind Greybeard. Stryker trots up to Teacher.

"Teacher, we need your men and women to come with us

urgently. We think the monsters may already be close to the city walls. Are you sure you are ready to meet the enemy?" he asks with urgency.

"Ready as we ever could be. Do not worry about us – we want to be here," Teacher replies, before addressing the tunny behind him. The giants stand fast, waiting for the words that will come out of Teacher's mouth.

"It is time we act on the choices we have made and run to the aid of the brave men and women who stand behind those walls in the city before us. We must run now with those who have already made their move. Follow me and be quick," urges Teacher, before making a move towards the city. The jotunn, bolstered by Teacher's words, roar and sprint as requested, intent on catching those who have gone on ahead. Stryker, caught out by their initial burst of speed, follows behind them.

The horn had been blown correctly; as the crow flies the sound produced from it works its way at a pace towards King's Mountain and the dragons who dwell there. Over plains, roads, rivers, fields and hills the sound travels, like a dog running to its master.

Meanwhile, on the floor of his cavern, Pengwellen is reading yet another book from his extensive library. His spectacles are firmly fixed on the bridge of his extraordinarily long nose and he flicks through the pages slowly, taking in the information offered by the book. Pengwellen gets a twinge in his ear as if a fly is flying in and out of it. Lifting his talon he screws it in and around the ear drum, trying to clear it of the annoyance.

Suddenly, a trumpeting type of sound booms through his cave, disturbing the dust that has settled in the cavern. It is the sound of the horn. The sound booms through every other dragon's cave as well, and they all sit up, understanding that the time has come to travel alongside Pengwellen into battle. Eventually, the sound stops, and every dragon is somewhat relieved because it is both deafening and irritating. And then another trumpet type of sound arrives and booms through the caves – this would be the second time Stryker blew on the horn. Stopping again, within a minute the sound generated by Igralf's turn on the horn arrives.

"I wish they would stop doing that," mumbles Pengwellen, holding his talons against his ears.

Another trumpeting sound bellows out and stops, and then another and another. Whilst the sounds have taken their time to travel to King's Mountain, Gendralf, Forester, Wattlespalf and Finn have all had turns trying to make the horn work as they think it should. Unbeknownst to them, it was working all along and dragons all round King's Mountain are beginning to get fed up with the booming interruptions invading their delicate ears.

"Dumb idiots, didn't I explain well enough?" Pengwellen grumbles, not acknowledging any blame for the imposition these men have caused. The dragon eventually closes his book, removes his spectacles and gives out a big yawn before stretching, as he always does in preparation for a move. Pengwellen puts the spectacles on the shelf where the horn, that has been causing so much trouble, once lay. Trepidation and tears engulf him as he knows his time draws closer. He has had a long time to accept his fate, but now more than ever he appreciates the gift of life. Memories flood back and he feels unfulfilled.

"I could have done more," the dragon mutters under his breath. Since he has been aware of the time of his death, Pengwellen has wallowed in his lair, frittering away what time he had left doing practically nothing. "Could I have done it differently?" he asks himself. What comes back is a resolute "Yes".

Looking around his lair, he observes the numerous items he has collected, stroking them with a gentleness reserved for the best of times. Books remind him of his knowledge; he could quite possibly have been one of the greatest minds in this world but now his knowledge is on the fringes of being lost.

"If the elves do go back to where they started and things change then I will live differently!" he exclaims. "I should do everything to make that possible." His resurrection will only be granted if he can ensure Finn and Beezle are returned to their age before the darkness happened, and he dearly hopes he can make it so.

Saying goodbye to his lair, he walks slowly to the cave opening. Pengwellen is greeted by a few dozen dragons on the ground below him. All are of a different colour and type but all have wings and the ability to fly. Many of the dragons have been excused from going to battle as their journeys would be too far and too difficult to make it to the battle on time, especially the land and water dragons, who were born without wings. Those who will not go into battle will be responsible for keeping the race of dragons alive. They will look after the dragonlings should their parents not return.

"We live on the cusp of one of the greatest battles since the first steps on this world were taken," Pengwellen announces, addressing his clan from the edge of the cave he calls his home. "Without us, this world might fall into a darkness so terrible that our kind might not be able to survive it. We must join forces with foes and friends alike to make sure that our cities are not defiled by those who want to dominate us. I ask you, come with me now and stop this enemy full of darkness. If you do, I guarantee you will become part of a history that our race can look upon proudly."

Pengwellen finishes his speech. Growls and roars ring out. Dragonfire shoots up into the skies, as all are in agreement with the old dragon and the cause. Pengwellen opens out his wings, beating them ferociously before taking to the air. Dragons at the foot of King's Mountain unfold their wings and follow Pengwellen up above the clouds. The sun shines brightly upon their backs here as the skies all around are blue. Speedily, the dragons fly, as flashes of blue, yellow, green and red skim silently above the green fields below. Echoes from the blowing of the horn still resonate out, leading the dragons to those that need them. The rumblings of the horn when blown travelled far beyond the speed of sound and the dragons are noticeably slower. The men were right to have summoned the dragons when they did, because it may not be until dusk or after that they arrive in Fricas to play their part in this skirmish.

"Goblins prefer to attack at night," Igralf reassures the others as they gain lost distance between themselves and Laureate. "It offers them an advantage, and they will need it against a city this large. If they are as close as we suspect they are, then tonight or tomorrow the city will be attacked, but not now."

"I hope you are right, dear friend," replies Forester.

"I am always right," reassures Igralf. "Do not fear."

Behind the city walls, against the parapets, the soldiers are bewildered as to why Warrior is taking his time over an attack. Whispering has ensued, questioning the tactics of such an army.

"Why are they waiting?" says one soldier.

"Maybe they want to take in the sun whilst the weather's good. Their skin isn't looking too great, and a bit of sun will sort it out no end," replies a second.

"Better a bath! The smell drifting this way is enough to make you sick," adds a third.

"Yeah, have a bath in the river, you mongrels!" shouts the second soldier over the parapets towards the waiting army.

"What are you doing? You can't provoke them like that," the first soldier remarks, clipping the second soldier round his helmet with his hand.

"Why do you think they're waiting, Old Jack?" asks the second soldier of an older man, large and muscular in frame, who is sitting on his own nearby.

"Well, they've been travelling the night, I suppose, and it is a big army, so they don't have much to fear. Take their time, I say," replies the stubble-faced, weather-beaten man trying to get some rest.

"Oh, that makes sense," comments the second soldier, admiring Jack's logic. Old Jack is generally considered wiser than the other soldiers, especially those who have the pleasure of his company now.

Whispers can be heard in the background as a soldier passes on information to other soldiers, bringing smiles and delight to everyone who hears it. Making its way upstairs and around walls, the information eventually comes to grace our three soldiers and Old Jack.

"Do not shout out what you are about to hear. Be aware that an army comes from the east to help us fight this terrible foe," a soldier whispers into the ear of the third soldier. The third soldier passes on the information to the second soldier.

But the third soldier forgets to tell the second soldier not to shout out the information, and to everyone's horror, the second soldier shouts, "Brilliant, an army is coming to help us!"

Warrior, who has been listening all along, breaks his motionless stance, moving his head in the direction of the parapets where the second soldier blurted out his disturbing revelation.

"General Glum!" he screams, ordering him to come. The general, who was very much asleep, wakes with a start, and as fast as he possibly can, runs in, out and over other blinny in order to get to his master. Glum arrives at Warrior's position, closely followed by his lieutenants. Warrior's pets, who have also been asleep, wake grumpily at the thudding footsteps of the goblin general. The pets hiss at Glum, watching his every step as he comes to face Warrior, who maintains his gaze towards the walls of the city.

"You called, sire." A breathless General Glum bows.

"Ready your men," shouts Warrior. "The time for battle has come. An army led by a foe I have had words with will arrive soon. By the time this army arrives I want this city razed to the ground. We can ill afford to have two armies with which to contend. I want your archers at the front of the line. Now!"

"Yes, sire. We will ready the army without hesitation." Glum grovels, before addressing his lieutenants. "You lot, inform the different divisions of our master's wishes."

The general and his lieutenants wander back in different directions to address and organise their respective men.

Dread fills the air behind the city walls. The second soldier who made the outburst may have given away the plot, and in doing so brought about their doom. But blame for this turn of events stretches right back to the King himself, because it was he who asked for the information to be imparted to his soldiers in the first place. Back in his room, realising that Laureate will most likely be too late to change the outcome for this city, the King looks at his armour.

Raising his eyes to face the ceiling and beyond, he pleads, "Creators, help us."

CHAPTER 22

THE BATTLE BEGINS – A HERO'S VIEW

The mounted men and giant warriors gather pace and miles under their belts, while foot soldiers travel at the best speed they can muster. Greybeard has stayed behind, only momentarily, to teach Beezle his last lesson before they too will fly forward. Perrywinkle sits in the background, watching and listening fervently to what Greybeard is about to say and do. At this present time they sit still on their horses as everyone else moves on into the distance.

"Beezle, you have one more lesson to be learned before we can be sure that if you are attacked you will be able to protect yourself well enough. Remember how I used my staff to deflect the fires of the dragon?" Greybeard asks as he dismounts Thundercloud. Beezle nods. "Well the trick I am about to teach you will provide you with a shield that Warrior himself would find hard to penetrate. Much like any other trick you have learnt, you must concentrate your mind upon what you want to achieve. Get off your horse," the old man orders. Beezle climbs down off his horse and faces the wizard. "Put your arm out at an angle in front of you, and bend your arm at the elbow as if your hand holds onto a shield." Beezle does so, following Greybeard's instruction to the letter. "Then say the words 'Radius shielded'."

Beezle repeats the words confidently, "Radius shielded." In an instant, the young elf holds what looks like a glass shield, light blue in colour, but transparent. Beezle moves his shielded arm above, below, behind and in front of his body.

"This shield weighs nothing," gasps Beezle.

Greybeard replies, "Put your arm out in front so the shield protects your body." Beezle obeys the old man. The wizard puts his palm out and mumbles a few words so the little elf cannot hear them. Producing a white orb the size of an orange, he suddenly thrusts it in Beezle's direction. The orb blasts against Beezle's magical shield, knocking the little elf backwards onto the floor. Beezle, stunned by the blast, shakes his head – his shield is still intact. He gets up, only to see Greybeard running towards him with his sword raised. Greybeard goes to strike the elf at the neck, but Beezle is not prepared – his shield is down and he will surely be beheaded. At that moment, as the wizard's sword flies purposefully towards Beezle, the little elf's shielded arm shoots up, as if possessed, to protect and deflect the old man's blade away. The little elf and Perrywinkle look at Greybeard, mouths open; neither can believe what they have just witnessed.

"This is the end of the lesson," Greybeard says with satisfaction. "Well done, young man." Beezle does not react; his eyes are still wide with shock. "Oh, one more thing… the shield will disappear when you say the words 'Radius departum'." Beezle's eyelids close and open again as he tries to gain control of his senses.

"Radius departum," the elf slowly recites. The shield disappears in an instant.

"Good, good," claps Greybeard, walking towards Thundercloud. "I want you to practise everything I have taught you. There are a good few hours before we reach the fields of battle and I want to make sure you are perfect."

Both the old man and Beezle climb back onto their respective horses. "You nearly killed me!" he says to the wizard.

"Oh no, just teaching you how effective that shield ought to be. It's a great little trick, isn't it?"

"But I could have died…"

"No, the shield, to its best ability, would not let that happen," reassures Greybeard. "Of course, I know more tricks that could have fooled the shield, but I am not one to use them unless it is necessary. By that I mean if I wanted you dead, you would be. Shall we make that move?"

The wizard gestures for his horse to move. Thundercloud shoots off at such a pace that Greybeard's olive-green wizard garment tails, his hair and his long grey beard fly behind him. Beezle and Perrywinkle clip their heels and urge their ponies to follow. The chase to catch up to the others is now on.

Whistling past foot soldiers, Thundercloud outpaces both Beezle and Perrywinkle's ponies. As Greybeard leaves them behind, Beezle uses the time to practice his tricks.

Perrywinkle, over these past few days, has perfected the

ability to write on a speeding pony. Sitting upright, he balances himself with a book in one hand and a pen in the other. Beezle practises his magic by throwing rocks. In his mind's eye, he visualises having to use his powers against the riders he has travelled with for quite some time. His magical rock throwing technique becomes quite violent as he throws rocks into trees so hard that they are uprooted. Beezle practises perfecting pick and throw, pull and catch, lightning and shield techniques; he needn't practice patience as it has been tested for days.

Soon, if the rod is to be believed, Beezle will be its master and together they will rule this world. Whilst he wants this, he has a slight feeling of unease. Greybeard and the others have been good to him. They may have shouted and disciplined, but equally they have spent a good amount of time helping him develop new skills. Beezle does not want to hurt these men, but he wants to be in control, believing that he is special and worthy of the rod and the red oric that he is yet to meet.

"Greybeard has said I am special – not in so many words, but he said I have talent. And talent must have the right tools to become the best," Beezle says to himself.

Thundercloud gallops along the well-trodden trading route. Despite the loss of time due to setting out so late after teaching Beezle his last trick, Greybeard is surprisingly close to Laureate's men. Laureate's cavalry have fallen behind the tunny, who now run on ahead valiantly, closely followed by Stryker, Forester, the dwarfs and Finn.

And then something happens that takes everyone by surprise.
Boom!

Everyone stops in their tracks. The blast comes from the southern side of the city. Sounds of destruction echo out for miles around, as smoke and dust rise high up into the air. The ground can be felt to rumble slightly by all outside of the blast. Laureate's men look at each other in dismay, unsure what to do with themselves. Greybeard sets off again, using the time to catch the others up. Everyone must continue their journey towards the city as they are too close now to give up hope. Upon seeing Greybeard's determination, Laureate follows suit, ordering his men to ride onward to help their brethren, but as the fricasian army sets off, there is another blast.

The second orb heads towards the wall

Boom!

Laureate's men stop again. More smoke, more rumblings and more sound heightens the tension of the current situation. The sun is covered by the smoke and dust, and a darkness lasting only a few moments envelops all that is near. Greybeard continues on his way, finally reaching the static Fricasian cavalry. The wizard stops in front of the shocked horsemen, seeking to reassure them that Warrior is not to be feared, or at least not to the extent that they fear him now.

"The blasts that have hit your city have come from Warrior himself. Warrior gets his magical power from an oric, much like the one embedded in my staff. Magic needs the energy of the man and the oric to work, and those two blasts will have drained a good part of his and his oric's already. He may have one or two more assaults on the city left in him before his magical energies run out. Warrior's body and oric must then regain their energy before he can cause damage of this magnitude again. It may take minutes or it may take hours to re-energise his oric and his body. But the time it does take gives us valuable minutes or hours to get on and protect this city. Now I implore you, we must move with the greatest speed we can muster."

Goblin roars, jeers and cheers can be heard by the riders and the tunny on the southern side of the city. It sounds as if they are on the move. Surely the blast cannot have provided a large enough hole in the wall to allow the little monsters to ransack the city?

A large, red orb-like ball floats along the city walls silently. It is the signal that Warrior told those goblins who travelled the valley close to Windrush to watch out for. Watching the orb are the creatures hoping to save this city. The orb has a grace and a beauty, so much so that some of the creatures are hypnotised by it. The orb stops when it reaches a certain spot on the north-eastern wall, the trajectory of the orb appearing to have been chosen. Pushing away from the stone wall it has hugged since its inception, the orb rushes outwards at speed before thrusting itself back towards the wall with the greatest of punches.

Boom!

The red, shining orb blasts through the stone in the north-eastern wall, turning it to dust. Dust fills the air, hiding the damage done. When the dust clears the damage can be seen. Riders and jotunn giants run and ride faster than ever before. Minutes pass before the dust settles, revealing the devastation. The part of the wall hit by the orb is no more. A clear path leads into the city. Goblins must be planning to infiltrate open streets via this entrance. Assumptions are right as minutes later blinny, from the valley close to Windrush, pile into the city. As expected, few soldiers protect this area, and most of those who did have been killed or maimed in the blast. There is one saving grace – many wooden gates stop their progression into the heart of the city as these gates are locked.

The dwarfs ride with Finn. Stryker and Forester ride up front close to the tunny. Finn is quiet and the dwarfs see tension brewing inside of him. The larger elf takes hold of the rod from out of his backpack; it sits silently, playing the innocent in his hands. If only Finn knew what it had promised his brother, he might have thrown it away days ago. Caressing the rod he looks to it to give him answers as to how and when he might use it. Despite his agility and prowess with bows and swords, Finn is unable to understand what skill might undo Warrior to enable him to use the rod effectively. His hopes lie in Lerwin the sword, Medrin the bow, his armour and the premethian liquid, which he has not even thought to use yet. Much like his Queen, the premethian liquid will tell him things about the future. The difference between the Queen and Finn is that he does not want to accept the responsibility in knowing details of another person's life and death. Uncertainty clouds his every thought. He has been told fate will guide him, but what if his fate is to fail? Deep in his thoughts, Finn is brought back to the here and now by Wattlespalf.

"Are you alright, Finn?" Wattlespalf asks, looking into Finn's eyes, which are full of anxiety.

"I'm not sure."

"What is bothering you?" asks Wattlespalf. Gendralf and Igralf also turn their attention towards him.

"How am I going to get the rod to touch Warrior's sword?" asks Finn.

"Let me ask you, how did you know to bring the jotunn warrior to her knees in the park?"

"I don't know."

"And how did you know to distract the draugar with Forester's bow in the Old Mill Inn?" asks Gendralf.

"I don't know," replies Finn.

"And how did you know to spear the fish in the river as expertly as you did when in competition with Forester?" adds Igralf.

"Concentration and instinct," replies Finn assuredly.

"Ha! Concentration and instinct," responds Igralf. "It has served you well so far, and it will no doubt serve you well when you need to make your decisions on the battlefield."

"Finn, believe us when we say that none of us will wilfully stray from you. We will try our utmost to help you fulfil what you have been asked to do," assures Gendralf.

"Wizards, lords, magical beings and your own King and Queen believe in you. You keep formidable company, Finn. I doubt these creatures will let you down and neither will we. You are truly exceptional and you must not doubt your abilities. Whether you were meant to be a warrior or not, this is about an act that you must carry out. The acts of others to help you do it will be as important as your own because they will clear the path, enabling you to do your work. Trust us as we trust you," philosophises Wattlespalf uncharacteristically.

Finn smiles nervously. "As long as you keep your end of the bargain, then I will have to keep mine, won't I?"

"Finn, do you see the forest up ahead?" Stryker asks, as he pulls his horse back in line with Finn and the dwarfs.

"Yes," replies Finn.

"That is Windrush," Stryker tells him.

"Windrush? Really?" grins the elf enthusiastically. Finn is back where he started before this mad set of events unfolded. It is ironic – he is within distance of the home Warrior destroyed over three thousand years ago, only to be coming back three thousand years later to fight the very same foe. Twinges of anger towards Warrior galvanise his resolve to end the monster's carnage.

Goblin roars, cheers and jeers continue. Screams of pain and death coming from fricasian soldiers intermingle with the joyous cries of the marauding army. Hundreds of burning arrows can be seen flying into the city. More screams ring out from those injured or worse, in the throes of death, as arrows pierce or burn them. Smoke, driven by fire, engulfs the city as old buildings and towers burn brightly. Fire is making its way closer and closer to the keep, and more importantly, the King. Laureate and his men cringe at every scream coming from the city, as they know one more kinsman has not survived to tell the tale.

Worse still, the goblins who entered via the north-eastern wall are making slow but steady progress, climbing up and over the gates before opening them to their masses.

Greybeard's army is just a few miles away from the gap in the wall where the blast occurred. Fricas is so close that the wizard's army can smell the smoke from fires and taste the dust from pulverised stone on their tongues. The jotunn who had carried on ahead, pause and wait for the others to arrive. Stryker, Forester, the dwarfs and Finn are not far behind. Greybeard arrives minutes later, as does Laureate's army. Right at the back Perrywinkle and Beezle have been left behind, their ponies are slow in comparision and they have also been preoccupied with writing or performing magical tricks.

"Stryker, Forester, dwarfs, Teacher, Laureate and Finn, come here. I need to speak with you all," orders Greybeard. "The time has arrived to take this army into battle. I would've liked the dragons to be here, but the battle has begun earlier than expected."

As if by magic, strong winds suddenly bear down on the men. All look up towards the sky and there before them is Pengwellen. The dragon's large wings beat, causing hairs on heads to fly in all directions. Through their screwed up faces the men squint, lips quiver and wind puffs up cheeks and dries eyes, resulting in distorted smiles for their airborne reinforcements. With long dragon teeth and a snout close to his head, Teacher is obviously uncomfortable, as is Laureate. This is the first time either of them have seen a dragon, and neither of them wanted one to get so close.

"Someone wish we were here?" Pengwellen asks. The dragon starts to beat his wings more slowly, encouraging himself to land lightly on his two back feet.

"Pengwellen, old friend. How did you get here so quickly?"

"Ah, we were fortunate enough to catch a strong wind blowing from north to south, and as a result, our flying time was cut by half," replies Pengwellen with a wink.

"Where are the other dragons?" asks Greybeard.

"Well, I didn't want to bring too much attention to us, so the others wait in the distance for further orders," replies Pengwellen wisely. "You do know that Fricas is getting a good battering from Warrior and his army, don't you?"

"Obviously!" says a slightly patronised Greybeard. "Did you see where Warrior is or where the goblins are in the city?"

"I did, as it happens; goblin and ogre foot soldiers have entered the city from the south. Warrior has not gone with them – he is still outside the city. It wouldn't surprise me if he is waiting for you, wizard," confirms Pengwellen.

"Hmm, more likely he is exhausted of strength and unable to join the assault. I mean, seriously, waiting for me? Why ever would he do that?" jokes Greybeard, knowing full well that he has already caused Warrior enough mischief for Pengwellen to be right.

Stryker pipes up, for he will decide what strategies to employ from now on in. "How many men do you have, Teacher?"

"About one hundred," he replies.

"And you, Laureate?"

Laureate looks up to the skies as he works out how many men he has available. "One hundred cavalrymen and one hundred foot soldiers."

"And you, Pengwellen… how many dragons have you brought?"

"I have forty dragons here with me," responds Pengwellen.

"So we have around two hundred and forty creatures here and now, with one hundred foot soldiers arriving in the next few hours. How many do they have?"

"Several thousand?" replies Laureate.

"So we're looking at around one creature to a minimum of twenty blinny," Stryker communicates to the others.

"Sounds fair," replies Gendralf with a hint of sarcasm.

"So, how do we break their attack?" asks Laureate. "It would seem that we have an impossible feat to overcome."

"Laureate, if you think like that then you will never overcome this foe," scolds Pengwellen. "Let us listen to our good friend before we make any judgements."

"Right," Stryker begins, looking out onto the smouldering city. "The goblins have entered through the north-eastern wall in front of us. I suspect that the blasts we heard at the southern end of the city attest to the fact that Warrior wanted the goblins to get in behind the city walls. After all, there are no places for Fricasian soldiers to run other than to the keep. If the only way out of the city is through the goblin hordes attacking you from all sides and all directions, then you have no escape. So I think the goblins will be actively working their way towards the keep. At that point the trap is set and the keep, along with all the soldiers gathered there, will be surrounded. A mass slaughter is going to take place."

"So, what do you want us to do?" interrupts Laureate.

"I think we should follow the blinny who entered the city via the blast. I would like everyone bar Laureate's men and the dragons to follow this route. Pengwellen, whilst we are making our way through the city streets, I would like you to pay a visit to the southern side of the city and burn, eat and rip apart any goblins who remain outside the city walls."

"Hmm, I like the sound of that." Pengwellen grins.

"Obviously, beware of Warrior. His power is enough to cause you great harm should you get in the way of his magic. Laureate, I would like your men to work your way along the city walls to the south, but I want you to keep out of sight. As the dragons whittle down the blinny outside of the city walls, they will no doubt panic and run. It will be the duty of your cavalry to pick off these stragglers."

"Yes," responds Laureate, "but I would like to come with you. After all, I would like to protect my King and I can show you the way."

"I was coming to that. We will work our way to the top of the city, close to the keep. Laureate, we will need you to guide us. Assuming that the little monsters will be within reach of the keep, we will need to secure the area around it before driving them back towards Warrior at the southern entrance. We must close all gates behind us, so that they might not come back into any part of the city so easily. Pengwellen, once the keep is secured, I would like you to split your dragons into two groups as you see fit. One group must carry on plaguing Warrior and his army on the outside of the wall. Upon our signal, I would like the second group of dragons to help guide the goblins back to the holes in the southern walls of the city. Once the goblins have been driven back out of the city, I would like your dragon brethren to greet them with the full force of their wrath. Greybeard, would you be able to put out the signal to the dragons, say a blast of light when we are ready for the dragons to aid us?"

"Of course," replies Greybeard.

"We need to regroup and reconsider our position when we reach the southern walls of the city. At this juncture we will be able to gauge how best to proceed. Our main concern is that Finn is protected at all times."

"Sounds like a well thought out plan. Is everybody comfortable with their role?" asks Greybeard of everyone else.

Nods and gestures of agreement are offered by everyone.

"What about my role in all of this?" a voice cries out from behind. It is Beezle.

"You will follow behind us and you will try to keep as far away from the fighting as is possible. Do you understand?" orders Greybeard forcefully.

"Yes sir," replies Beezle grudgingly.

"Right then, let us begin. I wish you all a good battle. May the Creators look kindly upon you," announces Greybeard, holding his staff up high.

Handshakes and hugs are exchanged as creatures separate to inform their respective armies of the plan now in place. Pengwellen flies back to the dragons. Laureate walks over to his cavalry. The rest head for the hole in the city wall in search of goblins.

CHAPTER 23

THE BATTLE BEGINS – A GOBLIN'S VIEW

Whilst Greybeard and the others get closer and closer to Fricas after their early morning meeting with Laureate and his army, Warrior's army is ready to wreak chaos on this city; not one goblin knows how the city walls will be brought down. Not even General Glum has been party to any information about how today's proceedings will develop. Warrior knows differently though, he has a definite plan at the forefront of his monstrous mind.

Removing one hand from the pommel of his sword, Warrior wraps his other hand around the grip of it tightly. Lifting his sword, he points it in the direction of the thick, seemingly impenetrable stone that forms the city walls. Concentrating all of his energy into action, a small orb-like ball, red in colour, whirs and develops at the very tip of the sword. The orb increases in size, getting bigger and bigger until it is the size of a small man. Goblins and ogres look on in wonder at the orb and ponder what something of this size might do; it will not be long before they find out. Warrior lifts his sword and balances the large red ball above his head as if it were as light as a feather. Thrusting his sword forward in the direction of the city wall, much like a fisherman would his rod when casting his float and baited hook, he releases the orb. Gliding through the air at a good strong speed, the red ball heads towards the southern walls of the city. Soldiers and citizens standing on the parapets run for their lives, knowing that whatever comes for them is not going to be merciful or kind. Of course they are right, as the red orb soon penetrates the centre of the wall, at which point it releases its devastating energy.

Boom!

Fricasian bodies caught in the blast fly all about. Arms, heads and legs flail and bend into positions they were not designed to withstand. Stone chippings and dust rise upwards into the skies, though interestingly, no large pieces of stone fly through the air or roll towards the goblin army as you might imagine. Dust soon clears, revealing that a huge chunk of the wall has been destroyed. A heavy gasp rings out as five thousand or more goblins look upon the devastated wall and admire the work of their leader.

Glum, rubbing his hands in glee, praises the monster. "Oh, master, that is a truly wonderful thing yer can do. Yer god-like in yer abilities."

Warrior does not listen to the grovelling of his general, and not satisfied that the hole is large enough to accommodate his vast army, he sets about creating another red orb. It is not long before he does so; raising this second ball full of energy and power above his head, he flings it forward towards the wall once more. Released and let wild, it travels much like its sister did. At a strong speed, this orb aims itself next to where the last blast took place. The army behind the wall braces itself for the imminent blast; soldiers and citizens alike crouch down closer to the floor, covering their ears and closing their eyes.

Boom!

The goblin army claps, cheers and dances. More and more dust ploughs into the sky, covering the sun momentarily, plunging this world into darkness.

Bobbucket looks up at the darkened skies and cringes. "Is this the end of the world?" he asks himself.

It will be for some, but the world is very much alive, though its future hangs very much in the balance. Behind the city walls, close to where the blast rang out, soldiers and citizens help pull others more unfortunate out of the rubble and retreat further back into the city.

"Come on, Billy. Off the floor with yer," Old Jack says, picking Billy – a soldier known well by Old Jack, from the rubble-strewn ground close to the hole in the wall. Billy gets up, puts his arm around the old soldier and hobbles alongside Old Jack, using him as a crutch.

"Thanks, Jack. I thought I might be a goner then. They're coming to get us, aren't they? I would rather live than die, even if it is only for a few more minutes," babbles Billy, dazed, confused and scared by the blast.

"We're not out of the woods yet, lad. You're right to say they're coming to get us. Those goblins will soon be here, and I don't want them close enough to either of us to cause us any harm," replies Jack, encouraging Billy to move faster.

With the walls breached there is not much hope for the Fricasian men now. Hope lies in the army that they have heard is coming to help them. The first sets of gates are locked behind retreating soldiers, who run onto the parapets of the inner city walls. Jack and Billy are the last of them to get through.

Warrior prepares a third and last red orb. This one feels heavier than the others, and he struggles to lift the sword up over his head before propelling it forward. Travelling straight ahead, it makes its way to where the other blasts boomed out. Breath is held, expectant goblins want to see more hate-filled purpose. Only there is a twist, because the orb veers away from its expected course.

"Where is that one goin'?" come perplexed cries from goblin men.

"He must've made a mistake," come answers.

"Nah, its goin' where he wants it to. Remember our mates goin' round the back? Well, looks like he's goin' to provide them with a doorway much like ours," replies another with half a brain.

Sticking close to the wall, the red ball of energy follows it around to the north-eastern side of the city. Warrior falls onto one knee, his energy drained by the orbs that he has created. Getting back up slowly, Warrior turns to his army.

"Bowmen, walk forward," Warrior commands. He is confident that there will not be an attack forthcoming from opposing soldiers who hide behind the city walls. Bowmen march to within shooting distance of the city. "Bowmen, halt. Get your arrows ready," he shouts to them loudly. A thousand bowmen dip and light a thousand arrows, all of them for the Fricasian people.

Boom! The third and final blast rings out at the north-eastern side of the city.

"Fire," Warrior bellows.

Twangs of bows are followed by the whooshes of flaming arrows as they fly towards the city – a thousand of them blanket the skies. Soldiers on the parapets crouch down and raise their shields above their heads. Citizens without the luxury of a shield hide against walls or in stone buildings close by, hoping that they are not caught. Like rain, the arrows beat down onto the city, piercing everything around it. The city is lucky that it is built out of stone, but some buildings have been built out of wood since its conception and it is they that welcome the flames.

From behind the small hill close to the valley where many goblin soldiers were lost last night, the wiry lieutenant peers over it, wondering what sight he might see. Disbelief and thoughts of miracles plough through this goblin lieutenant's head as he sees a wall replaced by dust.

"Oi, you lot come here and see what the master has done," he shouts out to his soldiers.

"How the heck did he do that?" replies Pompucket, who peers over at this wondrous sight. But no one can answer as science and magic are not subjects that goblins know well, and of course, they hadn't seen the orb approaching.

"Right, you lot – it looks like yer got what yer wanted. Seems we're goin' into the city now as opposed to tonight. We'll get away from this horrid, murderous place for good," the lieutenant says to the relief of his last remaining goblins.

Picking up weapons and putting on shoes, amongst other things, they ready themselves for an assault upon the city. After a few minutes, the goblins are ready enough to make a move up and over the hill onto the now white-dusted plains outside the city walls. Not long after, these stinking monsters find themselves at the site of the blast where once there was a wall. Climbing over bits of debris created by the explosion, the army jump up onto city streets that were hidden by the city wall minutes earlier. Immediately, they are greeted by an obstacle, this being a gate that has been closed shut and can only be unlocked from the other side.

"Whose good at climin' walls then?" asks the wiry goblin lieutenant.

"I am, I am," replies an over-eager goblin waving his hand in the air. This particular goblin dreams of becoming a lieutenant himself.

"Right, get up there, get over and let us in," commands the lieutenant, adding, "an' someone go with him." A less than happy goblin is volunteered by other goblins who use the unconventional but convincing method of pointing swords at his throat to persuade him. The two of them scale the gate and sit spread-legged on top of it. Looking up the street, the two goblins are none too pleased at what they see, because there in front of them stands gate, after gate, after gate, all locked and sealed.

The two goblin men realise that they are the ones who will have to open every gate, and now they wish they had not, or not been, volunteered at all. Jumping down onto the other side of this particular gate, the opening of it will be relatively easy. A large block of wood running the length of two gate doors sits suspended on two iron hinges. The two goblins each walk to one side of the gate and proceed to wrap their arms around the heavy block of wood. Pushing and pulling the wood up and out of the hinges, the goblins carry the block to one side before pulling back the gates to reveal the rest of the army.

The archers have done their work on the southern side of the city; fire is spreading through the lower end of Fricas, and many men work to douse the fires with water. Goblin archers fall off to the sides, exposing other divisions who have waited patiently behind them. Now, with the immediate view clear, the next wave of Warrior's army is to be let loose.

"General Glum, come hither," orders Warrior.

"Sir, what would you have us do?" asks Glum, speaking up for his lieutenants also.

"It is time for the foot soldiers and pikemen to storm the city. I want half of the archers to follow behind them. The rest must stay here. The closed gates in the city must be opened and the keep taken," Warrior hisses. "Do what you must to get there, if it means ridding the city of all and everyone, then so be it."

"Yes, sir! We'll do it with pleasure," replies Glum.

General Glum and his lieutenants wander back to their particular divisions, shouting out the orders to attack. Four thousand pikemen and foot soldiers march in the direction of the city. Row after row of growling, gurgling goblin men are itching for the fight which comes ever closer. All, that is, except for Bobbucket, who remains firmly fixed at the back of the throng, shaking with fear; as always, he hopes not to be involved in any fighting whatsoever.

Fricasian soldiers numbed with terror look down from parts of the city wall not affected by the blasts, while their fricasian sergeants try to rouse the men from their fear-stricken trances.

Only the blinny cavalry – around four hundred at best, half the bowmen – another five hundred or so, as well as cooks, cart pullers and the like remain with Warrior.

"Archers, line the walls. I want these goblins to pay for their intrusion," rouses one slim, bearded sergeant armed with a bow himself. The archers do as they are told but shake their heads, asking what impact they can make upon an army so large and organised.

Old Jack, resolute as ever, has taken a bow and quiver full of arrows from a dead comrade and is the first to take aim, saying to himself, "You ugly, self-satisfying mongrels. It will be a pleasure to fell you. If I live only for a minute more, I will be happy in the knowledge that I stood here against you."

Taking bows off shoulders, the rest of the fricasian bowmen aim at the approaching pack crammed full of vagabonds, thieves and murderers. Getting closer to the rubble left by the blast, blinny foot soldiers wait for the return fire of the Fricasians. Whilst the air is tense, victory is already in the minds of everyone marching into this city.

"Fire!" orders the fricasian sergeant.

A hundred or so arrows fly towards the goblin packs from the ramparts and parapets. The goblins look up at the skies and see the arrows making haste in their immediate direction. As arrows get closer and closer, individual blinny know that their time is nearly up, because within a second or two, an arrow will be embedded in their bony bodies. Goblins fall as arrows hit them, leaving some dead, some dying and some injured.

"Ready your bows. Take aim and fire," the fricasian sergeant orders with authority once again. Another hundred arrows head the aggressors' way, and another hundred arrows maim or kill their intended targets. But the aggressors are now here at the city wall and they have begun to seep into it. Some goblins scale the inner walls, standing on stones that jut out or running up the stairs of houses onto roofs high enough to enable them to climb onto the parapets. Some find ladders to step up and others climb ropes used to raise and lower heavy or cumbersome things. All this climbing and infiltrating is done with one aim in mind – to open the gates that will allow the other goblins and ogres to carry out their work. Whilst all this is happening, the Fricasian bowmen come under fire from goblin archers, making it harder for them to defend their fire-stricken city.

CHAPTER 24

POMPUCKET'S ROTTEN LUCK

"How long do you think it will take to catch up with the goblins?" asks Finn, walking next to Greybeard through the fields, towards the hole in the city wall.

"Oh, not long. The gates have held them back well enough to give us a good start. And they have confounded themselves by not locking the gates behind them. They are not the wisest of creatures," replies Greybeard.

"How wise are they then?" queries Finn.

"Hmm, from what I have seen I would say you are far wiser. Wattlespalf on the other hand..." Greybeard whispers with a mischievous smile.

"Oi, I heard that," Wattlespalf cries in the background.

The hole in the north-eastern wall of Fricas is a good enough place to start an offensive against the goblin hordes. The jotunn make the step up from the fields outside the walls onto the Fricasian street with ease. Horses have been left along the well-trodden path leading up to the city; for this particular part of the adventure they will not be needed. War on the streets is better achieved on foot. Smaller members of this unusual army must do a little climbing, as they step precariously amongst the rubble left by the blast. Using both arms, a little push up and the swinging of both legs is required to get one knee onto the street side of the wall. One by one, the men and dwarfs climb, pulling others up with a friendly hand until everyone, bar the elves and Perrywinkle, looks down onto the chalk-coloured hill from where they have just arrived. Wonderful agility is possessed by the three remaining, and just to show off a little, they all make one standing jump from the fields into the city.

"Smart alecs, all of you," moans Gendralf, wishing that he possessed the same sort of acrobatic skill. "And what is your next trick?"

"I can show you my tricks, if you want?" Beezle says, waving his hands all around and in the face of Gendralf.

"I do not want, thank you very much. And if you would be so kind as to stop putting your hands in the way of my eyes then that would be very much appreciated also. Bloody elves pretending to be wizards..." remarks Gendralf.

Locked gates had slowed down the depleted goblin army, and the expectation is that it will not be long before this small army, led by Stryker catches them up. The street is wide enough for two or three jotunn warriors to stand shoulder to shoulder; it is also low enough for these soldiers to comfortably look over the wall into the next street. If they ducked down low enough then the wall would hide the giant soldiers well. So it is that the jotunn lead the line in the early stages of this procession into battle.

At the back of the jotunn line is Teacher; he is feeling his age a little. The journey has been long enough to make his old, creaking knees ache, and he fears he may have to take on a smaller role in what is to come.

Up and up the cobbled path the tunny army walks, whilst behind them men, dwarfs and elves have trouble keeping up. The smaller creatures have to run every now and again, so that they might close down the distance that has opened up between them and the giants.

"Oh, I wish we had the horses," moans Igralf, whose little legs are having more trouble keeping up with the rest of the pack than the rest of the pack are having keeping up with the jotunn.

"What a luxurious necessity they are," dreams Greybeard, also pining for a saddle on a horse as he makes his way up the street using his staff to carry him.

Wooden gates as tall and thick as the walls on either side of the army are passed with alarming regularity; it is fair to say that the goblins have had a fair bit of climbing to contend with in order to get these gates open. It is not long before the jotunn warriors can see the blinny in the process of opening one of the gates up ahead. This gate is different, though, as it leads onto a street where houses are aplenty, and plenty of houses means plenty of fire and damage.

"Oi, there's somin' approachin' down the way," says a goblin looking down the street in the direction of the tunny warriors. All the other goblins look down the way, curious as to what might be coming to meet them.

"And they are big," informs another.

"What are they?" asks another.

"Big men, if yer ask me," warns Pompucket.

"Bigger than big. They're huge, and they have swords and shields. Oh no, oh no!" another screams, overtaken by fear.

"Open the doors, quick! There is somin' terrible out here, and I think they mean us harm," cries Pompucket, banging on the gates.

Indeed, the jotunn do mean them harm. Far from being the children the men and dwarfs had thought they might be, these warriors have tapped into a darker side of their nature much quicker than expected, if it had been expected at all. The jotunn get closer and closer to the three hundred screaming goblins. All are trapped in a corridor with quite possibly one of the most terrifying creatures they have ever had the displeasure of meeting. Wide-eyed and open-mouthed, goblins rush towards the gate, which is not quite fully open. Jumping over one another, they try to avoid being one of the first to be caught by the awful creatures running at them with such intent. And then, with a click and a creak, the gate is fully opened.

Goblins rush and push to get through the gate, and Pompucket is one of the first. The little monsters push so hard that many of them lose their balance, tripping, falling and crashing down onto the ground. The pile of goblins blocking the entrance onto the next street gets bigger and bigger with the passing of each and every second. As they scramble with such urgency to get away from the nightmare charging them, it is almost comical. Too many goblins are unable to get out of the corridor blocked by the pile, two or three feet high, of fallen blinny caught in the rush. All this and not one weapon has yet been raised to make an attack or defend.

The jotunn unsheathe their swords and press their shields against their chests. A hundred or so enemy soldiers trapped in a long line on this street close their eyes; holding their weapons outwards, they hope that they might make these monsters disappear. Jotunn drop their swords by their sides and instead push their shields out in front, bending forward to reduce their height enough to hit the little monsters hard.

"Don't hurt us. We never hurt a fly, any of us. We're good goblins, here to help," cries one of the disgusting little beasts.

"Good? You don't know the meaning of it. It is the first time I have met your kind, but you look evil and dangerous enough to make me believe that the stories told about you are true," booms one of the tunny soldiers upon hearing the goblin's words.

"We are misunderstood, that's all," says the terrified goblin.

"Misunderstood? I suspect you are more understood than many of the creatures that grace this world," replies the tunny soldier.

Impact is made. The jotunn run into and through the trapped goblin army. Bodies fly against the walls on either side. Goblins scream as some are sliced by swords, pummelled by shields and some fall underneath giant feet. As one would imagine, when a giant's foot rises, after being trampled on by a big weight, what is left underneath is not a sight for anyone squeamish. Carrying on, the tunny begin to slow, held back by the sheer amount of bodies in front of them. A lot of the goblins have been pushed further away from the gate leading onto the next street. Hope of an escape now lies in their ability to climb up and over the walls out of the city.

Until now, shields and armour against shins have protected the tunny. Two jotunn warriors pull swords from their sides and begin to thrust them into the crowd, cutting off or breaking legs and arms with abandon. This onslaught is relentless.

Archers at the very back of the trapped goblin army fire arrows upon the two jotunn soldiers attacking at the front. Arrows pierce the soldiers left, right and centre. As Igralf had suspected, arrows only serve to be a painful distraction to these giant men. Realising that they are being fired upon, the jotunn use their shields to protect themselves from these distractions whilst still carrying out their work without mercy. Other jotunn fight those goblins pushed to the sides of the wall, making sure that those at the front are not attacked from behind.

Flashes of blue, green, yellow and red fly above Greybeard and his men for a good few seconds. Pengwellen's brethren are on the move to the southern side of the city. The fighting stops as the dragons pass by and all manner of creatures look to the skies, wondering what created the shadows over the city. Pengwellen's view is far more impressive, able to see the fighting, the areas empty and deserted and those most vulnerable. He is disturbed by the amount of goblins and ogres infiltrating Fricas at this time and how easily the Fricasian soldiers are overpowered by their foes. Ahead of them, Pengwellen and his dragons can see Warrior. Behind him waits the rest of the army, which is small compared to those now rampaging through the city. Warrior too can see Pengwellen's approach. He did not envisage seeing dragons on the field of battle at all and he is perturbed by it.

"Can yer see them big birds comin' this way?" asks one short-sighted goblin, focusing his eyes as far as he can.

"Those aren't birds comin', they're dragons… and big ones," informs another.

"Oh dear, one of them is Pengwellen."

"Pengwellen approaches?" replies the short-sighted goblin, trying to focus his eyes even more.

"We are more than dead – we are deader than dead."

"What do we do? What do we do?" panics one.

"Warrior! Warrior will have him," reassures the short-sighted goblin.

"But he doesn't move. Why doesn't he move?" asks another.

"What, he isn't movin'? Oh no, oh no, oh no!" the short-sighted goblin screams, wondering what next.

Soldiers of all ranks are frozen to the spot and ready themselves for the fires that will engulf them. The goblins have witnessed what dragons can do before, and they are terrified by them. And they should be frightened – leathery hides and flame-filled guts will make easy work of soldiers on the ground, where they are helpless.

There is only one advantage to fighting a dragon: their main weapon is fire. A dragon's fiery breath can only cause harm from a short distance away and only for a short time. Whilst dragons might breathe their fire from the air, they have to get close enough to the ground to cause the damage they need to do. If by chance or by guile they can be brought to ground, then they are slow to regain flight, and in theory, can be attacked. Warrior knows this and looks at his pets. "You will be needed very soon. Be patient and wait for my call."

Trampling on those who have already been crushed by their own kind, jotunn, men, dwarfs and elves make their way over the pile of moaning and groaning goblin bodies by the gate. The blinny who have made it through unscathed huddle together in a large group, backing up into a park, brandishing their weapons in front of them. These goblin men poke and prod the air towards the attacking army led by Stryker, gesturing that they are prickly and will use force if anyone comes near them.

Greybeard, Stryker, Forester and the dwarfs have all seen this goblin show of strength before. In reality, they are truly terrified and stuck for what to do. Two hundred grunting, gasping, wheezers and heavy breathers stand in front of a jotunn army who have little time left to protect this city. The question running through everyone's mind is are the blinny so terrified that they will give up their weapons in favour of keeping their lives?

"So, who orders this army?" asks Greybeard.

Goblins gesture their deformed heads and long eerie fingers in the direction of the wiry lieutenant who has had a torrid time of it, leading this group through a horrific set of events thus far. Too much has happened and he had been hoping to get away with an interrogation from one so revered and hated as Greybeard. Yes, blinny have their own tales, and some know all about this wizard.

"Yes, I am the leader of these goblins," the lieutenant admits reluctantly.

"And what might you do now that you are more than matched by an army of fierce creatures bearing down on you?" patronises Greybeard, referring to the jotunn gathered behind him.

"We will fight to the death," announces the goblin lieutenant. Soldiers' heads turn, grumbling and mumbling behind their 'leader'. Displeased with his choice of words, the blinny do what they always do when they are unhappy with their superior – kill them. The goblin lieutenant turns round to face his men, and as he does so, he sees Pompucket's dagger thrust into his body. Dropping to the ground and writhing on the floor in pain, the lieutenant is left to die.

"We surrender, wise old Greybeard. We didn't mean to let it go this far. We've had such a rotten night, what with the ghosts in the forest killin' all of us. Honest," Pompucket cowers, pretending to be remorseful for his acts.

"Ghosts in the forest? Tell me about them, goblin. Did you get a glimpse of them?" asks Greybeard, his curiosity aroused.

"Oh no, we didn't see them. No, they were invisible. The fog covered them, but they were relentless, pickin' us off one by one. They had our ogres, and we fired our arrows only to have them come right back at us. Oh, it was horrible," laments Pompucket.

"Very interesting… very interesting indeed. Laureate, it seems your ghosts are real," Greybeard says, stroking his curly grey beard. "I think I would very much like to meet them."

"You're asking for trouble there," comments Laureate.

"Yes, I am, but I am more than familiar with it – trouble that is," retorts the wizard. "Stryker, do you want to clear up this mess, by that I mean the goblins?"

"With pleasure. Right, you lot, throw all your weapons into a pile by the wall," orders Stryker. "Teacher, could you kindly order your men to stop disembowelling our guests."

Behind Greybeard, the fighting between several jotunn and goblins still rages in the corridor, but the battle is close to its end as the blinny plead with their foes not to let the torture go on any longer.

"Oh, are you sure? They are enjoying themselves," comments Teacher with a smile.

"Too much methinks, but best to give the goblins some reprieve after the ordeal that they have suffered," replies Stryker.

Teacher tramples on the goblins who are still laid out across the gate opening, provoking more moans and groans. Most of them have managed to get themselves up and are in the process of brushing themselves down or putting dislocated parts of their bodies back into place. Teacher shouts for his men and women who were not privy to the surrender of the blinny to stop.

Not many goblins have been left alive. A dozen jotunn men and women have literally made mincemeat of the hundred or so who were trapped in the corridor. The few survivors huddle against the walls hiding their heads in their knees, disturbed by what they have seen. And when jotunn hands offer to help them up, so that they might rejoin the main group on the other side of the wall, the goblins greet the gesture with fear-filled whimpers and screams. It is quite understandable under the circumstances.

Soon, a big pile of weapons collected from goblins lies against the wall: swords, pikes, bows and arrows, daggers and axes. Pockets have been emptied and belts carrying swords have been removed, all in the name of surrender and the hope of a longer life.

"Here, we've done what yer've asked of us. We are helpless now – we won't do yer any harm. Can yer let us go?" asks Pompucket, maintaining his non-aggressive stance.

"Hmm, I don't think we can, goblin. We can't just saunter off and let you be. It would take you a good while to get out of our sight and we have little time to stand here and watch you. If we were to leave you here with all these weapons, then we would leave ourselves open to being attacked by you later down the line. No, I don't think we can let you go," informs Greybeard.

"Well, what yer goin' to do with us?" asks Pompucket a little more aggressively.

"I say we get Greybeard to turn them into men," suggests Gendralf.

"Oh no, not men!"

"Hideous creatures, all of them," cry the goblins.

"What about killing them all. Better dead than alive, I say," remarks Igralf.

"Anything but being turned into a man," the goblins continue in response to Igralf's idea.

"Well, actually, I would prefer being turned into a man over being dead," pipes up one of the goblins, who promptly receives a punch in the stomach for his blasphemy.

Whilst goblins wail and dwarfs suggest suitable punishments, Stryker looks at the houses lining the street, which are made of the same materials as the city walls. Indeed, many houses are embedded into the city walls, much like Greybeard's cave. The buildings are of an adequate size and with these particular abodes having only one front door, four windows and not much else, there would not be many escape routes for the little monsters imprisoned in them.

Stryker walks towards the houses, and rattling the front door handles, tests whether they are locked or not. Amazingly, all of the front doors are open. This can be explained by the fact that no one steals in this city, and no one murders or causes misdemeanours. Doors in this city are left open all the time because everyone is generally comfortable with anybody and everybody else. To have all the doors unlocked was still strange though. Locking a front door you never expect to come back to may have been the last thing on many a person's mind, or it just might have been a fortunate twist of fate. Needless to say, Stryker seizes the opportunity to use these abandoned houses for a practical purpose.

"Right, I think we need to hole you up for a while – to keep you all out of mischief. In light of this, I would like you to make your way into these very homely and very clean houses. Come on, in, all of you," Stryker orders. Mumbles and grumbles ensue, but after only a short while, all the goblins hobble, wobble and limp through the open front doors of their newly-founded prison.

"Look at this, clean and tidy and pretty... it's disgusting!" one goblin comments.

"Yer right, it's horrid this place. It's more horrid than when I dream about cuddling fluffy things," adds another.

"Hmm, dreams filled full of fluff. Terrible, terrible state of affairs – dreadful if yer inflicted with them types of dreams. I had them myself once upon a time. I feel for yer, honestly I do," empathises one goblin.

"How anyone could live in a place like this? It doesn't bear thinkin' about," shudders Pompucket.

"The cleanliness is making me feel very sick," wretches one goblin, looking at flowered papers on walls, books on bookcases, cushions on chairs and plants displayed as objects of beauty.

Grimacing with displeasure, some of the goblins are forced to sit down on the chairs, sofas or beds which are full of comfortable things, due to the lack of space in the houses. After much moaning and groaning at the prospect of being holed up in these houses for a time, those sitting down on sofas and chairs actually begin to let the weight off their feet. Most sit back and enjoy the sheer luxury of being able to do this, though none of them let on that this is the case. Pompucket, who is unlucky enough to be sitting on a chair, pulls a blanket from behind it and wraps it around his stinking body.

"Oooh, this is nice – I mean horrendous. Never want one of these things to touch my body ever again," he protests, before going into a deep sleep.

Others do the same.

CHAPTER 25

SAVING THE KING AND HIS KEEP

Goblin armies have pushed the fricasian soldiers further and further back into the city. Now they are at the keep and there is nowhere else to run.

"Push forward, men. These people are beaten. Soon we will own this city," boasts General Glum, who directs his men whilst they slither and slide around him.

The fricasians have lost a lot of soldiers and citizens to the merciless hordes, who continue to push ahead with ease. A consequence of the fricasian retreat, as gates are locked behind retreating soldiers, is that the space they inhabit becomes more and more cramped. The fricasian soldiers become more of a tight knit group. When they were spread out along the outer walls there was too much to guard with too few resources, which made it easier for the blinny to pick off the soldiers one by one. Now that the men have barricaded themselves into a smaller space around the keep, their numbers are condensed and less likely to be broken. They have found their niche and have begun to fight back.

"Come on, we can hold them off yet. Remember an army comes to help – let us hope that they are not too far away from us now. The longer we hold on, the better our prospects," rallies Old Jack from the top of the battlements.

"Well said, soldier," a voice shouts, echoing all around. Everyone gasps because these words came from the mouth of the King himself. He is outside the doors of the keep, dressed in his finest golden armour, sitting atop his favourite horse and surrounded by his own personal cavalry. "The army that comes to help is in the city. I have seen them from my tower and they should be here soon. Are these the last of our brave men?"

"Yes, sire," replies Old Jack.

"Then we must use you well, I decree that no one is allowed to die here, under pain of death," orders the King, winking to his more knowing cavalrymen.

"No, sire, of course not. You heard the King," commands Old

Jack, turning to his soldiers. "Now get on with repelling these little monsters below – before they repel us."

Soldiers on top of the last walls, before the entrance to the keep, are surrounded on all sides by goblins and ogres in the narrow streets below. Ogres try to break through to the other side of the gate using their clubs and their weight. Goblins climb the walls hoping to open the gates from the inside, much like they had done before.

"Bowmen, fire your arrows. Everyone else, grab what you can and pound them with whatever weapons you find," urges Old Jack.

Friscasian bowmen fire their remaining arrows down into the crowds below; citizens pass heavy objects up a line of people to the top, where men wait to throw them over the sides of the wall. Many objects, from bricks, small stone statues, kegs of ale, sides of beef, watermelons, blocks of wood and plant pots, rain down on blinny, squashing some and injuring others, but overall the effect is minimal.

The skies around Warrior teem with dragons, circling him and his army. Tensions are high on both sides; all creatures here understand the harm each other can cause. Pengwellen is first to make a move, diving down and down towards Warrior and his army in one swift movement. Close to the ground Pengwellen flies, giving out a burst of fiery breath which covers both Warrior and a line of the goblin cavalry. Pengwellen's approach has been so fast that blinny archers miss the chance to fire upon him, and his retreat is so swift that a line of fire still smoulders behind him. Twenty or so goblins and barghest are on fire or singed, though not enough so that they are unrecognisable or in any danger of dying. A sustained burst of fire, not one in passing, will inflict the damage necessary.

The old dragon saunters back up into the skies casually, once satisfied he is in no immediate danger. As he does so, dragon after dragon dives down in the direction of the plains, one behind another in a long line. The result is a sustained burst of fire passing over the goblin army. One after the other dragons fly past, releasing their breath. No one on the path that they follow can hide from it. When the smoke rises up off the ground and dissipates, it reveals a long line of dead goblins and barghest, blackened and charred. Caught lying down with hands generally covering their heads or standing with mouths still open as if surprised by the attack, their attempts to try and protect themselves from the slaughter were in vain.

The pets are unharmed, though, if a little dishevelled, and a little angry that it is they who are being attacked. Thick leathery hides protect these creatures, and it is obvious to Pengwellen that more will need to be done to get rid of them for good. Warrior stands as he always does, unmoved by the events around him. His armour is blackened but he displays no damage other than to the rotting face which has melted a little in the fiery heat, revealing part of the face plate behind it.

"When the dragons pass, I want you to take one out of the air," he tells his pets who, understanding his every word, grin excitedly at the prospect of being unleashed.

The dragons ready themselves for the next assault. Pengwellen is the first to go. Diving down, he directs his flight towards the easier kills, these being goblins and barghest. The old dragon will heed the wizard's words and be wary of Warrior from now on in. His first attack was cheeky at best, at worst irresponsible and dangerous (although he knows better). But for now, he knows Warrior is drained of magic and his brethren cannot be touched by him. Behind the old dragon, flying in a single line, is the rest of his clan. Five or six metres above the ground, close to the goblins, Pengwellen lets out his fiery breath. A yellow dragon behind Pengwellen lets out his breath a second or two later, then a red one, a blue one and a green one all follow suit, covering the same spot.

The dragons are making an impact upon the army on the ground with this assault. The blinny fire arrows from their bows, thrust pikes and swing swords, all to no avail, but the dragons have not noticed pets running at great speeds in their direction.

The attack is nearly at its end, and the last few dragons in the line await their turn to inflict damage. A young, inexperienced, yellow-coloured dragon flies a little too low, opening himself up to attack. Already in the vicinity of the advancing dragons, the pets see their chance. Three of them closest to the yellow dragon jump as high as they can, and use the large hands at the end of their very long arms to grab onto him at the neck, wing and tail, bringing him to a sudden halt. The halting of the dragon is so severe that the dragons behind him have to swerve and veer away from the body braking in front of them. The yellow dragon, under the weight of the pets, hits the ground. The pets hang on to him, unperturbed by the fact that they are crushed numerous times as he rolls. Goblin cavalrymen are nearby and immediately they pounce onto the opportunity that has presented itself. Barghest, seeing their chance, run bloody-minded at the struggling yellow dragon who is being systematically cut by pet talons; the barghest resolve that their teeth will join in soon.

Pengwellen views the desperate plight of the yellow dragon with horror, knowing that he can do nothing to save him. The best that might be done for this one is to end his torture. Diving down once more, this time it will be to end the nightmare of one of their own.

Outside the houses filled with goblin prisoners, preparations for an advance are being made.

"Laureate, can you guide us to the keep?" asks Stryker.

"I can – we are not far away from it, only minutes at worst," replies Laureate.

"Good man," says Stryker. Turning his attention to Teacher, Stryker says, "Teacher, we need some of your men to stay here and guard the goblin prisoners. We cannot have them escaping back into the city. I would leave only ten at most, I have a sneaky feeling that the goblins will not want to tangle with even that many of your men."

Teacher nods and walks over to his warriors, talking aloud to himself, "Ah, it is a hard thing for me to do, but do it I must if it keeps these murderers at bay." Choosing ten to stay will pose a problem, as all men and women present want to continue on with their adventure, especially after their most recent battle. Heads slump when they are picked, but the jotunn take their orders well and remain as professional as they have always appeared to be. Separating from the rest of the crowd, ten tunny warriors line up, shoulder to shoulder, outside the houses. Shields on arms and swords unsheathed are held in wait for any action that would prompt their use.

Setting off again, Laureate leads the army through a myriad of streets full of grey stone-coloured houses, some of which are set into the city walls. Every now and again, a glimpse of the keep reveals itself before disappearing behind a house, a tree or a wall. The jotunn have a better view, but they are distracted quite a bit. Washing lines between houses on either side of a cobbled street, or branches and twigs from the odd bush or tree, get in their way. Surprisingly, the climb through the streets up to the keep, situated at the very top of this city, is not long.

"The noises created by the goblins and ogres are getting louder. We are very close to their position now," Greybeard says to Finn. "The battle will become increasingly more dangerous from now on. Stick close to me, and do not join the front lines of the battle. You are our standard bearer and you must be protected at all costs."

"I will stick close," reassures Finn.

"That goes for you two as well," Greybeard shouts out to Beezle and Perrywinkle. "Especially you, Beezle – do not do anything stupid or dangerous."

"Humph," is the only sound Beezle makes.

Goblin noises prompt Greybeard's army to walk just that little bit faster until they arrive a few streets down from the keep. Laureate and Stryker both look around the corner of the building they stand next to. Up ahead, past another couple of streets is the keep wall, which is surrounded by Warrior's army. They cannot see the closed gate leading to the keep itself; that is around another corner.

The final gate leading to the keep creaks as it opens; cheers ring out as goblins and ogres pour into the keep courtyard. It wasn't Warrior's army who were responsible for opening the gate – that was the King's order. Sitting on his favoured horse, sword ready, he imagines that this is likely to be his last battle whether he survives it or not. Lines of cavalry sit immediately behind him, and his most trusted soldiers at his side. Behind the King and his cavalry, a few hundred foot soldiers, the last of his army, look out nervously at the goblins and ogres that have fought them back to this point with ease.

"Attack!" the King orders, flying first into the goblin throng, swiping and slashing with his sword.

The chance is now there for Stryker to order a surprise attack

Goblins attack the Fricasian keep

as preoccupied goblins and ogres enter the confines of the keep courtyard through the open gates.

"The time has come to assert ourselves upon the goblin hordes around these walls, but we must be stealthy as we approach. So follow me and be careful not to make a sound as you do so," Stryker orders.

Stryker tiptoes around the corner from where he has been looking out. Crossing the street, he presses himself against the walls of the houses. The rest of the army also makes their way to the other side of the street, slowly and surely. Stryker walks up the cobbled paths towards the keep wall, stopping only when he comes to a crossroads where this street meets another. Before he walks any further, he looks round the corner just to make sure that goblins and ogres have not spilled out onto this other street. Satisfied that there are no surprises awaiting him and his army, he rushes forward, urging others to follow quickly but cautiously.

Moments later, Stryker is at the end of the street. He peers around the corner that looks upon the gates leading to the keep and Warrior's army that besieges it. Stryker takes out his sword slowly and quietly; others take the hint and also make their weapons ready.

"Around this corner is our destiny. Let us roar now as loud as we can, so that they are surprised by us," Stryker suggests, changing tack; after all, the army is close enough to do some damage now. Stryker, followed by the others, runs out from behind the corner of the building and faces the blinny at the back of the throng. Giving out loud, booming screams, they immediately get the goblins' attention. After a short pause, though, the goblins begin to laugh and gurgle and lick their lips with genuine amusement. The ogres remain quiet – they don't get it. Stryker, Forester and the dwarfs are somewhat surprised and dismayed after the reaction that the jotunn got from the last lot of goblins, although the roars provided by the army could have been a little louder.

"A few men and dwarfs to take our army on – ooh, they're cheeky this lot. Do yer worst, yer scum," laughs one goblin.

"Yeah, who do you think yer are?" another goads. Stryker, Forester and the dwarfs look behind them, and to their surprise the jotunn are nowhere to be seen.

"Where are they? I thought it was a bit quiet," asks Wattlespalf. Everyone shrugs their shoulders. Wattlespalf rushes back to the building from where they have just come.

"Come on, it's starting! We are being made a mockery of out there. Why didn't you follow? Oh, never mind. Follow me now," the dwarf says, ordering the waiting giants, who had not heard Stryker's call to arms. Wattlespalf runs back to the others who are beginning to sweat anxiously. From around the corner the jotunn appear, walking slowly in pairs, with shields protecting chests and swords pointing ahead of them. The goblins, who had been confident before, look up and gulp at the large men and women who look down on them. Smiles are on other faces now as goblins try to take steps backwards – so do ogres, which is very unlike them. Not far behind the jotunn soldiers are Greybeard, Finn, Perrywinkle and Beezle.

Perrywinkle, eager to gain a good view of the action, climbs a tree a safe distance away from the soon-to-be warring armies, midway between the city wall closest to the keep and the nearest houses on the other side of the street. Perrywinkle finds a suitable perch on a strong thick branch of the tree. Camouflaged by many leaves, he pulls out his journal and his favourite pen from his backpack, opens his journal and flicks through the pages carefully with his wetted thumb until he comes to a blank page. The little man begins to write furiously, taking in all the sights, sounds and action.

"Who are these giant monsters approachin' with huge weapons?" screams one goblin, but there is no time to ponder as Stryker and the rest are itching to attack.

"Do you not know who we are? We are your judge, jury and executioners. We are vengeance for all the wrongs you have committed to other creatures and to the world. We will bear down on you with no mercy and no heart," shouts Forester, waving his sword.

Slow to react, goblins and ogres are faced with swords, axes and hammers that thrust at, chop and blow bodies left, right and centre.

In the courtyard of the keep, a similar story is developing as the King valiantly forces goblins back out of the gate doors with his fearsome cavalry beside him.

Goblin bowmen, seeing their compatriots in trouble, take aim from the back and fire arrows upon the jotunn, who are seen to be the biggest threat. Scores of arrows fly forward. The jotunn try to protect their bodies as well as they can with shields, but arrows come from all directions. Many arrows puncture legs, stomachs, chests, arms and shoulders of the five jotunn soldiers leading the line. The pain endured by the tunny is great this time – too many arrows have come too soon. Gritting teeth and screwing up eyes in anguish, blood trickles out from various parts of their bodies and some begin to feel weak.

Goblin pikemen and foot soldiers, seeing that the giants are wounded, seek to make easy kills. Groups of them begin to climb up onto the jotunn, slashing legs and arms, stabbing backs and necks. Ogres beat them brutally with their clubs, bones are easily broken. One tunny warrior falls forward, his life ended, onto the goblins beneath him, squashing them underneath his huge weight, ending their lives as well. Another soldier, full of arrows, tries to shake off the goblins and ogres attacking him, but to no avail. One by one the jotunn at the front are surrounded by Warrior's army and are overpowered by them.

"Help us!" the tunny holler, but there appears to be no one who can help. Stryker, Forester and the dwarfs are finding it hard to keep their balance, for the strength of the goblin army pressing forward is great.

Finn takes Medrin, the elven bow, off his shoulder; he has heard the tunny cry. Pulling back the bow string, the light blue, pencil-thin beam of energy resembling an arrow forms itself. The elf fires the energised arrow towards the goblins who climb and surround the tunny soldiers, as well as the ogres who strike them with their large, heavy clubs. Quick and fast is Finn's response, and beams of blue energy fly all around. Foes fall, releasing the injured jotunn from their mortal danger. Wounded jotunn at the front are pulled to the back of the line by protective hands, only to be replaced by others, full of vigour and unharmed.

Beezle looks at his brother – or more specifically, his backpack and what dwells within it. He is unable to get the rod out of his head now that his impending receipt of both it and the red oric looms ever nearer. The little elf feels hungry for them; his stomach twists and turns, and his mind feels squeezed and starved.

Beezle shakes his head as he tries to throw out the thoughts swirling around his head. Maybe if he partakes in the battle, tests his skills, he might forget about them for a little while. Climbing onto a bench close to the tree where Perrywinkle currently sits, Beezle is able to get a better view of the goblins and ogres ahead.

"I wonder which trick to begin with. I know, I think I'll start with the first trick I learned," he mutters, putting his arm out, aiming at one particular goblin and grabbing it whilst saying the magic words: "Grabius movus." But the goblin Beezle has chosen to take a hold of is no ordinary goblin, it is General Glum.

"What is this? Why do I feel as light as a feather?" asks Glum, rising above his army, confused as to what is happening to him. Having got his goblin, Beezle shakes him vigorously from side to side, forwards and backwards above the crowds. The goblins below watch the spectacle; a sea of heads follow every move, pushing and pulling stops and awe turns to twinges of fear. Only a wizard could do this and Warrior was not anywhere to be seen. High up into the air, higher than the tallest buildings, the large, chubby goblin flies.

"What is happening to meeeeee!" exclaims the goblin.

Beezle giggles; he loves his new-found abilities. Glum's big, worm-like lips curl as he is raised into the air at Beezle's whim. Once up, Glum comes back down at the greatest of speeds, until he stops – just short of squashing his goblin compatriots. General Glum is scared out of his wits and justifiably so. Beezle throws him up into the air many more times, higher and higher he goes at every turn. Glum is finally flung high up towards the clouds where he can see the dragons flying all around.

"Release me! Please let me go!" he screams.

"With pleasure," Beezle remarks with menace, releasing Glum from his spell. Down and down he drops, but this time Glum doesn't stop.

"I should have not wished for that," he whimpers, closing his eyes.

Splat is the sound made as the large, chubby goblin general drops onto a good dozen or more of his soldiers, killing them as well as being killed himself.

"Who's doin' this?" question some of the blinny. None have yet caught sight of Beezle, but what could they do? Wizards are notoriously hard to kill, and Beezle is well-hidden and well-protected behind Stryker's army.

Pengwellen and his dragons are not having the easiest of times. Warrior's pets make it difficult for the dragons to approach their targets at a height that will cause the maximum damage. Every approach made carries the real concern that pets could bring down a dragon or two. As such, goblin casualties have not increased as speedily as expected, with many still gracing this field of battle.

The one soldier that they have not dared engage in any real capacity is Warrior, who funnily enough, has not moved one inch during this conflict. Warrior appears to be waiting for something. The possibility is that his regeneration, after the creation of the orbs, has taken longer to complete than he would have liked, or he reserves his energy for something or someone else, maybe Greybeard. The dragons have kept one eye on him at all times, as they know Warrior might turn on them at any given moment. But his pets appear suitably capable of keeping the dragons entertained, and at this point, he probably feels no threat from them at all. Pengwellen flies back into the skies after another frustrating attack that has yielded little.

"Hold your attacks," he shouts to his dragons, giving him time to ponder the next move. "What is holding us back?" he asks himself. "Pets, is the answer. And what is the weakness of this breed? I don't know. Fire doesn't kill them." Out of the corner of his eye, he sees a chubby goblin being hurled high up into the sky (it is General Glum) around the area where the keep is situated, only to see him falling at a terrible speed that he could never have survived.

"This gives me an idea," he says, but the idea is discounted. if he was to drop a pet from a height, Warrior would surely catch it before it impacted against the ground. Another idea pops into his mind – one which is far more fiendish. He turns to his dragons, and communicating in dragonspeak, Pengwellen asks them to protect him at all costs, making sure that nothing can distract him from his purpose.

Flight towards the ground is attempted once more. This time Pengwellen wants to try something different, something that might well provoke Warrior but will further the cause. This big old dragon has his eye on one of Warrior's pets. Flying as fast as he can, the old dragon lines himself up in the direction of a lone pet who is currently outside the protective sphere of the main group. The pet, expecting Pengwellen to fly above him, gets ready to make a grab for this old beast. The dragon feigns the appearance that he is indeed going to fly over Warrior's pet, but as he draws close he lowers himself just a little more. Either side of him dragons breathe fire in all directions, protecting their lord. Stretching out his long neck and opening his mouth as wide as it can go, he waits until the right moment before closing his jaws around the beast's head. Pengwellen lifts himself and Warrior's pet off the ground, not stopping until he is very high up in the skies, where no one on the ground can see him.

The pet thrashes its arms, grabbing and squeezing Pengwellen's long nose, trying to find a way out of the dragon's mouth. If only the pet knew how high off the ground it is, it might think better and stay exactly where it is. Warrior tries to search out the old dragon carrying his beloved pet. A feeling of powerlessness overcomes him as he is unable to use his magic so that he may save it.

Hovering in mid-air, Pengwellen is joined by two other dragons, who each take hold of an arm in their mouths. These two dragons begin to pull away from each other, stretching the pet's arms further and further away from its body.

Inside Pengwellen's mouth, the muffled screams of the pet can be heard faintly trying to get out. Pulls turn to tugs as the dragons endeavour to rip this pet apart. Pengwellen bites down just a little bit harder on the pet's neck to secure it in position. Down on the ground Warrior looks on helplessly, though you would never know it by looking into the darkness beyond the mask.

Suddenly, a blue-tinted liquid rains down onto his armour, followed moments later by individual body parts that flap and thud as they hit the hard ground. One pet's arm can clearly be seen to have been chewed upon; the dragons had obviously been curious enough to try this potential new delicacy only to spit it out as unpalatable. Now only four pets remain.

Meanwhile, goblins and ogres are pushed back, further and

further away from the keep. The King and his soldiers fight well, energised with hope, knowing that this is the last chance they have to save both themselves and their city. Greybeard's men, led at this time by Stryker, are also in the ascendancy as Warrior's army begins to filter back down into the streets leading towards the southern walls.

The King and his men emerge at the entrance of the last gate protecting the keep, whilst goblins and ogres defend themselves from all manner of weapons. Laureate, who fights alongside Stryker and the others, smiles with relief on seeing his King well and in fighting spirits.

The King sits on his horse at the front of the line, his sword swiping this way and that whilst his shield protects him from incoming arrows, sword swipes and pike thrusts. Before long, the King and his men are outside the walled gate. Flooding onto the streets, they are quickly joined shoulder to shoulder by Stryker's forces. The two armies work together, ushering goblins and ogres further back and at a much quicker pace.

The jotunn who were injured earlier on in this battle are carried by compatriots through the gate entrance into the keep courtyard, which is now empty. They are laid down, given water, blankets and urged to rest.

"Close the gate," orders the King.

Slowly, on either side of the gated entrance, wooden doors close. Each door is pushed forward by four men until they are secured shut. A large iron key situated in a keyhole on the right-hand wooden door is turned by one of the soldiers. The key is turned anti-clockwise several times because the unseen iron block locking these two doors together is both long and strong.

Now there is no going back.

CHAPTER 26

DRAGONS AND GIANTS PLAY SHEPHERD

Unified soldiers bolstered by their renewed strength begin to push further forward.

"Greybeard, please alert the dragons," Stryker asks. Greybeard, staying close to Finn and Beezle under the tree where Perrywinkle sits, acknowledges Stryker's request. Raising his staff towards the sky, the wizard mumbles a couple of words, and with a *pop* a bolt of green light flies high up into the air. Reaching what appears to be a preordained distance, the bolt of green light explodes, producing spark after spark of green light, until after only a short while it fizzes out into nothingness.

Pengwellen's attention turns momentarily from spitting out the last of the blood and bones of his most recent kill (a second pet has been pulled apart by the dragons, much like the first. Pets are down to three), to watching the display being witnessed by the others. The hovering dragons who fill the skies immediately split into two groups upon seeing the wizard's signal. Pengwellen has already chosen those who will come to the aid of those fighting in the city. He did this after the initial meeting to discuss the plan of action, and he will not be joining them. The big old dragon's focus remains firmly fixed on Warrior, his army and his pets as there is much to be done. Pengwellen begins another attack, heading towards the ground once more.

Back at the keep, too many streets offer Warrior's army too many routes which they might use to hide or escape punishment for their actions. Anticipating this, Stryker has already formulated a plan. Removing himself from the front line of the battle, Stryker shuffles in between the other soldiers until he is surrounded by them no more. Teacher stands supporting his pupils, who fight the goblins and spike-wielding ogres as he thrusts his sword through the spaces between tunny soldiers. Despite his age, Teacher has been equally as successful as his younger charges, instilling fear and doubt in goblin minds.

"Teacher," shouts Stryker as loud as he can in the old giant's direction, hoping to gain his attention. Teacher turns round and Stryker gestures for him to come over. The old man pulls himself out of the throng and makes his way over to him.

"You called?" questions Teacher, wondering why Stryker wants him.

"Teacher, I need you to help me. Could you get a hold of some of your men and go back down the street we originally came up to get to this place? I need you to block every street shooting off the main road on which we stand, so that the goblins cannot stray onto them and escape. If the tunny guard these streets, the hope is that the blinny will limit themselves to following only the routes we allow them to soil. Would you be so kind as to do this?" Stryker asks.

"Yes, no problem. It will be a pleasure," Teacher replies. Turning to a section of his men and women, who stand well behind those tunny still fighting the goblin crowds, he taps a number of them on the shoulder and pulls them out of battle. One of them is Meena.

"Remember to keep your distance from the main crowd at all times. The dragons have been called upon and their breath is not to be taken lightly," Stryker warns. Teacher and around twenty jotunn make haste past Greybeard, Finn and Beezle before disappearing around the corner and down the street.

Stryker pushes his way back to the front of the battle, squeezing between his brother and the dwarfs. Hideous faces try to pull away from the army that advances against them, goblin weapons now defend where once they attacked. Swords and pikes stand vertically against chests and faces, protecting them from the swipes and thrusts of sharper, more skilled swords.

"Having a good day?" Stryker asks Forester, who stands to the right of him.

"A great day! It has been a long time since we partook in anything as intense as this," he replies, revelling in the moment.

"And look at how abundant the enemy is," adds Gendralf, chopping at a horrified goblin with his axe, lopping off his arm in the process.

"Truly the stuff of dreams," Igralf enthuses, swinging his large hammer at the retreating crowd. When Igralf's hammer connects with the bodies of those he touches, the power is enough to make blinny and even ogres fly off their feet. Up into the air goblins and ogres soar, landing back down six, seven or maybe even eight rows back onto the heads of other unfortunate and unsuspecting monsters.

"Dreams? A dream is a good meal and good ale. This swordplay lark is making me hungry," Wattlespalf states grumpily, taking a diagonal swipe from the shoulder of one stunned goblin, through the waist of another and the knee of a third with his sword. Two sets of stunned eyes belonging to those sliced by the sword look at Wattlespalf, whilst the third set of eyes squint with pain. Two are already dead and the third maimed as parts of bodies separate from other parts and fall to the ground in a heap.

Chances for the dwarfs and men to inflict maximum damage do not come often enough. The enclosed space this crowd inhabits makes movement quite restricted, but when the dwarfs and men are allowed, the enemy, faced with all this power, cannot get away fast enough. Greybeard watches patiently, but he does not lift a finger, his unwavering trust in those around allowing him to remain calm and peaceful. Kings, wizards, elves, dwarfs, giants and shape-shifters contribute to goblin carnage, whilst up above dragons waft their large wings, waiting for the most opportune moment to play their part.

Goblins at the back, unaffected by the battle, are pushed into the streets by others more affected and more terrified. Lieutenants, understanding that the advance is futile, order a partial retreat back into the city.

"Do not follow them. The dragons must have their way with the goblins now. Tell all of your men that they should regain their breath whilst they can. Battle will commence again soon enough," Stryker orders. Heavy arms are happy to let weapons fall to sides, slide back into sheaths and rest on shoulders. Soon, a short distance develops between the two armies.

Patience has prevailed; the dragons above finally see their chance to do awful things to the blinny whilst the other creatures below maintain a safe distance. Red, green, yellow and blue dragons smile menacingly into the eyes of those who have been brave and clever enough to look up into the skies. The dragons surround the goblin army on all sides, now they are trapped. Panic rushes through goblin blood, especially through the veins of those caught in the very centre of the tight, stifled crowd. They have no chance of surviving a dragon's fire, if or when they make their attack.

Anticipation as to what will happen heightens as the dragons get closer and closer to their prey. Smiling ghastly smiles, the dragons savour the fear that they spread amongst common foes whilst their friends watch on. Goblins and ogres, having been surrounded, swing their clubs in the dragons' general direction, but to no avail. Deep breaths are taken by these mercurial beasts in readiness for the act that they are about to commit. Similarly, deep breaths are taken by Warrior's army, on whom the act will be committed. And then, short sharp bursts of flame force their way out through dragon mouths into the crowd. Goblins and ogres duck down as far as they can, so as not to be caught out by the inferno that rages above them. Flames hover just above the ogres' heads, but they are hot enough to singe hairs on those most unfortunate. The dragons laugh evilly, enjoying the torture they are administering.

"You lot further down, help us! Move more quickly – my head is bein' cooked by awful firin' dragons," one terrified goblin screams.

"Ay, mine, too! Do yer not care about yer own kind, or do yer not have the head for understandin' that we must move back to where we came?" cries another.

A second burst of fire beats down on the goblin throng, but this time the fire burns a little more closely. Some goblins' heads turn red as the heat burns their skin, and some with fuller heads of hair find that their barnets are on fire. Hands wafting faster than fast try to cool the scorching heat they feel. Others pat their heads or empty flasks of ale onto burning hair in an attempt to douse the flames. The onlookers, standing further back, are amused by the dragons playing games with their foes. Giggles and sniggers sound out from those watching the absurdity ensuing within the goblin ranks.

"Who'd have thought it? Dragons burning the hairs on the heads of our enemies and the many changes to our enemies' faces in reaction to them," roars Igralf with a big, beaming smile.

"Oh, the confusion… then the fear," adds Gendralf.

"The frowns and the relief," continues Igralf.

"The ducking and the fleeing," Gendralf continues.

"And the smell, what a terrible smell," interrupts Wattlespalf, holding his nose.

"Hmm, yes – I suppose you are right. The smell of burning goblins is very much worse than the smell of goblins who are not burning," agrees Igralf, covering his mouth with his hand.

Screams and shouts have turned to action. Finally the goblin crowds move steadily, almost at a trot, as the march through the city, back towards the holes in the southern walls, begins in earnest.

Laureate walks over to his King, who has briefly climbed down from his horse.

"Welcome back, Captain Laureate," the King says with open arms. Laureate and the King both hug briefly before pulling away from each other to talk. "And who are these friends you have brought?"

"Sire, this is the army that approached from the east. They were riding to our aid and have been good enough to dispatch a good amount of the enemy thus far, including an army who sought to attack us from the north-eastern side of the city," comments Laureate.

"I am aware," the King replies. "Thank you all for coming to help fight for this city. I have no doubt that there is a larger purpose behind your presence. If we can play any part in helping you succeed in your mission, then we will with all our heart."

"Ahem," Stryker pipes up, getting everyone's attention. "Much work is still left to be done. We cannot rest on our laurels as we are only at the very beginning of this battle. We will need what is left of your army, and they must work hard alongside ours. The endgame is to defeat Warrior and to do that we must first clear a path through his minions to get to him. Can your men do that for us?"

"Consider it done," replies the King.

Teacher has secured the streets adjacent to the road the remnants of Warrior's army are being herded along. Jotunn soldiers see dragons hovering above the roofs of the houses they guard. Goblin crowds at the ends of the streets want to overflow into the paths of the giants who protect the borders, but on seeing the jotunn, bodies tremble and quiver. Heads turn and attention sways between dragons and giants. Frail minds consider what might be the worst of two fates. Those who see fire breathing dragons as the more potent threat run onto the streets covered by jotunn soldiers.

On one of the streets, furthest away from the keep, Meena and two others can see the mob that is the goblin army passing by slowly. Four or five goblins rush to the doors of houses lining the streets, turning knobs and pushing on doors frantically as they try to find a place to hide. After all, the tunny are too big to enter these abodes, but unlike those houses inspected by Stryker earlier, none of the doors close by are open. Fate or luck might well be playing its part in this battle. The blinny are left with no choice but to push closer towards the giants as they try to open doors to houses further up the street. Bows are pulled off jotunn shoulders. Meena is the first to warn approaching goblins to retreat.

"Get back into the crowd," commands Meena.

"Or else, what are yer gonna do, jotunn woman?" goads one dark, black-eyed goblin who carries on walking towards her, pulling menacing faces and flaring his teeth. Meena, who is not in any mood to be goaded or menaced, removes an arrow from her quiver, quickly aims and then shoots it in the goblins direction. A scream rings out as the large tunny arrow travels through the shoulder of the goading goblin.

"You shot me," the goblin wails. Other goblins start walking back towards the moving crowd and the dragons, scared that they will be next.

"Of course I shot you, you idiot. Really, the bravado you were showing and your mouthing off was enough that I should have killed you outright," replies Meena angrily.

"Bravado, eh? What does that mean? Mouthin' off? Well mouth this – I could still have yer," goads the goblin some more. Meena, hoping to teach him a lesson, pulls out another arrow from her quiver. The goading goblin flinches.

"Do you want this arrow to become a part of you?" Meena asks.

"Why not? Better an arrow than seeing the sour-faced look on yer face, yer miserable…" Before the goblin can finish his sentence an arrow pierces the top of his thigh. Screaming, the goading goblin falls to the floor and writhes in agony. Squinting with pained eyes, he grits his teeth and shouts, "Go on then… finish me off."

Meena stands over the pained, smelly beast below her and pulls out both arrows, twisting them for extra effect. The goading goblin puts his fingers in his mouth and bites down hard, high-pitched squeals fill the air as he does so.

"Get back to your brethren or your life might be ended here and now," orders Meena calmly, as she puts the arrows back into the quiver.

He looks up at Meena and at the other jotunn pacing the streets behind her with a defeated expression on his face. Meena puts out her hand, gesturing that he will be helped up should he wish to use her strength as a crutch.

"I would have had yer, yer know," he says, extending his wounded arm out. Meena grabs hold of his arm and pulls him up firmly, but as she does so, the goblin pulls out a large dagger from behind his back. Reaching as high as his arm will allow, he thrusts the dagger into her side, close to her belly, and slices downward until the blade reaches the top of her leg. Meena's eyes instantly reveal her shock. Her arm relaxes. Letting go of the goblin, he slides slowly back onto the cobbled floor.

"Told yer I'd get yer," he laughs and then groans in pain.

Jotunn soldiers run to her aid, laying her down on the ground carefully. Meena feels sleepy, her hands and neck feel cold, her heart beats more slowly, blood spilling from her side.

One tunny soldier runs back up the street from where the army originally came, to the wall close to the keep where Greybeard and the others stand. Another tunny soldier finishes the job that Meena started on the goading goblin – not much is left of him when he is done.

"Sir, Meena… she is grave. Help us," shouts the soldier running along the wall, repeating his words over and over.

Greybeard pulls out of a self-inflicted trance as he watches dragons breathe their hypnotic bursts of fire at Warrior's army.

"Meena? Meena is hurt?" Finn trembles. "Greybeard, we must

help her. The dangleberry potion – do you have it? Please help her."

"Soldier, take us to her," orders Greybeard gently. "The rest of you stay behind and follow the dragons down the hill."

"Can I not come?" asks Beezle, not wanting to lose sight of Finn's backpack, and more importantly, the thing that dwells inside of it.

"No, stay here with the rest," responds Greybeard. Beezle accepts it, but fidgets maniacally, trying to block out the obsession he has for the rod.

"Sir, we must be quick! She is dying," the panicked soldier reveals.

The soldier, the wizard and the elf all run back around the corner. The jotunn soldier, who is quite a bit faster, runs past street after street. He stops several streets down and points to the spot where Meena lies. Seconds later, Greybeard and Finn arrive. Here, they get their first glimpse of Meena's wounded body, prompting Finn and Greybeard to rush over to her. The wizard gets down on one knee and begins to examine the giant.

"It is true, she is deathly ill," reveals Greybeard, a little unsure if he is able to do anything at all for her.

"Please do all you can – she is a good person and too young to follow the destinies of those who have lived much longer lives. Too many have already lost their lives too soon," Finn pleads.

"Finn, prepare yourself for the very real possibility of this dangleberry not being potent enough to reverse the predicament she finds herself. The berry can only do so much – the strength and will of the creature it treats is paramount in its ability to help," Greybeard tells Finn with honesty, taking the wrapped dangleberry out of his backpack and holding it aloft.

"I'm sure she will fight all she can. Do you need water to make the brew?" asks Finn.

"No, no… the dangleberry on its own will be fine," Greybeard replies. The wizard puts the berry in his mouth and chews on it for a while. He does this to break it down and make it soft. Mixing his own saliva with the juices of the dangleberry, he puts his face close to Meena's and spits the liquid mixture into her mouth. After keeping the chewed dangleberry close against his cheek, he eventually pulls it out of his mouth. Playing with the fruit for a while in his fingers, he inserts the dangleberry into the wound inflicted by the goblin's dagger.

"This is the best I can do," Greybeard says after a pause.

"Do you think she will survive?" asks Finn, beside himself.

"I don't know," replies Greybeard solemnly, not holding out much hope.

"I know what I can do," says a resolute Finn. He takes his backpack off his back, opens it and dips his hand into its deep recesses pulling out the promethian liquid from within. Finn looks into the bottle at the clear, blue-tinted liquid inside. All forms of emotion boil inside him. The liquid had been the present he least wanted, but now he is compelled to use it, just this once, to satisfy himself that Meena will indeed survive her wounds.

Finn tips the bottle upside down so as to get some of the liquid onto the dropper. Removing the dropper from the bottle, Finn puts his head back and aims the dropper over his open mouth. A droplet forms at the very tip of the dropper, it hangs tentatively above Finn's mouth as if sensing his dread and desire to have it over and done with. Gracefully, one drop of liquid leaves the dropper and heads for Finn's mouth, landing on the tip of his tongue. Finn closes his mouth, and proceeds to secure the dropper back into the bottle where it belongs.

"I don't feel any different," he says, turning to Greybeard, who looks on silently. Even Greybeard hasn't been party to the wonders of promethian liquid, and he is intrigued as to how Finn might make use of it, or how the liquid might make use of him.

"Oh, there is a tingle on the nape of my neck and the tips of my toes," says Finn, describing this new experience. He kneels beside Meena, close to her face. The elf guides his hand towards her cheek, only to pull back as his mind wrestles with anxiety and the potential that he might see the death of a new-found friend. With one swift moment of bravery, Finn places his hand upon Meena's cheek. A snap and a bang cracks inside Finn's mind. White flashes intermingled with darkness replace thought. Finn is worried. Nothing has yet been revealed, or has it? Is the light and dark all that is left of Meena's life? No, it is only the beginning – now there is colour and a movement. A life runs fast forward through Finn's mind. His eyes flicker as information is transmitted. Emotions including happiness, sadness, anger and love surge through his soul. Finn has lived Meena's life from this point on and it is one filled with much joy and eventful times. The visions end and Finn smiles the most subtle of smiles.

Turning to Greybeard, Finn says, "She will have a good long life and with the right sort of folk."

"Good, good. So what did you see?" Greybeard asks, eager to find out more of what Finn saw. He stops short of patting Finn on the back, just in case there is some residual ability still left in him that may tell the elf some truths about the wizard, truths which are best left alone.

"I would rather not say, if that is alright by you. It wouldn't be fair to Meena to talk of such private things," replies Finn.

"What, not even a snippet?" asks Greybeard, a little disappointed.

"Oh, alright… she will own a cat at some point in the future," divulges Finn.

"Hmm, well that's not nearly enough to keep me interested."

"Sirs," Finn shouts, waving to two jotunn soldiers close by. "Please stay here and protect Meena."

"We would not think about doing anything else," replies one of the soldiers graciously.

Teacher, who has been running between the soldiers in different streets, makes his way to Finn and Greybeard, panting heavily.

"Will she be alright, Greybeard?" he asks, slightly out of breath.

"Apparently so," Greybeard replies.

"Oh, excellent, excellent," a relieved Teacher enthuses. "Shall we scare these monsters witless in reply?"

"I think you better had, although I suspect the dragons have done enough scaring already. How about terrify?" comments Greybeard playfully.

"Terrify, that sounds good to me," Teacher laughs. "Soldiers, you heard the man, beat your shields and give these monsters cause to fear us."

Jotunn soldiers bang swords against shields, and booming voices echo out from the almost empty streets. Hideous, deformed faces stop and look in the direction of the noise. For those who had not realised soldiers approached from the streets adjacent, they certainly do now. Herding them like cattle, these creatures are. Soldiers come from one direction and dragons from above, banging harder and breathing more fiercely so as to get their respective messages across – messages that are adhered to. Walking down the hill a good distance away is Stryker and his company, as well as the King and his men, content with this steady progress.

"It has been a good day so far," whispers Stryker to Forester.

"Yes, very pleasing. Let us hope that the rest of this skirmish runs as smoothly," replies Forester.

"Shall we meet this Warrior fellow everyone has been talking about and show him what Everlast has to say about him?" Stryker shouts out to the others. A resounding cheer indicates a definite yes.

As the army walks slowly down the hill, Beezle and Perrywinkle have been left behind. Perrywinkle, who has been writing furiously, looks up and sees that everyone has gone. Panicking somewhat, he stops his writing, closes his journal and removes himself from his seated position high up in his tree, before jumping down to the floor with the lightest of feet.

"Beezle, we've been left behind! They must have forgotten about us," whimpers Perrywinkle. Beezle does not answer, he appears as if in a trance. He is thinking about the rod. "Beezle!" Perrywinkle shouts at the top of his voice. This time Beezle does wake.

"What? What did you say?" Beezle asks, shaking his head as he tries to get the thoughts out of his mind.

"We've been left behind. Quick, we need to catch them up."

"Yes, yes… of course," replies Beezle, at which point both he and Perrywinkle begin to run in the direction of the others.

Just to make sure there are no stragglers seeking to escape their fate, every nook and every cranny is explored by the army full of men, dwarfs and jotunn led by Stryker. Blinny are relatively good at hiding, whilst seeking them can also be good fun. Swords are thrust into holes, under covers, around corners and inside things like market stalls or animal houses reserved for pigs, dogs and chickens. Whimpers heard and movements seen give away the whereabouts of these cowardly beings. Not that many are found hiding, though… shame.

Walking down the street, still able to see the harrassed goblin horde, the army stops outside a stable. The slate-roofed, wooden-framed stables are split into five separate bedding areas. Each has its own individual front gate lovingly painted with bright colours and flowery patterns. Horses would have looked out onto the streets and wiled away many hours watching the world go by from these stables. If those very same horses were here now they would be able to see a plethora of races coming towards them whilst others pass by. Next to the stables, on the side closest to Stryker, is a haystack, tall and pointed at the top, wide and round at the bottom. But this does not appear to be any ordinary haystack, as it shakes as if cold or frightened. Quietly, the dwarfs tiptoe over to the haystack, hoping to surprise what is hidden in it.

"You in there, come out and face your destiny," orders Wattlespalf, poking his sword into the shivering pile of hay.

"I would rather stay in here, clouded and covered, so that I at least do not get to see your deformed disgusting faces. And remove your sword from my belly – the point of it is causing me great discomfort," cries the goblin hiding in the hay. He sounds unlike his comrades; his voice is clear and well pronounced.

"Well, I never. A talking haystack, and one which is really quite rude. I shall remove my sword from your belly, but as for having a deformed, disgusting face, I'll have you know that I am quite handsome for someone of my race. Although, my main assets, those being my beard and my hair, have temporarily gone amiss," replies Wattlespalf.

Laughs ring out at the vanity the dwarf displays. Undeterred by the others poking fun at him, Wattlespalf looks around at them and says: "Well, I am and you know it."

"Enough of your idle chitter chatter. Show yourself!" orders Igralf forcefully.

The haystack shuffles, individual pieces of straw jumping off the top of the haystack, whilst larger clumps of straw fall from its sides. The goblin, after a little bit of effort, makes his way out of the haystack. Stopping and standing a few footsteps from his straw hiding place, this small goblin looks into the face of Igralf with tears running down his eyes. It is Bobbucket who, it appears, has chosen to hide as best he can, not only from the army that has just found him but also from the goblins he is meant to be fighting with. His best was obviously not good enough.

"Go on, just have it over and done with. I'm ashamed to be of the same ilk as these murderers. As much as I have tried to fit in and follow their ways, it has always been a futile exercise. And now, look at where my brethren have led me," cries Bobbucket.

"Indeed, look at where they have led you. You are a coward to complain now that you have been caught. Did you think about those you killed? Did you think when you were burning the houses of innocent people, leaving them with nothing to come back to? You disgust me!" shouts Igralf.

The goblin bows his head in shame; although he has never killed anyone or burned down anyone's house he has witnessed others doing it numerous times, which is bad enough, he thinks. Everyone stares at the little goblin and they display no empathy for him. Most faces are filled only with anger, hate and disappointment. Igralf raises his hammer in readiness of making the one blow that will end this sorry little monster's life.

"Are you ready?" asks Igralf.

"As ready as I ever will be." The goblin blubs and wails.

Igralf readies his strike, but just before he is about to pummel the seemingly ill-fated goblin, fate interjects.

"Stop!" shouts a familiar booming, bellowing voice. It is Greybeard's booming voice that shakes the air all around, he and Finn having returned from tending to Meena's wounds.

The goblin lifts his head and wipes away the tears covering his face.

"You, goblin, what is your name?" asks Greybeard.

"Bobbucket, sir," comes the reply from the goblin.

"Do you know who I am?" asks the old man probingly.

"Are you Greybeard, sir?" Bobbucket replies. "You look very much like the wizard I have read about in books and heard about in taller tales."

"You are very perceptive, Bobbucket, and what's more, it is not often that I meet goblins who can read. How did you acquire this skill?" the wizard asks.

"I used to wander to a village of man, climb into the roof of the local school and watch lessons from holes drilled through the boards covering the ceiling," Bobbucket reveals.

"What a very enterprising young fellow you are. I'm going to do you a favour and let you go," announces the wizard. "But before you do, remember well that you owe me a favour in return. I will come and visit you one day, or you will stumble upon me. On that day I will ask that the favour be repaid, and you will repay me. Do you understand?" grimaces Greybeard, looking at Bobbucket in a way that no one would dare say 'no'.

"Yes, sir. Thank you, sir," gulps a shocked Bobbucket, relieved and grateful for Greybeard's mercy. What does not twig in his mind is that what Greybeard has just told him will come true one day. Bobbucket has absolutely no idea that the wizard's 'favours' often entail danger. Whilst he has survived today's ordeal, he may have only been granted a short reprieve. Bobbucket wonders which way to run. The only escape route he knows is the one leading back down the hill, past his brethren who are being bothered by the nasty dragons and jotunn.

"Head down those streets," Greybeard says, pointing in the direction Bobbucket needs to follow. "Keep going and you will come to a hole in the wall, much like the one you came through at the southern end of this city. Watch out for the giants guarding your cousins who are imprisoned in houses, though, as they will not be as forgiving as I am," warns the old man. Bobbucket nods in acknowledgement and understanding of Greybeard's comments, and runs off through the streets in the direction told to him. Members of the army stand gobsmacked that the wizard has just allowed this goblin to get away. None are more surprised than the King.

"Why did you let the fiend go?" the King asks, his tone commanding and disapproving.

"In years to come I may need his help, and as such, he may be more useful to this world then than we might ever know now," Greybeard responds coolly.

"And what is that supposed to mean?" comes a terse reply from the King.

Greybeard does not reply; instead he turns away from the King and starts to walk down the hill. Dwarfs, men, Finn, Beezle and Perrywinkle, having caught up with the others, follow. The King does not dwell upon the impertinence of the wizard. He is more than aware that the old man's army has done more to dispel the threat of the goblin hordes than his own. And after all, a wizard can be dangerous if you meddle with him and make him angry.

The dragons and jotunn are a distance away now. The confrontation and conversation with Bobbucket had taken a short while, enough to prompt a catch up between those travelling with Greybeard.

"Might I ask what has become of Meena?" probes Forester, walking next to Finn, who is obviously preoccupied by many thoughts. Finn looks blankly at Forester. "You don't need to tell me if you don't want, but if you want company I will gladly walk with you," Forester continues.

"She will be fine. Her life will be a largely wonderful one," Finn says confidently, smiling. Now Forester looks blankly, wondering how the elf might know this. "Erm, I used the promethian liquid. I vowed never to use it, but now I have, I am glad that I did," Finn adds, elaborating further.

"The liquid you were given by the buggane? Ah, now it makes sense," replies Forester. "Just don't use it on me."

"I never want to use it again, Forester. Meena's life will be full of joy, but if I were to touch something more sinister then I fear I may be driven mad," states Finn, still of the opinion that the liquid is the least welcome of all the gifts from his Queen.

"Are you saying that I might be sinister?" replies Forester jokingly.

"No, no, of course not... although sinister things have found you during your life, and I am sorry to say that I am sure sinister things will find you for the rest of it."

"Hmm, I suspect your insight may well be right, Finn," Forester winks at the elf knowingly.

Finn looks down the hill at the dragons and jotunn teasing the goblins and the ogres. Nervously he comments, "It is nearly that time, isn't it?"

"Nearly time? Yes, it is nearly time. Let's take our time, eh?" smiles Forester, patting Finn on the back.

Beezle, who has been walking behind Finn and Forester,

wanders up to them in a jittery manner. Thoughts have been whirring round his head for too long – thoughts about the kindness of the strangers who have, over the past few days, become friends; thoughts of impatience driven by his new found skills; thoughts of gaining power and firmly taking his place in the history of this world. Beezle has convinced himself that he, with the help of the rod and red oric, can make this a better place. Too much time has been spent on battle, destruction, futile shows of strength and power, segregation, fear and hate. Races have been wiped out and others have endured the threat of annihilation; refugees fill cities, no one is sure of their place and the world changes on a whim. People here want stability, they want security, they want to know where they stand and they need a leader who will guide them.

"I will give them that," Beezle whispers to himself, forgetting that he is not a King yet. Tapping Finn on the shoulder, he asks, "Brother, can I have a look at the rod? I would very much like to hold it."

"I don't think this is either the time or the place," replies Finn calmly.

"But why can't I see it? There are no monsters here to take it, and anyway, I am more worthy of holding it than you. You wouldn't even be able to use it. I can use it because I am special enough to do so. So get it out and show it to me." A maddened Beezle twitches. "I am desperate to see it." Finn and Forester look annoyed and slightly unsure of Beezle's manner, his outburst taking them aback.

"Why do want to see the rod? You have seen it only a few times and you were not interested in it, as I recall. So why would you place so much value on it now?" probes Forester.

"It talks to me. I want it to be mine – I am desperate for it. I don't want to leave you all, but I fear I must," rambles Beezle.

Sounds enter Beezle's mind, they come from Finn's backpack. "Keep quiet, you foolish boy," hisses the rod. "You and I, we have a plan. You are spoiling it. Do not spoil it any more than you already have. We are nearly one again."

"One again?" asks Beezle, talking in the direction of Finn's backpack. Finn and Forester look at each other, perplexed and worried.

"Be silent! You are confused," orders the rod. "They will stop me from being with you."

"Stop you from being with me? Never! They will never do that... trust me and we will make Everlast great. We will make this a better place, you and I," rambles Beezle.

"Who is he talking to?" asks Wattlespalf, who has happened upon the conversation from behind Finn, Forester and Beezle.

"I don't know, but I am worried, friend. Something is afoot with Beezle and we are not party to it," responds Forester, showing concern.

Beezle stops talking and seemingly falls into a trance, no doubt instigated by the rod. He smiles at the sound of its voice, and his eyes glaze over. He ignores everything and everybody else, but still walks on beside Forester and Finn.

"Beezle, Beezle!" shouts Forester in the little elf's ear. Forester is ignored. He sees that Beezle is red in the cheeks and that his forehead sweats. He puts his hand across his brow as they walk. "He is hot. I think he must be weary and have a fever. The travelling, the climates, the battles, the lack of sleep may have been too much to bear for someone so young. But then I fear something else takes his thoughts. His words are very strange."

"Brother, what is wrong with you?" asks Finn, shaking him lightly, trying to wake him from his trance. "Forester, Wattlespalf, what shall we do?"

"I think we must lay him down to rest. Find him somewhere cool... maybe in one of the houses, away from danger," suggests Forester.

"Greybeard!" Finn shouts, unconvinced by this answer. Another opinion must be sought. The wizard has made it further down the hill than the others, but he stops at Finn's call. "Beezle is unwell; there is something strangely wrong with him." Finn turns to his brother and looks him directly in the eye. "Brother, we will see you are well. I would not be without you and will not allow you to be harmed."

Beezle hears the words of his brother; they are ones he has longed to hear for so many years. For a few seconds, Beezle breaks out from his trance. Touching Finn's chin in the palm of his hand, he says, "I would not be without you either, brother.

Our fates will be intertwined forever. Though we might be unable to enjoy each other's presence for a good length of time. I will not see my destiny and my happiness lost." Seconds later, his arm slowly falls away from Finn's face, and he becomes lost in his trance once more.

Greybeard walks back up the hill towards Finn and Forester, who are trying to stop Beezle from walking any further.

"He began talking about the rod. He was aggressive and pleaded for it to be shown to him," informs Finn, as Greybeard gets closer.

"The rod? Why the rod?" Greybeard ponders.

"He said it talked to him. That he was desperate to have it. That he did not want to see his destiny and happiness lost, and with it he would change Everlast," explains Finn, his explanation erratic; he is disturbed by what he has seen.

Greybeard thinks upon what he has been told. "We must take him somewhere from which he cannot escape. He must be bound tight and he must not get anywhere near the battlefield. If not, we might be undone," he warns.

"What is wrong with him?" asks Finn.

"He has been seduced by a great darkness. The rod and the red oric need a powerful third vessel to become whole. I suspect that they have chosen him to be their 'partner'. Beezle has great power in him, but he is wild and fanciful. He can be moulded, and I fear that if he gets his hands on this weapon, he may well be changed into a monster that cannot be controlled."

Stryker, Gendralf, Igralf and Perrywinkle join the others; they have been brought closer by concerned faces.

"What is going on here?" asks Stryker.

"We have a very big problem, brother," replies a shaken Forester, "and it is not Warrior."

"What do you mean?" probes Gendralf.

"A power that might prompt an apocalypse stands within our ranks," warns Greybeard.

"Let me guess. Could it be Beezle?" asks Igralf.

"How would you know that?" questions Greybeard, although he is not surprised the answer has been found so soon.

"Come on, you old fool. How could you not have seen it? The boy and his power... all of us could see he was special, but his manner – his manner is not right," shouts Gendralf grumpily.

Realising his huge mistake, Greybeard looks into the eyes of everyone around, searching for forgiveness as it was he who introduced Beezle to magic in the first instance. It is not hard for his men to forgive him. Greybeard has saved and protected these men for years and he has been faultless. A big mistake this wizard might have made, but they are certain that whatever happens, he will guide them to a good conclusion. Everyone, in turn, smiles at the old man, giving him a pat on the back in support and affection for him.

"Come on, old fool. If we are to die today, I think I speak for all by saying I would rather die by your side than any other. Let us see if we can correct the actions that have gone before," enthuses Forester.

"I second that," says Igralf.

"And I," says Stryker.

"I," adds Gendralf.

"I, as well," says Wattlespalf.

"I owe you my life," Perrywinkle informs.

"I apologise for my brother. If I had not let him come here, we would not be in this position. I hope I can repay you for your kindness and belief in me and my errant brother," states Finn.

"I thank all of you for your comments. I am so sorry, but as always we have no time to waste," says an ashamed Greybeard, bolstered by the friendship he has been shown. "We need to secure Beezle as soon as possible. Forester, could you ask the King where we might find a place so secure that no one could escape it?"

"A pleasure, sir," replies Forester, who walks a short distance back up the hill towards the King and his Fricasian army. Making his way towards the King and Laureate, Forester, makes himself known.

"Sire, I need to ask you a question," calls Forester.

"Please, ask it," replies the King graciously.

"We need a prison or a building so secure that no one is ever likely to escape it. Is there a building of this sort close by?"

"Well, actually, I don't know. My knowledge of the city is a little rusty. It is not often I leave my keep. Laureate, do you know of such a place?" asks the King of his favourite soldier.

"Yes, sire. Actually I do. That building over there, the sign outside that says 'Prison' is a sure giveaway." Laureate points to the left hand side of the road they travel down, patronising the others for their lack of vision.

"Ah, good man. Well spotted, Laureate," praises the King. "Why do you need this place?" he asks, turning back to Forester.

"We have a big problem. The smaller of the elves has been wooed by a powerful weapon. This weapon has the potential to do the greatest of good or the greatest of damage, and we must let him get nowhere near it. Sir, I will need four or five of your men to guard the boy. Are you able to do this for us?" asks an obviously concerned Forester.

"Of course, you may have the men. I will do anything to make sure that we are not compromised, and I will do anything to help the men who have come to help us. Please bring the boy and let us get him secured as well as we can do," says the King.

"Yes, yes. Thank you. I'll get him promptly." Forester runs back to the others, shouting for them to stop their advance as he does so.

Attempts have been made to try and stop Beezle from walking further. So far they have been unsuccessful, and the group has determined that he must be raised from the ground so his feet cannot carry him any longer. Forester catches up and points to the prison building a short distance back up the road. "There, that is where we need to take him."

Greybeard looks at the dwarfs. "Come on, you three. I think it should be your job to carry this young elf to the prison." The dwarfs huff and grumble. They are put out that they have been chosen to do the hard work when Greybeard could quite easily levitate Beezle back up the hill to the prison himself. Wattlespalf and Gendralf, not happy at Greybeard's request, each take one of Beezle's legs whilst Igralf takes hold of both Beezle's arms.

"Forester, I want you to go with the dwarfs, and I want you to listen to what I have to tell you. Wherever you may secure him, make sure his hands are tied and his mouth is gagged. It is very important that you do this. He must not be given a chance to recite or carry out magical acts," instructs Greybeard. "Did you hear that, dwarfs?"

366

"Yes we heard it. Bind and gag," they say in unison, repeating the wizard's instruction with a hint of sarcasm.

"I've also secured the help of five fricasian soldiers to guard him. I take it you want us to return to battle Warrior?" Forester asks.

"It wouldn't be the same without you," Greybeard replies with a smile.

"Good," enthuses Forester, glad that he and the dwarfs will not miss out on the final showdown.

"Stryker, Finn, Perrywinkle and I will carry onward. We'll need to oversee the proceedings at the southern walls," Greybeard informs.

"Can we get a move on? The muscles in my arms are beginning to ache," moans Igralf. "Here, Forester... you take an arm and relieve the weight from my ageing limbs." Forester quickly takes Beezle's right arm, apologising to Igralf for not noticing his discomfort. All four start to walk slowly up the hill towards the prison where five fricasian soldiers wait. Passing the King and Laureate, who are carrying on down the hill, Forester expresses his gratitude.

The prison is a stand-alone building, inset into the natural rock that makes up part of the wall in this city. A cave graced this place long before the city was built. Men found a use for it because the cave was not deep, rugged or full of rocks. With only one entrance and one exit it is a perfect place to have a prison. Strong stone covers its mouth now, with only a cast iron door housing a small window allowing persons to enter inside, and more rarely, allowing them to exit as well. Through the front door of this prison there are two recognisable parts: a corridor leading past the cells to the end of the cavern, and the cells themselves.

Eerie thoughts enter the minds of men who gaze inside it. Children are led through the corridor and into the cells as a warning when naughty. "Be bad and you might live in this darkness for the rest of your days," jailers tell them. Naughty children often cower when they hear those words, especially when the cell doors are locked behind them. The cell doors themselves are much like the one covering the front entrance. The corridor is lit by tall, thick candles, one standing outside every cell. There are five cells in all, one of which is still occupied, and mumblings and shuffles can be heard coming from inside it.

"Who's there?" a voice shouts out from behind the iron door of the occupied cell. Moments later, a face peers out through the small cell door window. A grubby, pale, gaunt man with green teeth and long, greasy tousled hair giggles for no reason. His clothing is dirty and torn; he wears what used to be a white tunic and white pants, but now they are more brown than white. "Been here a long time, one of the longest serving. What year is it?" the man repeats these words over and over again, before barking the most rasping of coughs. He is quite obviously mad and not very well at all.

"Shut your trap," says one of the soldiers, banging on the cell door with his sword.

Another soldier unlocks and opens the door to the last cell in the corridor. "Get him in this one." Forester and the dwarfs carry Beezle into the small open cell. There is nothing in it except for a chair, a metal bucket and a bed of straw lining the ground. The walls are wet and the smell inside is musty. It is a most unwelcoming space, and shivers run down Forester's back as he imagines the cell door closing and being thrust into darkness alone.

"Sit him on the chair," says Igralf to the others. "Have you got any wrist and ankle chains? We need to secure him," he adds, looking at one of the soldiers. The soldier nods and walks back out of the cell as he goes to find the chains. One soldier stands against each of the walls in the cell surrounding Beezle, who is now sitting on the chair. Eyes fixed, staring straight ahead at one of the walls, Beezle remains quiet. The soldier returns with the wrist and ankle chains. Forester and the dwarfs stand back, allowing the soldier to walk up to Beezle. Everyone is relaxed at this point. No one sees any threat coming from the young elf who is sitting motionless on his worm-eaten chair.

"At this rate we won't be too far behind the others. We should be able to leave in a few minutes knowing the job is done," whispers Gendralf.

"Get to those southern city walls, defeat Warrior, go home and rest," adds Wattlespalf. "What do you think he'll do with the rod and the red oric?"

"Don't know, I'm sure Greybeard has got a plan for it," replies Gendralf.

"He'll probably figure out a way to get rid of it, or hide it so we never need see it again," adds Igralf.

As the soldier kneels down, chains ready to lock around Beezle's ankles, the elf moves his eyes and looks down on him. Unbeknownst to the others, Beezle has been very much aware of what was going on and an unseen anger has brewed inside of him. The dwarfs' talk of the rod has incensed him so much that he is ready to harm each and every one of those trapped in the cell with him.

"Don't you dare take my destiny away from me," Beezle screams. "The rod told me you were going to do this!"

Beezle mumbles magic words under his breath and before anyone can get close enough to silence him, they are flung with such a passion that skulls and bodies crack against the stone walls of the cell. Greybeard hadn't taught the little elf this trick. Forester, Wattlespalf, Igralf, Gendralf and the soldiers are hurled, almost in unison, so that each of them is knocked unconscious. Beezle's rage is confounded only by the fact that he has no one left in this room to harm, unconscious bodies lying all around. He looks down on them without love or hate. He is indifferent to them now – not a foe, but not a friend, either. Standing up, Beezle walks to the open cell door, through it and along the corridor.

"Let me out," the mad man in the cell closest to the exit pleads. Beezle looks at the mad man with aggressive eyes. Mumbling magic words, Beezle's finger lights and then lightning strikes the lock, opening the door to the mad man's cell. Beezle leaves the prison. The mad man, stunned by what he has seen, opens and closes his prison door; he has been here so long that the very thought of leaving his 'home' scares him. By the time he draws courage to leave his place of residence, Beezle is nowhere to be seen – he has gone.

The walk down the hill is a hurried one. Apart from finding the odd goblin hidden away or in the process of hiding, nothing of any note happens upon Greybeard or the men who walk with him. Dragons and jotunn herd goblins and ogres back to the hole in the wall quickly and without incident.

Shouts, screams, curses and calls are all pitted in the direction of the dragons and giants, but the words have no effect on them.

Casually and calmly, fire breathes down on sweaty goblins and swords prick those who might break formation. All the others who walk behind the dragons and jotunn need do is watch avidly and close the gates where necessary.

Rows and rows of dark, grey stone terraced houses pass by; some are straight and some are slanted, depending on age and how they are set against the slope of the hill. The houses are two to three floors high, surrounded by parks, fountains, markets and towers. Bigger houses, much newer in age and made out of lighter brown and cream stones, have gardens and iron railings on the outer edges of their land, marking out their territory. Trees, monuments, flowerbeds and benches dot the paths down the hill so that there is always something to see or be seated on. Views to the outer limits of the city are obscured sometimes as high-sided city walls dominate and buildings are grouped closer together.

Out of houses, towers, market stalls and trees, soldiers and citizens appear, having hidden earlier in the day when the fighting was too fierce. Scowls on faces and the shaking of heads greet these men and women who had been quick to run when others had not, but they are easily forgiven. Soldiers and citizens rejoin the army, bulking up the forces who think they might be ready for their final battle.

Everyone can see Pengwellen and the dragons darting up, down and hovering in the skies above as they maintain their assault on the enemy outside the city walls. The dragons disappear every now and again as the city walls hide views of the plains on the southern side of the city. All that can be seen from behind the city walls is that much fire has been expelled from dragon mouths as wisps of smoke and flame billow up into the sky. The blinny panic when they see that the vast majority of the dragon army still awaits them and they wonder why it appears Warrior has not done anything to repel these beasts. Push and shove they might, but the dragons and jotunn have their way because the streets and roads are filled tightly, so much so that thousands of little (and large) monsters cannot move their arms to reach for their weapons.

"We are very close now," Stryker says to Greybeard.

"Yes, can you feel the butterflies?" replies Greybeard.

"Every time," answers Stryker.

"So, what's the plan?" asks Greybeard.

"There isn't one." Stryker smiles. "Yet!"

"Time is still on our side. When we get to the field of battle, you will have a better view," comments Greybeard.

Gate after gate is locked behind the travelling army, the doors to each set protected by only two soldiers. Down and down the city roads the men travel, until finally the large hole in the southern city wall becomes visible. Stryker walks up to and calls out to one of the dragons who has herded goblins and ogres to this point.

"Yellow dragon, I need to tell you something but I need to do it in private," shouts Stryker. He makes a point of alerting everyone to the forthcoming conversation – including the goblins, who get increasingly worried that something terrible is going to happen. The yellow beast, intrigued by what Stryker might have to say, leaves his dragon compatriots. He flies a little way up into the air before perching himself on top of the nearest and clearest inner city wall. Stryker runs, jumps and climbs up the large grey wall until he too reaches the top.

"Yellow dragon, please can you put your ear near to my mouth?" asks Stryker gently. The dragon winds out his long, thick neck and turns his graceful head until his ear is perfectly positioned to receive a message from Stryker. Stryker pushes his face up to the beast's ear and begins to whisper. Chuckles and grins envelop the yellow dragon as he hears what Stryker has to say. Stryker ends his chatter, and upon finishing the conversation, climbs back down the wall as quickly as he can. Wings beat and winds form as the yellow dragon rises up from off the wall back into the air. Rejoining his group, he recounts the conversation had with Stryker in dragonspeak and all of them laugh a very frightening, sneaky laugh. As the crowd of goblins and ogres reaches the entrance to the hole in the wall, Stryker walks up to them.

"Run!" Stryker shouts, ushering goblins and ogres away. Warrior's army does so gladly. The dragons and the jotunn soldiers who have been guarding the goblins and ogres hold their positions. That is, until the enemy have made their way out through the hole and back onto the plains, where the dragons rise high up into the air and begin to stalk them.

Goblins followed by ogres run frantically, screaming and shouting in all directions. Some run, limp and hobble towards Warrior, while others do the same towards the cliff edges hiding the river below or head towards the woods and Laureate's cavalry and foot soldiers, who lie in wait by the eastern walls of the city.

Dragons, who had minutes ago played the shepherd, now play the hunter. A dozen or so dragons beat down on the goblins and ogres running from the city with one purpose – to show strength so malevolent that these little monsters do not want to remain on the field of battle. Fiery breath beats down with such intensity that it scorches and chars everything in sight. The plains close to the city are awash with flaming orange and yellow tones, beautiful to watch but deadly to anything caught within its swirls. When the fire, smoke and dust settles, goblins are blackened, their skin colour blending in with their dark black eyes. Clothes hang off them like scorched rags, hair is all but gone and lungs are filled with a smoke that makes them cough and splutter wildly.

Stryker looks out from beyond the hole in the city wall for the very first time. Through the smoke and crowds, he sees Warrior and he is awesome, remaining still, hands on the pommel of his sword whilst chaos ensues around him. The pets who nuzzle and worm around him are an enigma to Stryker and many questions run round his head. They will be tough to beat, he thinks. Stryker is joined by others, everyone wanting to get a glimpse of the one thing that has caused so much upheaval, pain and death. He looks all around, at the dips in the plains, the sky and the clouds, the distances between walls, Warrior and the woods, goblin positions and the city. Stryker looks at dragons, jotunn and men, then at Greybeard and Finn, who must now be protected at all costs.

"Where is my brother and where are those pesky dwarfs?" Stryker asks, talking aloud to himself. "We don't have long before we will need them."

A strategy must be formulated, or at least a plan that might develop. One thing that is very much apparent is that this is it – what happens now will dictate this world's future, for better or for worse.

CHAPTER 27

MEETING WARRIOR ON FRICASIAN FIELDS

Forester regains consciousness. Lying on his back, his eyesight blurred, his first view is of the dark, damp ceiling of the cell. Forester blinks slowly but regularly, trying to refocus his eyes. To the left of him, still unconscious and snoring loudly, are Igralf and Wattlespalf, as well as three of the five soldiers – all of whom appear content in their dreams. To the right of him are Gendralf and the other two soldiers. Like Forester, Gendralf is awake but not yet ready to lift his heavy carcass up off the floor. His muscles and bones still ache from the hammering given to him by Beezle.

"Oh no, Greybeard is not going to be pleased about this turn of events," panics Forester. "Gendralf, you do know Beezle has escaped?"

Gendralf looks left and right then groans, dismayed at his sudden realisation.

"Greybeard is going to boil the waters of the sea when he hears about this," Gendralf comments.

"How long do you think we have been here?" Forester asks, still lying on his back.

"I have no idea. A while?" replies Gendralf.

Forester summons the strength to get up. Rolling round onto all fours, he then jumps up onto his feet. Gendralf rolls off his back and onto his belly, picking himself up with his big, strong arms. Forester gives Wattlespalf and Igralf, who are both snoring heavily, a light kick up the bum in the hope that they will wake from their slumber. But in response to being kicked, both Wattlespalf and Igralf grunt and groan before resuming their long, loud, maddening snores.

"Oi, you two, wake up. We've lost Beezle. We need to get out of here and tell Greybeard that he has gone," Forester shouts, kicking both of them just a little bit harder. Gendralf attempts to do the same to the two soldiers who lie next to him, but it is not long before he realises that their lights will definitely be out for a good while yet. Finally, with a little help from Forester's encouraging words and boots, Wattlespalf and Igralf rumble out of their deep sleep.

"Tell Greybeard that Beezle is gone?" bellows a shocked Igralf, becoming wide-eyed and bushy-tailed, brought about by his concern over Beezle's disappearance.

"How long is it since we were beaten unconscious by the blighter?" wonders Wattlespalf.

"We don't know; we assume a while," responds Gendralf.

"And how long do you assume that while to be?" asks Wattlespalf.

"A… long… while," replies Gendralf slowly and not so surely.

"A… long… while?" probes Igralf.

"Long enough for Beezle to have got away from us, and for us to be letting him get even further away with all this talk and twaddle about how long we have been here. Now shall we make a move? Beezle could already be on his way to recover the rod for himself."

Everyone is aware that Beezle's escape could well turn out to be catastrophic. Words between the four are soon replaced by action – all of them are in agreement that they must warn Greybeard and the others that Beezle is at large. At last, four runners rush out of the cell at such a speed that horses would be proud. Up the corridor and out through the exit back into the open air, along the cobbled paths and down the hill they run.

Dispersed and whittled down by dragons, those goblins who have managed to reach their brethren standing behind Warrior reorganise their ranks. This city has not been good to them. Warrior's army, so close to sealing victory and a hold on Fricas, have lost General Glum to Beezle's magic and have been pushed back by giant soldiers and dragons in the most degrading of fashions. Dragons have also got rid of two of the five pets, and numerous archers and cavalrymen have been burnt to a crisp by wave after wave of the dragons' breath.

Warrior's lifeless stance has led many to think that he has somehow abandoned his men, and that nothing lives and breathes behind the spiky-armoured exterior now. But the dragons still do not dare get too near to him, and goblins still rally behind him, hopeful that he will honour the promises he has made to them. Then, without warning, Warrior lifts his sword high up into the air as if reaching for the skies. A pulse of colourless energy booms outwards and upwards like a mushroom growing at an unnatural pace. Caught and immediately stunned by the pulsating energy, dragons begin to fall from the sky, flapping and flopping, round and round, down and down, sky to ground.

Above the city, the dragons have unknowingly switched their allegiances, now they are Warrior's weapons of destruction. Like falling rocks, buildings crumble under the weight and force of the stunned dragons. Each and every dragon is lost, bodies winded, wounded or worse, dead, lying in shallow holes or wound around buildings. Dragon heads and necks stretch out as if offering the blinny an easy cut, openly inviting anyone and everyone the chance to end their lives quickly.

The last to fall, of course, is Pengwellen, who knew all along that this was going to happen. The pulse of energy catches him, enveloping the old dragon. His ears burst as if trapped under a sea of water, and he is unable to breathe, with the weight of the force pushing him downward, his wings frozen and flightless. Darkness pervades every pore, his eyes close and nothingness engulfs him. Pengwellen falls and falls, his body landing between the city and Warrior. The ground shakes as he hits it, and his body ripples. Lifeless and losing colour at such a pace, it could well be that this dragon is dead already.

Stryker and Greybeard look on horrified. Pengwellen's life has been interwoven with theirs, and the thought that death may have found him leaves them with a sudden sickness and sadness. Worse still, one division of the army has been lost. Hearts dip in this moment, as the task ahead will be a lot harder without them.

Then a noticeable breath causes Pengwellen's belly to rise and fall, alerting Stryker, who tugs on Greybeard's cloak in order to gain his attention.

"He is alive," Stryker whispers to Greybeard.

Stryker decides there and then to advance from behind the city walls onto the field of battle in order to protect the old dragon, or at least what is left of him.

"Teacher, get your men ready – archers at the back, foot

soldiers at the front," orders Stryker. "Laureate, do the same. I want your cavalry at the front and your foot soldiers behind."

"Yes, Stryker," shout both men.

"Greybeard, how do you…" Stryker stops short of saying anything else, Greybeard has left his side. The wizard has begun to make his way out of the city towards Pengwellen, more disturbing is that he heads in the direction of Warrior also.

"Greybeard, you old oaf – what are you doing?" Stryker shouts out.

"Why, I'm off to engage in something I've been meaning to do for a while now. Don't worry about me. Just concentrate on what you need to do. I'll be fine, trust me," assures Greybeard. Slowly and resolutely Greybeard walks onwards, holding his staff by his side; it walks with him, back and forth with every step. Grass on the battlefield touches the tips of his toes over his sandals, and air glides over his fingertips. Greybeard can feel everything and revels in the sensations as if these might be his last moments.

Warrior shudders at the very appearance of the old man. What happened only days ago on the edges of the woods, near Paledon, is still raw in Warrior's mind. Certainly the singular foe that approaches from the city has already summoned doubt within this monster. How were they able to drive back a goblin army of so many with so few? Was Greybeard right about being too strong for him? Little does Warrior know that Stryker masterminded the events inside the city; if Warrior thinks Greybeard is the only figure posing a threat then this monster would be wise to think again. Nonetheless, Greybeard approaches in his direction and he must be dealt with. The armoured soldier is unsure how to handle this wizard. Where will his weaknesses lie? Three thousand goblins still remain loyal to Warrior, and now that he has finally rejoined the battle, they feel assured that he will deliver them to their destiny. Warrior is not too sure, though. Gesturing with his gauntleted fingers, Warrior points at the bowmen and then at Greybeard, ordering them to fire upon the olive-green cloaked old man who walks ever closer.

Stryker, after allowing Teacher to organise his soldiers, determines that he has something to tell the old giant. "Teacher, I have noticed you becoming wearier as the journey and the battle has progressed."

"I was hoping you would not have noticed. My dreams are being realised at this moment in time, and I do not want to give them up," replies Teacher, as if he has been caught out on a lie.

"I am sorry to do this to you, but I must. I cannot let you become involved in this final battle. Your soldiers have been well taught and they will do well by you, but you cannot join them. I have another very important role for you to play instead – I want you to protect that man over there," Stryker says, pointing at Perrywinkle. "Greybeard, as you may already be aware, has chosen him to tell this tale after it has ended, or at least if it ends in our favour. He has given Perrywinkle a chance to redeem himself and I suspect he also admires Perrywinkle's skill. He must be given the chance to fulfil what has been asked of him. Will you do what I have asked of you?"

Teacher looks at the tunny men and women who are prepared to sacrifice their lives so that others might live. He feels some shame that he will not be there with them, and that he an older man, might have a greater chance of surviving today when others much younger will not. But he has also read between Stryker's words: he could be a hindrance. His actions, should he be allowed to fight, might cost others their lives; he could hold them back or he could be left behind.

After a few reflective moments Teacher nods. "Yes, I will stay with the young man and keep him safe."

"Good, I am glad that you above all others will keep him out of trouble," Stryker says with a serious smile. "Perrywinkle, Teacher will be joining you as you watch these final events unfold. He will protect you should anything nasty or unexpected try to harm you."

"That is a very kind gesture. I should think I need a seasoned soldier much like yourself to fight alongside should we be attacked. I was hoping to make my way up onto the city walls to get a decent view. Shall we find a place to sit together?" Perrywinkle asks Teacher.

"No time like the present, I suppose," Teacher sighs. Patting his soldiers' shoulders, Teacher says his farewells with a tear in his eye. "All of you, do well… I am sure you will relive past glories and revel in the pride of your ancestors." Eventually, there is no one left to whom to say goodbye, and Perrywinkle and

Teacher climb the stairs against the city walls to the parapets and pick a perch from which they can watch the battle, warts and all.

Stryker walks out from behind the protection of the city walls. He and the army are some distance behind Greybeard now. Jotunn foot soldiers walk immediately behind Stryker as they are the most formidable and most frightening; the goblins have already had a taste of their might and are not happy or pleased that they must face them again.

Behind the jotunn foot soldiers are the fricasian cavalry, all one hundred horses led proudly by the King. Laureate follows his King with the remaining five hundred or so fricasian foot soldiers and citizens. He is joined in full by those cavalrymen and soldiers (having just arrived from their long march) who stayed close to the eastern city wall, picking off goblins and ogres as commanded. At the back, a row of fricasian archers are followed by a few jotunn bowmen. All march out of the city, leaving no one to guard it, bar those soldiers who have stayed behind to watch over goblins imprisoned in houses and the locked city gates. This truly is a last stand.

Talking of city gates, Forester and the dwarfs scale the last of them. It is quicker to climb the walls, rather than wait on slovenly soldiers following strict procedures to open the gates just a little, enabling them to pass through. Running as fast as they can, they reach the holes in the southern city wall. A mass of bodies marching forward hinders their view of what lies ahead, and they cannot see Pengwellen or Greybeard – or Stryker for that matter. After a few seconds, regaining some of their lost breath, the running resumes.

Red hues scorch the horizon as the last rays before sunset burn away the day, shining in the eyes of both armies, north advancing on south. In the deep blue blanket that stretches over the earth, a wondrous full moon wakes and begins its journey. Greybeard passes Pengwellen, and as he does so, he strokes the old dragon's head. The big blue dragon does not look well at all – his breathing is erratic and he is wheezing, struggling to find the air to fill his lungs. His fall was hard and painful, and who knows what damage has been done to the unseen parts inside of him. Pengwellen's right eye opens just a little at the wizard's touch. Greybeard smiles at the old dragon, then he looks back at the army following, comforted that they will offer him at least temporary protection.

"They're coming to protect you," Greybeard tells the old dragon. "I will not let you die so soon. I have a little dangleberry left, but not enough; I could help though."

"Don't fret, Greybeard, save your potions – there is life left in me yet. Be assured that I still have a part to play in this tale," informs Pengwellen, coughing and spluttering as he talks.

"I dare say you have, old friend," the wizard replies. "I will respect your wish. I will leave you to play your part. I have errands to run, don't you know." The old man winks. With sadness in his heart, the wizard walks onward and ever closer to the goblins.

Goblin archers aim their arrows as Greybeard comes into shooting distance; they fire upon the wizard who carries on at a leisurely pace, as if taking a long stroll. Arrows shoot up, over and down, gliding casually, death-headed tips seeking out their final resting place. Raising his staff, the wizard mumbles, "Arrows originatum." On the utterance of these words, the arrows hurtling towards Greybeard begin to take a different route. Wave after wave turns around to face the sky once more. Up and over they travel, heading back to where they originated. Goblin archers look at each other and then panic, scrambling to get out of the way of the arrows that come back at them. This is more than unexpected. Screams and shouts beckon their master to do something, and not to be outdone, he answers their prayers. With one upward swipe of his sword, Warrior sends the arrows back up into the sky. Up and up they travel until eventually they disappear, showing no sign of ever coming back down again.

Perrywinkle looks up at the sky from his perch on the city wall. Dumbfounded, he asks Teacher, "Do you think that those arrows have actually touched the stars?"

"I don't know, Connor, but being a wizard does appear to have its advantages. Who else could say that they fired an arrow into the sky only for it to never come back down again?" responds Teacher, wondering what other remarkable impossibilities will be performed before the day is out.

Warrior, the otherworldly soldier with the decomposing face tied to his helmet, continues his assault on Greybeard and calls upon his cavalry.

"Let your barghest feed on his flesh – make sure he is dead before you are done with him," he shouts out to riders sitting on barghest beasts whilst pointing in Greybeard's direction. Warrior's three remaining pets sit by his side, disappointed that they have not been called into use because they are sure that they can drag this old man down. 'Barghest have nothing on us,' they think.

Forester and the dwarfs have finally caught up to Stryker; they are exhausted as you would expect after a long run and a series of climbs.

"Where have you been?" shouts Stryker to his brother.

Forester puffs and pants, unable to speak a word. He is very much out of breath and so, instead, Igralf pipes up, "Beezle."

"Yes, Beezle is tied up in the prison, safe and sound," interrupts Stryker, finishing what he thinks are wasted words and fully understood.

"No, no. Beezle… Beezle is gone," corrects Igralf.

"Beezle is gone?" a worried look crosses Stryker's face.

"We do not know where. We were attacked by him and left unconscious," says Forester, adding breathless words to the developing conversation.

"My brother has gone and he harmed you in his escape? The rod, it has changed him for the worst," cautions Finn, who has been listening to the worrying words.

"It does pose somewhat of a problem moving forward," adds Stryker. "Best we keep an eye out for him and best we tell Greybeard at the first opportunity."

Goblins riding barghest fly forward towards Greybeard. They are many, one hundred or more are keen to savour the wizard's flesh. Barghest mouths open, teeth grinning with a frightening purpose that would scare most, but Greybeard walks on, undeterred.

Forester, upon seeing Greybeard's peril, shouts over to Finn. "Finn, get your bow ready. Greybeard could well be in grave danger." Forester takes his own bow off his shoulder and prepares the first arrow, ready to shoot.

The King and his cavalry break ranks, trailing left and right around Stryker, Forester, the dwarfs and Finn. Forming an attack on the goblin cavalry, they hope to deflect attention away from Greybeard.

Barghest snap and growl, long legs trot ever faster, excited at the prospect of felling their proud prey. One barghest at the front of the pack is already within distance of Greybeard, and one goblin sword is raised ready to strike down his foe, as are his barghest's teeth. At the very moment of impact, Greybeard stops and slams the bear-headed staff into the ground. There is no quake, rumble, or any spectacular wizardry visible, but unseen forces saturate the barghest, from the ground, up through their feet, changing fur and flesh, until finally it reaches the beasts' minds. Greybeard's invisible trick is quite extraordinary as it stops the barghest in their tracks. Their eyes lose their hate and anger, and their interest in the wizard is lost. Placid and useless, they wonder what to do next, and confused goblins dismount, wondering what is happening.

"Here, what's goin' on?" one annoyed goblin says.

"Bare yer teeth and do some gnashin'! Yer no use to us like this, yer bleedin' vermin," another goblin comments, hitting his barghest steed with his rusty sword.

"I've never seen anythin' like it. They must've eaten somin' – somin' that makes them behave in strange ways," remarks another, trying to offer an explanation as to what has happened.

"Eaten somin'?" questions one blinny, whilst kicking his barghest steed, trying to get a reaction out of it.

"Stop sniffin' me," another orders, as a barghest wipes its snotty nose upon his clothing.

The blinny poke, prod, kick and curse for what seems a good while, but nothing appears to have any effect on them. Greybeard has somehow tamed the barghest because now they lollop around and lick each other rather than snap and growl. The barghest act more like cows than the hunters they are known to be. One of the beasts has even had the gall to lollop up to and lick Greybeard who was, until a minute ago, dinner.

Perrywinkle, who is writing furiously into his journal, writes while watching the action ensue. Breathlessness captures both him and Teacher – the action they are witnessing is both intense and captivating. Anticipated outcomes have been turned on their head; it is unbelievable and bizarre.

"Imagine taming barghest. I've never seen that before." A gobsmacked Perrywinkle gawps.

"I've never seen barghest before, never mind seeing them tamed. By the looks of them they were never that ferocious anyway," responds Teacher. "Ugly creatures, mind."

"Hmm, well, they are renowned for being awful, imposing and deadly. Mind you, Greybeard has a reputation for being so, too," jokes Perrywinkle. Teacher looks blankly then begins to laugh.

"That's hilarious," he says, appreciating the joke just told by Perrywinkle, "I can see what you mean by that. He is quite scary at times, I don't doubt."

Annoyed goblins turn their attention away from the barghest to the wizard.

"Oh, what are we worried about anyway? We don't need our rides – one old man couldn't take on all of us now, could he?" comments one goblin, who has not heard of the wizard in tales. "Come on, boys, let's have him for dinner."

"Yeah, yer'll pay for bein' here. Yer a brave old man, I'll give yer that. Brave as yer might be, yer couldn't have all of us... but one of us will have you," adds another, waving his sword.

If we remember rightly, Greybeard has played no part in this battle thus far, keeping his powers very much to his chest and his energy high. Allowing others to initiate necessary evils has led this old man to be less feared by those who choose to stalk him. Goblins gather and swords swipe aggressively, blades edge nearer to the wizard's face. *Whoosh, whoosh, whoosh* come sounds from behind. It is the sound of Finn and Forester's arrows flying furiously to their end, the end being the bodies of the blinny who creep in the direction of Greybeard.

"Arrows! Arrows are flying in our direction. Retreat, retreat," screams one of the blinny somewhat belatedly, as goblins fall all around, before being pierced by one himself. "I'm dying, I'm dying," he screams some more. "Please help me."

Greybeard looks back with a smile, waving at Finn and Forester in appreciation of their support, confident that their intervention was fated.

The army has reached its position ahead of Pengwellen. Archers are well within distance to attack the dismounted cavalrymen of the goblin ranks. Enemy soldiers now pay with their lives for indiscretions past, and now more than ever,

Forester and Finn's anger (as well as that of fricasian and jotunn archers) is directed towards them.

"Pushus Farum," Greybeard says, arm extended and hand wide open as he walks on. Using the power of his words, he deflects the attention of the goblins, throwing them off balance and into the paths of arrows that fly from behind the advancing wizard.

Warrior, who stands close to the main goblin throng, his pets sitting beside him, is uneasy. He knows now that this wizard will not be killed at the hands of his army – he must be confronted by someone stronger. Warrior must engage the enemy, and with that thought, he retreats to the one place where he will gain his advantage. Suddenly, he is gone.

His pets immediately sit up and begin to whine as if abandoned. The goblins look in all directions for reassurance; their guidance has gone, and they are now leaderless. Minutes pass. Has Warrior decided that the wizard is too strong for him after all?

'No' is the answer. Warrior faces the darkness and the nothingness of the 'other' world. He then turns back to the doorway he has just walked through and imagines that he is standing face to face with Greybeard. Hovering slowly round, it is only seconds before his request is granted. Standing centimetres away from Greybeard's face, although worlds apart, he can see the wrinkles, lines and tales making up this man's skin. Warrior is intrigued, and he spends much time watching Greybeard's cool exterior turn to one of mild fear. The old man looks all around, sensing Warrior's presence – he anticipates what is going to happen, but has no expectation as to when. Warrior cups his hands close to Greybeard's face, and in his mind he takes it and fixes it upon the face plate of his helmet. The rest of his vision is too terrible to go into any great detail, but obviously, Warrior's new face plate leaves Greybeard with no face at all.

"Come on, monster. Show yourself!" Greybeard shouts, hoping to get a response. "Even goblins are greater than you. If you read the books of this world you would know that they are considered above all others to be the most cowardly, but you take the proverbial biscuit."

Warrior, unaffected by the wizard's taunts, imagines himself behind Greybeard and slowly he rotates around him. The monster knocks on the door three times so that he can be let out, back into the world where the old man stands, and more purposefully, so that he can surprise the wizard from behind. Warrior points his sword very slightly out from the 'other' world into Everlast. Greybeard's white oric stands tall by his side; it sees the point of the sword entering back into the world and calls out, letting its master know that Warrior is behind him. Warrior thrusts his sword at Greybeard's midriff but the wizard, heeding his oric's call, turns in time to avoid being cut. Instead, the sword catches his olive-green coat, ripping it as it does so. Turning around to face Warrior, Greybeard grabs hold of the hand holding the sword and tugs hard, pulling Warrior with all his might back into Everlast.

"So you made it back here without having the courtesy of looking directly into my face when you did so. You really do beggar belief. Who taught you to be what you have become? Manners and etiquette were obviously not drilled into you," comments a very grumpy wizard. Warrior remains silent.

Pets and blinny in the main throng are relieved to see their leader appear once more – they are not abandoned. Reinvigorated, they compose themselves and are ready for battle, driven on by their admiration for the monster.

Warrior, stunned by Greybeard's foresight, and not knowing that it was the old man's oric that had warned him, is immediately hit in the rotten face-covered armour plate by the bear-headed staff. The force of the growling bear is enough to dent the face plate. A second blow hidden by Greybeard's flowing green cloak is administered to the monster's stomach, his armour dented once more. Warrior bends forward in reaction to the blow, exposing the armour on his neck and back. Skulls of warriors and kings taken by the monster click and clack around his neck with every sharp movement made. A third swing of the wizard's staff hits the back of Warrior's exposed neck, beating him to the ground. Skulls are crushed as his body falls against the well-trodden field, points of the armour protruding outwards piercing it. This would be the perfect opportunity to release the power of the rod, but Finn is still closer to Pengwellen, far enough away to be of no use at this juncture.

"Have you had enough?" Greybeard booms at Warrior. "No, of course not – we will not be done with you until you are dead, will we?"

"Ha! Not be done with until you are dead. You will be dead soon enough, and I will honour your face when you are – I am in need of a replacement," cackles the monster.

Regaining his composure, Warrior gets up off the ground, fractured and broken skulls falling away from around his neck. Swinging his sword as hard as he can at the wizard, his blow is blocked by the old man's trusty staff. Staff and sword meet, creating red and white sparks as orics compete to better one another. Staff then sword, then staff again trade blows; the battle between these two could well be long and fruitless.

"One part of this battle is won," roars the King to the cheers of his men. The King's cavalry has overpowered the rest of the goblin cavalry; those left have run away, though most lie on the ground, pierced by swords or filled with arrows.

"The battle has not ended, though. We must ride to the aid of our compatriots who go to fight the main goblin army. They are outnumbered but not outmatched. Let us tip the balance in our favour," rouses the King. With that, the King's cavalry leave their position and head towards those fricasian and jotunn soldiers who travel on foot to battle.

Igralf has joined Laureate and the fricasian and jotunn foot soldiers with a purpose. Running alongside those at the front of the line, Igralf growls madly at the greater goblin pack, comprising ogres and pets also. Goblins especially are unsure as to whether they should run away or stay put to enact the victory foretold by Warrior. Goblin archers fire the last of their arrows, quivers have emptied quickly, having tried to delay and hinder the inevitable. Fricasian and jotunn foot soldiers joined by Igralf run forward, stopping only to hide behind shields when arrows come close. Some giants and men are hit and deemed redundant, left behind to tend to their wounds; some, as always, are not lucky enough to survive. Jotunn and fricasian archers follow behind foot soldiers, reciprocating goblin aggression.

Getting uncomfortably close to the enemy, giant soldiers, confident of their new-found dominance, roar and beat shields as they have been taught. There are still thousands of goblins left, certainly enough to say that the odds remain firmly fixed in their favour, but they are unsure of their enemy. Sixty jotunn soldiers and the rest, who rush ever nearer, have worldly winds behind them. Jotunn are worth ten men, confidence is high and they are oh, so fierce.

Igralf stops and shouts at the top of his voice. "Hold your advance. I have a gift for these murderers." The jotunn and fricasian soldiers stop in their tracks, much to the surprise of the enemy soldiers, who anticipate a full-blooded attack. Igralf takes a number of steps forward and begins to issue forth his message, which rings out around the battlefield. "Monsters, see this hammer? Its name is Clobber..."

"Clobber? We'll clobber yer. Dwarfs are good for nothin' but clownin' and cleanin' things closer to the ground. Go home, little man, and find me a gem," taunts one pointy-eared goblin in the crowd. Oh, how this goblin should have kept quiet.

"So you think dwarfs are only good for mining gems, eh? Think my height is a hindrance, do you? Do you think that because you are taller than I am, that I am somehow a lesser being?"

"Me thinks I have struck a chord. Do my words hurt yer?" patronises the pointy-eared goblin. Igralf goes redder than red with anger – the goblin's words have indeed touched a nerve.

"Your words only hurt me insofar as the one who delivers them says them without any thought of his own faults, goblin. Look at you, able to think but unable to read. You have hands but you use them to aid destruction when they could be used to create the most wonderful things. You have a heart but yours looks inward, hoping to satisfy your own desires as opposed to opening it out to others," philosophises Igralf, rather than being drawn into an uncontrollable rage.

"Arghh, shut yer mouth, little man. You might yet defeat us by putting us to sleep with yer words," grimaces the pointy-eared goblin.

"I'll save you my words – just understand this, you rotten ingrates," Igralf grumbles. Raising his hammer high above his head, he strikes it down with the force of one of the Creators themselves. The last time he did this on the playing fields in the jotunn town his charge was restrained, but this time his hammer's full fury is unleashed.

The ground swells and quakes at the hammer's touch. Ripples as tall as the largest waves produced by the seas force earth, stone and all that is buried below onto the well-trodden grasses above. Swells of earth crash forth, and goblin feet once sturdy and strong shiver uncontrollably as they try to run away. Faces shake and rumble, skin ripples from toes to chests. Weapons vibrate, numbing the hands that hold them. Unable to escape, unsettled earth, stone and grasses climb above the goblin lines, crashing down on them as if they have been caught in a squall at sea. Bodies are swallowed by falling ground, buried underneath it never to be uncovered. Hundreds are gone and the rest have fallen to the ground shocked and trembling, crying for this hell to end.

"The goblins have been felled. All of you pierce them with your swords before they re-root themselves and stand in our faces once more," cries Laureate.

From behind the earth-filled waves, fricasian and jotunn soldiers run and jump over mounds of soil, hoping to catch goblins and ogres dazed, confused and hopeless. The King's cavalry has arrived and also joins in the fray.

Only pets stand tall, untouched by Igralf's magic. Undeterred by the approaching army of giants, horses, men and one powerful dwarf, whimpering pets begin their attempt to help their beloved master. In order to get to him, though, the pets must get past fricasian and jotunn soldiers who hide the bitter battle between wizard and Warrior behind them. Afraid that Warrior might be overpowered before they can help protect him, they wonder what next? Pets are otherworldly, and if they were to be left on this land without their master they might not survive. Such is the desperation of these animals that they would risk their lives to be close to the armoured Warrior, who pits his wits against an unarmoured but accomplished fighter in Greybeard.

Parting themselves from the goblin ranks over mounds and hills created by Igralf's hammer, the pets encounter and engage enemy soldiers, who hack and thrust weapons towards them. Running forward, the pets break through the front lines of the army. Long-armed, long-fingered hands slash and swipe at horses' bellies, jotunn legs and fricasian faces. The pets filter through the throng, and as they do, soldiers fall. While these animals might kill and maim, their main focus is reaching the other side, for they want to be close to their master. The damage done to jotunn and fricasian soldiers is nowhere near the level of which they are capable.

Avoiding thrusts of swords and flying arrows, the pets dodge, dive and jump as if time itself slows for them and them alone. So fast do they think, that these dark, dangerous animals anticipate everything and everyone around them, before everything and everyone around has even struck upon the thought that the pets already know the answer to. But despite this, the dragons had taken two of the pets, they had found a weakness.

Stryker, Forester, Finn, Gendralf and Wattlespalf have fallen far behind the pack of soldiers led by Igralf, who have already engaged their goblin foes. Instead they have joined the wizard. Both Greybeard and the monster have taken a rest from fighting, standing a short distance apart from each other. Elf, men and dwarfs all move forward, like wolves in a pack circling prey.

"Stay back," Greybeard commands. All of them take steps back, heeding the warning. "Shall we see what you're really capable of," the wizard remarks, issuing a challenge to Warrior. He aims the head of his staff at the monster. Mumbling magical words, "Fistir incrediblis," the wizard delivers what must be an invisible punch into Warrior's chest as the spiky-armoured solider flies backwards, crashing onto the floor with a loud thud. The wizard then swings his staff. Warrior, as if connected to the staff by an invisible piece of string, moves in the same direction as it. His spikes, which are embedded into the ground, plough through it as he is dragged along the grassy floor by Greybeard's magic.

"Wow, I've got to say that is very impressive," claps Perrywinkle from the sidelines.

"Indeed, his approach and finish are perfect," adds Teacher.

Flying off his back and into the air, Warrior lands on two feet, steadily and surely. The man-masked monster thrusts his sword high up above his head, and as he does so, Greybeard flies high up into the air; now the wizard appears to be the one possessed. Through the clouds and into the darkening skies he travels. Ice begins to gather around his nose and beard; a very cold, strong wind causes him to feel chilly and his toes begin to go blue. Warrior, satisfied that the wizard has a long enough drop, releases him from his oric's spell. With that, Greybeard can feel himself falling.

"Where has he gone?" questions Finn.

"How far can he go?" asks Wattlespalf.

"Oh, I hope he is alright up there," adds Forester.

"I had a ride on a giant bat once, and I've got to say that it was mightily chilly above the clouds. He's not going to be pleased if his feet get cold," informs Stryker.

"Whooahh!" the wizard screams as he falls down and down, the ground getting nearer by the second. "I need some help, old friend. Can you stop me from falling, or else I fear I will become a part of the ground, literally." The oric, responding to its master's call, flickers and sure enough Greybeard's descent begins to slow. Greybeard floats down gently before landing safely on the ground, much to Warrior's annoyance. After a brief standoff, the wizard and the monster, both quite irked by the fact that they have been caught out by each other's magic, begin to run towards each other, swinging their magical weapons in front of them.

Clink and snap, snap and clink sound, as metal from the sword clips the wood of the staff, and the wood of the staff clips the metal of the sword. Exchanging blows, it is tiring to watch these two stand face to face, sidestep, wrestle and cross weapons. Neither loses concentration or pace for fear of their existence being dramatically shortened.

"Finn, get the rod in hand and ready yourself to use it," shouts Greybeard. Finn takes the pack off his back and fumbles nervously inside, trying to find the rod amongst the other things trapped in there with it. Eventually, triumphantly, he pulls it out. To his surprise the gems in the rod light, pleased to see the red oric in Warrior's sword, for which it has waited for such a long time.

Warrior, unsure as to what the rod represents, has noticed the writing emblazoned on it and knows instantly that it is ancient and powerful. The red oric, trapped in the armoured beast's sword, lights brightly and squeals with pleasure. Drawn towards the rod, Warrior's sword, controlled by the red oric, tries to elevate and pull itself closer to it, all without the spiky-armoured soldier's express permission. Knowing that something is desperately wrong, Warrior knocks three times into the air and retreats back through the doorway into the other world, dragging Greybeard by the scruff of the neck with him.

As the wizard is pulled back, he manages to calmly and clearly leave several words with his companions before he passes through the portal. "Do not lose faith. I am only one."

"No!" screams Finn. "Where has he gone? Don't go!"

Everyone looks dumbstruck, numb, and unable to comprehend what has just happened. A good few seconds pass before Forester breaks the silence.

"Greybeard told us at the beginning that Warrior has the power to disappear and travel to different places," laments Forester. "I fear he is in the place where Warrior sometimes dwells, and it cannot be a good place... far from it."

"Greybeard!" Stryker screams, hoping that he will be heard and that Greybeard will follow his voice back into this world.

"Greybeard!" Igralf and Wattlespalf join in, hoping the same.

Pets break through the last lines of the army, run to safety and immediately stop as they see Warrior disappear again. The three pets now sit on a hillock awaiting their master's return. 'Why travel to a place, when that place may not be the place to travel to at all,' they think.

The wizard takes in his new surroundings, the darkness of the other world stifling his senses. He has never been here before; indeed he has never read about it or even heard of it. Rocky terrain lies underfoot, and sand and dust seeps into the spaces between his still cold, naked toes. He is struck by the barrenness of this world, which appears to be in a permanent state of dusk. Mountains on both sides of him remind him of a prison, unmovable walls bearing down and always inescapable. A black river weaves its way around many rocks to an unending horizon and beyond.

Greybeard is intrigued by the doorway, which follows Warrior's every step. Its image is fixed on Finn, Stryker, Forester and the two dwarfs who shout out Greybeard's name, concerned as to where he might be and what might have happened to him. The wizard's appreciation of this land and the doorway behind comes to an abrupt end. His attention quickly returns to Warrior, who thrusts his sword at him. A red beam of light reflects off this monster's armour, generated by his red oric

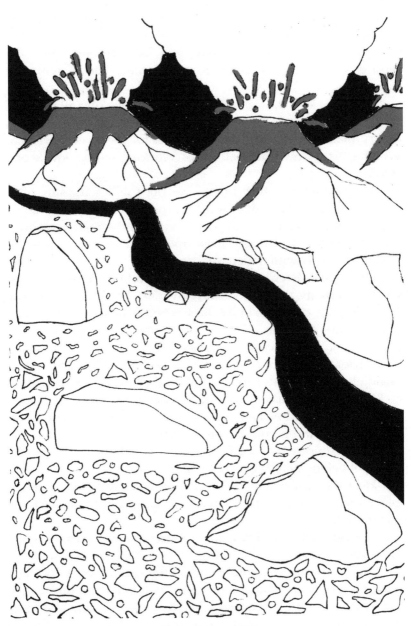

The 'other' world

which is still lit, excited at finding its mate. Warrior swings his expectant sword at Greybeard, prompting a block from the wizard's trusty staff.

"What is this world to which you have brought me?" the wizard shouts out to Warrior as he trades blows with the monster.

"Beautiful isn't it, wizard?" Warrior says, looking all around.

"You don't know the meaning of it, monster. This is a dull, dreary place at best, with little about it for me to ever want to visit it again," Greybeard patronises, blocking another swipe of a sword.

"You will never return to your world, I will make sure of it. Know this before your demise – the world you and your friends once knew will be one with this place, and the many creatures that inhabit this world will feast upon the creatures in yours," Warrior foretells with a menace.

"Did your master tell you that? Do you know monsters past have tried many times to subvert Everlast and failed to do so? The will of the creatures in it is far beyond your scope. There will only be one outcome – I have no doubt in my words and I promise you will succumb to the same fate."

Warrior says nothing, instead he is driven into action and raising his sword, flies forward in the direction of the wizard.

"Who is your master?" questions Greybeard.

"He is yours, mine and everyone's. He found this world and has set his sights on yours," replies Warrior.

"Found this world?" asks a bewildered Greybeard. "So he does not belong here? He is not one of you?"

"He is the master, and his green light will shine over each and every one of us," retorts Warrior, striking a blow against the wizard's staff.

"A green light, eh? So he is a wizard," the old man whispers to himself.

Minutes pass as weapons try to outwit each other. Avoiding a blow, Greybeard is unaware of a doorway following him, much like Warrior's, and is shocked when he whirls around and faces it. Stumbling, he falls back some distance, his head hitting a sizeable rock and knocking him unconscious.

Warrior, pleased with this lucky turn of events, looks down on the unconscious wizard. He puts his face close to Greybeard's body and looks up and down it with a sadistic sort of glee before focusing his eyes on the wizard's face. Again, Warrior dreams of this old man's features being his own. But there is a problem – Greybeard is not dead. Warrior, however much of a monster he might be, is not one to cheat. Greybeard must be awake and killed outright in battle before he can claim his prize.

"Now why did you go and do that, you inconsiderate oaf? You know that I am very busy. Now I will have to waste my time fighting you all over again, though this time I'll chop off one of your arms or legs. I'm sure you would agree that I should have the advantage when we restart our fight." A disappointed Warrior looks past Greybeard's body laid out on the floor; instead he looks at the doorway behind the old man and focuses his attention more closely towards Finn, who holds the rod. Whilst he will not cheat those he values for their faces, Warrior will quickly dispatch anyone of no consequence standing in his way by whatever means.

New, enthralling, feelings of excitement rush through every part of this man-masked soldier. The item held by the elf must be very powerful. If the red oric belongs to him and wants to connect to the rod, then he should embrace their union, Warrior thinks. There is time yet to finish off the wizard, although this old man must be bound.

"We cannot have you roaming around discovering things that you should not be discovering, can we?" comments Warrior.

Close to the river, a rock which is a little taller and a little wider than Greybeard seems to be the perfect place to tie him up. Grabbing hold of the old man's grey hair and wrapping it around his hand, Warrior begins to drag him towards the rock. Over dust, sand and small stones Greybeard's body is pulled before Warrior stops, letting the old man's hair fall. The man-masked monster picks him up and balances him against the rock. Mumbling to his sword, he asks that it bind the wizard to this rock. No sooner said than done, a thin red mist, emanating from the red oric, weaves its way around the rock and around Greybeard. Round and round it goes, trapping hands to sides and body to rock. The misty red ribbon is secure and tight – Greybeard will never escape it as long as the oric serves this master.

"Don't move. I'll be back for you shortly. I need to deal with your friends and finish off your army. I will not be long," Warrior cackles, cupping Greybeard's face in his hands before turning his back on the old man. "Succumb to the same fate?" huffs Warrior. "My master and I control each and everyone's, you foolish old man."

CHAPTER 28

WHERE HAS THE WIZARD GONE?

Perrywinkle has forgotten to write events into his journal, so many things have gone on and he wants to make sure he doesn't miss anything. "Teacher, I need a recap of what has gone on before. Can you help to remind me?"

"I can try. Remind me of what happened first off?" asks Teacher.

"Well, Warrior felled the dragons from out of the skies."

"Ah yes, and then Greybeard walked out of the city towards Warrior without anyone else to protect him. Stryker's army full of fricasian and jotunn soldiers marched out of the city, some distance behind your wizard, to fight the goblins. Hmm, remind me some more."

"Enemy arrows flew at Greybeard, but then Greybeard threw them right back at the goblins," adds Perrywinkle.

"Then Warrior made the arrows fly high up towards the stars," interjects Teacher. "Greybeard tamed the barghest sent by Warrior to kill him."

"The King and his cavalry, with the help of Forester and Finn, cut down the goblins who rode them," Connor continues; things are flowing now. "Warrior disappeared from this world and then returned to fight Greybeard, after which blow after blow was administered by both. Greybeard got the best of Warrior though, I think." Perrywinkle falls silent, maybe things weren't flowing through his mind as well as he thought they were.

"Igralf struck the ground with his hammer and caused the earth to move and grow and eat goblins for dinner. Fricasian and tunny soldiers bore down on the goblins caught in Igralf's mess. Otherworldly beasts ran through our soldiers' lines so that they might escape. Stryker, Forester, Finn, Wattlespalf and Gendralf surrounded Warrior, only to be called back by Greybeard," informs Teacher.

"And then... Greybeard and Warrior were gone," Connor says solemnly.

"So what do you think has happened to him? Where do you think he has gone?" asks Teacher.

"Oh, I don't know. I don't think there's anyone I know of who I could ask about where they have gone… another world perhaps? But Greybeard can look after himself. I expect his disappearance is only a temporary one. I do hope he is alright." Perrywinkle worries.

"So do I," Teacher says hopefully.

Friends look around in all directions, weapons readied in anticipation of a surprise attack.

Surviving dragons begin to wake and climb down from buildings, or stand once more on the field of battle, shaking heads and bodies. Not many are left. With broken wings and legs limping they wander over to each other, showing concern and camaraderie. Pengwellen does not move. His fall had been particularly severe, although he is awake and can see what goes on in the distance. He longs to be involved, better that than lying down impotent and injured, but at the same time he knows better. This old dragon still has a very, very important part to play in this tale.

Igralf, Laureate, jotunn and fricasian soldiers fight the remaining goblins and ogres. They are rampant, confident and brutal. Hammer blows dealt by Igralf strike down those around him, and some are squashed beneath the weight and the force of it.

"Come on, rabble – have you got nothing else to give? A waste of my time, all of you," Igralf bellows at the goblin hordes. "My grandmother could beat you lot with her cooking spoons. Ha!"

"Igralf, it looks like you are enjoying this just a little too much," shouts Laureate with a smile.

"Enjoying it? Too much like a long run to me, laborious and time-consuming, but good for the body and the mind. I would much prefer an ale to grace my lips, though." Igralf laughs.

"Oh, how can you say that, dwarf? To be involved in a battle like this, it reminds me of being young again," says an invigorated King. "I feel feisty and invincible. It's such a long time since I thought as well of myself than I do now. Laureate, when you get to mine and Igralf's age, you'll appreciate these times. Life becomes so repetitive. It is magic to be in the here and now."

"Oi, less of the age, King. Go out and find what you need, that's what I say. I'm as young as I was yesterday," Igralf responds, forcing his hammer into the stomach of an errant goblin.

"Sire, what of the others? How are they fairing? Are we winning on all sides?" Laureate asks. The King looks around from his elevated position towards Warrior but he cannot see him... or Greybeard, for that matter. All he can see are Warrior's foul pets lying around, and friends of Greybeard standing in wait for something to happen.

"They are gone, Warrior and the wizard. The scene is strange, but your friends appear well, Igralf," informs the King.

Igralf is slightly concerned by the King's words, but his need is to remain alive and battle those in front so he tries to think less of what might be happening elsewhere. His friends and Greybeard can look after themselves, that is for sure.

The pets, having abandoned their goblin 'friends', remain calm as they wait; lying down they scratch their bodies on the short, dust-filled grass. Long arms and short legs stretch out along the floor, saving their energy for battles yet to begin.

Meanwhile, Finn, never one to request something until he needs it, feels it is time to test out his sword. The elf has waited in trepidation of this moment, but the prospect of Warrior returning to exact damage means needs must.

"Sword, please tell me what is about to happen," asks Finn, not quite sure what words will activate this ancient piece of old metal. Nothing, nothing at all, happens for a few seconds or more – it seems an age to Finn, but finally, after a few more seconds pass, a blue flame engulfs the blade.

This old sword had chosen to take its time to light; bundled away for thousands of years, it had learned to sulk in its solace. 'How dare no one pay me the attention I deserve. Don't they know I have fought alongside the most legendary elven leaders and warriors? I mean, locked inside a box for an age, it is hard for one's mind to be occupied for so long. Oh, how I was bored,' it thinks.

Finn looks at the others and quickly realises that they cannot see the flame, its gaseous beauty being only his to behold. It makes sense that this sword does not alert others to its purpose, for if an enemy were to know its magic then the sword's master might be put into an unnecessarily perilous situation. The others continue to mutter amongst themselves as Finn raises the blade of his sword until it is parallel with his face.

Grudgingly, the grumpy old sword, in two minds as to whether it should do anyone any favours, does reveal the future. Finn sees clear black and white images form on the blade: Forester points into the distance, and Stryker looks in the direction of Forester's gesture. Stryker and Forester debate with each other in a colourful fashion. A discussion of two minds and two different opinions ensues. Finn cannot hear their words – the sword offers only a vision with no sound, not even a whimper. The vision of Forester looks at the dwarfs; he asks them a question to which the dwarfs respond with a nod of the head and an unheard comment from their mouths. And then the images dissipate until only the reflection of Finn's face remains. Hoping to relive the visions he has been given, he immediately turns his attention to Stryker and Forester. Watching them with a hawk-like intensity, he is instantly rewarded.

"Stryker, what do you think the pets wait for?" Forester asks his brother, seeking an answer to his bewilderment, pointing in their direction as he does so.

"I don't know. I suspect that they wait for their master," Stryker suggests, unsure as to whether his assumption is right or wrong.

"I think we should finish them off. We don't want them to join the fight when Greybeard and Warrior return, as they are sure to cause problems," Forester says forcefully.

"We need to protect Finn. If we leave him we may put him into a dangerous position. We have a better chance of protecting each other if we stick together," Stryker replies, his palms open, believing his words to be the truth.

"But the dwarfs are more than capable of protecting him – they are equal to us and more," responds Forester. "I just feel that if we don't tackle them now they're going to be a bigger hindrance later. And anyway, who knows when Warrior and Greybeard might return. We could have this over and done within minutes," Forester insists. "Gendralf, Wattlespalf, you can protect Finn, can't you?"

Gendralf and Wattlespalf both nod, and Gendralf reassures the two shape-shifters by adding, "Of course we can. Finn would be in safe hands with us by his side."

Finn is understandably overawed as he sees the images from the sword unfold before his very eyes. The experience makes him keen to experiment further, and so he stares into the blue-flamed blade once more. "What if I were to change the history prophesised by the blade?" he says to himself. "How would the sword react then, and what would the consequences be? Tell me what will happen next," he asks it politely. This time Lerwin reacts more positively. To be asked to reveal a possible future twice in a matter of minutes, when it took more than a few thousand years to answer the last question asked, was very exciting, very exciting indeed.

Lerwin's shining steel blade once more reveals events to come, and Finn is transfixed by what it might tell. The images begin with Stryker and Forester starting to remove their clothes, belts are undone and weapons are laid on the ground. The dwarfs heckle Stryker and Forester, but then joke-filled banter turns to embarrassment as the two shape-shifters begin to remove their shirts. The dwarfs turn away and look at Finn. As Finn talks to the dwarfs, suddenly his face shows pain, squinting and the blood drains from his face as his mouth opens in a silent scream. A gauntleted hand appears from nowhere, landing on Finn's shoulders as his body lurches forward. The gauntlet holds his shoulders back as a blade pushes through his chest. More and more of the blade comes into view and then, as quickly as the blade had appeared, it is gone. The blue-flamed aura around the sword recedes and the images end.

Terror fills Finn's face, but what he knows now can surely be changed, he thinks. The decision has been made, Stryker and Forester will face the pets, better now than when Warrior comes. Finn turns to Stryker and Forester, who at this moment remove their belts, which hold sheathed swords.

"He's coming... he will be here in a matter of seconds and I might be dead. The sword has told me," screams Finn, making sure that all can hear what he has to say. Finn twitches and turns all around like a mad man possessed; his sword is ready, in hand, pointing in front of him, waiting for Warrior to make his move.

Time stands still for the others. Images and ideas flash through dumbfounded minds searching for an answer that will counter Warrior, but nothing comes. Instead instinct begets wit. Stryker and Forester pick up their swords and rally around Finn; at least they had not yet removed their shirts and pants. Gendralf and Wattlespalf goad Warrior.

"Come on, you savage. You think that killing men unfairly makes you strong and fearful. Greybeard was right to say you are a coward," rants Gendralf. There is no response.

A thought enters Stryker's mind and it is a chilling one; he shudders, not wanting to grasp the truth it might tell. "Finn, did the sword tell you anything about the whereabouts of Greybeard?" Finn shakes his head.

"There was nothing. All I saw was Warrior's hand coming out of thin air, his sword already in the process of killing me," replies Finn, still twitching and turning. Finn is afraid for his life but he has indeed changed the future predicted by the sword – he is still here and Warrior is nowhere to be seen.

Behind the door separating this world from the other, Warrior waits for the right moment to strike. His attention is firmly fixed on Finn; he wants the rod and he must do everything to get it. The spiky-armoured monster's eyes, hidden behind the face plate, watch Finn through the doorway. He sees terror and anticipation in Finn's face, yet he does not understand why.

"Why do they behave the way they do? Why do the others band around the elf? Do they know something that I do not?" Warrior says to himself. The portal from the other world glides around Finn's form, guided by Warrior's thoughts. Position is crucial if he is to dispatch Finn with one blow, but the group of bodies makes it hard to get a clear thrust with his sword. Warrior stops himself.

"Why do I hesitate? The great and good have fallen at my feet and perished, and I have been told that I am he who cannot be defeated. How can I not trust my master's words? Why does doubt enter my very being? I must not let it – it is a trick. I am gifted," he mumbles, reasserting himself. His moment of doubt is replaced by confidence. Warrior already has the wizard where he wants him, and he is by far the most dangerous of these creatures. Glancing over at Greybeard for only a second, making sure he is still unconscious, he then turns back to the doorway. Warrior need only walk through this door, picking his spot close to the dwarfs who stand in front of Finn. Finn's back is turned. The monster knocks on the doorway three times, readies his sword and forces his way back onto the battlefield.

As soon as he passes through, the rod senses that its partner, the red oric, has come back for it and glows more brightly than ever. Holding the device in the hand that does not hold his sword, this change alerts Finn, though Gendralf is the first to see Warrior himself. An arm, a leg, and then a head appears from nowhere, close to Finn, who has turned away from the monster.

"He's here. He has come back to face us. Ready yourselves – I will hold him off for as long as I can," shouts Gendralf, rushing towards Warrior with his axe above his head. Warrior is more than twice as tall as the dwarf heading towards him. In his haste the monster has forgotten to look down at smaller things, and is initially caught unaware by Gendralf. Gendralf, using this advantage, strikes the axe down on Warrior's foot. Creating sparks as metal hits metal, Gendralf's axe cuts through the armour as if it were butter. Warrior looks down at his foot and then at the dwarf. Unmoved, he feels no pain at all. For a wound so severe you would expect blood to be seeping from it, but there is nothing, not even a drop.

"What manner of beast are you?" gulps Gendralf. "This axe is enchanted – it has cut through your foot and yet you do not flinch or flail. And where is our wizard?"

"I am one whom you could never understand or harm. My greatest challenge, that being your wizard, has been overcome. You are all alone. Your skill and your magic could never replace his. Not one of you concerns me. I would run, never to return if you are coward enough, or offer your lives to me and have done with them. Maybe I will honour you by putting your skull around my neck or by placing your face on my helmet," replies Warrior.

Shoulders drop for a moment. Is it really possible that Greybeard is dead? If he is gone then surely the battle has ended and further fighting is futile. But a message left by the wizard rings out through all. He is but one and the others left are as important to the cause as he. Do not give up hope, their hearts tell them, despite being at odds with their minds.

"You are a liar," retorts Gendralf. "Greybeard is in all of us. Our combined magic and belief, with or without our old man, will still provide you with your contest."

Warrior swipes his sword in anger at the direction of Gendralf's head. 'What will make them give in?' he thinks. Gendralf is not quick enough to react, and as the sword nears his neck, he closes his eyes. Seconds later, Gendralf opens them, wondering why his head has not left his shoulders.

Another blade has joined in the fight, saving Gendralf in the process; only a centimetre or two separates his throat from Warrior's blade. The blade that has rescued Gendralf's life belongs to his brother, Wattlespalf. With a wink, Wattlespalf gestures for Gendralf to escape. Gendralf does so by rolling across the grassy floor, away from Warrior, with his axe in tow. The axe-holding dwarf looks up at the sky and thanks his lucky stars, and his brother in the same breath. Wattlespalf, fearing that he might be open to a counterattack from Warrior, quickly retreats as well.

Meanwhile, the pets, although a distance away, have once again begun to run towards their master now that he has reappeared. Stryker and Forester prepare to change – Stryker now sees how Forester was right to assume that the pets would be a hindrance and makes a mental note to listen to him more often. But how best to face them? These creatures are not of this world, and knowledge of them is limited to what has been witnessed on this field of battle.

"What creature do you suppose will have the best chance of defeating these dark, vicious-looking beasts?" Stryker asks Forester.

"Brother, I have absolutely no idea. What about a bolheffer? The spikes on our body would stop these things from getting a hold on us, our tails could cause some damage when swung, and our beaks would surely be enough to break these monstrous servants' bones," suggests Forester to a less than impressed Stryker, who shakes his head.

"Not to mention that they are the slowest beasts in the land. The pets could sleep for a number of hours before we got anywhere near them. If we are distracted for too long, Warrior may gain an advantage," Stryker insists. Whilst Stryker feels he must listen to Forester more often, sometimes he is better off not listening to him at all.

"Well, what do you suggest then?" Forester asks Stryker, expecting a less than brilliant idea to be put forward.

Stryker thinks for a few valuable seconds. "What about a scallopodile?"

"No, no, no," interrupts Forester. "What if I said it might be a better idea to fight fire with fire and change ourselves into one of these pets?" Forester feels quite clever and self-satisfied that he may have done enough to outthink his brother.

"Hmm, I suppose we can give it a try. It will give us at least a good start to test these creatures' strengths and weaknesses," agrees Stryker, seeing the sense in Forester's words.

"Dwarfs, protect the elf from Warrior. The approaching distractions will do more harm than good if we do not fight them now. We will be very close by. If we see that you are in trouble then we will come to your aid as quickly as we can," shouts Stryker.

And, so it begins – the transformation is not pretty, but it is quick. Stryker and Forester's limbs, torsos and heads, push and pull, lengthen and shorten, widen and thin; their skin colour changes and their fingernails turn to talons. Within seconds, Stryker and Forester are changed. They retain their own faces, as opposed to assuming those that grace the pets, as they need eyes, which pets haven't got.

"Come on, brother. Let us fly and rid this world of these animals," Forester calls out.

Stryker and Forester run and intercept one of the remaining three pets, who is only a few dozen metres away from Warrior. Like fighting dogs, the two of them jump on top of the pet and begin to rip it apart with their new-found talons. The pet gives out one shrill scream, alerting the others who are now within reach of the spiky-armoured monster, the elf and the dwarfs. The other two pets turn around, unaware that their brother has been brought down, and horrified at what they see they stop their advance and run back to help him. The tactic Forester and Stryker have employed, however uncouth and brutal, has worked. Four hands with five deadly fingers on each of them dig deeper into exposed flesh. The pet, unable to take the pain from the assault waged against it, stops breathing and slumps to the ground in a heap.

"That was too easy," shouts Stryker over to his brother.

"Hmm, told you so," boasts Forester playfully, but then suddenly Stryker is attacked from behind by Warrior's remaining two pets. Sharp talons rip through his leathery skin and small, pin-like teeth bite into his shoulder and leg. Blood spurts all over the ground as the two pets do to Stryker what he and his brother have just done to one of their kin.

"Stryker! No! Do not touch him. Brother, hang on to your life – I am coming to help you," screams Forester. Forester quickly jumps to the aid of his brother, grabbing hold of one of the pets by the neck. The other one continues its assault on Stryker, who lies on his back flailing his arms, trying to protect himself from the blows dealt. Forester squeezes his long-fingered talons around the throat of the pet. He raises his long arms high up in the air, making it impossible for the pet to touch the floor. The pet struggles desperately to be let free, asphyxiated by the shapeshifter that has assumed its form. It gurgles as it searches for even the smallest pocket of air to breathe.

Meanwhile, Warrior, who we thought was fond of his pets, is unmoved by the death of another of them at the hands of Stryker and Forester. It appears that they are now surplus to requirements, and he was never that fond of them at all. Instead, the monster's sights are firmly fixed on Finn and the rod. Wattlespalf and Gendralf stand between Warrior and his intended prey.

Stryker, still defending himself against the one pet, is back on his feet but he is bleeding heavily. The pet hears Stryker's heartbeat fading and rejoices in what it believes to be a kill, readying itself for one final attack. Forester has taken his second pet scalp, and lowering his arm, he loosens his grip from around the now dead pet's neck. Seeing his brother stumbling to his feet, he runs as fast as he can and attacks the last pet alive.

Bowing out of the battle, Stryker is left battered and bleeding. Lying on the floor, his body returns to its most normal of forms.

Naked and covered in blood, he curls up into a ball. Stryker sweats, though he is getting colder. The marks on his shoulder, back and legs will leave memorable scars of today's events, although he might be worse than just scarred at the end of this day – he may well be dead. Forester must protect Stryker and finish this fight alone.

Gendralf and Wattlespalf fight Warrior together, the elf staying back, waiting for an opportunity to fulfil his purpose. Finn holds the rod in one hand and Lerwin in the other. The rod burns brightly as it seeks to reunite itself with the oric. With each attack, Gendralf and Wattlespalf try to distract Warrior long enough for Finn to reach in and attempt a joining of the two, but Warrior is too strong and the dwarfs' attacks are easily defended.

"The rod… I want it much like you," the red oric whispers to the monster. "We are one, me and it. Together we will be more powerful than the master. You can guide us. You could be the third and complete the circle. Take it from the elf. Take it from him as quickly as you can."

"Be more powerful than the master? But the master is the master, and I will not rise against him… although being connected to you and the rod will mean that we can fulfil the master's wishes quicker," Warrior resolves, hoping that the voice behind the green light will be pleased with him.

Warrior fires lightning spells from the tip of his sword but they miss their intended targets. The red oric, displeased with Warrior's blind allegiance to his master, has done this on purpose.

"Do not hurt my partner," his oric screams. "Your spells might harm him, and we cannot have that. Be careful – kill the boy and the dwarfs, but leave my rod alone!"

Every attack administered by the dwarfs and the elf ends in them being pushed back further and further towards the dragons, who are too weak to be of any help at all.

"I'll tell you what, this Warrior fellow has got some puff to fend off the three of us as he has done," comments Wattlespalf.

"Yes and we're getting closer to the dragons. We need to make sure he doesn't begin to slaughter those that remain," adds Gendralf.

"Finn, have you got enough breath inside of you to carry on against this beast?" asks Wattlespalf.

"Plenty enough – I will not rest until he is disposed of," replies Finn.

"Ha, good man! Keep your energy up for as long as you can," Gendralf encourages. Changing the subject he asks, "And what of Stryker and Forester? Can anyone see if they are alright? My eyes are not what they once were."

"Brother, they may very well be dead. Better to concentrate on the here and now," responds Wattlespalf.

"I can see only two of those things in the distance, and they are fighting one another," replies Finn.

"What, one of them is dead?" asks a concerned Wattlespalf, his heart feeling as if it is stuck in his throat.

"I didn't say that. Maybe he is injured," replies Finn. "Shall we give this monster something to worry about, rather than worrying about things which we are not in control of?" adds Finn.

"Aye, lad, I'm with you," replies Gendralf.

"Yes, let's cut this beast to shreds and feed him to the chickens," answers Wattlespalf.

The two dwarfs and one elf throw themselves back into the exchange with Warrior with renewed determination, though tired limbs and minds provoke mistakes, and protecting themselves from Warrior's heavy strikes is draining. Soon the dwarfs and Finn find it hard to carry on. Warrior, on the other hand, is brimming with strength and confidence, and he finally senses victory. Again, Finn, Gendralf and Wattlespalf distance themselves from the monster.

"What do we need to do to get that rod to connect to the red oric in that sword?" Gendralf pants.

"I don't know, brother. We are doing everything we can to distract this monster but to no avail. It is as if he knows what we are going to attempt before we do," replies Wattlespalf.

"If this is the case then we have no chance, and Finn needs one," Gendralf remarks.

"Brother, do not despair. We must keep doing what we are doing... a chance must arise soon," encourages Wattlespalf.

"I'm exhausted, Wattlespalf. I don't know how much longer I can last," admits Gendralf.

"Just keep going. Are you alright, Finn?" asks Wattlespalf.

"Yes, I'm fine. I promise you I will try harder to finish this," assures Finn.

Wattlespalf attacks Warrior from the right, but pulling back his sword in preparation for a strike, he leaves his body exposed. Warrior seizes the opportunity to counter, and with his huge heavy-armoured leg he kicks Wattlespalf in the stomach. The dwarf flies many metres through the air before landing on his back. Wattlespalf looks up at the dark skies above. He sees the stars and the moon, and at the same time he thinks he hears music. He cannot move. Closing his eyes, the dwarf will play no further part in this battle, and will have no further memory of it.

In the same seconds, Gendralf attacks from the left, holding his axe high up in the air. Before he is able to lower the axe and cause Warrior any harm, the butt of Warrior's sword hits him hard in the face. With a crack to the bones of his skull, it is not clear how badly he is hurt. Gendralf stumbles backwards before falling forward, his face firmly pressed against the floor, unconscious.

CHAPTER 29

THE END AS WE KNOW IT

Only Finn remains. Forester is otherwise engaged, Stryker and the dwarfs have fallen and Greybeard… what has become of him? Finn retreats backwards, step by step, until a good distance separates him from the monster, who looks even more threatening now that he has to face him on his own. Lerwin is gripped tightly in his right hand, and the rod held equally as tight in his left.

"This is your chance. Take the rod from him. Let us all be one," the red oric hisses. Warrior walks step by heavy step towards Finn.

"Give me the rod, boy. Make this easy and I will make your death come around more quickly," offers Warrior with a menacing cackle.

"I will not. You will never have it," replies an impertinent Finn, gritting his teeth.

"Boy, someone of your race is no match for me. They died with a whimper and I dare add that you will, too," taunts Warrior.

Finn reminds himself of the horrors this monster has committed. He reminds himself of his father and the friends he loved and left behind. Looking all around, he sees the devastation this beast has caused: a damaged city, friends wounded and dying, dragons wandering aimlessly, others grounded and dead, jotunn and men decimated, fighting bravely for their lives against a hideous enemy. Finn is appalled.

"My race did no one any harm. We lived away from everything and everyone – we were hardly a threat. Why did you do what you did? What did you gain from it? What do you hope to achieve?" shouts Finn.

Warrior is silent.

"Come on, tell me! You must have had a reason to kill us. Look at you, you're battling men now. Why are you doing it?" screams Finn, his eyes fierce and frustrated.

Warrior remains silent; he is not going to be drawn into an exchange of words. He has revealed too much to Greybeard already. He knows what the end result might be, but he does not know what he will be asked to do and when. He knows only that he must obey the wishes of his master.

Battling with his emotions, Finn realises that he may be the only one able to stop Warrior. He has no time to ask Lerwin about his future as Warrior is almost upon him. Feeling his legs push forward, Finn runs at the giant in front of him, and he growls and roars with anger, his sword outstretched.

Everything goes silent and slowly for everyone else. Perrywinkle and Teacher's stomachs churn. Goblins, ogres, giants, men and Igralf stop fighting and turn to watch Finn's attack. Forester and the last pet stop trading blows. The pet, sensing bad things and put out that his owner did not try to save its brothers uses this chance to retreat, running into the woods nearby. Pengwellen lifts his weary head in disbelief that this elven boy has, with all and everything against him, chosen to retain the dream held by others.

Stryker looks up from his position. Proud but ultimately fearing for Finn, he begs the Creators, "Protect him, and guide him well."

Jumping high up into the air, Finn uses his agility to travel over and above Warrior, who can only look up as he flies by. Landing close to Warrior, who now faces away from him, he thrusts his sword into the heavily-armoured soldier's back, twisting it as he does so. Warrior does not reveal even the slightest gesture of pain.

"What will kill you?" Finn screams at Warrior, wanting an answer.

Finn thrusts his sword into Warrior's back again and again and again. The spiky-armoured soldier stumbles from side to side – it appears that the ferocity and repeated menace of Finn's attack has wounded Warrior fatally. Letting down his guard, satisfied that he might well have done enough, Finn lowers his sword and bows his head. Breathing heavily, he is obviously worn out. And then a sickening laugh escapes from the giant soldier. Turning around quickly to face Finn, Warrior's swiftness with the sword that follows him surprises the elf, and he buries it deep into Finn's right shoulder. The shock and the pain of it causes the elf to drop Lerwin. His sword falls to the ground. Finn is helpless.

Warrior has outwitted the elf. By feigning an injury he has caught Finn off guard, his elven armour doing little to protect against the harsh blow. Finn becomes instantly dizzy. The pain of the wound is unbearable – it burns. Unable to contain or control himself, the elf falls backwards onto the ground. His eyes remain open.

The spiky-armoured monster cackles madly, "Nothing will kill me, elf! Your time has come. Although you have fought valiantly, you would have done better to surrender yourself to me before any of this ever started. Now give me the rod and have done with it."

"Never," whispers Finn, resolving to keep a tight grip on the rod until the very last moment.

The battle is over.

Heads bow and hopes fall. Many a creature's eyes close as all hope edges away. Tears envelop the bravest of hearts and the most optimistic of minds. If there has been any moment on this journey when no one imagines they can beat this monster on his rampage, this is it. Finn is surely dead now, and those who believed in him as a saviour curse themselves for allowing to trust any part of it.

Warrior looks down on the brave soul who faced him alone. Maybe the elf, over Greybeard, should have the honour of emblazoning his face plate. Warrior bends down onto one knee and steadies himself with his sword, which pierces the ground close to Finn's right hand. He looks closely at the face which stares back at him, eyes open but lifeless.

Finn floats into a dream. A shining light and an elven face too far away to make out talks to him. "I have waited a long time to deliver this message. The time my wife has foretold has come and you, I know, are in grave danger. Your quest is not yet over, and there are a number of things left for you to accomplish before you can pass out of this world. I promise you this – your wishes will be granted, only be careful what it is that you wish for. All will become clear in time, and though truths will reveal themselves to you more slowly than you would like, be patient. Now is the time to take the rod in your left hand and strike the oric in the sword. Once done, run as fast as you can," the voice says forcefully. The face travels far forward until Finn recognises that it is his King. Bolstered by his monarch, Finn's left hand closes its grip on the rod. His hand and his body twists from left to right in one quick movement, taking the kneeling soldier by surprise. Finn, whilst in control of the movement, is driven by an instinct rather than a planned understanding of what he is doing.

Finally, oh finally, the rod clinks against the red oric. No sooner done than liquid metal rushes out from the end of the rod. It swirls around the red oric as if to caress and protect it. Warrior's sword cracks and shatters around the oric, giving the liquid metal more space to cover its partner. Lightning crackles through the metal of the sword.

"You are not our master," the rod and the red oric hiss in unison. "You have been deceived – we have another."

Warrior's hand is caught up in the energy. The rod and the red oric do not want this monster to touch them, and instead, cause him pain. Cast aside, Warrior removes his hand from the sword. Likewise, Finn removes his hand from the rod. Warrior's sword cracks further as it is pulled apart, the red oric literally shedding itself of the skin it has worn for such a long, long time.

"Your time is up, Warrior. I have done what I set out to do. If Lord was right, your power will be lost," reveals Finn.

The elf lifts himself from the ground. Picking up Lerwin, he begins to run as his King had ordered, towards Pengwellen and the other dragons, who are not too far away. Creatures all around scream, "Run! Run elf, run! Do not look back. Something terrible is on its way."

Warrior, not wanting to let this killer of his rampage and of his otherworldly master's dreams go, chases Finn, intent on murdering him at the very least. As the chased and the chaser run away, Warrior's sword shatters amidst an explosion that emanates out from the tempestuous joining of the rod and the red oric. Shards of metal fly in all directions.

Finn, who is still within range of the shattering sword, is cut and pierced all over his body. Small, sharp darting pieces of metal shooting through the air cause him to dive on to the ground in the hope of protecting himself. Warrior has not escaped his sword's wrath – in fact, he has had the worst of it, and to confound him further, his armour and the body inside it appear not to be protected by the red oric anymore. A large shard of his prized sword cuts through the hard, shiny metal plate protecting his back. The other end sticks out through the armour protecting his chest, the shard sticking firmly in his soft torso. A yellowy green-coloured blood covers the shard and drips onto the grassy floor.

Stopping to look down at his now beaten body, Warrior shakes, shocked that he has been violated, and even worse, by his own sword. Dropping down onto one knee, he looks at the ground, his arm and the weight of his body supported by one raised knee. Without prompt he grabs hold of the large shard of metal, and pulling on it, he gives out a series of deafening roars, until finally it is out of him.

Propelled by the explosion, the rod and the oric fly high up into the night sky, close enough to the clouds to disturb them, creating a light pitter-patter of rain. Travelling in the direction of the fricasian city, it is not long before they begin their descent. Down and down the joined rod and oric tumbles. No one knows that they are in the air, let alone descending at a speed, except for one creature, of course. Down below, close to the eastern wall of the damaged city, behind the dragons and everything else, the red oric and the rod can see their new master looking up at them. A small figure dressed in green, sitting on a small black pony, waits. Happy and relieved that the rod has kept its promise, Beezle holds out his hand and guides this new magical vessel to him. Together at last, Beezle holds the rod and red oric to his chest lovingly and beams the biggest smile you might ever see.

The master now has his weapon, but who is the master and who is the weapon? Only time will tell.

"I told you we would be together," hisses the rod.

"You have made me happier than I have ever been," says Beezle, a tear forming at the corner of his left eye. "So now we are one, what should we do next?"

"We could make our way a little closer to where your brother battles Warrior?" suggests the rod, wanting to see how the battle will end.

"Yes, why not. There is little time to do anything else today,

The rod and red oric seek out Beezle

anyway," replies Beezle, snapping the reins of his pony, urging it to move forth.

Finn looks back at Warrior; he is obviously in pain.

"Ha ha, it looks as if you have been undone, monster. The rod and the oric didn't want you to lead them, did they? They took away your power and made you flesh and blood just like me. What's more, they wanted you dead as well, by the looks of you. Who's going to look after you now?" Finn aggravates his opponent.

"I'm going to kill you, elf. You and your friends have done well to take everything that we had achieved and worked hard for away from us. For that my final wish is to make sure you go to a place from which you will never return," replies Warrior.

"You will never have me, and you will never deliver me to the place of which you speak," Finn says defiantly.

Stumbling to his feet, the spiky-armoured warrior walks only a step or two closer to Finn before falling down once more. To add to his dilemma, a staff held by two hands, an olive-green-cloaked arm and the end of a very long grey beard appears out of nowhere, literally.

"Greybeard… Greybeard is back," murmurs Finn. A smile stretches across his face.

The misty red ribbon that tied the wizard to the rock had released him from its hold the second Warrior ceased to be the red oric's master. The wizard was awake and saw Warrior as he left the other world, and at that moment knew how to get back into this world.

With two hands, Greybeard pushes the staff in front of Warrior's rotten face before it is pulled back against his throat, strangling him. Warrior tries to struggle, but his armour is too heavy and his wounds have drained him of stamina. He is getting weaker with every breath; the oric that gave him strength and would have saved him is gone.

"Finn, stand up. Take your sword and strike Warrior through his heart," Greybeard urges the elf. Finn, in pain and weak, raises himself off the ground, gets to his feet and begins to stumble over to Warrior. He puts one foot in front of the other as quickly as his feet will carry him, which is not that quick at all.

"Don't dilly dally – be quick about it. I haven't got all day you know," commands Greybeard. Trying to block out the pain, Finn grits his teeth and mumbles the words to an elven song. Without a thought, the elf stands in front of the monster.

"Warrior, I do not want to be your executioner, but it appears fate dictates that I must be just that. You still have the chance to repent – the Creators may look on you more kindly if you do. Is there anything you want to say? Have you words you want us to hear before you go?" asks Finn.

"Save your words. I am someone who can never die – my master has willed it. It is you who will be killed by my hand very soon," responds Warrior nervously, hoping that his words are right.

Finn plunges his sword into Warrior, twisting and turning it as he does so, much like the last time he tried; the elf releases his anger and frustration onto this killer of so many creatures – elves, men and dragons included. Warrior screams, he has not felt these sensations for a long time, not since he was child when terrible things were done to him as part of his training. The spiky-armoured soldier's vision of the battlefield is replaced with a strange white light. Dizziness, a feeling of being drained, displaced, and becoming something other than what he believes himself to be pervades every cell in Warrior's body. He is dying.

Pulling Lerwin the sword out of Warrior, the elf turns around and walks away. Tears envelop the elf's eyes; the man, the soldier, and the killer Finn has become are all overtaken by the boy who began this tale. He never wanted any of this – all he wanted was to go home. His innocence is lost, tainted, and he tries to regain some semblance of what he once was. Surely his part in this tale has been fulfilled and now he can forget, but he knows that to forget is impossible. His life has been changed forever. For this moment, though, he will be a boy.

The monster struggles against Greybeard's hold, anxious to deny Finn of his victory. He feels his life ebbing away more quickly.

"I can never die... I can never die. Master, help me – I am dying. I have served you well. Where are you now when I need your assistance?" Warrior mutters over and over as if his chanting will reverse the inevitable. He whimpers and cries when he realises that he will be unable to fulfil his last wish.

Warrior slowly becomes limp, and after a minute or so, Greybeard releases him and lets the monster's lifeless body crash onto the hard earth.

Cheers ring out from all around. The blinny who have battled hard in the name of their saviour realise that it is they who have been beaten once again – another false prophet has been felled. Dispersing hastily, running back down the hill towards Paledon with their remaining ogres in tow, they hope that they are not followed and that their lives might be spared.

Fricasian and jotunn archers would have picked off those running away as a deadly final gesture, warning them never to come back again, but quivers have been emptied of arrows. Disappointment can be seen in the lines of their faces. It is doubtful these horrid little creatures will never show their faces again. The annals will be written in mind of this battle being yet another black mark against this race's reputation. Another question has been raised as to why these creatures must be allowed to live at all.

"Well, that's enough of that," huffs Greybeard, feeling as if the job has finally been done. He looks around at the chaos. The old man's distaste is plain to see. Why these events must occur is a mystery to him, but they do, and it is a catastrophe of life that is all too regularly witnessed.

Greybeard waves to a naked Stryker, now comforted by his brother, who has brought Stryker's clothes to him. Stryker returns the wave, smiling, glad that it is over. He is helped up by Forester and slowly, once Stryker is dressed, he joins the wizard.

Wattlespalf and Gendralf have woken from their Warrior-induced sleeps. Clutching their broken bodies and broken noses, these two dwarfs have begun the walk towards Igralf and the army, which was almost decimated. Many men and jotunn cry for their lost. Brothers, sisters, sons, daughters, nephews, nieces, mothers and fathers are no more, and families begin their mourning. They wonder what things would be like had events unfolded differently. What futures would the fallen have had if the here and now had never taken place?

A cheering Teacher and Perrywinkle, who have run from their elevated position on the battlements, are now a close distance to

Finn. Both comfort and congratulate the elf on his achievements.

"Finn, are you well?" asks Teacher. "Do you know what you have done?"

"I've got to say you were awesome, Finn. You really do deserve the title of hero," adds Perrywinkle, glad that the end to this adventure has come and that he is still alive. Finn, now unaware of anything other than pain of both mind and body, falls to the ground and closes his eyes. Pengwellen's long-nosed face is only metres away.

"Finn will be alright – you needn't worry about him. Heroism is a tiring business, that is all," Pengwellen mutters, using some of the strength he still has left to talk. Teacher and Perrywinkle are glad of the old dragon's reassurance.

Greybeard's eye is caught by Beezle. The little elf has travelled in close, but is far enough away from the others to infer that he is not a part of this group. On his black steed he watches all and sundry. Beezle silently caresses his new-found teacher and friend.

"Beezle, I'm so glad to see you. I see you have the rod and the red oric. Here, bring them to me. In time, I will need their help to send you and your brother back to where you came from," Greybeard shouts out in his friendliest and best booming voice, understanding that something must be very wrong. After all, this young elf should not be here; he should be detained elsewhere. No one has had the chance to tell Greybeard of this significant change of events. What is worse, much worse, is that it is he who holds the rod and the red oric. Beezle ignores Greybeard – he is more interested in his brother and his condition. He does not want him to be fatally wounded and his concern is clear.

"Beezle, do you not want to come and comfort your brother?" asks Greybeard, hoping that he might lure him in to take a closer look.

"Do you think he will be alright?" Beezle asks the wizard.

Greybeard looks over at Finn's battered body and then back at Beezle. "He will make a good recovery," reassures the wizard.

"Good, I am glad of it," Beezle responds, relieved and trusting of the old man's words.

"So why don't you come over and keep him company?" urges the wizard.

"I'd rather not. Look, you've taught me much over these past days I have spent with you. For that I must thank you. But I fear that you will not teach me everything I need to know… not now. Too much has passed between us for that to happen. My new friend and teacher will tell me more than you ever could. I feel it. And what is more, they need me – I have never felt that before. The rod and the red oric are mine, and I must insist on keeping them."

"Beezle, the rod and red oric are not yours. It is you who belongs to them," protests the wizard.

"You don't understand, old man. You really don't," retorts the little elf.

"Please, pass them to me before your life takes a terrible turn. I will have to take them away from you if you do not," warns the old man.

"No, they are mine!" screams the little elf, his voice turning to thunder.

"You have left me no option then," Greybeard mutters under his breath. Swinging the bear-headed staff in Beezle's direction, the wizard shouts, "Lightening stun." Suddenly, a white flash of energy in the shape of a sword flies through the air towards the little elf.

"Radius shielded," shouts the elf, his words full of panic. But the elf is too late. Greybeard's blast is too fast and Beezle's shield too slow to react. The white blast of energy hits Beezle in the chest, knocking him off his horse. Still grasping the rod and red oric, he falls onto the floor.

"Quick," Greybeard hurries the others. "We must get to him before he wakes."

Before anyone can make a move, demented cackles can be heard coming from where Beezle lies.

"Did you really think that your silly little trick would harm me enough to buy you some time?" goads Beezle, getting back up onto his feet. "Think again, because they won't let me be parted from them, you know. They will always keep me safe. I am already filled with power, and by the time we've finished – the rod, the red oric and I – the world will be a much happier place. Until that time arrives, all I ask is that you look after my brother, I will… "

"Cagus containum," bellows Greybeard, pounding the ground with his staff and interrupting Beezle's flow in the same instance.

The earth cracks around and about Beezle. The elf looks perplexed by what is happening as bars of white energy emerge from the cracks in the ground, surrounding Beezle and his horse, stopping only once they have taken the form of a cage.

"Silly little tricks, eh? You talk far too much and profess greatness before you have even attained it. Your weapon is powerful – you, my boy, are not. Now, please, give me the rod and red oric before it is too late."

"What do I do? What do I do?" Beezle whispers to the rod and red oric, fear making him grasp his teachers as tightly as he can.

"You must listen to us, listen to us both," the rod and red oric advise. "We are going to teach you ancient, dangerous magic. You must listen to every word we tell you – you may die if you don't."

"Alright, I will do anything you tell me to do, just get me out of here," begs the elf.

"Put us in front of you and move us round in a circle," instructs the teacher. Beezle does as he is told. "Recite these words in your loudest voice, 'Shalfar, Forenum, Timus'. Do it now!"

"Shalfar, Forenum, Timus!" screams the little elf as loud as he possibly can. And, with that, Beezle, his horse, the rod and the red oric disappear into thin air, leaving the cage of white energy empty. All around, creatures including Greybeard gasp and gawp at what they have just witnessed. With his disappearance, Beezle has taken away any chance for Finn to be reunited with his father and friends, who now remain firmly in the larger elf's past.

"We will soon meet again, little elf. I wonder what monster you might have become by then," Greybeard mumbles to himself after his initial shock. The old man drops to his knees, resting his staff on the floor. "Warrior may well have been a threat not to be ignored but he was conquerable. The fate of this world might well lie firmly in your hands now, Beezle. I suspect you will not be so easy to overcome."

The wizard has spoken too soon. Warrior, who had been thought dead only minutes ago, is up, walking and not very far from Finn. The red oric had been with him for a long, long time and its energy, easily given, was not so easily lost after all. As it lived on under the stewardship of another, it left its mark on the one it had left behind. Teacher and Perrywinkle are the first to see the horror approaching; they are also the first to unsheath their swords and advance towards him.

Warrior does not have a sword anymore, but he has his will. Perrywinkle and Teacher have run on ahead of where Finn lies and now stand in front of the monster. Weapons raised, they ask in unison that Warrior does not move any closer. Teacher has age against him but Warrior is smaller, and his life is surely close to its end. Any battle between the two must now favour Teacher.

"Stop your advance," orders a resolute Teacher.

"Move away, giant – you are still no match for me even in my withered condition. Let me do my work upon the elf or I will do it upon you," Warrior replies defiantly.

"I said stop your advance or I will cut you to shreds," Teacher warns, as Warrior comes deathly close.

The monster's large gauntleted hands push against the giant's chest. At the same time, Teacher's sword pierces Warrior and travels right through him. The soldier grunts with pain before pushing Teacher to the floor; as he does so, the sword held by the giant slides out of Warrior's body, bringing forth more blood.

"You ingrate, did I not warn you?" Warrior says, his words slow and pained. "Feel my boot for your insolence." Warrior raises his foot, as if ready to stamp on Teacher, and then, at his side, he hears a shout.

"Leave him alone. If you harm someone, do it to me," pipes up Perrywinkle. "Or I swear you will die by my sword."

Looking up at the spiky-armoured monster, who now clutches his side where Teacher's sword entered, Perrywinkle is overawed and out matched. The little man stands as firm as he can, although he shakes and trembles with fear.

"Accept your end and leave us be. You are dead, you must know that."

Warrior lowers his foot and turns to face Perrywinkle. The little man's words ring true. Sensing his end, Warrior realises that his energy must be directed back onto the elf or his initial resolve will be undone. Perrywinkle holds out his sword and attempts to stab the dying solider in the legs so as to disable him, but Warrior has no time for Connor, and with a swipe of his right hand, he slaps the little man down onto the ground. His route to Finn, who is lying down close to Pengwellen, is now clear.

Greybeard, initially unaware that Warrior had approached, gets up off the ground and readies his staff. Arms outstretched, Warrior is within seconds of completing his final wish of murdering Finn.

Then, suddenly, the monster is gone! Had he at the last moment retreated back into the other world? No. Pengwellen had exacted what would be his very last lunge. He wasn't telling lies when he said he still had an important part to play in this battle. The dragon had measured up Warrior's size, and without a moment's hesitation, he had devoured the errant soldier before he ever had the chance to exact his revenge on Finn. Munching on him for a good long while, he swallows down his heavy meal, leaving absolutely nothing behind except for one long, loud, solitary burp.

The crowd, made up of many different creatures, cheer and clap once more; jubilant sounds not heard for many years in this city ring out for the victorious dragon.

The day is done and now it has ended. The moon and the stars are here to stay, well for a night at least. Enough death and destruction has been cast on this day to last many lifetimes over; all creatures would agree on this – well, most of them, anyway. In the midst of the celebrations, Pengwellen the hero, breaths his last breath. His predetermined life, told to him by the elven Queen, has been fulfilled and all acts asked of him completed.

CHAPTER 30

THE FUTURE IS NOT BRIGHT

After the battle, when all had left the field having graced and dirtied it, a walk back up into the city had been followed with another right back down again. All the goblins held in the houses, of which Pompucket was one, were frog marched to the edges of the city. Here, they were set free with nothing else but a kick up the backside and a warning for the future. A generation of goblins, it was hoped, had learnt their lessons; one of them was not to worship false gods who promise everything but ultimately deliver nothing. How long they will remember this lesson, who knows? Not long one might think.

And now, surrounded by darkness, birds sing again. Owls hoot in the woods not far away from the city, their calls drowned out by louder sounds, which take the attention owls seek away from them. Music blares out from the keep that was so very nearly destroyed today. The music is so loud that it can be heard well into Windrush Forest, attracting animals of all kinds, who dance and play on the edges of their homelands under the bright light of the moon. Mice, hedgehogs, snakes, foxes and more sit side by side, putting aside their differences for one night only. Tonight they will be friends and they are eager to enjoy each other's company.

Hooded figures, many in number, also join the woodland animals. Dressed in all the colours of the forest, they too stand together listening to the music on the outskirts of Windrush. Happy that today's bloodshed has ended in celebration and not outright despair, the hooded figures reflect on things to come. Tomorrow will pass, as will the coming weeks, months and maybe even years, without so much as a sword directed in anger, but there will come a time when battles greater than this one will not be avoided. The hooded figures lament the fact that their anonymity and undisturbed solitude will not last, and that they will be drawn back into the world once again. For now they enjoy the music and what time they have left before a need for sleep beckons them back into the forest.

In and around the keep, fires and candles burn, lighting up the stone walls of this large, imposing building so that the beacon of hope it has become can be seen for miles and miles around. For those who are left, survivors of violence and loss, it is a celebration, but one that is bitterly marred by images of friends and family who were not so fortunate to be in the here and now.

Tonight, in the long hall of the keep, ale flows freely. Long tables intermingle with smaller tables, and benches filling every available space are crammed with different folk all recounting their experiences and telling tales of their kind. The music is wild and loud, full of flutes, lutes and drums. The three dwarfs carry a number of flagons full of ale in each hand, dancing and singing on tables to the musician's tunes.

Finn and Stryker sit next to each other on chairs covered with comfortable things. Both are unable to move much. Bruises and cuts combined with the pain from their wounds make it hard for them to do anything at all. Only rest and relaxation is called for. Stryker has dozed on and off all night, the amount of blood loss he suffered has made him overly tired. It is harder for Finn, he is unable to sleep, although he would very much like to. He thinks of what his brother might become and why his brother let himself be seduced by the rod. More than that, why did Beezle not return them to the time in which they belong? How he misses his father and his friends. At the same time, Finn can understand and answer some of those questions running around his mind, but thoughts of what Beezle might become scare him.

"Are you alright, Finn?" groans Stryker, waking again from a short nap, repositioning his beaten body on his chair.

"Yes, fine," replies Finn. Thoughts about Beezle recede.

"Ah, you two – a fine pair you make," laughs Forester, appearing out of the crowd in the hall.

"Bugger off, you," shouts Stryker, although he is unable to shout loudly. He is less than impressed with his brother's amusement at his and Finn's expense. "Can't you see we are not well?" Forester pats Stryker on the back with an evil sense of purpose, knowing his brother will be pained by it.

"Oh, you will be alright, Stryker," Forester says, feigning concern. Stryker, hiding his pain at Forester's impromptu patting of his open wounds wants to cry. Not wanting to give Forester the pleasure, he grits his teeth instead.

"How are you fairing, hero?" Forester asks, looking at Finn proudly.

"Oh, not too bad… considering that my body is broken and cut to shreds," Finn says sarcastically.

"Shall I get you both some ale? It might sharpen your mood and help you to forget that your bodies are in pain," Forester offers.

"No, thank you, but I might sharpen a sword and pain your body so you can experience some of mine," Finn says, smiling back.

Stryker laughs in response, only to grimace in agony. "Even laughing hurts."

"What did you say?" Forester asks, unable to hear Finn over the music.

"No, water is enough for me, thank you. My throat is still dry and in need of wetting," replies Finn, raising his voice.

"Stryker, do you want me to top you up?" asks Forester, taking hold of Stryker's flagon and trying now to be a little bit more helpful.

"Why not," comes the reply.

"Why not, indeed… numb your pain. I knew you couldn't resist," laughs Forester.

Greybeard approaches and bumps into Forester, who gives the old man a clumsy hug, flagons clinking and clunking as he does so.

"Hello, you two. How are you both fairing?" asks Greybeard, his voice slightly raised to counter the noise of the music and laughter in the background.

"Very well, sir, considering the circumstances," Finn groans.

"Oh, it could be a lot worse. Not much, but it could," responds Stryker, also full of moans and groans.

"Indeed, it could, but it is not and you two are stronger than I ever thought you would be. Fortune has looked favourably upon you both," bellows Greybeard with a mischievous glint in his eye. "We're going to be here for a good few days because of you two. I suppose being who you are your wounds need more time to mend." Finn and Stryker, understanding of Greybeard's lack of charm and lack of understanding of others, roll their eyes.

"Moving on, have you any preferences as to where you want to travel next? I have some errands to run and some questions that need answering, but we do have time to take in some sights if you would like," asks the wizard, aiming this question at both, but a little more towards Finn.

"No preference. Everlast is always open," Stryker answers first, home being wherever he is at any given time. Finn does not offer an answer.

"And what about you, Finn – what do you want to do? You are quite welcome to travel with us, if you dare," Greybeard asks again with a smile on his face and a shuffle of his shoulders, amused somewhat by his own humour. "There is always something or someone on the boil that must be dealt with. The biggest foe I have seen yet is the one you have defeated today. So, it can only get better from here on in," the old man reassures, wanting Finn to join him. The world is not a place for an elf to be left on his own. Too many would want to exploit Finn. He is unique and needs to become worldly-wise, especially in this time.

Finn is silent. He thinks of how he should deal with his exile away from where he is most comfortable.

"Finn, my promise still holds true. I will, if you still want, get you back home, only it will take a while longer than I initially thought. I fear your journey here has only just begun – your brother has seen to that. The rod and the red oric, if I had them, may have revealed the answers to our dilemma quickly. It has seen much. The information it holds may have led us on a path that could undo everything that has already been done. We may even have had a chance of resurrecting the whole elven race. Not to worry, though... there are many clever people and clever wizards in Everlast who might be able to help us to the same end. All of us could pay them a visit, if you would like," assures Greybeard.

The elf ponders some more before making a sound. "I would like to see this world – the better parts, and what makes them special. Though I would like to avoid fighting if at all possible. And..." Finn pauses, "I would like to make a journey to Windrush sometime. Not necessarily soon, but I foresee that I will need to go back to my village or at least the ruins of it at some point in the future. I feel that we will find something there. Maybe we will find your answer. Oh and the sea… I love being close to the sea. Can we go there? I would like very much to spend some time watching it." A whole world has been unleashed. With so much to see and the resurrection of the elves a possibility, once Finn begins to realise that it might not all be doom and gloom, his mind begins to flow with ideas.

"Anywhere, everywhere and all of those places – especially Windrush. I have a feeling we will find something other than ghosts there," Greybeard enthuses, pleased by Finn's answer. "I can certainly show you the best of this world as well as the worst. We could see the Rolling Rocks of Pratius, or the Shining Star Mines, or visit the towns above the clouds of the Neverwitch Tree. I might even be able to introduce you to the Great Sea Bull who resides in the ocean. It is a long time since I visited this friend."

"A Great Sea Bull? But they are only found in legends." Finn is bewildered but very excited, at least in a very reserved kind of way, as he is unable to show much emotion or movement in his bruised and battered face and body. "Greybeard?" continues Finn, swiftly moving on from excitement to something more serious. "What of my brother? I am worried for him. Where do you think he might be? What do you think he might become?"

Greybeard looks away, not wanting to answer the questions posed by Finn. His eyes show an element of fear and his mind wonders whether or not to lie to the elf, knowing this would do him an injustice.

"I cannot answer your questions. My heart wants him to be alright and to believe that sometime soon we will encounter him in a better state of mind," says Greybeard, half answering the question.

"And what does your mind and heart really tell you?" probes Finn further.

"Finn…" Greybeard closes his eyes as if pained, his smile dropping to concern. "My mind and my heart tells me that we are all in grave danger. Your brother has a dangerous weapon in his possession. I need to speak to a number of people to find out how dangerous it is. I know too little of it, but it is bothersome. No, it is terrifying. If the rod really does become his teacher, bearing in mind that the rod may have been forged by a magic more ancient and more pure than my own, in his current state of mind I can only predict bad things."

"I have those same thoughts," agrees Finn.

"I, too, am bothered by this," reveals Stryker, looking at both Finn and Greybeard in turn.

"Please do not be unduly concerned," Greybeard reassures. "Beezle is young in mind and not experienced in magical things. A long time must pass before he is fluent in the ways of wizardry. What I taught him is practised by novices the length and breadth of this land. To master everything he needs to know will take a long, long time, even with his talent for it. We too have things to be taught. Our learning, I hope, will take a lot less time to understand, enabling us to devise a plan to counteract his threat more fully, if he becomes one. Warrior also provided me with some very interesting information about his master today. I believe the one who is behind all of this is a wizard, and as such, I will arrange a meeting of the wizards' council to discuss what I have learned. I hope they can provide us with some useful guidance."

Forester comes back with one flagon of ale each for his brother and Greybeard. Grudgingly he has brought a flagon of water for Finn, although he was very tempted to switch this for something stronger. They are joined by the dwarfs, who are tired from dancing and generally acting the fool. They put their faces up against Finn's and kiss him heartily on both cheeks.

"Ah, Finn, you are truly the soldier we needed today. I just wish we got to see the last of it," slurs Wattlespalf, having partaken in too much ale, cupping his hands round Finn's black and blue face.

"You have saved this world. Anything, anything you want, we will help you get it," offers a swollen-faced Gendralf, his nose broken and bruised.

"Ay, methinks you will be a King one day," adds Igralf.

Perrywinkle, who has also partaken in too much ale this night, provides Finn with his thoughts. "Finn, Greybeard has asked me to write a tale worthy of the folk who have valiantly fought in this battle. Whilst Greybeard is the instigator, you, I think, are its main character – nay, the hero! I have, in my time, been a thief, I have been a coward..."

427

"You might have been but you are not now," interrupts Wattlespalf in his drunken stupor. "Now, you are a great man and you have proved it today. You were very valiant standing up to Warrior."

Perrywinkle lifts his hands, waving away the compliment. "No, Finn is the great man. Along with our most esteemed Greybeard. And let's not forget all of you. You have changed my life and all of you will feature well."

Finn is overwhelmed by the attention of those he has looked up to on this adventure. Raising his voice, he says, "Please, all of you…" The floor of the hall falls silent. Dragons peer their heads through the large open doorway into the hall, as Finn's words resonate across the room. "The compliments you give me are all very well, but the heroes of today's events are many. Everyone who has fought and survived, and those who lie still on the battlefield, are all heroes. Since I arrived here, I have been captivated by the generosity of spirit in men, dwarfs, giants, Otso and the wizard, all who were once strangers to me. Without any of you we would not be here now. It is I who must thank you for my life, and you who trusted and guided us all to the victory we now celebrate."

Greybeard smiles, proud of Finn's spirit; whilst the elf might talk of others, he is without doubt more deserving and more majestic than most. The hall breaks into applause, not only for Finn but for everyone else, too. The wizard saunters off after the clapping dies down – he has many people to thank as well as to offer condolences to. Teacher and the King are in his sights and he is quick to catch both of them.

People still arrive through the open doors of the keep. One of those late to arrive is Meena. She is walking and well again, the dangleberry potion has done the work it was supposed to do and to the very best of its ability. Finn's eyes light up when he sees her. He wants to leave his seated exile and rush to her warmth.

Her blue eyes shine, her dark hair graces her back and she is beautiful. A long, red, flowing dress, kept in her backpack, much as girls might for an occasion like this, has replaced her bloodied soldier's garb. She is mobbed by friends, happy to see her well again. She laughs, and smiles and talks for a while, giving them the attention they need, but her eyes drift to meet Finn's time and time again. Eventually Meena is able to get away from her kin and rushes towards Finn as fast as she possibly can.

"Finn, I heard about your exploits. It sounds like you were very brave, and I hope you will get better soon." She smiles, touching him lightly under his chin, mindful of the hurt he must feel.

"I will, thank you. If it weren't for you there might have been enough dangleberry to make me better quicker," he jests. "Anyway, I'm told by the wizard my wounds are not life threatening enough, and that the pain will make me a better man. Seriously though, I thought you were going to die and I am glad that you didn't. However brief our acquaintance I feel that you are already a good friend."

Meena gives Finn a peck on the cheek, and Finn blushes.

"Thank you, Finn. You have become a friend to me too, and one that I would like to know for a good while longer. Anyway, tell me about everything I missed. I'd like to know how it ended."

The drinking and the music carries on well into the night. Dragons lie in the courtyard outside the keep and on the streets, supping ale out of barrels and eating as many cows as can be mustered. The beasts within them might have also eaten a soldier or two, but don't tell anyone. Dragons, like other creatures inside the keep, lament and celebrate in the same instance. Wounds will heal, but the thought that Pengwellen, whose life was so intertwined with theirs, will never rejoin them is too much for many to bear. Time will heal the feelings that dog them, but it could never be the same without him.

The worry is that the peace they have been used to under Pengwellen's wing could now be thrown into disarray. Factions and clans within dragon ranks have been suppressed for hundreds, nay thousands, of years. Without Pengwellen, fierce rivalries may be brought to the surface once more. Tonight, though, they like the others, seek to forget and rest after the hardest and most brutal of days.

Back on the plains where the battle took place, the creaking of old wood can be heard if you listen hard enough. Ankou has arrived, but not on the rickety old cart he was seen with by the Mayor of Paledon. Ankou, fed up of travelling here and there between the worlds of the living and the dead, has brought another rickety old cart, but one that is much longer and holds many more travelling dead. With only the same two horses pulling the cart, men, jotunn, even goblin and ogre souls are guided by many more skeletal assistants helping them onto it. Whatever differences these creatures might have had in the world of the living have been forgotten as they wait to be taken to the world of the departed. In single file they will wait patiently for many hours – it might even be days before they are taken, such is the size of the line. When the cart is full, the skeletal assistants jump onto the back of it before disappearing into another world, a world unknown, followed by flying dragons too big to fit into the cart. One of them is Pengwellen.

In the melee of souls awaiting rescue, two stand away from the rest of the queue. Unwilling to be taken, Laureate has chosen another path; he wants to be with his King and will become a ghost. So it is that he walks back towards the city. What use he might be is unclear yet, but of use he aims to be. The other is Warrior.

Unmasked and out of his armour, this monster reveals its true form. Those who fought Warrior would be glad that they never saw what lay behind the armour; souls would have been better taken then and there, than to live knowing it existed. Far from wanting to be taken or being wanted by Ankou, Warrior is given another route. Out of the darkness of night and from nowhere in particular, a green light shines. Warrior, attracted by its glow, walks towards the light. An open hand covered by a black glove gestures for Warrior to come to it, and Warrior grasps hold of it. And then he is gone.

In another part of the land, away from the city on the edges of fricasian territory, over the fields, through rivers, under trees and around hedgerows, there is a black horse with red eyes standing alone outside the entrance to a cave. Inside this dark, dank cave, where water drips from sodden stone, animals, insects, birds and bats creep, fly and scatter on the floors, walls and in hidden holes. The sound of music, hailing from the fricasian keep, filters into the cave. Musical sound is caught, contained and amplified inside this hole, bringing glee to the creatures that hide within its dark recesses. One creature sits on top of a rock.

Covered in darkness, Beezle caresses the rod and the oric.

Beezle's new teachers, more dangerous than anything ever known before them, vibrate as cats would purr – they are happy to be in their new master's hands. The red oric shines its soft red light, exposing Beezle's smiling face.

"Beezle, Beezle, rod and oric," the novice wizard sings to the tune of the music coming from outside. Rocking the rod and oric to sleep, much like a baby, he thinks of those he has left behind and how they tried to take him away from his new teacher. Expressions of calm and contentment slowly turn to a frown, distorting, twisting and screwing up his face. Beezle transforms himself from a beautiful elf into something far more sinister. Filled with a seething anger so intense, Beezle's breath becomes heavy and spittle shoots out onto the floor through his gritted teeth.

"Tomorrow is the beginning of a new tale," he announces with menace.